Dancing on the Edge of the Roof

"Sheila Williams's debut delivers with her runaway heroine. All aboard!"
— *Romantic Times*

"[It] kept my heart and mind dancing through the pages. Sheila Williams, with her talent for detailed storytelling, expertly takes the reader on a poignant and humorous quest for self."
— LORI BRYANT-WOOLRIDGE, author of *Hitts & Mrs.*

The Shade of My Own Tree

"Once you've read a Sheila Williams novel, you'll be a fan."
— *Kentucky Monthly*

"An enlightening novel about surviving a life of domestic abuse . . . Williams carries this off in an elegantly sparse style that's laced, incredibly enough, with humor."
— *Cincinnati Enquirer*

"Poignant, humorous, and thought-provoking."
— *Cincinnati Herald*

"Weaving social commentary into the normalcy of everyday life, Williams interchanges humor and heartache in even the most mundane of activities."
— *Louisville Cardinal*

"Williams weaves another great story about a woman seeking self-discovery."
— *Booklist*

On the Right Side of a Dream

"Williams has written an entertaining sequel to *Dancing on the Edge of the Roof*."
— *Booklist*

BOOKS BY SHEILA WILLIAMS

Dancing on the Edge of the Roof

The Shade of My Own Tree

On the Right Side of a Dream

GIRLS MOST LIKELY

.

Girls Most Likely

A NOVEL

Sheila Williams

ONE WORLD

BALLANTINE BOOKS / NEW YORK

A One World Books Trade Paperback Original

Copyright © 2006 by Sheila Williams

Published in the United States by One World Books,
an imprint of The Random House Publishing Group,
a division of Random House, Inc., New York.

ONE WORLD is a registered trademark and the One World colophon is
a trademark of Random House, Inc.

LIBRARY OF CONGRESS CATALOGING-IN-PUBLICATION DATA
Williams, Sheila (Sheila J.)
Girls most likely : a novel / by Sheila Williams.
p. cm.
ISBN 0-345-46476-1
1. African American women—Fiction. 2. Female friendship—Fiction.
3. Reunions—Fiction. 4. Reminiscing—Fiction. I. Title.
PS3623.I5633G57 2006
813'.6—dc22   2005055528

Printed in the United States of America

www.oneworldbooks.net

246897531

Book design by Casey Hampton

This book is dedicated to the memory of my mother,

MYRTLE JONES HUMPHREY
1930–2004

And in the sweetness of friendship let there be laughter, and sharing of pleasures. For in the dew of little things the heart finds its morning and is refreshed.

— Kahlil Gibran, *The Prophet*

ACKNOWLEDGMENTS

When you have many thanks to give, it means that you've had many blessings. I would like to thank my agent, Alison Picard, and my editor, Melody Guy, for their advice and encouragement. Thanks also to Danielle Durkin, Gillium Hailparn, and Margaret Sanborn at Ballantine Books for their support and assistance.

I extend my appreciation to my personal circle of "girls most likely" for their smiles, encouragement, and e-mails—there are too many of them to mention by name, but you know who you are. I cherish you all: Good friends are treasures of the heart.

Special thanks to my "experts": my dear friends Leslie Sawyer, who allowed me to borrow a hilarious experience from our childhood for this book (I won't say which one), and Michelle Hopkins, television co-anchor, who patiently answered my questions about her industry. Any mistakes made or liberties taken with their information are entirely my responsibility.

Special thanks to my family: my sister, Claire; my children Bethany and Kevin; and to Bruce—who is always there. *Girls Most Likely* is dedicated to the memory of my mother, Myrtle Jones Humphrey. Mother believed that I was a "girl most likely" to be successful in any field I chose. For that and for her love, encouragement, and guidance, I will always be grateful.

—SJW

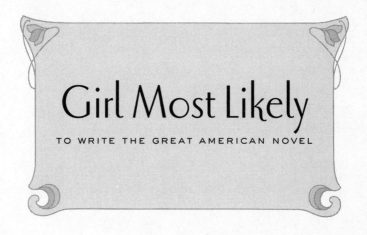

Girl Most Likely

TO WRITE THE GREAT AMERICAN NOVEL

Vaughn

ONE

I thought that I was fearless until the piece of paper that every sane adult over forty dreads arrived in my mailbox on a June afternoon: the invitation to my thirtieth high school class reunion

PURPLE TIGERS, CLASS OF 1971
IT'S REUNION TIME!
DATE: FRIDAY, AUGUST 25
TIME: 7:00 P.M. UNTIL ???
PLACE: THE IMPERIAL ARMS
BE THERE OR BE SQUARE
RSVP TO DARLA MARTIN-GILMORE BY AUGUST 5
WE LOOK FORWARD TO SEEING YOU!!!!

Damn it! I said to myself, fingering the white envelope trimmed in purple. I wondered if the French Foreign Legion was still in existence. I hadn't used my high school French in over twenty years but there were refresher courses. Maybe it wasn't too late to join the Witness Protection Program.

Why, for God's sake, the Imperial Arms? It had seen better days. Like forty years ago. And the buffet wasn't *that* good even *then*.

You have some choices, my conscience advised. *You can kill your-*

self now or mark the envelope "Addressee Unknown" and drop it into the mailbox . . . or you could go.

Oh grow up, I answered back. *What's wrong with suicide?*

I would be fifty in a couple of years so I figured there weren't many things left in the world that could really scare me. After all, I was on my second marriage. I was not afraid of the dark—I outgrew that when I was four. I will admit that I am the only mom who sits at the bottom of the bleachers at my son's football games. Heights make me queasy. And yes, cancer and Alzheimer's worry me. So I eat broccoli and do crossword puzzles to keep the gray cells from getting squishy. But other than that, I thought I was fearless. But there's nothing like the invitation to your thirtieth high school reunion to put ice cubes in your intestines.

Maybe I could run away from home.

"Hey! What's up?" My son, Keith, or "Jaws" as we call him because of his feeding habits, joined me in the hallway. He was chomping on an apple, talking with his mouth full, and holding a jar of peanut butter in one hand. Life was normal.

"What's with the psychedelic envelope?" he asked, with a burst of laughter in his voice. Bits of apple went everywhere.

"High school reunion," I answered. "And clean up that mess!"

"Ho, ho! How many years is it, Mom? Thirty-five? Forty?"

"Thirty, thank you. Get it right," I retorted.

"You're *old*."

"If you don't watch it, I'll stop feeding you," I warned him.

"Purple Tigers? Oh, this ought to be good. You old-school fogies limping around the dance floor to Al Green . . ."

"No, the Temptations, Sly and the Family Stone, Earth, Wind and Fire," I countered. I was remembering the wonderful music. "And there isn't anything 'old school' about it. It's just *real* music where people actually play the instruments. You know, musical instruments? Saxophones, trumpets, guitars?"

Keith shook his head and took another monstrous bite.

"Yeah, yeah, whatever. You're going, right?" He patted me on the top of my head.

One of the lovely things about having a nearly grown son is that when he gets to be taller than you are, he treats you like an armrest.

"Go away, shoo," I said, pushing his two-hundred-pound frame toward the kitchen where it belonged. "Don't forget we have to talk about that football camp this evening. Oh, and that girl called again." I call her "that girl" because she has one of those amazing names that I can't pronounce. "La" on the front end and an "ishelle" on the back end. As my great-grandmother would say, "Mercy!"

"OK, but you should go, Ma. You don't look too bad for an old lady. A little short but . . ."

I love compliments.

"Beat it before I throw something at you," I yelled after him.

I looked at the invitation again.

Had it really been thirty years? It seemed like only yesterday that I had nearly been suspended for . . . Now I *was* sounding like an old-school fogy. Of course, it had been thirty years. I'd been to college, married, had two babies, divorced, married again, had one more baby; worked at three companies, one university, and one junior college; done innumerable loads of laundry, been a room mother three hundred times, cheered soccer, football, and volleyball games; and made more chili and Rice Krispies treats than I care to think about. Not to mention the gray hair that I religiously color every four weeks and the extra ten pounds I was carrying around—OK, fifteen pounds.

Oh, yes, and those babies grew up. Becca was in San Francisco preparing to make me a grandmother. Yikes! Candace had just finished her master's degree and was spending the summer in Italy. Keith was headed toward his senior year in high school.

And there were the other things.

Thirty years ago my parents still lived on Greenway Avenue in a little beige stucco house. Our German shepherd, Ranger, held court in the backyard and Mrs. Adams poked her nose over the fence complaining about his barking. My oldest sister, Pat, would have been in the bathroom in front of the mirror combing her hair this way and that. My youngest sister, Jean, would have been in the window seat, coloring. Grandma Jane lived on the next block; the Methodist minister lived around the corner.

Time didn't march on, it flew at light speed. Dad was gone now, and Mother sold the little house and lived in a condo on the other side of town. Pat and her family live in Denver and Jean is stationed in Washington, D.C. My baby sister is a major in the U.S. Army. Grandma's gone, the reverend is gone, and Ranger was the third of several dogs by the same name, all of which were buried with pomp and circumstance and heartfelt tears in the backyard beneath the old maple tree.

Thank God for the memories. My high school yearbooks rest on top of the bookshelf in the family room. Keith leafs through them and makes fun of the way we dressed "back in the olden days," especially our afros. Of course, everything comes back, and now that bell-bottoms are on the runways in New York, my long-haired son looks at my high school picture with more respect. We were trendsetters.

I pick up the book from 1971, which is my favorite year. I flip through it whenever I want to feel good. It's like a worn house slipper, completely broken in. It is like meat loaf and mashed potatoes made with whole milk and butter. And I always open it to the same page. There we are. It's the picture of the National Honor Society and we're standing in the front row: me, Audrey, Reenie, and Su—best friends since elementary and junior high school. Inseparable. We are wearing plaid jumpers with pleated skirts, V-neck sweaters, and knee socks. Cheerleader skirts. Afros and hooped earrings. Dashikis. And smiles. Lots and lots of smiles, real ones. Life was full of possibilities then.

On the day we graduated we promised to stay in touch, but we scattered. Our times together grew further apart but were no less cherished. And I think all of us would agree that the times we spent together growing up were some of the best times of our lives. Those were the days when we weren't afraid to experiment or make mistakes. Those were the days before our lives would need revision, before our souls would need restoration. Those were the days before we learned that we wouldn't live forever, the days before regrets. And, in many ways, those were the last days that we had friendships so close that our skins inhaled the fibers of the mohair sweaters we borrowed from one another.

Irene, Audrey, and Susan were the girls I grew up with. The girls who turned the double-Dutch ropes when I was nine, who invited me to their slumber parties and told me their secrets, some of which I've kept to this day. In high school, they got their own page in the yearbook because they were the "girls most likely": to succeed, to marry a millionaire, to be rich and famous, and to negotiate world peace. They were the girls most likely to do everything wonderful. I was on the fringes of their lives, basking in the reflection of their friendship and taking advantage of the benefits that came with being seen with them.

We were born in the early fifties. Our mothers named us after their favorite movie stars: Susan Hayward, Irene Dunne, and Audrey Hepburn. And like the screen queens, we were told to behave ourselves and do what was expected of us: white gloves and a hat to church on Sunday; Fisk, Spelman, or Howard; a "good" job teaching school or working for the government (thirty years in and a pension out), or, God willing, marry a doctor and not have to work at all. Of course, we were colored then and things were changing in the world.

Neither our mothers, or Mesdames Hayward, Dunne, or Hepburn, ever dreamed that when we grew up not only would we be *black* (we're African American now, but that is another book) but we would not teach or go to Fisk or work for the state *or* marry doctors. Instead, we wore afros, pitched out our bras (I have since had to retrieve mine for the safety of myself and others), wore blue jeans with holes in the knees, took the pill, and raised our fists high in the symbol of Black Power. We *did* inhale and we lived lives that neither our parents nor society ever planned. Our mothers and fathers, who had tried so hard to make decent Negro women out of us, were horrified at first. But I think Susan, Irene, and Audrey might not have minded as much. Now, we are Su, Reenie, and Audrey (Audrey is *not* the kind of girl who takes to nicknames). My name is Vaughn and I'm the fourth member of the group. My name doesn't come from a screen queen. My mother, conveniently, has amnesia on the subject. The expectations, however, were just the same.

I, however, wasn't voted most likely to do anything. I was raised to be a "good girl." And I was. Until I learned that good girls finish behind good guys—dead last. So I rebelled. Unlike my friends, I ended up being the girl most likely to be suspended, arrested on a picket line, or having her editorial censored.

This is a great picture. Reenie is darling, her long black hair pulled into a ponytail that falls around her shoulders. She's petite but has an hourglass figure, the only one of us who can look sexy in a plaid jumper and knee socks. Even in the black-and-white photograph, her eyes sparkle and you can see dimples in her pale cheeks.

Audrey is tall, thin, and elegant, just like her namesake. This photo was taken on game day so she's wearing her cheerleading uniform: dark purple sweater with the tiger on front; short, purple skirt, pleated; bobby socks and snow-white sneakers. These are the old days, before Nike. Her dark hair curls gently around her face in a soft afro, her almond-shaped eyes and smooth cheekbones give her face an exotic look. We called her Cat Woman sometimes. She was the only girl we knew who had hazel eyes, and if she was angry at you, they glowed.

Su is also tall but sturdy-looking, not willowy like Audrey. Despite her love of Kathleen Cleaver and Angela Davis, Su didn't give up her neatly pressed hair for anything. It falls to her shoulders in a perfectly arranged pageboy, expertly curled and sprayed by her hairdresser aunt. She's not cute like Reenie or elegant like Audrey. Su is striking. Her brows are naturally arched, her nose strong and wide, her smile engaging. Su was a majorette, so she's wearing the short-skirted cream dress with the purple Tiger emblem on front and white boots with tassels. On anyone else, that getup would be tacky. On Su, it looks like Givenchy couture.

And then there is me.

I was the original "in between kid," not as tall as Audrey, not as short as Reenie; not as brown-skinned as Su but not as fair-skinned as Reenie. No one in the world is as skinny as Audrey was then, no one in the world as shapely as Su. I wore braces, which is why I'm smiling with my mouth closed. I would be described as a little lumpy, medium height, caramel-colored, with average features. I had a Kathleen Cleaver–style afro that happened to look good on Picture Day, which was a miracle. I could never get the hang of picking out my hair.

Oh, look at the boys.

Paul Smith, Jimmy Davis, what's-his-name, his family lived on Atcheson. Giles something, he was killed in a car accident, I remember now . . .

It takes only a few minutes for those pictures to bring back the memories, both good and bad. The boy over there, wearing the dashiki and the huge afro, he's a corporate guy now. And there's Errol, the last I heard he was still in Lucasville for murdering somebody. The boy wearing the matching sweater and trousers, he was Beverly Gibbons's brother, right? Smart, black Ray Charles–style glasses, always carried a slide rule. What's the word my son uses now? Dork? Geek? I think Su told me that he chairs a university chemistry department. Good for him.

Oh, yeah, and there's Su's boyfriend, Bradley Garcia. Yes, things have changed.

I love this picture; it's one of my favorites. I like the ponytails and the knee socks and the fisherman knit sweaters. I love the cheerleader and majorette uniforms and the afros. And I love the way we look straight into the camera. Our eyes are clear, our smiles full of hope, humor, and confidence. We know there will be dragons to slay. Our youth and our ignorance are the swords. Our friendship is the shield that gives us courage. I love the warmth in our smiles and the stories behind them: Reenie, Su, and Audrey had been nominated for homecoming queen. I was a National Merit scholar. So was Audrey. We were all stitching the hems of our dresses (taking them up, of course) for the dance. And the Purple Tigers had won their last football game against Newark. And there were other stories yet to unfold.

Looking back on when I
Was a little nappy headed boy . . .

It all started because of Timmy Early. Timmy was a sixth grader and the head bully at Gateway Elementary School. Timmy was so bad that he bullied the other bullies. Even some of the teachers were afraid of him.

I was Timmy's favorite target.

At the time I could not understand why, out of all the kids in school, *I* was the one who got Timmy's undivided attention. I was chased home and threatened at least once a week. Now, with nearly forty years of hindsight, I realize that it's a miracle that I wasn't bullied *more*.

I started kindergarten at the age of four before the law changed and said you had to be five. I was a good fifteen pounds lighter, one and one-half heads shorter and nearly a whole year younger than most of the kids in my class. I had sandy brown–colored hair that turned pumpkin orange in the summer; an overbite that required braces in an era when braces looked like—and were—instruments of torture left over from the days of drawing and quartering, and I was very nearsighted. OK, I was damn near blind. I wore glasses with lenses thicker than bulletproof glass. I could read on a high school level, which didn't endear me to some of my classmates, and I had the annoying habit of getting A's and B's in every subject except arithmetic. Add to this charming stew the fact that I had, and still have, the athletic coordination of an apoplectic baboon with attention deficit disorder. I was always chosen last for the kickball team. I might as well have had a sign on my back that read "Beat me up— *please!*"

About the only thing I could do well was run and, thanks to Timmy Early, I did a lot of that.

I was running from Timmy the day Irene Keller saved my life.

It was late fall. I was flying down Sherborne Drive heading for Greenway Avenue. I was at least half a block ahead of Timmy when one of my shoes came untied, I slipped on wet leaves and fell. By the time I stood up and grabbed my books, Timmy was practically breathing down my neck. I was scared and gulping air so fast that my chest hurt. When I glanced over my shoulder to see how close Timmy was, I ran head-on into Reenie.

"Ow! Vaughn! Watch where you're going!" she yelped, rubbing her ankle where I'd stepped on it.

"Sorry," I gasped out, stealing another look at Timmy, who was rounding the corner. He was grinning. He wore the kind of look a wolf might get just before devouring a plate of lamb chops.

"I'm really sorry, I gotta go."

"What are you running from? Miz Harris's dog get loose again?" Reenie asked, looking past me for the boxer that escaped from our neighbor's yard at least once a week.

Didn't she see the bloodthirsty fiend who was getting ready to murder us both?

"Timmy Early!" I yelled at her as I prepared to take off again. This was no time for a conversation. "He's gonna beat me up if he catches me! You'd better run, too!"

Reenie snorted.

"Run? From Timmy?" She shook her head in disbelief. Her dark curls danced around her shoulders. "I'm not afraid of Timmy Early."

"Well I am," I told her and kept going. I was nearly home, not far from the corner of Sherborne and Greenway, headed toward the white colonial and safety when I realized that I didn't hear footsteps and panting behind me anymore. I knew that I'd regret it, but I skidded to a stop and took the chance of looking back over my shoulder.

Timmy wasn't chasing me anymore. He was talking to Reenie Keller.

Curiosity may have killed the cat but satisfaction brought him back, at least that's what we said on the playground. I was still so scared that my stomach was in knots, but I was more nosy than scared, so I inched back toward Reenie to hear what was going on.

Timmy, tall for his age, muscular, and as dark as Hershey's chocolate, was looming over Reenie, who was, even in those days, tiny and slim with skin the color of weak coffee with too much cream in it. Timmy had his back to me, but I could tell by the way his shoulders were hunched up that he was about to pummel Reenie into the ground and dig his heel into her throat. I was a real 'fraidy cat when it came to physical violence, so I started to run the other way and justify my cowardice by saying that Reenie had brought this on herself. I mean, I warned her, didn't I?

But I'm a product of Baptist Sunday school, and even though we were taught about turning the other cheek, we Baptists knew the Bible stories. We were taught that Jesus didn't put up with any stuff and created a big mess when he chased out the money changers, and Zipporah helped Moses out when she turned back that angel. I say all this to say that I didn't run away, I decided to sacrifice my life to Timmy in order to save Irene. I figured that I would get into heaven easily with this act of heroism.

By the time I was close enough to see and hear what was going on, I realized that it wasn't Irene who needed saving. It was Timmy.

Irene was waving her finger in front of his nose. Timmy looked scared enough to fart.

Reenie Keller was about the last person you'd expect to see facing down Timmy Early. She looked like a dove squaring off with a rhino.

"You touch Vaughn, I'll have your butt dragged down the street and thrown into Alum Creek!" Her eyes were blazing and her expression was completely serious. Even her voice, small and high-pitched in those days, was strong and very firm. I believed her although I wasn't sure how tiny little Irene could ever drag Timmy anywhere. Not to mention the fact that we weren't supposed to use the word *butt* in our house. I was enthralled.

"I can beat you up before you tell," Timmy replied. But he wasn't convincing.

"Humph," she commented unimpressed. "You touch me, it'll be three times as bad. I'll call my biggest brother, Calvin, he's away at school. He'll come home and help! And he'll be mad, too, if he has to miss a party to do it!"

Timmy just about pooped in his pants. All the color drained out of his face. And that is saying something.

And no wonder.

I had forgotten that Irene Keller was the fourth youngest of the five Keller children and the only girl. There was Calvin, JC, Jimmy, and Ernie. The Keller boys were legendary. They played every sport well and the older boys wore their Southeast High purple-and-white football jackets everywhere. They were closer than fingers on a fist. And they were fiercely protective of their little sister, Irene Darling. That's what they called her, Irene Darling.

Nobody messed with Irene Keller. Nobody.

"She's my friend," Irene lied—she hardly knew me. "And if you mess with her, I'll get Ernie, Jimmy, *and* JC to kick your behind all the way to Bexley." She cocked her head to the side in a defiant tilt. "And don't think I won't either."

Her arms were folded across her chest. I don't think I've ever seen anyone look so brave wearing polished navy leather Buster Brown Mary Janes along with a perfectly pleated skirt, matching jacket, and curled pigtails with white ribbons. St. Michael the Archangel never looked as formidable as Irene did on that fall afternoon.

Timmy Early slinked away. As he approached me, I shrank to the side to let him pass. He didn't looked scared anymore, but he was angry.

"I'll git you one of these days, count on it," he said. He glared back at Reenie. But he kept walking.

"I-I . . . thank you. It's really nice of you to do that. Would-Would your brothers really beat Timmy up?"

"My brothers would beat up Timmy Early just for something to do. He never comes around me 'cause JC told him not to. Now he won't bother you anymore either."

"You saved my life," I said, meaning it. "I was so scared . . ."

Reenie crinkled up her nose and smiled.

"My dad says that if you save someone's life, they are your responsibility." She studied me. It's not as if she didn't know who I was, but Reenie played with another crowd at recess and I played alone or with the other outcasts. "So I have to watch out for you for the rest of your life. Or at least until you're thirty." I remember thinking with pleasure that I would have Irene's company when I was an old, old woman of, say, twenty-seven. When you're nine going on ten, thirty seems like a very ancient age.

At the corner we said good-bye and went our separate ways. I checked both Sherborne and Greenway to see if Timmy was lurking anywhere near, then sprinted the rest of the way home.

At dinner all I could talk about was how Reenie Keller faced down Timmy Early and saved my life. Nobody was interested.

My sister Pat was unimpressed. She was in junior high school and wasn't interested in anything except for boys, Marvin Gaye, and boys. My youngest sister, Jean, was also unimpressed, mostly because she had a boo-boo on her knee and Mom was fussing about it. Daddy was about the only one who was remotely interested in my epic tale. But even he had other concerns that didn't have much to do with how my life was saved or what I would do tomorrow if Timmy was lurking around the shrubs in Reverend Charles's yard.

"Early. That's the family over on Merry Hill? The father's an NCO and stationed in Korea?"

"I don't know, Daddy, but . . ."

"Bob, it's Marjorie Jolly, remember? She went to Eastwood with Betty?" Betty was "Aunt Betty" to us, Mom's older sister. "She married the guy she met at Lockbourne. He was from Memphis or somewhere like that in Tennessee?"

"Oh, yes, I remember now." Dad's brow wrinkled. He returned his attention to the *Dispatch*. It was always important for him to be able to identify who the families were and where they were from. You would have thought he was tracing the lineage of a racehorse.

"She has too many kids . . ." I thought I heard my mom say under her breath as she started clearing the table. How can you have too many kids? To me that sounded fun, you'd always have enough kids to play games with. Twenty years later, when I was a mother, I understood what she was talking about.

"You should tell Mrs. Allen or Mrs. Webster," Mom said, yelling over the running water. "They'll do something about Timmy."

Pat looked at Mom and sighed loudly.

"Mom, that never works! That'll make Timmy want to beat her up more! Being a tattletale is so useless."

"No, Patricia, your mother's right," Dad chimed in. "You should tell someone in authority, Vaughn. Let Mrs. Allen know that there's a problem."

Just put "Kick me" on my behind, I thought miserably. I am the middle child. Patricia gets the glory, Jeannie gets the attention. Vaughn with the strange name was left to fend for herself. Until now. *Now I have Reenie.*

"No, it's OK now," I finally said. "Reenie Keller took care of it. Told Timmy her brothers would beat him up if he came after me again."

"You mean, Dinah Keller's little girl?" Mom was finally listening.

I'd been playing with my food, trying to scoot the green peas, which I hated (and still hate), to the edge of my plate so I could slip them into my napkin and stash them in the trash.

Dad's brow rose. *Had he seen me?*

"Yes, ma'am," I answered. The peas slid perfectly into my napkin. *Yeah!*

"She's a pretty little thing," Mom commented, turning back to her dishes. "Looks just like her mother."

"Yes, ma'am," I murmured. My thoughts were far away. "She's going to look after me until I'm thirty." Just saying this made me feel better about nearly everything. I had never had a guardian angel before. It made me feel as if I belonged somewhere.

The next day, at recess, I was invited to play with Reenie and some of the girls from Miss Innes's class. Miss Innes had the coolest fifth-grade class at Gateway. She was one of the younger teachers, enthusiastic and still hopeful, not yet disillusioned by the system. We kids thought the other teachers didn't like her. But the kids loved her. I wasn't in her class, but being invited to play with girls who were was like having the tooth fairy come and having a birthday at the same time.

At ten-fifteen, I was jumping double Dutch with Reenie and her friends, including her cousin Dyanne and Susan Penn. Let me revise that sentence. I was hanging around with Reenie, Dyanne, Susan Penn, and the other girls watching *them* jump double Dutch. If my life depended on skipping through those turning ropes, I would be dead.

For the uninformed, double Dutch is a style of jumping rope that uses two ropes moving toward each other in alternating beats. If you're turning the ropes, you'd better be ambidextrous. If you're jumping, you'll need the coordination of a flamenco dancer and a gymnast because it takes timing, skill, and physical coordination. I had none of these things, so every time I stepped into the sacred circle of turning ropes, I got tangled up in them and nearly strangled. And when I was up to turn them, they hit the ground with a thud because I couldn't get the rhythm straight, which is interesting because I can play Rachmaninoff on the piano. But I cannot turn the ropes for double Dutch. Like I've said, I have the athletic coordination of an apoplectic baboon. Of course, my clodhopper shoes didn't help either. It felt as if I were jumping wearing two buckets of concrete on my feet. But that is an issue (yet another one) that I need to take up with my mother.

"Vaughn, can't you even jump?" one of the other girls cried in frustration as my size-six oxfords got tangled up, yet again, in the ropes and we had to start over.

"Sorry," I whimpered out for the twentieth time. Recess was only twenty minutes long and they had wasted five of them trying to keep the ropes turning when I jumped in. We'd wasted another five minutes learning that I couldn't turn the darned ropes.

"Get out, it's Dyanne's turn," Evelyn ordered, her deep voice filled with frustration. "Su, you're after her."

Humiliated, I slinked off to the side and stood in the shade against the fence. My first and probably last adventure with the cool girls in Miss Innes's class was over. They wouldn't waste a recess period on me again. And Reenie Keller would have to find someone else to watch over until we were thirty.

But it was Susan Penn's voice that I heard next.

"Lyn, don't be a meanie. You turn the rope too fast. Vaughn, come on back and try again. Reenie, you turn with me."

"It's my turn!" Dyanne exclaimed, stomping her foot.

"Yeah! Dyanne's next," Evelyn agreed. "Vaughn had her turn and messed it up!"

"It's OK," I said, trying to keep the peace. I didn't want to jump again anyway. There are few things more embarrassing than not being able to jump rope in fifth grade.

"Vaughn didn't finish her turn," Su shouted at Evelyn as she and

Reenie began to turn the rope. The plastic rope hit the pavement with a rhythmic click-click-click-click, crisp and sharp like rim shots on a snare drum. "Go on, Vaughn." Reenie and Su slowed it down a bit so I could jump in without hanging myself. Su coached me in a soft but strong voice, just loud enough to be heard over the staccato of the ropes.

Take your time, listen to the ropes . . .

"I don't care, it's my turn, I'm goin' in," Dyanne repeated and she bent her knees and poised her body, preparing to launch herself between the moving ropes.

"It's Vaughn's turn," Su said forcefully, glaring at Dyanne.

"You're not the boss of everything, Suz-Ann," Evelyn taunted. "We can do what we want."

In a split second, Su and Reenie pulled the ropes completely straight. Dyanne froze.

"And it's *my* rope," Reenie said. Looking at me, she said, "Go *ahead*, Vaughn."

And that is all that needed to be said. Evelyn and Dyanne pouted. But they didn't say anything. And they moved away and let me go another round in the center of the turning ropes.

Su and Reenie were best friends and the most popular girls in the fifth grade. They were inseparable; if you saw one, you saw the other. They were both smart and quick. They were almost always the first girls picked for any playground games. Su was tall and strong. She kicked, hit, or threw the ball as far as the boys could. Reenie, despite her delicate appearance, was the fastest thing wearing Buster Browns. She was like quicksilver.

Physically, they were opposites: Reenie was short, Su was tall. Reenie was pale, the color of vanilla ice cream, Su was the shade of milk chocolate. Both were good-looking, although in high school, Reenie would become "cute" while Su grew into "attractive." She was tall and muscular with a square jaw, dark eyes that seemed to see miles into your soul, and a beauty queen smile, although this was in the days when no Negro girl was considered for Miss Ohio.

Reenie spoke quickly in her high-pitched voice, running words then sentences then paragraphs together without taking a breath.

"Goodness! Irene!" Miss Diggs, the art teacher, would exclaim. "Slow down, please, I can't understand what you're saying!"

When Susan Penn talked, people listened. Su had the voice of God.

She had, and still has, the kind of voice that can sing a baby to sleep or stop a freight train. It isn't too low and it isn't too high. She was nearly eleven years old but when she answered the telephone, folks assumed they were talking with a grown-up. In church, her strong alto was nearly legendary and she sang with the grown-up choir. In class and on the playground, her speaking voice with its adult timbre and English teacher–style articulation had fooled lots of us into thinking that Miss or Mrs. So-and-So was right behind us and we'd better straighten up. It is the voice of an angel but not one of those flighty things, white with fluffy wings and a harp. Susan has the voice of a female archangel, a voice that can warn the sinner that judgment day is near and sing a joyful hymn all in the same song.

Su became my other guardian angel that day. She and Reenie took me under their wings, giving me a place to hide and heal when the taunts and the teasing got to be too much. My awkwardness and small size, thick-lensed glasses, and funny-colored hair had put a bull's eye on my back.

Sticks and stones may break my bones but words will never hurt me.

I had learned through hard experience that this adage wasn't true. The scratches and bruises from the sticks and stones healed quickly. The wounds from the words took longer. But thanks to the protective circle of Reenie and Su and, in later years, Audrey, the words didn't hurt as much and eventually didn't hurt at all.

Evelyn pushed me when we lined up to go back into our class-rooms.

"Four-eyes," she whispered loudly. The kids around me giggled.

"Bitch," I told her back. Su had told me to call her that.

It was the first time I was sent to the principal's office. It wouldn't be the last.

TWO

If you tell my son, I'll deny it, but there are advantages to being called to the principal's office. Just don't make it a habit. If you're called down once or twice in your elementary school life, it's no big deal. If you're sent down twice a week from grade two on, you're headed toward a career in crime. Having a two-ton bully like Evelyn Edwards tattle on me raised my standing ten feet among my fellow fifth graders. Getting sent to Mrs. Webb's office for saying a bad word, and not just any bad word, the *b* word, was another plus. This was the mid-sixties and the midsection of the country. Even the really bad boys in the school weren't using the *b* word yet. Timmy Early, Bobby Henry, and the other members of the rough-and-tumble crowd watched in awe as I was escorted, not sent, *escorted* to the principal's office. Only really bad kids were escorted.

Mrs. Webb, who had rarely heard me open my mouth in front of a group much less use a word like *bitch*, was at a loss. I remember the amazed look she got on her face as she listened to Mrs. Ayles explain what had happened. Then they went into the hall and whispered.

"Are you sure that it was . . . Vaughn Jones?"

"I'm positive. Evelyn isn't the most reliable child, but Brenda, Jennifer, Earl, and Eugene all said the same thing."

Mrs. Webb turned and gave me a funny look. As an adult looking back on that, I recognize it as the "What the hell is going on?" look.

I wasn't paddled. I wasn't even suspended. I was given a good talking to and kept in from recess for two weeks. Su felt bad and promised to make it up to me, but I wasn't feeling bad about it at all. I had become infamous. From that day on, the kids looked at me as if I were a force of nature. No one was sure what else I might be capable of, so the words that used to hurt me—"four-eyes," "buck-tooth," and "peewee"—were used less often. I mean, if I could let a word like "bitch" roll off my tongue, what else was I likely to say? Even the boys began to treat me with more respect.

Mother and Dad, stunned when they'd heard of my transgression for using a word that (a) I had never heard of until Su told me to use it and (b) was not used in our home, also put me on punishment of sorts. I was to go directly to my room after school. I tried very hard to look unhappy when this sentence was handed down. My room . . . the place where peace and quiet reigned (as long as my little sister, Jeannie, wasn't around), the place where my crayons and coloring books were, the place where my pink plaid diary resided with its formidable-looking but flimsy lock. My room . . . the home of my Nancy Drew mysteries. For me, it was heaven. I was almost fifteen by the time Mother realized that sending me to my room was no punishment at all. Su and Reenie kept me in touch with things by passing notes to me between classes and stopping by to see how I was doing when they "happened to be in the neighborhood." Since Reenie lived on the opposite end of our neighborhood and Su didn't live in our neighborhood at all, it was a stretch. But I appreciated the support. I finally had real girlfriends. And the moment I was paroled, I was invited over to Reenie's house.

I can best describe the Keller home using television sitcom analogies from several decades. It was like *Ozzie and Harriet*, *The Cosby Show*, *My Three Sons*, and *The Simpsons*, all rolled up into one. Reenie's mother was a homemaker, but that's about as close to Harriet Nelson as she got. She was tiny and pretty like Reenie, with a long coil of black hair that she tried to pin up with little success. She didn't work outside of the home, but with four active sons and one high-maintenance daughter, she wouldn't have had time any-way. If she wasn't cooking something, buying groceries, picking up JC, dropping off Ernie, or doing laundry, she was playing mediator between Jimmy and Reenie, changing a bicycle tire, cleaning up dog poop, or serving as referee for the kickball games that the Kellers had in their huge yard that backed up onto the railroad tracks. That doesn't include playing jazz music very loud on the hi-fi and tum-bling exercises on the living room floor. My mother says that Ree-nie's mom used to be a tomboy.

For me, visiting the Kellers was like entering the Looking Glass world of Alice or visiting the realm of Scheherazade and the Arabian Nights. Their household was as different from mine as Tom Sawyer is from Miss Marple. My mother's dining room table shone with pol-ish and was always dust-free and empty except for the centerpiece. The living room was not lived in; we peeked in on our way upstairs. The adages about floors clean enough to eat a meal on? That was my mother's kitchen floor. The sounds in my house were Patty's voice on the phone, a low murmur, as she sat at the top of the stairs in the hall, Jeannie's high-pitched whining because something didn't go her way, and the soft rumble of my father's voice from time to time. There was the occasional slammed door, but our mother didn't tol-erate bursts of temper so that was a rare event. The paraphernalia of a home that sheltered three girls and one grown woman included pink foam hair curlers, bobby socks (but never on the floor), boxes of Kotex quickly stashed out of sight, a stray Barbie high-heeled shoe, and Coca-Cola, bottles not cans. There was the smell of freshly pressed hair, Tabu, and furniture polish.

Not at Reenie's house. From the moment you walked in the door, you were bombarded with sights, sounds, and smells that all seemed to be at odds with one another. But when you think about it, there was no other way that the Keller house could have been with all those boys! There was stuff everywhere. All kinds of stuff—socks, tennis shoes, balls, bats, homework, schoolbooks. There were parts of Boy Scout uniforms from the blue of the Cub Scout to the dark khaki of the Eagle. There were science projects on the dining room table instead of linen runners and centerpieces, there were cages in the corner of the upstairs hall with hamsters and guinea pigs in them (to protect them from the dogs) and you had to watch where you stepped when you walked upstairs because there was nearly always something on the steps that could trip you. Tinker Toys and demolished erector sets, miniature racing cars and roller skates, muddy footballs (there are no other kind) and other "stuff" that defied description.

There was music playing all of the time because there were two hi-fi players and each of the Keller kids had a transistor radio. You walked in the front door and the sound of Rusty Bryant's saxophone floated over from the living room; up the stairs, JC played the radio as loudly as he could without getting yelled at (and there was lots of yelling at Reenie's house); and in the soft pink-cotton-candied aura of Reenie's room we listened to Mary Wells's smooth as honey voice croon about "My Guy." And the soft fragrance of the Chanel No. 5 that Mrs. Keller wore or the aromas of freshly baked or fried delights wrestled with the sharp stench of dirty socks that had fallen under the couch and the ripe smell of drying mud on the bottom of football cleats. There was always lots of noise, yelling, laughter, and thumping and bumping.

Reenie's house was small, cluttered, and noisy. It was the most chaotic, unorganized mess you ever saw.

And I loved it.

"Reenie, close that door, Duchess will get out. JC? Are these your socks on the counter? JC? Did you hear me ask you a question?"

"*Mom!* The toilet's backed up again! Ernie's filled it with crap!"

"Don't use the word *crap*, Jimmy. JC! The socks!"

"Mommy, Vaughn's here!"

"Hi, sweetie, how's your mother?"

"*Mom!* The toilet's spilled over! Ernie did it!"

"I did not!"

"Did too!"

"Did not."

"Yes, you did!"

And on and on. It was like a three-ring circus, overflowing toilet and all. Ernie would sit on the cat, JC and Jimmy were dispatched to clean up the bathroom floor and plunge the toilet, and Reenie and I helped Mrs. Keller with the sugar cookies and brownies that she was making for PTA. The furniture was worn and usually covered with athletic socks and homework papers (unfinished). The front hall was the favorite sleeping spot for the various dogs and cats that found their way home with the Keller boys, including a collie that was blind in one eye, a piece of dog that looked like a Chihuahua mix, and another large black-and-white fur ball that followed Reenie's oldest brother, Calvin, home one day eight years before and stayed. Its name was . . . Furball.

And if Mr. Keller, a city bus driver, happened to come home in the middle of this gumbo, he would, just like Dr. Huxtable, look around at the mess, trip over the dog (like Rob Petrie tripped over the foot stool), scrunch up his face and say, to no one in particular, "Where is your mother?"

Walk on by . . .

Reenie and I sang along with Dionne Warwick and Mrs. Keller as we sliced out the cookies and poured the brownie batter into well-greased pans. She opened the huge door of the Tappan range and handed us pot holders.

"Be careful now, don't burn yourselves . . . that's right, Vaughn, leave yourself some room . . ."

We felt so grown-up, centering the pans in the oven, feeling the 400-degree heat on our faces.

Walk on by (don't stop) . . .

"There!" Mrs. Keller wiped her hands on her apron and reached for the cigarette that was sitting in the ashtray next to the sink. "Let's see . . ." She squinted as the smoke curled up around her face. "I'll set the timer for . . . twenty-five minutes." A button was pushed, Mrs. Keller exhaled. "Good! Twenty-five minutes and not a second more. You girls go on upstairs and play for a while. I'll call you when the bell goes off."

We zipped through the living room and flew up the stairs, avoiding the ones that had sneakers or baseballs or rulers on them. One thing about the Keller house, it really had that lived-in look. We tromped down the narrow hall, again dodging sneakers and boy junk. A Chuck Berry poster covered one door, football schedules covered another.

JC stuck his head out. Behind him, I could see the bunk beds, covered with clothes. Dionne Warwick had been drowned out by Junior Walker and the All-Stars.

"Hey, Irenedarling, ya gonna give me some of those cookies you baked? Hi, Vaughn." JC's words all ran together in a big rush like Reenie's. You had to listen real carefully to catch what he was saying. Hard to hear with the music blaring.

"No, and if I think you took one, I'm tellin' Mom," replied Irenedarling in a firm voice. You did not mess with Irenedarling.

"Awwww, Reenie, just one . . ." whined JC. He gave her a huge Kool-Aid grin. His dimples were like craters in his fawn-colored cheeks. His dark eyes sparkled with mischief. "Only one . . ."

The door to Reenie's room slammed close. And I was in a different world. In the first place, it was quiet. In the second place, it was soft, pink, and neat. There weren't any socks, pencils, homework papers (finished or unfinished), dogs, cats, or shoes in sight. The canopy bed was crowned with a beautiful pink floral fabric that matched the tied-back curtains. In addition to the bed, Reenie had a matching nightstand, dresser, mirror, and rocking chair. I think she must have had the full set of Nancy Drew mysteries, even beyond the *Clue of the Tapping Heels* and the *Mystery of the Brass-Bound Trunk*. The books were arranged in her bookcase in their proper numerical order. And, wonder of all wonders, Reenie had two Barbie trunks, the black one and the new hot pink one, and four (I counted them), *four* Barbie dolls, two with ponytails, two with the new bouffant hairdos. Each doll had its own outfits, shoes, jewelry, everything. And its own carrying case. I had one Barbie doll that I'd gotten for Christmas and she was already ruined. Jeannie had decided to practice her hairdressing skills on her—the ponytail had been unwound and then set on rollers with Dippity-Do. The synthetic blond hair turned green. Even with the salvaged ponytail, my Barbie would never be museum quality.

We'd been given one Barbie doll each for Christmas. Pat groaned when she got hers, "Mom, I am too *old* for dolls! I wanted another

mohair sweater!" ("Wish I could find that damn doll now," my sister
has said more times than I can count. "Now they're collectibles.")
Jeannie pulled the legs and arms off her doll and uncurled her hair.
Don't ask me how she did that. Then, with her Barbie maimed, dis-
membered, and nearly bald, she turned her attention to mine.

Reenie's room was too wonderful for words. We sat on the pinker-
than-Pepto carpet and played with the dolls and the Barbie house
and the Barbie car and the Barbie beauty shop. And despite the in-
terruptions from JC, Jimmy, and Ernie, we had a wonderful time. I
still sigh when I think about it. Reenie had a lot going for her: brains,
beauty, and personality. She had the most wonderful clothes. But
those weren't the things I envied her for. I was jealous of her Barbie
doll collection and her brothers.

The cookies and brownies came out of the oven, the kitchen was
cleaned up. No automatic dishwashers; we were the dishwashers,
sink scrubbers, and floor moppers. If I did that much work every time
I used my kitchen now, I'd be dead.

Mrs. Keller stuck her head inside the door.

"Girls, get yourselves ready to go. I'll drop you off at Su's on my
way to take Ernie to Boy Scouts. Then I'll swing back by and we'll
head downtown. Hurry up now!"

"Downtown." The word had magical connotations. For us it was
like going to the Emerald City. The boulevard widened, the traffic
increased, the streetcars converged, and the buildings got taller and
taller until the LeVeque Lincoln Tower loomed ahead just before
the Broad Street Bridge. Going downtown meant that we got to
dress up, not as much as on Sunday, but you didn't go downtown in
just any old thing. Downtown meant inhaling the warm, deep smell
of roasted peanuts from the Planters peanut store on High Street,
window-shopping at Madison's wondering if we would ever be rich
enough to wear sleek, cloth-buttoned suits with mink collars and
Jackie Kennedy pillbox hats. Downtown meant walking past the ornate lobby of the Deshler Hilton or the Neil House and trying not to
gawk at the gilded lobby with its plush chairs and the sophisticated
people coming and going. It meant waiting at the corner of Gay and
High with crowds of people on the sidewalks, people who looked dif-

ferent from the ones who lived in our neighborhood. People who walked fast and wore business suits and hats. Women wearing heels and carrying alligator handbags. Downtown meant spending nearly the entire afternoon in Lazarus, riding the elevators, watching the light turn from red to green and back again, starting at the first floor with the perfume and the hats and the jewelry, and ending up on the sixth floor, a magical place that transformed itself in late November into a children's paradise because it was the toy store in town and every child dreamed of spending eternity among the dolls and the electric trains and cowboy outfits and Lincoln Logs. And, if it was near Christmas, the Town Street windows of the department store became a wonderland of music, color, and movement. The mechanical puppets bobbed, twirled, bowed, and danced to piped-in music and the sounds of delight from little children. I was pretty much out of high school before I stopped gawking at those windows. But even when I came home from college and later in my life, I'd stop by the corner of Town and High to see the Christmas windows. They're all gone now.

On this particular Saturday, Mrs. Keller was taking us downtown with her while she ran some errands. Su, Reenie, and I were old enough to go with her and, if we were very good, we would be allowed to visit the hallowed sixth-floor Lazarus and the third-floor junior department (where all the really cool clothes were) by ourselves. We were so excited about the opportunity that I think we were afraid to breathe the wrong way. We felt so grown-up and sophisticated. That was our new favorite word: sophisticated.

It amazes me now to think of how much freedom we had and we didn't realize it. We thought our parents were too strict. And yet we walked all over our neighborhoods, alone and in groups, and no one ever bothered us, unless you count Timmy Early and friends. Our parents told us not to talk to strangers and we obeyed them, but "strangers" were a small exclusive group because we knew everyone who belonged in our close-knit community and it was pretty easy to figure out who didn't belong. Wedged in between all-white Bexley and Alum Creek on the east and the business district and downtown on the west, our enclave, bordered by Nelson Road, Leonard and

Hamilton Avenues, and Livingston on the south, was friendly, busy, and safe. Teenage girls could walk past the bars unmolested. It was "yes, sir" and "yes, ma'am" regardless of who you were speaking to because everybody knew who your people were. If you were disrespectful or got caught doing something you shouldn't, the news reached your home long before you did. There were spies everywhere.

"Hi, baby!" a hairdresser would call out from Benson's Beauty Parlor on Long Street.

"You be careful crossing that street now," a wino would remind us in a firm voice, index finger wagging. "You gals don't want to be runned over."

"Aren't you Carol Jones's girl? I went to Sunday school with her at Centenary."

"How's your daddy getting along at the post office?"

Reenie's mother dropped us off in front of the apartment building where Su lived with her mother. Dinah Keller looked at her watch.

"I should be back in fifteen minutes, all right? Now, you girls meet me right here at the curb at a quarter after, y'hear? No fooling around."

"Yes, ma'am," we said in unison.

The blue Chevy rolled away. Ernie, who'd been sitting in the backseat with us, pushed his head out the window and stuck his tongue out at us.

We looked up at the third-floor east windows where Su lived. The curtains were drawn and the windows closed even though it was a mild day.

"Did she say she was coming?" I asked Reenie. "It looks as if no one's home."

"She called this morning," Reenie replied, frowning in the bright sunlight. "But she was whispering. Said her mom had . . . a headache." Her dark eyes met mine.

I pushed the button for apartment 310 several times before the buzzer came on. Reenie and I pushed the door open. We were remembering the last time we'd picked up Su and the curtains were drawn and her mother had a headache.

So many balloons float over your head when you are young.

They carry the trials and treats of life that you aren't old enough yet to understand or appreciate—the pains and pleasures that require girth and guts to deal with. Things like "sex" and "cancer" and "abuse." And "hangovers."

"You know Barb drinks," I'd heard my mother say to my father once when she thought I was upstairs. *Drinks what?* I remember thinking.

"How is your mother?" Dinah Keller had asked Su once.

Su's eyes flickered but she answered quickly, with a smile that came too late, "Oh . . . she's fine."

Barbara Penn was tall, dark, and elegant like her daughter, a striking-looking woman with a warm smile; bright, almond-shaped eyes; and a dancer's lithe figure. She'd studied in New York and she'd modeled with the Ebony Fashion Fair. Miss Penn was sophistication personified. She was the only person we knew who read the *New York Times*.

"The bee's knees" as my great-grandmother would have said. Her short hair was colored auburn and cut short and spiky and she wore black Capri pants and smoked cigarettes at the end of a long black holder like Audrey Hepburn in *Breakfast at Tiffany's*. When she spoke, her words were softened around the edges, and when she said "New York" we thought it was the most fabulous thing. Not like the flat, harsh "New Yawk" that we heard come from our own lips. Barbara Penn could scat like Ella Fitzgerald and we often heard her singing along to the jazz LPs she played in her tiny apartment when we went to pick up Su or were visiting her. She'd seen Duke Ellington in person, had cocktails with my daddy's favorite singer, Dinah Washington. She had studied dance with Katherine Dunham. When she was younger, she was good enough to perform in *The Nutcracker*, but Columbus wasn't ready for a colored Sugarplum fairy. If we were good and had permission, Su's mother pulled her tap and ballet shoes out from under her bed and let us try them on.

"Be careful, girls, with the ribbons, I mean," she would instruct us. "The fabric is very delicate." She would run her manicured finger-tips over the soft pink ribbons of the toe shoes, stroking them as gently as she would a baby's cheek. A giggle. Then a sigh. "When I put on my toe shoes, I was almost six feet tall! A good height for a basketball player, Madame would tell me. *Tres mal pour la danseuse.*" She smiled at us but the fondness of the memory was not in her eyes. They were sad. She shrugged her shoulders. *"Eh bien . . ."*

Su's mother was the only mother we knew who could speak French. She was also the only mother we knew who didn't have a husband. Our mothers were Mrs. Jones and Mrs. Keller and, when Audrey joined us, Mrs. Taylor. Su's mother was always "Miss Penn."

When she was nineteen, Barbara Penn left town to study dance in New York City. When she returned, four years later, she had a reputation. Eight months later, she had a baby. She did not have a husband.

"Shhhh." Su's finger went to her lips. "Momma's . . . not feeling well, she has a headache." She beckoned to us. "Have a seat on the couch, I'm almost ready."

Su's footsteps were barely audible as she floated down the hall to her tiny bedroom in the back. Reenie and I sat, huddled together, nearly knee-to-knee and looked at each other and then at our surroundings. The blinds were closed and the curtains pulled over them. There was no light in the room except for the tiny bulb beneath the hood of the stove in the galley kitchen ten feet away. There'd been dishes in the sink and a pair of high heels peeked out from beneath the armchair across from us. Nylons hung over the kitchen chair along with a brassiere, skirt, and other pieces of clothing. There were several glasses on the table and ashtrays filled with cigarettes. There had been a bottle there, too, but Su had swept it up and tossed it into the trash can on her way to the back. The room was stuffy and the gloom took on a life of its own. It was still and quiet. I shivered. The only sound I heard was Reenie's breathing: fast and quick.

The first time we'd come to Su's apartment, the blinds were open and the curtains pulled back. Daylight streamed in and Miss Penn still had all the lamps on.

"I'm trying to keep the electric company going!" she'd told us with laughter in her voice. "Let there be light!"

We feasted on Vienna sausage hors d'oeuvres and cherry Kool-Aid spiked with 7-Up "to make it seem like pink champagne." We danced to one of Miss Penn's LPs and learned to snap our fingers as loudly as she did. She talked about mythical people we'd only read bits and pieces about in *Jet*, like Adam Clayton Powell, Eartha Kitt, and Ruby Dee. She asked us what we were reading and when we told her about Nancy Drew, she said that we should read "Jimmy" Baldwin, but no, maybe we weren't old enough yet. The small combination living room–dining room–kitchen was accented with modern dark pumpkin–colored chairs, a lacquered coffee table, oblong and unusually shaped glass ashtrays, and modern art hanging on the white walls, splashes of color in red, teal, a crisp black and sharp cloud white. We had art history lessons.

"Look at this shape, girls, look closely now." Barbara outlined a brown shape with one slender index finger. "It looks like an African sculpture, doesn't it? Picasso was influenced by Dogon art. That's a nation of people who live in West Africa. Excellent wood carvings. And look at this . . ."

The haunting portrait of a young woman dressed in a deep red gown had our attention. The woman's dark eyes were fierce in some way but not threatening. And her expression was strong and wise.

"This is called a self-portrait," Su's mom continued in her smooth, eloquent voice. "Frida Kahlo was from Mexico and she used her art to show her feelings, to show what was going on in her life. You read her story in her eyes, in the way she's painted her face . . . see here?"

Reenie and I were enthralled. Su was proud. Just sitting in Miss Penn's living room was more educational than visiting the art museum downtown.

"Su? Suze that you? Whozat the door?"

The voice that uttered those words was rough and hard and the words were slurred and crackling.

"It's nothin', Momma," Su's voice came from the hall. I heard a door open. "Just Vaughn and Reenie, we're goin' downtown. Mrs. Keller's taking us."

"Zere any gin lef'in dat bottle? Huh? Shit . . . where'z my cigarettes?"

This was not the same smooth, cultured voice that had told us about Lorraine Hansberry's plays and Romare Bearden's collages.

"Where you goin'?"

"Downtown, Momma, remember? Mrs. Keller—"

"Shit. Susie, where my cigarettes?"

Mrs. Keller's car horn sounded in the distance. I heard Su's voice again but didn't catch her words. The door closed and Su appeared.

"Come on, let's go."

She quietly closed the door to the apartment. We ran down the two flights of stairs and out the main door into the sunshine. I gulped down deep breaths of air and Reenie blinked her eyes. We tumbled into the huge backseat of the Chevrolet, chattering and giggling, comparing our shopping lists. Reenie chattered on about the hair stuff that she planned to buy at Kresge's where we usually spent most of our time and nearly all of our money when we went downtown. I talked about the newest Nancy Drew mystery that I had permission to buy, *The Haunted Bridge,* and how I had to pick up something at Will-Call for my mother. Su talked about her shopping plans, too. And we tried hard not to notice the dark circles under her eyes and the fading tracks of tears that had dried on her cheeks.

THREE

When I look back on those days, I wish I had the eyeglasses that I wore when I was ten. The lenses were as thick as Coke bottles, they weren't as clean and they weren't adjusted for bifocals, but they saw the world more plainly, if that's possible. And the thoughts that ran through my head in those days were unedited. I hadn't learned yet to embellish with grace notes and trills or to use the "delete" key.

Su Penn was tall, pretty, smart, and had a voice like a meadowlark. Anyway, that's what the music teacher said. We'd never heard a meadowlark so we had to take his word for it. Su could jump rope, climb to the top of the jungle gym without getting dizzy, push me higher on the swings than anyone besides Earl Smith (who was only trying to make me fall out), and she could actually understand fractions, a concept that reduced me to tears and had Reenie tearing up her homework night after night.

We loved her because she was brave and funny. And because she was our friend. She was strong but vulnerable and we felt that we had to protect her. We got huffy with the kids who whispered bad things behind Su's back. It didn't matter to us that Su's father, whoever he was, was not around and hadn't married her mother. We liked her interesting, sophisticated mother.

Reenie and I watched the world go round from the level of a half-size person. We saw things and we didn't see things. We heard things and we ignored them. And we protected Su when we had to, putting Band-Aids on the wounds that we saw in her spirit. We had no way of knowing then how deep they were and how long they would take to heal, if ever.

For a while, the child wrestled with the dark and fought off the shadows. But eventually, the monsters in Su Penn's life surfaced like sea dragons and began to crawl toward shore.

It started with little things.

The steady click-click-click of the double-Dutch ropes set the beat for the count: "two-four-six and eight. . . ." Su put her hands on her hips as she jumped, her feet barely touching the ground. She grinned at us and did a complete 360-degree turn. We clapped our hands. Su was the tallest of us with long arms, skinny legs, and feet "like skis" she'd say sadly looking down at the size eight and a half shoes she wore. But neither her height nor her spindly legs and arms kept her from dancing through the ropes like a prima ballerina.

"Dag, she's wearing that same white blouse today that she wore yesterday." Evil Evelyn's voice carried over the counting and the clickity-clack of the ropes.

"*With* the same skirt. It's got somethin' on it, too." This comment from Reenie's cousin Dyanne.

"Mommy says that Su's mother . . ."

Reenie and I ignored the comments; we weren't old enough yet to understand what they all meant. Neither were Evelyn or Dyanne, who were only repeating what they'd heard adults say. But Reenie and I both knew that something was wrong with Su and with her mother. And with the uncluttered optimism of children, we tried to shield her and take care of her ourselves as best we could.

These were the days of lunch boxes or sack lunches, and most of us brought what we thought was the most unappetizing mess imaginable from home. Peanut butter sandwiches with thick layers of chunky Jif alternating with smooth layers of dark grape jam on Wonder bread. An apple as big as your head ("for fiber," my ahead-of-her-time health-conscious mother would say), and white milk. Bologna and cheese with old-time thick bologna that actually had flavor, and salty potato chips and Oreo cookies. We sat together at the corner of a long table in the gym on the side that Miss Cousins patrolled during lunch period. We compared the misery of menu choices that our mothers had thought would be "good for you" and wished that we could have nothing but Fritos and chocolate milk like Donna. Our lunch boxes opened and closed at exactly the same time, but we were talking and giggling and plotting so much that it was awhile before Reenie and I noticed that very little actually came out of Su's Minnie Mouse lunch box. It had been several days of white milk (which we bought at school) and crackers when I said, "Su, aren't you hungry? You didn't eat much."

Su's head bowed quickly.

"Mommy packed me a big sandwich but it's . . . too much, I'll just leave it for later." She nibbled on the crackers and we quickly forgot about it and moved on to talk about Gloria and her chicken pox and David and ringworm.

But after Su passed out in gym class and had to spend the afternoon in the nurse's office, we realized there hadn't been sandwiches in her lunch box, that all she had been eating were crackers and milk. On the days she stopped at my house after school, she gobbled up cheese, crackers, fruit, and milk that my mom set out as a snack as if she hadn't eaten in weeks.

"My goodness! Susan!" Mom would exclaim, pouring out another glass of milk. "You must be having a growth spurt!"

"You're really lucky," Su would say when she'd get ready to go home after she'd helped me work through fractions. Who invented those damn things, anyway?

"You can only have three-fifths, Vaughn! *Not* five-thirds! Here, let me show you . . ."

We both squished ourselves flat against the wall as Patty flew down the stairs without even saying "Excuse me!"

"Lucky? What do you mean, 'lucky'?"

Su's dark eyes had circles under them. Again. She turned her head to look around my mother's off-limits living room, the dining room table where Jeannie was now doing her homework. Just beyond, my parents' voices hummed above the sound of pots clanging and something sizzling in an iron frying pan.

"Your house, it's really nice. Your mom, too."

My mom? I'm sure I looked at Su as if she had just found water on Mars. There wasn't a more boring, straitlaced, by-the-book woman on the earth than my mother. (I had no idea then how lucky I was.) And our house was, well, it wasn't exciting either. My sister Patty was a teenager now, which meant that she was more rude and self-absorbed than usual and she hogged the telephone. Jeannie was going through a bratty stage, again, but I was never allowed to pop her in the head, which was my misfortune for being the middle child. There were no Picassos on our living room walls and we had to take piano and ballet lessons—a misery for me with my two right feet and lack of balance and coordination.

"Su, what on earth are you talking about?"

But, of course, we didn't know then that Su was sometimes starving, her only meal being the snack she had after school at my house or at Reenie's. We soon learned that she washed out her own clothes every night in the sink because her mother hadn't been to the Laundromat in two weeks. Reenie and I took the day-to-day routine and order of our homes for granted. What we thought was boring represented safety and security for Su. We didn't know it then. It wasn't until much later in our lives that I heard from Su's own lips the bad waking dreams of a child left alone.

School was out at three-fifteen sharp; the bell rang not a minute before, not a minute after. The shrieks and laughter of children released from prison for the day echoed throughout the playground, the sounds bouncing off the walls of the houses that bordered Gateway Elementary. The patrols guided us across the streets with their orange flags and we meandered home in the sunshine, clumps of little people here and there moving down the streets. Su spent the afternoon at Reenie's that day; she told Mrs. Keller that her mom was working late. Dinah Keller, who always cooked enough dinner for two armies instead of the one she fed regularly, asked Su to have dinner with the family. She called Barb Penn both at work and at her apartment but she didn't get an answer, and after Su assured her that it was OK since "Mommy already knows where I am," Dinah forgot about it.

"We had round steak and gravy. Mashed potatoes and string beans, I still remember those string beans," Su said years later. "Just that one simple home-cooked meal made an impression on me." She'd turned her dark eyes toward me and, despite the professionally applied TV makeup and perfectly cut hair, I saw the ten-year-old girl she was when I first met her. "Mrs. Keller even put a tablecloth on the table! And JC, no, it was the other brother, Ernie, spilled grape juice all over it! What a mess!" We laughed. Reenie's brothers seemed to take turns spilling and dropping food on the dinner table or on the kitchen floor.

It ain't the glitz and the glamour that you remember. It's the string beans, the spills, and the round steak.

They played Barbie's after their homework was done and they called me to make sure I had survived my ballet lesson OK. (I had.) Then Mr. Keller came up and said that it was getting late and it was time to drive Su home. He'd bundled the girls up into the car and rolled down Greenway toward Clifton Avenue and Su's apartment building.

Su's stomach was jumpy as the Chevy rounded the curve and the apartment building came into view. She'd only stayed so late at Reenie's (and told that lie about her mother working overtime) because, lately, Barbara Penn had taken to coming in from work very late; so late, in fact, that sometimes Su walked all the way to Ohio Avenue and spent the evening with her aunt. Barbara hadn't given her a key ("You're too young for the responsibility," she'd said). So Su was locked out. But there was a light on in the front room of the top-floor east apartment and Su's stomach calmed down. Mommy was home!

But Mommy wasn't home. The light was just on. Had it not been, Cal Keller would never have dropped off Susan and driven away. As it was, he and Reenie waved back at her as she stood just inside the door of the apartment building. And the huge Chevy turned down Brunson because Mr. Keller had to pick up another carton of milk from Rosati's. It was eight o'clock on a Wednesday evening and it was dark.

Su bounded up the steps, the sound of her hard-soled Mary Janes echoing off the plaster walls. Her book bag bounced off her hip as she ran and she smiled thinking of a cup of hot chocolate with marshmallows—her mother's favorite nighttime snack whether it was warm or cold outside.

She turned the doorknob to the apartment. The door was locked. She pressed the door buzzer then tapped on the door.

"Mommy? Mommy, I'm home!"

The green metal door remained closed.

After ten minutes of pounding, tapping, and yelling, Su realized that her mother wasn't home. And that she was alone. She didn't really know any of the other people who lived in her building. Not well enough, anyway, to knock on their doors. Mrs. Givens and her boys had moved out of apartment 308 and it was too dark now to walk all the way to Aunt Leila's on Ohio Avenue. Her grandparents' home was out of the question. They lived way up on the Hilltop.

Mommy would be home soon, wouldn't she? The little girl had not learned the word *hopelessness* yet. And so she sat, cross-legged, in the corner next to the door of apartment 312, huddling against the wall, shivering against its icy, rough hardness, waiting. Waiting.

In the night, even in the lighted landings of Building C, the familiar sounds of the neighborhood, of Clifton Avenue and of Long Street one block over, became dark and spooky. Cars raced up and down the street, not in groups, but one at a time, the roar of the large V-8 engines startling Su with their intensity, then leaving goose bumps on her arms as their sounds faded into the night. The downstairs door opened and closed several times; each time Su started and moved to stand up and peer over the railing into the hall below.

But what if it wasn't Mommy? What if it was a stranger? In the context of a community where everyone knows everyone, the mere idea of a "stranger" was horrifying. She'd wait, that's what she'd do, she'd wait. And she did wait. And she pulled herself into a tighter and tighter ball each time heavy footsteps clumped in and out of the building. When a faceless person climbed the stairs to the second floor, Su nearly jumped out of her skin with fright. Those weren't Mommy's footsteps, light and clicking. Barbara's high heels made a distinct snappy sound on the hard linoleum. These were the large feet of a man, maybe Mr. So-and-So in 210? Or that man who came to visit his mother in 202? Su's breath caught in her throat as the thumping steps came closer and closer, finally stopping at the top of the landing on the second floor. By then, Su was hardly breathing at all.

The buzzer rang, and a door opened. Voices. A television playing in the background.

"It's 'bout time you got here! Did you pick up my Viceroys?"

The metal door slammed shut, sending small tremors into the hall and up the stairs to the floor where Su sat.

She exhaled. And her heart started beating once again. Mommy had taken her Cinderella watch to the jewelry repair because one of the hands had fallen off. So she didn't know that she'd been sitting in the cold, empty hall for nearly two hours.

It was nearly midnight when Barbara Penn came home. Su didn't hear her at first because she'd taken her heels off, climbing the stairs in her stocking feet. When Barb reached the landing of the third floor, she wondered about the child who was sitting there. Through a fog of gin, she saw a skinny, brown-skinned girl with huge, red-circled eyes set in a drawn, frightened face. The child looked up at her with a small smile and tears rolling down her cheeks. Barbara Penn was baffled.

The gin said: *"Whose child is this?"*

The child said, "Mommy? Where've you been?"

The gin replied, *"Oh. That child."*

Barbara Penn didn't speak. The gin that flowed through her system permitted her only enough energy to open the door to the apartment, stumble to the couch, and lie down. The child closed and locked the door behind her and trudged to the bedroom at the back of the apartment. When she got up in the morning (Mommy had taught her how to use the alarm clock) she smoothed a twice worn blouse with her hands and checked her favorite green-and-red-plaid skirt for food stains. She rummaged around in a forgotten laundry basket for a clean pair of underwear but had to wear the red knee socks again. There wasn't any milk in the refrigerator. Mommy hadn't been to the store yet, so there wasn't any cereal or bread either. The crackers were gone.

And that was the day that Susan Penn fainted in gym class because she hadn't had anything to eat since dinner the day before. Shortly after that, Su went to live with her aunt Leila and her life evened out into a boring, secure routine of three meals a day, clean clothes, soft sheets, a supporting hand, and library visits.

"The best days of my life," Su told us years later.

We were kids, so we were never told what actually happened blow by blow. But as Su later came to find out, the information card in Mrs. Webb's office had a "In case of emergency" section. Once the principal called Su's mother at work and at home, and got no answer, she called the third number on her list, Barbara's sister, Leila. But then, Ann Webb would have called Leila Penn in any event. They had known each other for years and belonged to the same sorority. They'd grown up on the Hilltop just blocks from each other. Within a week, Su was living on Ohio Avenue with Leila.

"It's only . . . for a little while," Su had told us, not meeting our eyes. "Only until Mommy . . . feels better." The "little while" turned out to be nearly ten years because Barbara Penn never really did feel "better." For the next twenty years, she floated in and out of her daughter's life, bringing with her guilt and disruption, broken promises and excuses.

Much has been made about the innocence of children. Looking back on those days through a mist of soft towels that smelled like Cheer and nights when the only worries I had were whether I could finish problem number twenty in my long division homework, I know that while the times were precious and my responsibilities few, innocence had nothing to do with it. I played day to day with children who did vicious things, who called people names, who bullied and teased, and there were thefts and murders and painful secrets swept beneath the rugs. On the playground, we perpetrated treasons and mean-spirited slights and were, somehow, forgiven these transgressions because we were children and children are supposed to be innocent. But we weren't then and children aren't these days either. We were naïve and untested and unaware and as yet unexposed to many of life's realities, horrors, and pain. But innocent? Attila the Hun could not have been more merciless than ten-year-old girls who, for reasons only understood among themselves, decided to shun a friend. Naïve, yes. Innocent, no. The age of innocence never existed. And the age of naïveté began to wind down.

I guess we were lucky. We weren't rich and we weren't poor. Most of the time the electric bill was paid and we always had milk to drink, Borden's had home delivery then. There was a streetcar that ran up and down Long Street, the long antennae sparking as the car wound its way around the curve below Woodland on its way to the turnaround at Nelson Road. You could buy a milk shake at Gray's Drugstore and Mr. Rosati's produce was pretty good. These were the days before he had to put bars up. My grandmother used to cash her checks there. The store is gone now. Progress. The biggest trauma in my life then was the fact that Mom wouldn't let me drink chocolate milk after recess (somehow she got the idea that I was allergic to chocolate). I still wore glasses but it wasn't the end of the world anymore because of Reenie and Su.

We lived on the east side of town because if you were Negro (I was born colored but it was the sixties, we were Negroes) that's where you lived, either the east side or Linden. But that's where your doctor lived and your lawyer, and the dentist was around the corner as was the minister and the pharmacist. Oh, sure, my dad drove carefully and stopped for a full twenty seconds at each stop sign in Bexley when he took us to ballet lessons. And when we were teenagers, our parents told us, "Stay out of South Utica and don't let the sun set on you in Grand Lake." But still we managed. Our parents worked hard to keep us fed and clothed. And insulated for as long as they could. And fought for the right for us to be left alone. Chipped away at the things that would have taken away our dignity. We were children and had no idea, really. We saw but we didn't fully understand. We stayed away from certain places and situations but were too young and easily distracted to grasp the import of the ghosts that whispered around us. We knew that we were colored, and we knew that other people were white. But we lived in a soft cocoon of family, community, and discipline.

At nearly ten years old, in November 1963, life was good if you wore the right pair of Keds (I didn't), could jump rope without tripping (I couldn't), or hung with the "in crowd" (I did). One out of three wasn't bad.

We didn't know it then but the times were changing. Fast. And even at nine and ten years old, we were about to be caught up in the earthquakes of our world, and nothing would ever seem the same again.

Mrs. Ayles's fifth-grade class had just finished bathroom break. It was Friday, Art Day, and our desks were being cleared for artistic ventures that were sure to result in water, paint, or clay all over the floor and all over my clothes. We wore old shirts or smocks to keep our clothes clean, but that never worked for me. I invariably spilled something on myself or someone else and made a mess that soaked through the old white shirt with the torn pocket that Mother had given me from my father's closet.

Mrs. Ayles clapped her hands from the front of the class.

"Class, let's get quiet now." Her eagle eyes spotted Billy Porter headed toward the coatroom. "Billy? It isn't time for that, come out of there this minute." Billy was one of the endless Porter children and nearly as bad as Timmy Early. But even he didn't mess with Mrs. Ayles. She was six feet tall and three feet wide and had a voice like a foghorn. I'd never heard a foghorn, of course, having lived my entire life in landlocked Ohio, but my dad grew up with her and had been to sea with the Merchant Marines. So when he said "Lilly Ayles has the voice of a foghorn," it must have been true.

"Paul, go to the sink and wash your hands, please," Mrs. Ayles ordered.

"Why?" Paul asked impertinently. And bravely. In those days, adults did not reason with children or worry about stifling their independence. They gave orders and you did as you were told.

Mrs. Ayles gave him a look that could uncurl his hair and said, "Because you were picking your nose. Now go wash your hands and then go sit in the chair in the corner."

The entire class broke up, giggling and hooting. Paul was embarrassed. He picked his nose so often that I thought he'd forgotten he was in a room full of people.

Paul ended up in the chair in the corner. That wasn't so bad, but the chair was near the coatroom and when he thought no one was looking, he'd pick his nose again and wipe it on whoever's coat was closest.

I know, this is nasty, but it was fifth grade.

"Now, class, we're going to work on our watercolors again. We have about an hour. Get your cover-ups out and make sure your desks are clear. Patricia, Nathaniel, Jill . . . Randolph, please help me get the paint and paper out."

The anticipation of an afternoon away from fractions and long division was enough to make me want to jump out of my seat. I cleared my desk and my dad's shirt was already buttoned halfway down when I noticed Mrs. Ayles was standing at the door of room 10 chatting with Mrs. Webb. They were talking in very low voices, which wasn't unusual. But the principal had tissues in her hand and her eyes were wet. That was unusual. Mrs. Webb was the most composed, poised, and perfect woman you could ever imagine. Nothing ruffled her feathers no matter how hilarious, no matter how sad. If she was crying, then something was really wrong. And when Mrs. Ayles turned to the class, she was dabbing her eyes with a handkerchief, too.

Behind her, Mr. Walker, one of the janitors, wheeled in a TV set mounted on an elevated stand.

Mrs. Ayles moved to the center of the blackboard and clapped her hands together.

"Boys and girls, let me have your attention, please. I want you all to take your seats. Quickly now, this is very important. Mr. Walker will set up the audiovisual system. Something has happened."

It was like the buzzing in a hive before all the bees fly out and sting whatever is in sight. We scurried around, chairs banging against one another, desks scraping across the floor. Normally, Mrs. Ayles would have said "Quietly now," but she'd forgotten that. So we were fussing and talking and picking at one another until, finally, all twenty-five of us settled into our seats. We looked at one another with excitement. It was a rare occasion when we got to watch TV in class.

The huge black-and-white TV hummed until it warmed up and then Mr. Walker spent what seemed like an hour moving the rabbit ear antennae this way and that until the picture cleared into fuzzy but recognizable images of black, dark grays, and light grays.

Mrs. Ayles's voice carried over the sound of the humming set.

"Girls and boys, I want you to listen very carefully. Boyd! Sit down, please! This is a very important moment. Our president . . . President Kennedy has been shot . . ."

It was the first time in my life that I could equate an actual sound to the word *gasp*. Twenty-five ten- and eleven-year-olds and three adults inhaled collectively and expelled the air in an uneasy chorus. We turned to one another with jack-o'-lantern faces and whispered the once familiar word as if the pronunciation had been changed overnight by Webster's.

Shot.

Cowboys and gangsters were shot in black-and-white movies. Frankenstein was shot, the Werewolf, too, with a silver bullet, according to folklore. Robot aliens were shot with ray guns in sci-fi movies and my dad and grandfather went hunting every year in late November and shot deer.

But presidents weren't shot. Not since McKinley, anyway. Especially not this president.

We passed messages to one another back and forth down the rows of honey-colored wood desks. We traded notes and watched the blurry images on the screen of the black-and-white TV as Mr. Walker tried to steady the picture, as if by making the transmitted image crisp and perfect he could change the reality that it depicted. The sound of static filled our ears, the intermittent "snow" on the screen transfixed us. As the lumpy shapes solidified into recognizable letters and people, we stopped chatting and held our breaths. Perhaps this horrible thing hadn't really happened. Maybe it was a mistake.

I wasn't paying attention to time then, but during what would have been our art period, Walter Cronkite's face appeared on-screen again. Someone handed him a piece of paper that he read for what seemed to be a long time. Then he looked up with a sad face that reminded me of Uncle Franklin's basset hound.

"From Dallas, Texas, the flash, apparently official. President Kennedy died at one p.m., Central Standard Time, two o'clock Eastern Standard Time."

We were still holding our breaths.

"Some thirty-eight minutes ago."

There was nothing else that he could say. Like us, he was without words, too sad to go on. He made a face and took off his glasses. The broadcast continued but I don't remember anything else about it.

Mr. Walker bowed his head and closed his eyes for a moment. Mrs. Webb paused in our doorway. Tears were streaming down her face. Mrs. Ayles's flower-trimmed handkerchief was soaked. Still on-camera, Mr. Cronkite wiped his eyes.

And for the first and last time in the tenure of room 10, fifth grade, Gateway Elementary School, Mrs. Ayles's twenty-five students sat, perfectly still and perfectly quiet, wondering how such a thing could happen in their world and what could happen next.

FOUR

To every thing, turn, turn, turn
There is a season, turn, turn, turn

At the opposite end of the country, in the exotic state of California (if you're from Ohio, *any place* else is exotic), a place called Haight-Ashbury attracted young people from everywhere who smoked a weed called pot instead of Lucky Strikes and preferred long hair, jeans, and tie-dyed shirts to knife-creased khakis, short-sleeved checked Oxford shirts, short hair, and roller sets. Oh, and no bras of any kind.

More than a world away, men in arms were on the move. One army moved out, one army moved in. And quietly, almost without us noticing, one by one, the older boys in our neighborhood began to disappear. The heavy wool purple Southeast Tiger football jackets were exchanged for khaki green, sneakers for polished black combat boots. The green rain forest sliver of a country became a permanent resident on the front page of the newspapers. My grandfather showed me where it was on the old globe that he kept in the dining room next to his smoking stand. French Indochina. But now it was called something else.

And in the Georgia where my grandmother grew up, in the North Carolina where Su's uncle and great-grandmother still lived, and in the Alabama where Reenie's father was born, the nearly four hundred years of Christian patience and good humor of colored people wore out. The Negro would not be denied. And in another five years, he would be black.

You do not have to be at the epicenter of an earthquake to feel its effects. Our little cocoon of status quo was about to be buffeted by hurricane-force winds, ripped open and challenged to a duel by the forces of change coming from south, west, and east. How could we have known when we were so young, that these events would help shape us and the times during which we reached womanhood? That the names, places, and dates would ring in our minds for the rest of our lives? That they would change the direction of the winds that pushed us along our paths? It was because of all these things that we did not do what was expected of us. The landscape was scraped clean by those harsh winds of change and we were left with few landmarks or signposts. We would have to make it up as we went along.

> *What happens to a dream deferred?*
> *. . . does it explode?*

It was as if the murder of President Kennedy blew the lid off Pandora's box. But my father said that her box was like a stew pot left on the stove too long. It had simmered and it had boiled. Now it was spilling over.

During these years, our family dinner conversations were dominated by our parents talking about a reserved but determined man from Atlanta, the tall boisterous Texan who lived in Washington, and the slip of a country with the strange name that was like a monster gobbling up young dreams and hopes by the hundreds, then by the thousands, sending them home in flag-draped coffins. My sisters and I ate quietly. Sometimes we listened; sometimes we were lost in our own thoughts: of Beatles, boys, Barbie dolls, and bras.

Public events and puberty, we went from cooties to Maybelline overnight.

Su, Reenie, and I were sixth-grade girls now. We were "the big girls," looked up to by the little first and second graders, held in awe by fourth graders, and openly envied by the fifth graders who couldn't wait to be the big kids on campus when we moved on to junior high in the fall of 1965.

It wasn't only our way of thinking that began to change. We looked different. We felt different. The change was subtle for some, dramatic for others. I got my period—a rite of passage that would be a pain in my butt for the next forty-some years—but not much else. Reenie, Su, and some of the other more "mature" girls got boobs, which didn't seem quite fair to me. They got to buy bras and, like nearly everything else we did in those days, we turned bra-buying into an event. We went downtown on the bus, browsed through the "women's lingerie" department at Lazarus, and were "fitted" for brassieres. I'll rework that sentence. *They* were fitted. I was strictly an observer. Unless I was able to snitch one of my sister Patty's, I was braless—and not in the traditional sixties sense of the word either. My mom didn't believe in training bras; she said that the real thing would be more than enough once I really needed it. At eleven years of age, that pronouncement made me feel inadequate and left behind. Now, of course, I am amazed at how brilliant my mother was.

So I went along for the ride, making mental notes of the brands and the styles for future reference. Mom assured me that someday I would have bras of my own. This was the pre–Victoria's Secret era, when bras came in only two colors—white and black. And black was not considered a proper color for a young girl. (There may have been a few bras made in the "nude" color, but those weren't considered appropriate either.) In fact, I believe that one of the sales policies of the Lazarus lingerie department was a prohibition on selling black brassieres to women under the age of twenty-one.

Our mothers now allowed us to wear our hair "down" sometimes instead of confined to plaits, barrettes, and ponytails. For Su, this meant freedom for her thick, shoulder-length, chocolate brown hair. One of her aunts was a hairdresser, so Su's hair always looked as if she had just stepped out of the chair. Reenie's braids hung to her waist, but she was determined to look "older," so this meant a haircut. Dinah Keller snipped off eight inches and Reenie's hair was pulled back into the timeless Barbie-style ponytail that she still wears sometimes. My hair, a straw-colored wiry mess, was best left in the single ponytail that Patty combed out for me every morning. Mother refused to do my hair because I was tender-headed and cried. Patty was gentler with the comb and brush unless she was mad or on the telephone with her boyfriend.

My teenage sister was always on the telephone. Her boyfriend, Gregory, whom she was forbidden to see, was eighteen and a senior at Southeast. Mother thought he was too "mature," which, of course, made him even more attractive. He was headed to Fort Knox after graduation. Mother and Daddy didn't know it, but there had been talk of an elopement. I overheard that word late one night when Patty thought we were all in bed and she had sneaked down-stairs to talk on the phone. Of course, I told Reenie and Su. The intrigue surrounding that kind of secret was way too good to keep to yourself.

"Elope." Reenie said the word as if it had magical properties.

Su's eyes gleamed.

"That is so romantic," she gushed. "Your sister is lucky. Gregory Bradshaw is soooo cute." These were the days when boys were not at-tractive, handsome, or even good-looking. They were *cute*.

"Not like his brother, Karl," Reenie's voice came from below us. We were at Su's, the house where she now lived with her aunt Leila and her cousins. Su and I were stretched out on the bed, looking at the *Seventeen* magazines I'd borrowed from Patty. Reenie was sitting cross-legged on the floor, reading *Ebony*. We had sneaked in a bag of Cheetos and cans of Fresca.

"He's not that bad," Su said in Karl's defense. Su thought Karl was, well, kinda cute.

Reenie's dark ponytail flipped as she turned around, her face scrunched into a frown.

"He farts all the time and scratches his butt, *Susan*," she said sharply. Reenie always called Su "Susan" when she was serious about something.

I giggled.

Su blushed.

"That isn't him, that's Timmy Early, *Irene*," she shot back. She gave me a wide, fake smile. "Timothy Harrison Early who thinks that Vaughn Rene Jones is . . . gorgeous." She blinked her eyes. Then she and Reenie dissolved into cackles of laughter.

I moaned. Boys had begun to look a little different now. Well, some of them anyway. They were getting taller and broader and they seemed more afraid of us than they used to be. And, I write this with a "sigh," now they seemed to like us. I had found out, to my horror, that Timmy Early, the monster who had chased and bullied me mercilessly, thought that I was . . . cute. Which meant, of course, that he never left me alone again. It was torture.

"Is she going to do it?" Reenie asked me.

"Is she going to do what?" I was wondering if that was the Supremes' real hair or wigs.

"Is she going to elope with Gregory Bradshaw? Pay attention, Vaughn!" Reenie was exasperated with me.

"Oh. I don't know," I answered. And I didn't. Patty and I were four years apart. As far as she was concerned, I was less important than a piece of lint on her sweater. I wasn't old enough to be a confidante and I was too old to be cute like Jeannie. The middle-child blues. But every once in a while now, my sister looked off into space more often than she used to. And she knew that I had seen her on the telephone late at night against Mom and Dad's instructions and that I hadn't tattled. So, at least it seemed to me, Patty combed my always tangled hair more gently now and let me borrow her Emeraude cologne if I asked her nicely. But she still didn't tell me anything.

"That would be so romantic if they ran away together," Reenie gasped out, leaning back against the bed. "And they get married and then he goes off to the army . . ."

She stopped there and she went back to the magazine she was reading. Su and I exchanged glances but didn't say anything. Diana Ross's *"Baby, baby, baby, where did our love go?"* tickled our ears. But our thoughts were someplace very different.

And then he goes off to the army. And then he goes to a place called Vietnam like Reenie's brothers Calvin and JC. Reenie got letters and postcards from her brothers sometimes. We all had snapshots of them hanging on our bulletin boards or tacked up on the wall. They were smiling, their heads cocked to the side, faces lean but strong. Reenie had a formal portrait of both of her brothers in their dress uniforms. They looked so handsome and strong. They were so young. Mr. and Mrs. Keller were prouder than they could say, but Dinah Keller's coal black hair now had strands of gray in it, and she teared up when either Cal or JC's names were mentioned. Su's older cousin was there, too, and Patty had told me that after something called boot camp, her boyfriend, Gregory, was going to a place called the Mekong. On Sundays, from the pulpits of St. Dominic's, St. Paul's AME, Second Baptist, Centenary, and other places, prayers were asked for and given on behalf of "our boys" who were fighting three-quarters of the way around the globe.

The sixth-grade spring dance was held in mid-May of every year. Only sixth graders were allowed to go. It would be our first evening event and it ended at eight p.m. We were all going to wear stockings. Bobby socks were OK for casual occasions and school, at least that's what *Teen* magazine said, but nylons were required for p.m. events. That presented a small problem since they were expensive and prone to runs. Also, my mother and Reenie's mother had to be convinced that we were old enough to wear the coveted leggings at all.

"I don't know, Vaughn," Mother said, studying me with the practiced eye of a woman who'd realized that she'd lost control of her first daughter and wasn't ready to concede the loss of the next one. "You're only eleven . . ."

Well, hell (I did not say that then, this is the fifty-year-old talking), I had started school a year early so I would always be at least six months younger than the rest of the class. Reenie was having the same problem. Her mother hadn't been able to accept the fact that her precious little only girl was not a little girl anymore.

"Mom, all of the other girls . . . Su, Reenie" (that was a small lie) "Dyanne, everyone else will be wearing them!" I put out my case. Surely Mother wouldn't want to be among the minority of out-of-touch moms whose girls were wearing anklet socks to a sixth-grade dance!

My mother would not be moved. Her arched eyebrows rose in unison.

"If everyone jumps off the bridge into Alum Creek, Vaughn, are you going to jump, too?"

Oh, Lord, please don't let me ever say that to my children, I remember thinking. My son informs me that I break this resolution all the time.

"Mom!" I wailed.

A woman warrior in shining armor wearing a red corduroy jumper saved the day.

"Mother, for goodness' sake!" Patty's voice came out of nowhere. "It's the dance for the sixth graders. You know, like a graduation dance." My older sister shook her head with feigned exasperation. "Vaughn can't go dressed like a little girl. This is like a coming-out party. She's going to junior high school in the fall, Mom! She's almost twelve!"

My mother looked from Patty, who was a little taller than me with boobs, hips, the slightest blush of pale lipstick, and the cutest Twiggy-style haircut, to me: skinny, knock-kneed, peering desperately out of thick-lensed blue cat-eyed glasses, my hair going every which way. My mother's pity was written all over her face. She probably figured that I had enough problems without her adding to them by making me wear white lace-trimmed anklet socks to a dance.

"Oh . . . all right . . ." she gave in.

I was delirious with joy and grateful to Patty forever.

We were ready two weeks ahead of time. Dresses had been purchased or stitched (my mother was a genius on the black iron Singer sewing machine), shoes polished, an afternoon of manicures scheduled (clear polish only); stockings (and lipstick, which we weren't allowed to wear) purchased during an all-day shopping expedition downtown. The anticipation of attending our first grown-up dance was overwhelming. We consulted one another constantly, passing notes in class, attending hastily arranged conferences at the corner of Denbridge and Greenway, telephone calls after school.

"Should I borrow Patty's beige Capezio T-straps?"

"Cutex has a darling pale pink nail polish. What do you think? I could put it on in the car, then Mom wouldn't know."

"The telephone is never for me anymore," Patty grumbled, handing me the receiver. She gave me the evil eye. "It's always for Vaughn."

Only one thing remained for me to do. I had to learn how to fast dance.

Su was practically a professional. After all, her mother had been a ballerina once. Plus, she had cousins in high school. Reenie was the fourth child in a family of boys—there were few skills she hadn't picked up, including throwing a softball like a boy. Reenie always knew the latest dances.

And I had Patty. But I also had two right feet. Ballet lessons had done wonders for my posture but very little for my sense of rhythm or coordination.

"Vaughn, it's on two and four, not one and three. Ow!"

"Sorry," I murmured, trying to keep my focus. Right foot back, left foot . . . no, double-step . . . then right, no . . . left foot . . .

"Two and four, Vaughn! God, I give up! You're hopeless!"

"Patricia, watch your language," Mother's voice rang out from the hall.

"Yes, ma'am," my sister said through clenched teeth. To me, she said, "*Hope less.*"

It was five days before liftoff. This was a case for the girls most likely.

"We only have till Friday to teach Vaughn how to fast dance," mused Reenie at recess on Monday.

We sat on the outside steps of the utility room watching the other (younger) kids playing on the swings. Sixth graders didn't play on the swings anymore.

"Five days, that's not a lot of time. We've been trying to teach Vaughn to jump double Dutch for almost two years and she still gets caught in the ropes," Su commented. I winced. Su gave me a small smile. "Sorry, Vaughn."

"It's OK," I sighed. "Patty's right. I am hopeless." The sad prospect of spending the evening trying to disappear into the gymnasium walls was a sorry one. But I was still trying to find two and four, move my arms, *and* avoid stomping on my partner's toes. No way could I be trusted not to make a complete fool of myself in five days.

"Let's play hopscotch." Su snatched up a handful of pebbles and bounded over to the two remaining hopscotch courts, their yellow lines and numbers fading into the oblivion of the worn-out black-topped playground surface.

We took turns, maneuvering our feet onto the open spaces, rolling the pebbles into place if we could.

"Two, four, seven . . ." I hopped on one foot from square to square, going from left to right and back again until I tipped through nine and out. "All right!" I clapped my hands together and looked up. "Reenie, it's your . . ." Reenie and Su were staring at me. "What's wrong?"

Su glanced at Reenie, grinned, then cleared the hopscotch grid with one sweep of her size eight and a halfs.

"Hey! What are you doing?" I exclaimed.

Reenie was grinning, too.

"V, did you see what you just did? Skipped through those obstacles like you were dancing on water," Reenie said, her hands on her little hips.

"Yeah, so?"

"Soooo . . ." Su mocked me. "If you can skip through that maze without tripping over your own feet, you can fast dance. Let me put the rocks down and you move your feet into the squares that are empty. Only, you're dancing, not skipping. Here, we'll sing like the Four Tops . . ."

Sugar pie, honey bunch, you know that I love you . . .

It was a comical sight: Reenie and Su sashayed through the dance moves just like Levi Stubs and the boys. But it worked. I danced through that hopscotch court and didn't trip once, nor did I fall over my own feet.

And when the cutest boy in sixth grade asked me to dance, I accepted and did a respectable job of moving around the floor. Tony was impressed and so was I. And so were the other kids who kept waving at me and saying, "Hey, Vaughn! You dance good."

I waved back and said "thanks" even though I didn't know who I was talking to. In addition to the new dress, the stockings, the clear nail polish, bangs, and the covert application of mauve lip gloss, I had taken off my glasses. They were stashed safely under my sweater, which was folded neatly on a bench. If no one sat on it, I was home free. I was as blind as a bat with a blindfold in the dark. But I was cute that night and that's all that mattered. It was wonderful.

Of course, Su had the undivided attention of the new boy, Bradley something, and Reenie, like the queen bee she was and still is, danced with everyone and held court by the punch bowl.

"Have you got a boyfriend?" one of her admirers asked.

"I don't want to be tied down," she'd commented later with a dramatic sigh. Elizabeth Taylor has nothing on Reenie when it comes to romance.

Su's reaction was the opposite. She was ready to get married and have babies.

And me? I just soaked it all up and enjoyed it. I wasn't Vaughn the smart kid or Vaughn the four-eyes that night. I was just a cute girl named Vaughn. I wrote down every moment of that night in my diary, every word and gesture I could remember. Including the moments that came after the dance.

My dad, who'd picked us up on his way home from work, listened to our chatter without comment after he'd asked us, "Did you girls have a good time?"

He dropped us off at Reenie's. We tumbled out of the car, Su and I carrying our little tote bags for the slumber party we were having. Like the Marx Brothers, we bounced, skipped, tumbled, and danced up the front walk. We didn't notice that all the lights were on at Reenie's and that there were cars parked out front and in the driveway. The front door was open and through the screen we saw people milling around in the hall.

"Are your parents having a party?" I asked, noticing one of our neighbors standing in the kitchen patting Reenie's dad on the back.

"If they are, I didn't know about it," Reenie answered.

It wasn't until we got inside that we realized this was a party without music, cocktails, bridge, or laughter. Several of the adults noticed our entrance and Mr. Clarke tapped Abraham Keller on the shoulder to let him know we were there.

I knew the moment he turned around. The warm spring air was soft, fresh, and light. And very quiet. And Mr. Keller's face was red and puffy and looked as if it had been hit by a baseball bat.

"Reeniedarling . . ." He rushed toward us, wiping his eyes with the back of his hand. "Reenie . . ."

Reenie stepped back as she looked up at her father.

He swallowed. He looked at Su and me and didn't say anything more.

But Reenie knew, too.

Before that moment, I had not ever heard Reenie Keller's voice sound so quiet or so serious. And I don't think I have since.

"Where's Mommy?"

"Mommy's . . . upstairs, baby, she's . . . lying down. Reenie, honey, Calvin's been . . ." He choked.

He did not have to say it. In the living room, someone had draped a strip of black ribbon over PFC Calvin Keller's portrait.

At eleven years old, you haven't worked out the concept of death yet. It isn't real. You find dead birds in the park, squirrels get squished crossing the road, and flies and grasshoppers die. I'd yet to keep a lightning bug alive more than an hour or so in a mayonnaise jar even if I did punch holes in the lid.

But that's not real death.

I had been to funerals for as long as I could remember. My great-grandfather died when I was five and I went to the funeral; I wondered why he didn't move. My great-great-aunt died when I was six and on and on. My maternal grandfather passed the year before. So I was used to death, I thought. I knew how to behave at funerals. You wore dark colors, you sat up straight in the church, and you did not cry loudly. My mother's rules.

But Grandpa Jones was nearly ninety, his sister was nearly one hundred, and my grandfather was in his late seventies—these people were old. Only old people and animals died, right?

They still played "Taps" in those days. And even though it wasn't regulation, several of the band members from SE High stood in the back and played along with the army officer's coronet. JC was given leave to come home. I did not recognize him. His once round face was thin, dark, and lined. He looked like an old man. His eyes were filled with pain. It hurt to look at him. Mrs. Keller was inconsolable. She stood, silently, dressed in black. I don't think she ever stopped crying. The minister handed her the flag and, for a moment, I thought she was going to throw it down. She didn't, but she held it away from her body, as if it were poisonous.

We listened to the minister's words, something about death being in the midst of life—or was it the other way around? We saw Mr. and Mrs. Keller, JC, Jimmy and Ernie and Reenie, each throw a handful of dirt on top of the coffin. It made a sick, strange sound. And because it was May, the birds sang and the sky was blue. Life was going on. But it was going on without Calvin.

And we wondered about this death thing. We thought we'd figured it out. We'd live nearly forever; I mean, old people died, but they were sixty and seventy and a hundred. But now Calvin was dead, killed in a place we heard about only on the news. And he was barely twenty. That wasn't right, was it? *Was it?*

As we walked back to our cars at the cemetery, I looked over at Reenie, who was dabbing her eyes again. I saw Su in the distance, her face quiet and thoughtful. I knew we were all thinking the same thing. Life seemed to be going along. The sun was still shining. And on Maryland Avenue, the traffic sped by. The man pumped gas at the SOHIO station on the corner. But everything was different now.

These were the years where we learned that there were other kinds of death besides the death of the body. There was the death of the spirit, the death of the soul. Dinah Keller's coal black hair turned white and she did not bother to color it. When Reenie speaks of her mother, even today, she says, "Momma wore that silver hair like a widow's veil. She hated black, so after the funeral she put the black suit away. But her hair turned white, she was only thirty-eight, and she said she'd never color it. It was her badge of grief for Cal."

And JC, who returned to a place called Da Nang, always carried his grief with him, too. It's called survivor's guilt. He felt guilty that Calvin had died. Guilty that he had lived, even though he knew that his parents would never have been able to recover from the loss of two sons. He felt guilty that he came back without a scratch, not even a sniffle. And JC was guilty all the rest of his life. He made the military his career and retired as a light colonel. He has that straight bearing that all military men retain; he is crisp and polished, always looks as if he is about to salute. He doesn't talk about Vietnam. He doesn't believe in post-traumatic stress syndrome. And yet there is something in his eyes. He married one of Patty's girlfriends. And even now, his wife, Vicky, says that he has nightmares. She dreads it when *Apocalypse Now* or *Full Metal Jacket* come on cable. Because Vicky knows that JC shouldn't watch them, but Vicky also knows that JC will watch them and that he won't sleep for weeks afterward. It's been nearly forty years. Some wounds really don't heal.

My sister did not elope with Gregory Bradshaw. He served two tours in Vietnam and came back to her in one physical piece. But his mind was broken, a pile of oddly shaped, jagged-edge fragments. He was hooked on heroin. His hands shook when he tried to light his cigarette and sometimes he talked to himself. He came to visit Patty once during the summer that she was home from college and I thought he was a scarecrow. His face was gaunt and rough as if it had been strip-mined. His voice hoarse from the drugs, cigarettes, and alcohol. He was a toothpick man. And Gregory's eyes? They were dark and sad and haunted.

We still see him, here and there around town, pushing a grocery cart from Kroger's. Everything he owns is in that cart. Most of the time he doesn't know who I am when I wave. But he always recognizes Patty and stops to talk with her. She gives him some cash if she has it. Once, as he rolled his cart away, I saw a tear coming out of her eye. I know that he was her first love and will always have a special place in her heart. I just wonder what their lives would have been like if his soul had not died in Vietnam.

Death was no longer something that happened when you were old. It didn't happen just to people you did not know. It wasn't a dark, hooded figure who came by appointment when you had decided that you were old enough or sick enough or both. Now we knew that it came on its own terms and in its own time, keeping both a secret. And it didn't just kill the body. The minister was right, death was all around us, out in the open and hiding in the bushes. It was there, right at our elbows, waiting, watching, coming. Life, for us, would never be the same.

FIVE

In the fall of 1965, we started seventh grade at Poindexter Junior High School. Overnight we went from being the big kids on campus to "little seven-bees." It was exhilarating and traumatic, enlightening and overwhelming. We loved every minute of it.

It took a journey of epic proportions just to get there. We had to walk—rain, sun, sleet, or snow: carpooling was not a term our parents were familiar with. On good days it took about forty-five minutes, give or take, allowing for stops at the carryout to buy candy and pop, detours to avoid stray dogs, and unscheduled loitering with intent. In bad weather it took forever. But we had some of the best times of our lives struggling along, trading stories, shooing away stray dogs, spying on our neighbors, and trading insults with boys we thought were cute.

Our first day at Poindexter was frightening. Poindexter Junior High School was big. Built in 1910, the school's imposing front faced Champion Avenue and sprawled across nearly one block with its outbuildings, heating plant, and playgrounds. The lunchroom was a cavernous place where the staff, ruled by Mrs. Atkins, ran the lines like military generals with proper Southern manners. The green trays moved down the line like Fords in an assembly plant.

"What you want, baby? Speak up now."

"Move along there, honey. You want these greens or not?"

From day one, I got lost. We had "schedules," a class with this teacher in this room, the next class with another teacher in another room. The bells rang; we looked at the schedule in our hands and took off, usually in the wrong direction, to find the next class.

Reenie, Su, and I tried to coordinate schedules so we could see one another during the day, but it was no use. We had different homerooms and conflicting schedules. We got caught up on our long walks home and on Wednesdays and Fridays in Mrs. Bingham's sewing class.

But we were young and we adapted and we had a good time. There were sock hops and basketball games (and basketball players) and we got to wear our hair "down" more. We sneaked our transistor radios into our bags and sang along with Gladys Knight and the Supremes and the Temptations every chance we got. And we began to seek and find the places in the world where we felt most comfortable.

Su's alto singing voice landed her a spot in the choir. It was a mellow voice, warm but imposing. When Su spoke, you listened. She sang solos and she did the school-wide announcements over the PA system.

"Poindexter eighth graders, please note that Mr. Brown's American history class will meet in room 301, that's three-oh-one, during seventh, eighth, and ninth periods today and tomorrow. Mr. Bannister and his crew are making repairs on the registers. Remember, if you have American history during seventh, eighth, or ninth period, you should go to room 301." Su didn't identify herself during these life-changing announcements. All around us, we'd hear other students say "Who's that?" We began to call her "the Voice."

"I'd be scared to death to talk over the PA," Reenie said, looking at Su with admiration. "I'd be afraid that I'd make a mistake and everyone'd laugh at me."

"I wouldn't be able to open my mouth," I commented. I still died a million deaths when teachers called on me in class, even when I knew the answer to the question. I couldn't imagine putting a microphone in front of my face and just talking into it. I was sure that my throat would close up.

"Aw, it's not so bad," Su said. "I kinda like it. Maybe I can work for a radio station someday when I graduate from high school."

Reenie's natural curiosity and her eye for color, shape, and design put her yards ahead of all of us in home ec and science classes. By eighth grade, Reenie was using *Vogue* patterns to make her own clothes. She could even do invisible zippers and linings! And she was way ahead of us making simple yellow cakes from scratch and a Johnny Marzetti casserole to die for. Reenie took advanced cooking, following the hard recipes from the cooking teacher's personal collection, including *Mastering the Art of French Cooking*. Not only that, but Reenie was a science whiz. She didn't mind the nasty, squirmy things we studied in general science class. She wasn't afraid to mix horrible smelling things together and get something weird and wonderful. And me?

I was nearly always late for math class (both seventh and eighth grade), and a cool but exasperated Mr. Cummings gave me multiple detentions to break me of the habit. I napped in American history (Mr. Green had the voice of a metronome) and passed notes in social studies. I was fine in home ec as long as we didn't have to put in zippers in sewing or blend something in cooking class. And phys ed? My two right feet did not help much in Mrs. Watson's gym class. It was one of the few classes that Reenie, Su, and I had together, so we spent most of the period talking. And I was the one who usually got caught. My report cards had writing in the Additional Comments section: "Vaughn talks too much." "Vaughn would perform much better in class if she would stop scribbling and pay attention." My parents were not amused. I spent most of eighth grade on punishment. In my room.

There was one exception: Mrs. Shelley's English classes. The courses that put Reenie to sleep and struck Su as good for nothing fascinated me. The first semester of seventh-grade English was sentence structure and diagramming. Lord, deliver me, please, from sentence diagrams. Their charms are completely lost on me, then and now. My lines were never straight, I put adverbs where prepositions should have been, and English class was after Mrs. Serge's

French class, so I mixed past tense English with pluperfect French and had an unholy mess on my papers.

But the second semester was literature. Not *Alice and Jerry*, literature, real stories, real authors. I didn't like Charlie Dickens's *Great Expectations* much but I reveled in his use of words. So many of them! I tried to find the deep meanings in the short stories that we read and interpreted Robert Frost and Edna St. Vincent Millay. How did a candle burn at both ends? I didn't know then that I would live long enough to find out. I wondered why e.e. cummings didn't like capital letters. I was intrigued by those poor Brontë girls and thought that Captain Ahab probably needed a cup of sassafras tea to calm his "innards." That was my great-grandmother's cure-all for most forms of internal disruption.

I graduated from *The Clue in the Jewel Box* to *Rebecca*, Shakespeare, Langston Hughes, and, especially, those books and writers that Mom thought were too mature for me to read. I haunted the Eastside branch of the public library, bribing Patty and Jeannie to check out books for me since I was always over the five-book limit. It was glorious. And it was at this time that I began scribbling stories of my own. If old Herman could write a story about a mean-spirited white whale and get it published, I could, too. Get published that is. I had then and have now absolutely no interest in writing about a whale.

"I mean, who cares?" exclaimed Su as we drifted out of eighth-grade lit class. She shook her head uncomprehendingly. "As Diana Ross would say, 'where did our love go?' Emily Dickinson needed a boyfriend."

Reenie yawned.

"Can you imagine staying home for the rest of your life? Not going anywhere? No shopping, no traveling, and wearing white all the time?" To Reenie, fashion faux pas were crimes serious enough to warrant police intervention. "White. I don't get it. And her poems are short, too!"

"Thank goodness," Su mumbled. "I don't think I could stay awake if they were any longer. V, I don't understand why you like this stuff."

I blushed.

"I dunno. It's kinda neat . . . you know, the way Dickinson puts the words together to talk about things. It makes you think. Like when she writes about never seeing a moor . . ."

"What's a moor again?" Reenie interrupted.

"And why do we care?" Su added under her breath.

I was slow on the uptake.

"It's a, well, we don't have 'em in Ohio, they're like . . ." I shuffled through my papers. "Here, wait a minute, hold this." I shoved my algebra book into Su's arms. "I looked it up . . ."

I missed the look and the rolling eyes that passed between Susan and Irene.

"OK, a moor, 'chiefly British—an expanse of open rolling infertile land . . . a boggy area of wasteland . . .'"

"I can't believe you looked it up in the dictionary!" Su said, laughing.

"Vaughn, for God's sake, nobody cares about a darned *moor*! Cheerleading tryouts are tomorrow, we have more important things to think about besides that stupid moor!"

"Oh, yeah," I said, now awake. "Sorry."

Well, of course, what was wrong with me?

It was ninth period, Su and I were headed to math class, Reenie to Ohio history, and then an afternoon at the hairdresser's and another practice at Reenie's before bed. It was fall of our eighth-grade year, 1966, and we were eligible to try out for cheerleader. We were determined to wear the short, black, pleated skirts and black wool sweaters with the "Tiger" on the front. It would be the pinnacle of our junior high school careers. It had been days since we'd talked or thought about much else.

A tall, slim figure appeared on the landing in front of us. She glanced our way briefly, waved, then turned, and headed up the stairs to the third floor. We slowed down so we could watch every move and stay far enough away so we could talk about her and she wouldn't hear us. She was tall and skinny with caramel-colored skin and light reddish-brown hair that she wore in a long, thick ponytail. Her eyes were the color of my little cousin's dark gold marbles. She had fantastic clothes: pleated skirts in every color and pattern, matching sweaters, jumpers and knee socks, several pairs of loafers, and, which made us even more envious, she had at least four pairs of the coveted Capezio T-straps, in black, nude, navy, and red. She always looked as if she'd stepped out of the pages of *Seventeen* magazine with her perfect hair, perfect outfit, stylish shoes, and handbag to match. (We were carrying handbags now.) She was pretty and smart and she had been a cheerleader at her old junior high school. She could even do the Chinese splits.

We hated her.

Her name was Audrey Taylor.

She'd moved to town over the summer when her father retired from the army. They'd lived someplace in California before. To us, California was a magical place where the sun always shined and there was water and something called surfing. It was the place the Beach Boys (whom we didn't listen to) sang about and which we recognized on the maps in geography class. But we'd never known anyone who'd actually *lived* there. We were jealous. Audrey was the eldest in her family; she had a younger sister and brother, and her parents had bought one of the nicest houses on Clifton Avenue. Her father drove an Oldsmobile. Her first day at Poindexter, she was placed in all the advanced classes because her test results indicated that she was a "gifted" student.

"What does that mean, 'gifted'?" Su snarled. "Gifted. Humph. I saw her paper in algebra, she had the same answers I did."

"You copied off her paper!" I exclaimed.

"No, V, I *saw* her paper. "

"So what if she can do Chinese splits," Reenie mumbled, her dark eyes cutting into Audrey's back like knives. Reenie could do a very respectable split, but, so far, the Chinese splits had eluded her.

The soft fawn and slate gray mixed with cream plaid of Audrey's skirt swayed as she stepped onto the last step. Her matching fawn wool sweater was draped over her shoulders. She wore a crisp white blouse. Her purse, a cute little structured thing, hung from a long skinny strap. It was gray, too, just like her matching Capezio T-strapped shoes.

"She has a new pair of T-straps!" Reenie's envy was now in high gear.

"Gray ones," Su gushed.

"Nice . . ." I murmured. I didn't have even *one* pair of the coveted shoes.

The object of our surveillance disappeared into room 320.

"She's trying out for cheerleader," I said. "I heard Mrs. Watson tell Miss DiSanto that she's guaranteed a spot. That she's never seen a girl so well coordinated."

"Was she talking about her clothes or her cheerleading?" Su snickered.

"We'll see about that," Reenie snapped. "I'm ready for Miss California."

The bell for ninth period rang and we scurried off to class.

"See you after school on the east side of the playground. We can walk to the beauty parlor together," we yelled to one another.

They weren't salons, spas, or hair design studios then, they were beauty parlors and they dotted the landscape of the near east and near north side of the city, one every other block or so, often paired with a barber shop. The Beauty Shoppe, Cleopatra's Palace (I am not kidding), Fashionetta Beauty Box, and Miss Gladys's Beauty Bar, to name a few. Like churches and funeral homes, your family pledged loyalty forever to one or the other of them. My maternal grandmother, my aunts, and my mother had spent the better part of many mornings sitting in Miss Gladys's chair. And it would have taken an act of God (or one hot comb burn too many) to get them to change.

"Honey, I wouldn't take my poodle to Norma Tallmadge. I told her to put a little red in it and I came out looking like Lucille Ball!"

Su's aunt had a chair at Miss Gladys's, Reenie went to Fashionetta just down the street in the Williams Building, and, or so we'd heard, our nemesis, Audrey Taylor, and her mother and sister went to a new shop that had just opened on Cleveland Avenue.

When you opened the door to Miss Gladys's, you walked into a hive. And every beautician was a queen bee. They wore white uniforms and matching shoes just like nurses. And, like bees, they were in constant motion, shampooing, combing, rinsing, setting, curling, and pressing. There was no such thing as "downtime." It was as if the circus had come to town: bells ringing, water spraying and swooshing, pressing combs sizzling, and curling irons clicking and clacking like the pistons of a train picking up speed.

Twelve women in white answering phones, smoking Winstons, drinking Coca-Cola from bottles, gossiping—and all the while shampooing and rinsing and styling twenty plus customers in various stages of developing glamour. Heads were pulled this way and that, hung over shampoo bowls or propped in front of industrial-strength dryers. Some were tilted to the left, the ear folded over as the soft hair behind it was heated into sleekness.

In the middle of it all was Miss Gladys, who owned the beauty shop and the barber shop down at Twentieth and Long with her husband, Harold. Miss Gladys was a full-figured woman with a petite-figured voice. The contrast was ridiculous. But I'll tell you what, when Miss Gladys opened her mouth, the entire shop got quiet. She had power, that woman. Her prowess with a pressing comb was legendary. The queen of all the queen bees, Miss Gladys was pressing and curling hair before Eve wore a training bra. And she set an excellent example. Her hair was always perfectly straightened, curled, and colored coal black, an eternal mystery to my mother, who was fighting a losing battle against strands of gray.

"Now, will you tell me how Gladys hasn't a gray hair in her head and she's older than smoke?" my mother would exclaim in frustration whenever she looked at herself closely in the mirror.

Miss Gladys was tall and imposing and, with her snowy white uniform, she looked like a religious figure we'd seen somewhere before. Reenie thought it was at St. Catherine's Catholic Church on Main Street. Miss Gladys had the premier station in the shop, and from there she ruled. She also had every hair gadget, gizmo, pomade, cream, conditioner, and doodad known to beauty supply.

She had ten curling irons with different size barrels. And, make no mistake, these were not your momma's curling irons with mild heat and electricity. These instruments of beauty were heated over natural gas burners until they reached a temperature (known only to the beauticians through ESP) that could put a curl on your head that would last two weeks if you were careful and didn't sweat your hair out. She had five hot combs and a row of jars with different colors of grease in them. I could use the word *pomade* but we called it "grease": pale pink grease, lightweight teal blue grease, thick vanilla custard–colored grease, and on and on. Miss Gladys would finger through your hair just before pressing it and choose a jar based on what she felt. I asked her once how she decided on the clear amber–colored grease that she used on me.

"Baby, I just know, that's all. The good Lord gave me the touch."

And that was that.

You brought your lunch if you were going to Miss Gladys's because, chances are, you would be there awhile. That afternoon I remembered to pack a snack so I wouldn't get hungry. But Miss Gladys seemed to be moving right along. I checked the clock: 5:30. My hair was dry, and Miss Gladys was like the Roadrunner when it came to pressing and curling. Things were looking up. I might be home in time to practice with the girls one more time! Su had already left the shop and Reenie's hair only took Miss Stamps, down the street, an hour to do even if you counted sitting under the hair dryer.

But the fates were against me.

"Anybody want a fis' sandwich? I'm makin' a run to Frazier's."

Lord Almighty.

My spirits plummeted. No way was I getting out of this place before eight.

Miss Gladys's husband, Harold, took the orders. Frazier's Fish, a hole in the wall wedged in between Johnny's Market and the Miami Bar (where folks took their liquor very seriously) and across the street from Harold's barber shop, had some of the best fish in the city. If it had gills or swam, Frazier's could fry it, steam it, boil it, or grill it. They had vats of homemade tartar sauce in the back and bottles of hot sauce on the counter. There were only two booths in Frazier's, it was strictly a carryout place. And one of the places that their fish was carried out to the most was Miss Gladys's beauty parlor and Mr. Harold's barber shop.

Actually, fish (or fis, as they were usually called) sandwiches from

Frazier's were the primary reason my father didn't go to Mr. Harold for his haircuts. Well, one of the reasons. My daddy loved Frazier's fried perch sandwiches, but there were limits.

"Goddammit!" my father had exclaimed when he thought there were no children within hearing distance. "Every time Harold cuts my hair, I come out smelling like fish grease and have a tartar sauce stain on my shirt!"

"Mike, watch your language!" Mother scolded him.

Mr. Harold stacked his clients up like planes waiting to land at Port Columbus, and half the time he forgot who was next, so curse words flew when folks got bumped from their place in line.

Not only was the fried fish a distraction for Mr. Harold, but God help you if there was a basketball game on. Creative haircuts were seen every week on Long Street and Mt. Vernon Avenue, especially in February and March, because something Mr. H. saw on the TV made him yell "All right!" and nick the poor guy in the chair.

This happened to Reenie's father, but only once.

"Ow!"

"Um, you know you're getting a bald spot, don't you?" Mr. Harold had offered hopefully. Reenie's father was in no way nearing bald.

The story was that Mr. Keller called Mr. Harold a few names we hadn't heard at Second Baptist, left, and never went back.

"Let me have a shrimp basket with extra coleslaw."

"Harold! Make sure he fry that perch crisp, you understand? I don't like it all limp."

"Fis' sandwich and slap some tartar and hot sauce on there."

Half an hour later, curling irons were held in one hand and fish sandwiches, fried shrimp, and forks of coleslaw were held in the other. By the time I came out of Miss Gladys's, I looked OK but smelled like fish grease, hair grease, and French fries. Oh, and one more thing.

"Vaughn." Mother's nose twitched as she smoothed my hair. "Your hair looks nice." She shook her head. "Gladys did a Frazier's run, I can smell it. What did you get on yourself?" She pointed to a quarter-size red spot on the back of my blouse.

Miss Gladys was accustomed to having a little fish with her hot sauce. I sighed. The price of beauty was high.

The day of the cheerleading tryouts was warm, sunny, and clear. Excitement was in the air. The whole school buzzed with anticipation. In the hierarchy of junior high school royalty, the boys had their basketball team. For girls, the queens of the school were the cheerleaders.

Tryouts were held at the end of the day and the girls most likely to be the next Poindexter Junior High School "reserve squad" cheerleaders were lined up and ready. Even I was prepared. We wore white gym shirts and navy shorts, bobby socks and sneakers. Of course, Reenie, Su, and I had spent the previous evening in the beauty parlor so we were glamorous as well. But we'd managed to get in a quick practice session and even I was able to smoothly go down into the splits. All around us were cases of the jitters with one notable exception: *her.*

Audrey Taylor stood just opposite us. I don't think I'd ever seen a gym blouse that looked as if it had been starched before. Her socks were evenly turned down, her sneakers (Keds, of course) were pure white and obviously brand new. I had sent mine through the washing machine twice with bleach and, at best, they were a comfortable but imperfect shade of dull ivory. The little gold hoops that hung from her ears sparkled in the light and her hair was pulled back into its usual ponytail, but she had added a black and orange ribbon, Poindexter's school colors. She looked as calm as a cucumber.

I looked at Su who turned to Reenie who rolled her eyes.

We just hated Audrey Taylor.

A whistle blew and Mrs. Watson, the adviser for the cheerleading squad, marched out between the rows of cheerleader wannabes.

"All right, ladies, let me have your attention, please! Here's what we're going to do!"

Amy Watson was the cutest teacher in the school even though she was old. (She was thirty-two years old at that time, nearly twenty years younger than I am as I write this. But it's all about perspective, and when you're twelve going on thirteen, anyone older than eighteen is a fossil.) She taught physical education, health, and biology.

We thought she was wonderful. She had a friendly but no-nonsense manner. And she had been a cheerleader at SE High and at Central-State where the cheerleaders were divas. No one knew more about cheerleading than Mrs. Watson.

"Have you all been practicing the cheers we taught you?"

A chorus of "yes" in alto and soprano encircled the teacher. She beamed.

"Good! The varsity squad will lead you. The judges and I will observe and we'll begin!"

We went through three different cheers as a group, and then Mrs. Watson broke us up into smaller groups and led us through one more. I kept up pretty well but it was nerve-racking. The judging committee (made up of the basketball coach, Mrs. Watson, Mrs. Arnold, who'd also been a cheerleader at Central-State, and the vice principal, Mr. Culpepper) studied us all with serious expressions. Then they would whisper among themselves and write furiously on yellow pads. It was hard to keep from tripping while watching them because you were worried about what they were writing.

Then came the really hard part.

We had to audition individually in front of the entire group. Reenie, Su, and, of course, Miss California, stood tall and smiled confidently. I was ready to pee my pants. Doing anything publicly was always my downfall. I could do the splits, do a backflip, and keep up with the cheers. But only if the group was around. Not on my own. My heart pounded in my chest as Mrs. Watson went down the line and each girl moved front and center for her moment.

"Irene Keller."

Reenie bopped over to the designated spot and smiled at the judges. Reenie, at thirteen, was still petite, bosomy, with great legs and a pretty face. Her black hair was pulled into two ponytails that hung past her shoulders and, Su had whispered to me, she had borrowed a tube of her mother's lipstick (Tropical Coral Passion) to emphasize her mouth.

She went through the moves without a blemish and gave the judges a sweet but saucy smile when she was finished.

I sighed.

"Susan Penn."

Gone were the toothpick arms and legs, the knobby knees, and the ski-length feet. Su was nearly five feet six inches tall by then; she had a slim, athletic figure and her pencil legs had morphed into shapely ones. Her feet were still pretty long (size nine now) but it wasn't as noticeable since she was tall. Her coffee-colored hair, curled, styled, and sprayed into place by her aunt Leila, was perfection. When she finished her audition, she beamed at the judges and thanked them for their time using "the Voice." The judges were impressed.

Could I just disappear into thin air? I thought. *I'm near the end of the line, maybe I could just slink off to the side of the building and . . .*

"Vaughn Jones."

I barely heard my name because the blood was thumping so hard in my ears. In my own defense, I went through the cheers all right even if I was a little, well, stiff. The problem was no one could hear me. You see, my heart was stuck in my throat. I saw Mrs. Watson frowning when I had finished.

"Um, thank you, Vaughn," she said evenly.

Coach and Mrs. Arnold were scribbling rapidly on their notepads. I was doomed.

And then it got worse.

"Audrey Taylor."

Could I just die now?

The contrast couldn't have been more dramatic.

Audrey looked as if she'd stepped out of a catalog for gym wear. She had a slim, elegant figure, the kind that would in ten years grace runways in Milan and *Vogue* magazines on every newsstand. Every hair on her head was in place; it was warm outside but she wasn't even sweating, er, perspiring. (Mother says not to say "sweating.") She smiled at the judges and executed each and every move with perfection. Her voice was loud, clear, and her enunciation (Mrs. Watson was very big on enunciation, no mumbling was allowed) was sharp and crisp. When she finished, she smiled again and bowed toward the judges' table.

Well, I'm finished, I said to myself. There were only eight slots and sixty girls had tried out. Even if the judges didn't choose Connie, Crystal, Monica, or Deborah, I still didn't have a chance. Su, Reenie, the new girl, Audrey, and Tina Burroughs were shoo-ins and nearly everyone else was louder than I'd been. When it was over, I was relieved but sad. I knew that my friends would go on to the heights of glory that were possible in junior high school. And that I would remain a lowly and ordinary student.

I did remain an ordinary student. But not left behind. The circle of friendship that Susan, Irene, and I had created in fifth grade only strengthened. Our friendship transcended cheerleading practice and school queen competitions. And it was that year that it expanded to include Audrey.

SIX

"I guess we'll have to make friends with her," Reenie said, glancing down the row of green lockers at the solitary figure who was packing a book bag. "She's on the cheerleading squad."

"Connie Lopez says she's really not that bad, that she's kinda nice. She doesn't really think she's cute." This comment came from Su but her tone was not very convincing.

"Monica says she's siddity," I commented even though I thought Monica was even more siddity than Audrey appeared to be.

"I heard that she's *fast*," Pam Sterling interjected over Reenie's shoulder. "First, she went with Bobby Harris, then she went with Leonard Wade, and now, Karen said that Jennifer said that Richard said she's going with Lymore Johnson."

Our eyes were larger than basketballs on hearing this piece of gossip.

The boundaries of appropriate behavior were well-defined if you were "going with" somebody. There were all sorts of things that you could do and shouldn't do. And the terminology just didn't do them justice. "She's going with so-and-so," my dad would say, teasing me. "Where's she going?" "No, Dad," and I would try to explain, launching into a dissertation of what "going with" meant. My father would walk away, a confused expression on his face. In retrospect, it's a concept only a teenager can understand.

The term *fast*, however, had lots of implications for bad behavior. And all of them were lining up in the Audrey Taylor column.

The word *fast* as it related to girls (and it always seemed to relate to girls) was dangerous and delicious. It meant that you were doing things with boys that were scandalous and, probably, against our religion. Reenie and I were Baptist, Su was AME or Methodist, depending on which aunt she attended church with. Whichever transgressions Audrey was committing were probably against all of our faiths. The problem was that we were thirteen and nearly thirteen years old, it was the late 1960s, and since we knew nothing (and I mean, *nothing*) at all about boys, sex, or anything else related to either of them, well, suffice it to say that being *fast* was a bad thing even if its substance was fuzzy and covered with fog and we couldn't define it. It was as mysterious as Dracula's castle on a stormy night.

On the basis of unsubstantiated rumors, Audrey Taylor became a subject of intrigue and fascination.

We were so engrossed with our petty character assassination that we didn't notice that our target was approaching.

"Hi."

We jumped six feet.

"Oh, hi, Audrey," I said.

Reenie and Su murmured greetings.

"I, um, well, since we're all on the squad . . ." She stopped and looked at me, the lone outcast, but continued anyway. "I, well, my mother wanted to know if you would like to come over to our house after school one day. Since we'll be cheering together and everything. Umm, you, too, Vaughn."

Well, that's big of her, I remember thinking wickedly. Of course, I had no intention of turning down the invitation, afterthought or not.

I said that I'd have to check with my mother, which was true, but, of course, she wasn't going to say "no." My mom and Audrey's mother went to Sunday school together when they were children back in the days of Moses. That was practically a Good Housekeeping Seal of Approval.

Reenie and Su offered grudging acceptances of Audrey's invitation as if they had something better to do, which they didn't. God, we were such nasty bitches then.

And, in Audrey's case, it was so undeserved.

We were young but had already begun to learn that things were not always as they appeared, and that people wore masks to keep the outside from coming in and what was inside from coming *out*. We just weren't mature enough to apply that reasoning to Audrey yet. She was pretty, polished, and poised. She came from comfortable circumstances. She was the envy of all the girls and the desire of all the boys. We were jealous. Nearly thirty years after our junior high experience, over alcohol and nicotine, as we discussed various stages of marital attachment and detachment, teenagers, spreading hips (except for Audrey's), graying hair, and the benefits of hormone replacement therapy, Audrey reminded us that on that fall day in September of 1966, what looked like poise and conceited self-confidence was really terror, uncertainty, and the desire to please at all costs.

Our community was close-knit and had been for generations. Our parents, grandparents, great-grandparents, uncles, aunts, and cousins lived in the same neighborhoods, attended the same schools and churches, used the same barber shops and beauty parlors, went to the same parties, doctors, and dentists. Some of our fathers and uncles had served in the War together. Whole families had histories that were intertwined. It would have been hard for anyone to be the new girl at our school. Harder still for someone as nearly perfect as Audrey.

"You guys looked so . . . happy. You were having so much fun!" She'd sighed and popped the olive from her martini into her mouth. "Huddled together at the lunch table. Talking bad about people!"

Su and I grinned. Reenie's eyes widened as if she didn't know what Audrey was talking about.

"V was always giving a lecture about this or that obscure who cares piece of trivia that she'd found in one of her dusty old books." Audrey winked at me.

I pretended that my feelings were hurt.

"Obviously, you all had no appreciation for erudition and high-brow thinking," I commented in an arch tone. I raised my nose in the air.

"Oh, please." Su sighed.

"And the giggling and the gossiping and the walking home to-gether from school, I missed all that," Audrey continued. "Every time Dad got transferred, we were pulled up by the roots like potatoes and dragged off to a new town, a new school, and a new start." She blew out the smoke from her cigarette in one long *whoosh*. "I hated it. I was so shy, I had to make friends all over again. It was awful."

By the time she'd settle in, her father got new orders, the brown boxes would appear in the living room, and the Taylors were off on another new adventure.

At four and six, it didn't mean much. As long as Mommy is around, little kids are just fine. Even at seven, when Major Taylor got his orders for Germany, it wasn't so bad. But then, it seemed, Colonel Taylor was transferred every year, or so it seemed to Audrey. And by the time Audrey got to Poindexter, she was feeling like a train case.

You couldn't cry about it. You couldn't complain about it. Not that Audrey's mother ever did. She'd learned a long time ago that when you married an army officer, you were part of the package—and not the most important part. You were an accessory, as were your children. You had no identity, no vocation (and absolutely no ca-reer), and no name. You were the wife, Colonel Taylor's wife. The house and furniture were his, the car was his, the children were his, and *you* were his.

But things began to look up when Lieutenant Colonel Taylor re-tired and moved to his wife's hometown to take a job at Lockbourne Air Force Base. Finally! A real home, not on a base somewhere, a real school, and the chance to make real friends.

Except that it didn't happen right away and, since young people are impatient, Audrey began to feel left out. She joined the choir and the art club. She tried out for cheerleading and made the squad. At lunch, if she noticed a group of girls from her homeroom sit-ting together, she would smile and set her tray down. But no one said much.

No one except the boys, of course. So she talked back. And earned the reputation of being fast. By then, Audrey was ready to give up.

"And we weren't even kissing then," Audrey said years later, rolling her eyes. "How the hell can you be fast when you're not even kissing anyone? You all shoulda been shot. Gossipy bitches."

"Siddity, gossipy bitches," Reenie chimed in. "Get it right."

"It took all the courage I had to speak that day," Audrey remembered. "I just wanted friends, you know. Friends I could keep for more than an eighteen-month tour."

The invitation to the Taylor house was accepted, of course. We were eaten up with curiosity. The Taylors' home was one of the largest in the area, it was practically considered a mansion in the 1920s, and we'd heard bits and pieces about how it was richly decorated and how they had a maid and everything. We were also dying to know more about Audrey's family. Her younger sister, Andrea, was in the seventh grade and was everything that Audrey was not: loud, tomboyish, outgoing, and sloppy. She wore the same beautiful clothes that Audrey did, but on Andrea, or "Andy" as she preferred to be called, they were usually grubby or torn by the end of a school day. Their brother, Thompson, was younger still and of no importance at all. I tried to gather advance information.

"What was she like, Mom?" I asked. "Mrs. Taylor, I mean. When you knew her."

My mother, appropriately skeptical of my sudden interest in anything that she had to say, frowned and turned sideways so she could mold her meat loaf and figure out what I was up to.

"Why do you want to know about Ellie Howell?"

"Is that her name?" I asked, intrigued.

My mother was suspicious.

"It was then. She is *Mrs.* Taylor now," Mother added, emphasizing the "Mrs." as if I would forget and call her "Ellie" by mistake. "We went to Sunday school together."

"Oh," I commented. "Was she . . . a nice girl?"

Mother gave me another "I don't know why you're asking but I'm suspicious" look and turned her attention back to the wonderful-smelling ground beef, onion, and oatmeal concoction she was mashing into a loaf pan.

"She was a very nice girl," she said. "There were . . . hmmm . . . three of them, the Howell girls, I think, no. Four. Anne, Miriam, Eleanor, and Catherine. Anne and Miriam were twins, I think Anne plays bridge with Aunt Betty. Ellie was my age, we were in the same class. Cathy . . . I didn't know Cathy very well, she was much younger. And then she died young." Mother frowned. "I don't remember why."

"What was El . . . er, Mrs. Taylor like when you knew her?"

"Vaughn, I'm not sure what this is about but . . ."

"I'm just wondering. We're going over to Audrey's house tomorrow after school. If that's OK."

"That's fine, just make sure you do your homework. And tell *Mrs.* Taylor that I'll call her."

"I will," I agreed. Mother was shutting down, I knew I wouldn't get anything else useful from her, so I turned to leave, grabbing my geography book and papers.

I was in the doorway when Mother's voice reached me again.

"Ellie was a fun person. She laughed a lot and asked all kinds of questions in Sunday school that got us into trouble, like if Adam's sons got married, who did they marry? She was a wonderful girl." The loaf pan was bounced against the counter to settle the meat mixture. "Adventurous. Just delightful. Not like she is now," Mother continued, talking more to herself than to me. Only later did I remember those words.

When Audrey opened the heavy mahogany doors of her home, Su, Reenie, and I entered with our mouths open. We felt like the Tin Man, Scarecrow, and Cowardly Lion passing through the gates of Oz for the first time. To paraphrase Truman Capote, the only thing wrong with Audrey Taylor's house was that it was perfect. Other than that, it was perfect.

Despite *Leave It to Beaver* and *Father Knows Best,* Ellie Taylor was the only mother we knew who actually did wear a dress, heels, and pearls around the house. She even wore rubber gloves when she washed the dishes. Mrs. Taylor was tall and thin with the same greenish-gold eyes that Audrey had. Her hair was neatly curled and sprayed into place and she was even wearing lipstick, something my mother did only when she was going to work or out with Dad. As she floated past us, I caught a whiff of perfume. Shalimar, I recognized it. Patty's boyfriend had given her a bottle for Christmas. My mom never wore cologne around the house.

"Hello girls! It's wonderful to see you! I keep after Audrey to bring her friends home but she never does." Mrs. Taylor stroked Audrey's blushing cheek and gave her a smile. "Let's see, you're Susan, I remember your grandmother, what a grand lady she is. And Reenie, tell Dinah that I'll call her about the PTA Halloween party at the boys' school." Her eyes turned toward me and she beamed. Her voice was warm and soft. "And you must be Carolee's baby, Vaughn. I would have known you anywhere. You look just like your mother." She gave me a Chanel scented smooch on both cheeks. Carolee? No one ever called my mother Carolee to her face except Grandma and Aunt Betty. Not only that, but the last time I checked I looked nothing like my mother. "Oh, wipe your feet, dear."

We all wiped our feet even though it was as dry as Ezekiel's bones outside and had been for weeks. But I could see her point. I'd never seen a hallway like this, ever. No microbes anywhere on that floor.

Black and white tile, a mural on the wall leading to the upstairs, and two matching ferns on either side of the staircase. The floor was gleaming in the late-afternoon sunshine, and there was the faint smell of furniture polish beneath the sweet sauciness of the French perfume. It was only four forty-five but the chandelier was on. Yep, it was just like Oz.

Audrey was still blushing as she closed the door behind us and moved toward the stairs. "Come on, let's go up to my room . . ."

"Oh, no, Audrey, not that way!" Mrs. Taylor exclaimed, glancing at her watch. "It's almost five, the Colonel will be home soon. I need to sweep the steps, you girls use the back staircase, please. Will you?"

"Sure, Mom." Audrey switched gears in midstep and we tromped through the hall toward the kitchen, where I was nearly blinded by the shining chrome on the stove, refrigerator, dishwasher, and sink. Nearly everything was white. The floor was so shiny and so slippery that we skated across it, dissolving into giggles as we bumped into one another and made our way upstairs.

"Audrey! Did you leave your homework in the folder for the Colonel?" Mrs. Taylor's anxious voice followed us.

"Yes, Mom!" Audrey yelled back.

The next thing we heard was the roar of the vacuum cleaner and a thumping sound as Mrs. Taylor attacked the immaculate carpet one more time, cleaning the clean.

Reenie, Su, and I exchanged glances as we walked down the quiet, white-carpeted hall, our eyes scanning the large paintings that hung beneath little lamps that seemed to have been made just for them, peeking through the open doorways into rooms that looked as if they'd jumped from the pages of the home and garden magazines that my mother adored reading. This house didn't seem real.

"Audrey, your house is . . . beautiful," Reenie gushed in a low voice. Su simply nodded and I whispered "It really is." There was something sacred about the hallway, it was churchlike in its quiet, cool neatness. It didn't seem right to speak in normal voices or to breathe normally.

"Thanks" was all Audrey said. She opened a door at the end of the hall. "This is my room, come on in."

Reenie's neat and color-coordinated pink and white bedroom looked like a West Virginia junkyard compared to Audrey's room. Her furniture was white, and there were soft, lavender-colored draperies and a matching bedspread and canopy. The carpet was white and she had her own bathroom. It was white, too. Her dolls were arranged, by size, in the window seat. None of them looked as if they'd ever been played with. She had every Nancy Drew mystery from *The Secret in the Old Clock* to the newest one and her *Teen* and *Seventeen* magazines were arranged chronologically on the bookshelf. There were flowers—irises, I think—arranged in a vase on top of the bureau. When no one was looking, I touched one of them. They were real. I thought about my room at home with its lumpy twin beds, the bedspreads crooked because I was always in a hurry in the morning, the pillows squished against the headboards. Mutilated Barbie dolls sat on the floor in the corner and books were everywhere, haphazardly stacked on my bookshelf and in a Tower of Pisa beside my bed on the side that didn't face the door where Mom could see them.

"Who's the Colonel?" Su asked shortly after we'd finished a juicy conversation about what we thought Brenda Rodgers was doing with Nowell Johnson behind the candy store on Atcheson.

"Oh, that's my dad," Audrey answered. "He's . . . he was in the army. He's retired now."

"Your mom calls him 'Colonel'? That's strange." Reenie was rarely one to mince words. Su nudged her. Hard. Reenie's eyes widened. *What?*

Audrey didn't raise her eyes from the magazine she was flipping through. "She, uh, she was really happy when he was promoted so . . . I think she just likes calling him that."

"Oh, you have the new Four Tops album!" As usual Reenie's thoughts and words ran together. She'd been flipping through the records. "JC's girlfriend has it, it is bad."

"I'm dying to get it but I haven't saved up enough babysitting money yet," Su said wistfully. Her eyes lit up when Levi Stubbs's voice filled the room.

"You have Gladys Knight, too!" Reenie's voice was filled with excitement and envy.

Audrey blushed again, something she did a lot, I'd noticed.

"Yes, well, my mom bought it for me . . ."

We listened hungrily then started practicing dance steps we'd learned at a party the previous week. I was still saving up for the album. Most of my babysitting was for Jeannie, but Mom didn't consider babysitting Jeannie a job because she was my sister, so I had to scrape together a quarter here and a dollar there from other odd jobs, including working as a substitute cashier in the lunchroom from time to time. At the rate I was going, the Four Tops would cut their next album before I could afford to buy this one. Audrey's perfect clothes, perfect room, and perfect mother were getting under my skin. She seemed nice enough, but I decided that it was just too much pressure to have a friend who had everything *and* had the nerve to be humble about it.

But jealousy is a funny thing. It doesn't always work in the way we think.

There was a knock at the door and Mrs. Taylor peeked in.

"Audrey, the Colonel will be home in fifteen minutes. *Please* be on time, all right? Please?"

Be on time for what, I wondered.

"Yes, ma'am," Audrey murmured. "I always am." Only I heard those words.

"You girls having a good time?" Mrs. Taylor asked brightly.

We answered in a chorus of "yes" and she shut the door.

"Are you supposed to go somewhere?" Su asked Audrey. Audrey never did answer the question.

At 1745 Zulu—five forty-five p.m. to you and me—Lieutenant Colonel Wallace Taylor, Jr., Retired, stepped into the perfect hall of his perfect home. Just minutes before, Mrs. Taylor, Audrey, and her brother, Thompson, also known as Tommy, scurried into the living room, straightening their clothes, patting hair down, and clearing throats. Audrey's mom frowned as she tried, without success, to smooth a cowlick that had escaped from the elastic of Audrey's ponytail. One of Tommy's buttons was missing. Mrs. Taylor sighed, then her attention was diverted by a dead leaf on the practically perfect philodendron plant on the end table. She snatched it off and tucked it into her apron pocket. The front door clicked and Audrey, her mother, and her brother quickly came to attention. Judging from the way they acted, you would have thought that General Eisenhower had arrived.

The Colonel was not exactly what I was expecting.

In the first place, he was short. Let me rephrase that. He was smaller than the average man. Nope. That doesn't sound right either. I'll try again. He was, well, short. I have nothing against short people. But the Napoleonic complex is a real thing. Audrey's father was a whole head shorter than Mrs. Taylor, who towered over him in her high heels. He was slight and had the smallest hands I'd ever seen on a man. My dad was a solid, stocky man with large hands even though his fingers were delicate enough to play the piano. The Colonel's hands were downright teeny. His black hair was cut very short and his reddish brown face was cleanly shaven except for a pencil-thin mustache. He wore a dark suit, white shirt, and deep maroon tie. His shoes were polished to shine like patent leather. The Colonel was perfectly turned out. My mother said that he had a Continental look. I thought he looked like a twit. I'd expected a large burly man with a commanding voice. Instead, the Colonel was a flyweight who spoke in a low tenor. But his words, both in content and delivery, were razor sharp, the meanness emphasized by a clipped Philadelphia accent. He did not greet his wife with a nuzzle or a squeeze like my dad, who fondled Mom's behind when he thought we weren't looking. In fact, the Colonel barely seemed to notice Mrs. Taylor at all. She might as well have been a breathing hat rack. He handed her his briefcase and fedora, marched over to his chair, took a sip of his drink, and lit his cigarette before sitting down.

Mrs. Taylor was smiling so hard her cheeks looked as if they were going to crack. Tommy struggled to stand still and shifted his weight from one foot to the other. He smiled uncertainly at his father. Only Audrey did not smile. She stood perfectly still. I couldn't see her face, but if I had to guess, I would have said that her eyes were aimed directly at her father. Only Andrea escaped the review because she was taking her weekly piano lesson.

The inspection began.

"Thompson, no papers today?"

"No, sir." Reenie and I exchanged glances. It sounded so funny to hear a ten-year-old respond to his father like an army corporal.

"Is this your reading assignment?"

"Yes, sir."

"Have you finished it?"

"N-no, sir." Tommy was nervous.

One dark eyebrow rose as the Colonel's eyes bored into his son.

"This assignment is to be completed before lights out tonight, is that clear?"

"Yes, sir."

The temperature in the room was glacial.

The Colonel flipped through a few more pages then stopped. He frowned and put down his drink. Then he looked up at Audrey.

"Audrey Jean, front and center."

At school, Audrey Taylor was the most poised, calm, confident person you could imagine. Nothing shook her up, nothing. As they used to say, "butter wouldn't melt in her mouth." She is still that way. But there is a reason for everything. This was the day we learned what it was.

We were more than fifty feet away and Audrey's back was to us, so we couldn't see her face, but we could see that her knees were wobbly and her hands were balled up into tight fists. It was the first time I ever saw Audrey Taylor's shoulders droop.

"Audrey, I have reviewed your American history quiz." The Colonel's tenor echoed off the walls of the cavernous and pristine living room. "I am disturbed by the B plus grade that you received. It is unacceptable. Entirely unacceptable! It is a mark of inattention and laziness. Do you have anything to say about this?"

Anything to *say*? Reenie, Su, and I exchanged glances but remained silent. *Unacceptable?* I had studied for that quiz until midnight (from beneath the covers; Dad believed that if you hadn't figured it out by bedtime, that was just too bad) and I was grateful for the B minus that I got. I enjoyed history, but Mr. Buchanan's tests were difficult.

"No, sir." I could barely hear Audrey's voice.

"Wallace, Audrey studied very hard for that test. If you remem . . ."

The Colonel stopped Mrs. Taylor's voice with a glance. She lowered her head and folded her hands across her apron.

"This is what happens when discipline is lax, Audrey. When you don't have proper leadership." He looked over at Mrs. Taylor again. Her head was still bowed. "Sloppiness, lack of focus, and poor marks. All of them unacceptable. I expect nothing less than excellence. *At all* times. You will be confined to quarters until further notice. No visitors. There will be an A on the next test. Is that clear?"

"Yes, sir," Audrey barked. She sounded as if she was on *No Time for Sergeants*. But there wasn't a laugh track.

"That will be all. You are dismissed." The Colonel glanced up at us for a second then looked away. We were guests in his home yet he didn't wave or speak to us or do anything to indicate that we were standing there on the landing. He might as well have been looking at the paint on the wall. I shivered. Colonel Taylor had a cruel face.

"Yes, sir."

"Thompson!"

"Sir!"

Audrey left the room as Thompson stepped forward to receive his dressing-down for God knows what. She floated up the stairs. We were too stunned to say anything to her.

She gave us a ghost's smile, said "Come on," and headed back down the hall toward her room. We followed her in silence. Her face was composed, dry, and blank. I would have been sick to my stomach and crying my eyes out. But the expression in Audrey's eyes was unforgettable. It was the first time in my life I ever saw hatred in someone's eyes.

My dad had been in the army, lots of dads had. World War II left few able-bodied men behind. In fact, Reenie's dad and mine were in Italy at the same time, part of the 301st supporting the Tuskegee Airmen. And yes, my dad was neat and organized and arranged his shoes in a perfect row in his closet. It was probably the result of his army training, although I'll bet my grandmother would have disagreed with that assumption. But neither Reenie nor I could imagine our fathers having us line up every day for inspection and humiliation. Mr. Keller was the kind of man whose easygoing manner and generous laugh would not allow him to keep a stern demeanor for long. And my father, a quiet, gentle man who had a passion for baseball and Bach, had a warm and hopeful spirit. There was no room in his days between his job, baseball innings, and grace notes for petty criticism and sham military exercises.

Audrey was confined to quarters for six weeks.

There weren't any TV or radio psychologists then. Not that we needed them. It didn't take a Ph.D. to figure out the reason for Audrey's studied perfection. Her obvious lack of faults was not the fruit of her desire to be better than anyone or to become a saint. Audrey's single-minded desire to please, to be the best, and to overachieve arose from a more basic need: survival. Despite his later protests to the contrary, the Colonel's brutal domestic regime was not designed to encourage his children or his wife to do well or feel good about themselves. It wasn't about them at all. It was all about him.

Before we visited Audrey's home, we had started calling her "Mary Poppins" out of sheer meanness and jealousy. We called her that because, like the character, she appeared to be "practically perfect in every way." We stopped doing that. Because now we knew just how high a price she was paying for that perfection.

We were too young to realize it at the time, but we were becoming the girls most likely to be cheerleaders and earn straight A's and date the cutest boys and wear the most stylish clothes. We were envied and emulated and asked out everywhere. We were popular. Our friendship, already in its fourth year, was legendary and yet I'd bet that most of our classmates didn't know, and still don't know, that it had its roots in empathy, support, and determination. Reenie became my friend because Timmy Early kept chasing me home from school and she felt sorry for me. We strengthened our ties with Su because of her tenuous life with her troubled mother, we tolerated Reenie's Marie Antoinette flightiness because of her grab-the-day philosophy adopted after the death of her brother. And we dropped the petty backstabbing and envy we'd had for Audrey like a hot potato and pulled her into our circle. All her life she would be practically perfect in every way. And we loved her even more because of it.

SEVEN

So now the great quartet was complete: Reenie, Su, Audrey, and me. If you saw one, you usually saw the other three. And whenever one of us was alone, someone would tease, "You actually came out by yourself?" We complemented each other in ways that weren't obvious to us then. But now, looking back, I see the delicate scales of our friendship tipping first this way, then that way. Our personalities and our lives overlapped.

Su and Audrey were studious and measured, not given to impulse or exaggeration. They were hardworking and pragmatic, overachievers before the term came into common use.

"Susan! Are you going to eat that piece of chicken or dissect it?" Reenie would ask in frustration when we ate together. Su examined her food carefully before taking a bite, cutting this way and that with her knife and fork, studying with interest any veins or other formations that she came across.

Audrey was fastidious, too, cutting her meat up into a zillion little pieces. Sometimes it annoyed the hell out of Reenie and me, sometimes it didn't.

If the teacher assigned a five-page paper, Audrey wrote ten pages. If you needed four examples of iambic pentameter, Audrey found eight. But she had an analytical way of seeing the world and sometimes it helped us see things more clearly, too. To put it politely, Audrey could cut through the bullshit and find the diamond. She is the perfect editor.

"This is a good idea here, V, but you don't need the last two pages," Audrey commented once after reading a paper I had written. "Why don't you take this sentence and do a whole paragraph on it, too?" Bless her heart; she had thoughtfully circled the noteworthy sentence in red ink. I groaned about having to write more on such a boring topic, whatever it was (I've since forgotten), but I followed her advice anyway and got an A. Thanks, Audrey, for pointing that out to me. I never would have seen through the fog to find that sentence.

Reenie and I were the emotional ones, the artsy-fartsy, fly-by-the-seat-of-your-pants girls. We were the dreamers. And yet, even with our esoteric way of thinking, Reenie and I could see things that Su and Audrey couldn't. Reading between the lines was our specialty. We could feel vibrations that spreadsheets, statistics, and therapy could not uncover. Su and Audrey analyzed, Reenie and I sensed.

"What's really wrong with Audrey?" Reenie asked after we saw Audrey's perfect house and bedroom and met her perfect family. It would turn out to be a loaded question.

I was the space cadet, falling over the object in front of my nose because I was looking a hundred yards away.

"Goodness, Vaughn!" Audrey exclaimed after I tumbled into her as we walked home from school. As usual, I wasn't looking where I was going.

"You'd better start paying attention," Audrey warned. "You're going to miss something important that's right under the booger hanging on your nose!"

Boy, was she right about that. But I made myself useful reading every book I could find, trying to know everything, and scribbling in my notebooks, not to mention writing love letters (for a small fee) for my girlfriends, a valuable talent if you have girlfriends who were as popular as mine were. Unfortunately, Miss Norman intercepted one of these in sophomore English and read it aloud to the class. I tried to disappear behind the large world history textbook.

"Vaughn, I don't mind you acting as Cyrano de Bergerac for your friends, but in the future please proofread your work. 'I love you passionately and deeply, signed You Know Ho.' " I have been an obsessive proofreader ever since.

Reenie, of course, was our straight-talking no-nonsense glamour queen, and if that sounds contradictory, it is. But the girl who was always late because she needed one more spritz of hairspray or another wave of her magic mascara wand was also the girl who could change a flat tire, deconstruct Buddhist philosophy, and cook up a pot of chili for the football team without using a recipe or measuring cup. Reenie could balance pragmatism with Cinderella's dreams and somehow it always came out all right. Well, except for one area of her life: boys. Reenie was the original "boy crazy" girl. When it came to love, she was deaf, dumb, and blind.

"And stupid as a turnip," she would remark years later when she reviewed her romantic career. In love with love, that was Reenie.

We made our friendship work. Audrey merged into our clique, and in no time it seemed as if she'd always been there. As for me, the original misfit kid, I found a place to be, a place where I belonged even though it seemed I didn't have as much in common with these smart and beautiful girls. But fitting in wasn't what was important in our friendship, being there for one another was.

And for that reason Reenie would always hold a special place in my heart. It's not that I love Reenie any more than I do Audrey or Su. And I could say that it's because she rescued me from Timmy Early, which was a blessing. (Speaking of blessings, he's a preacher now, if you can believe it. Last time I saw him, he told me to have a "Blessed day." I reached into my purse to make sure my wallet was still there.) Or maybe it's because she was the first of the "girls most likely" to become my friend. It could be that, too. But it isn't. Reenie will be my soul mate friend forever for one very special reason: We were baptized together at Second Baptist Church. You don't forget the people who were dunked with you in the baptismal pool—ever.

Church attendance was part of our lives then. It wasn't bragged about piously and there weren't any sanctimonious pronouncements about personal relationships with Jesus or being saved. It was just what people did, as normal as my dad going to work on Monday and Mom checking in on Grandma on Tuesday afternoons. On Saturday nights, my sisters and I got our hair done, took our baths, and laid out our Sunday school clothes, making sure the patent leather shoes were polished to a blinding shine. On Sunday, it was breakfast, Sunday school at 9:30, church at 11:00 and don't be late.

Su's family was a hodgepodge of faiths; her grandmother was a shouting Pentecostal, one aunt and uncle attended Centenary Methodist, Leila went to Mt. Vernon AME. Audrey's family was staunchly AME, St. Paul's. Reenie's family was a hodgepodge like Su's. Mr. Keller had been raised Catholic but rarely went to Mass. He said his church was his easy chair; his hymnal, the sports pages. Dinah Keller wasn't big on popes and kneeling and genuflection and, besides, she'd attended the Baptist church since she was a kid. She attended Second Baptist and brought Reenie and the boys with her.

Now that we were teenagers, Mom and Dad allowed Patty and me to sit separately from them as long as we behaved ourselves. Patty did behave. I didn't. On the second and fourth Sundays, Reenie and I sat with the junior choir, passed notes, and whispered until it was time for us to sing. On the first and third Sundays, we ran to the corner store after Sunday school, hung out with our friends (kids from Centenary, Love Zion, and St. Paul's) who were also supposed to be in church and weren't, bought hard candy and gum and slipped back into church in time for the sermon, the passing of the collection plate, and, on first Sundays, communion. The only reason we didn't get into real trouble was because our parents sat in the front of the huge sanctuary and we sat in the back. This strategy worked for a while.

One Sunday, it broke down completely.

It was a third Sunday, one of the Sundays when we sat in the back, sucked on hard candy, wrote notes to each other and any cute boys sitting in the vicinity, and caught up on the gossip that might have occurred since we talked on the phone the night before. There was usually enough candy, cute boys, and gossip to take up the entire hour-and-a-half service. This Sunday, however, we had an added bonus: L Davis and his cousin sat three rows ahead. L was, hands down, the cutest boy in the Second Baptist Church Sunday school program. He was tall, cute (a prerequisite), and played basketball. He had dimples. I still sigh when I think about him. His first name was a mystery. Mrs. Keller said he was named after his uncle, Lawrence; my father said, no, he was named after his grandfather Lucretius. It didn't matter. Reenie and I and all the other junior high school girls at Second thought he was darling and we didn't care what his real name was. "L" was good enough for us.

Anyway, he was sitting within striking distance of our famous rolled up notebook paper fastballs and within the crosshairs of Cupid's bow. Reenie had decided that he should be her next boyfriend. I had thought about asking him myself, but once I learned Reenie was interested, I let that dream go. No way would he have chosen me over her. On her behalf, I scribbled down a few sentences to let him know that someone thought he was really cute and passed them to Reenie for review.

"Not just 'cute,' " Reenie whispered. "Think of another word besides 'cute.' " As we tried to think of just the right word, Reenie forgot and cracked her gum. "Sorry."

The sound reverberated in the quiet room, bouncing off the stained-glass windows dedicated to the memory of parishioners who'd died in the sixteenth century or something, and hit the ears of Reenie's aunt Edith, who turned around to look at us. She was not happy.

We studied page 498 of the hymnal to avoid her gaze.

Aunt Edith sat in the same pew every Sunday and wore the largest hats you can imagine. She had more hats than my grandmother, if such a thing was possible. Edith Keller had red hats, blue hats, green hats, and purple hats. She had a hat to match every coat in the winter and every dress in the summer. She took her religion seriously, saying "amen" very loudly when something Reverend Tharp said agreed with her and "Well . . ." equally loudly when it did not. She sang the hymns with a lot of enthusiasm and volume but without any talent. All Reenie and I needed to do was catch a few bars of Aunt Edith wailing "Onward Christian Soldiers" at the top of her lungs and we would dissolve into uncontrollable laughter, which we had to expel silently until our stomachs hurt and our faces were drenched in tears.

This Sunday, Aunt Edith's daffodil-hued confection tilted our way and we caught a glimpse of a disapproving eye before we concentrated on the lyrics to "There's a Balm in Gilead."

"Shhh . . ." I warned Reenie. "I thought you spit out that gum."

"I forgot!" Reenie quickly covered it with a tissue and stuffed it into her purse. "OK, now what about 'gorgeously handsome' instead of 'cute'?"

As a survivor of Mrs. Shelley's English composition class, I'd been indoctrinated in the rules of sentence diagramming and economical word usage.

"Now, class," Mrs. Shelley would elocute deliberately in firm but soft, well-modulated tones that held only a hint of the South Carolina pinewoods where she was from. "You must choose your words carefully. Don't be wasteful. And watch the overuse of adverbs." Always, her eye would fall on me for this cardinal sin. "Vaughn, you must discard some of those adverbs!"

"The adverb's out," I whispered to Reenie and drew a line through it. Reenie snorted and handed me another small piece of paper. "OK, no 'gorgeously.' But it did sound good."

It did but I finished the note without it, signed Reenie's name, and passed it to her for delivery. Reenie Keller made good use of her position as the only girl in a family of boys. She could curse like a sailor, run like the wind, and throw a curveball when she needed to. The note was balled up into the proper shape and readied for its pitch.

On any other Sunday it wouldn't have mattered much if the note went astray. We would have ducked, giggled, and retrieved it during the call for the offering. But this Sunday, Reverend Tharp finished his sermon with an invitation for those who wanted to accept Christ as their Savior and be baptized. Reenie and I weren't paying attention. She molded the paper ball in her hand, swayed a little from side to side just like the players in the World Series on TV, and let it rip.

It ripped right onto Aunt Edith's daffodil hat.

"Oops," Reenie said.

We started to duck but before we did, Aunt Edith turned around, saw us sitting there with expressions of near panic and hysterical rapture (also known as near hysterical laughter) on our faces and stood up, calling out to Reverend Tharp and gesturing back to us.

"These girls want to be baptized, Reverend! Back here! See?"

"No, no . . ." I started to say, shaking my head. Reenie nudged me in the ribs. I closed my mouth. She was right. There was no way to back out now. The eyes of three hundred fifty people, including both of our mothers, my father, my sisters, two of Reenie's brothers, and my grandmother, were on us.

Reverend Tharp beamed.

"How wonderful! Two young people! Young ladies! Come forward, young ladies!"

"Reenie!" I hissed through clenched teeth as we marched down the center aisle toward the pulpit. "What have you gotten me into?"

Don't get me wrong. It wasn't that I intended to remain an unbaptized heathen all my life. You don't go to the Baptist church without an intention to be baptized. Someday. But I was twelve, preoccupied with school, boys, music lessons, boys, hair, makeup, and boys. Getting baptized was on one of my "to do" lists, just not the one that I'd expected to get to in the next twenty years. So here I was, standing in front of the entire congregation, the living embodiment of Christian commitment.

I was scared to death.

Mother and Dad quizzed me on the drive home.

"Why didn't you tell us you were going to join the church?" Mom said as if I'd forgotten to mention that my head had fallen off. "I'd have told your grandfather to come. He'd have wanted to be here!"

Patty thought it was funny. Jeannie didn't understand what "baptized" meant, so Mom and Dad spent the rest of the drive home explaining. I, of course, should have been listening, too, but, as usual, I wasn't. I was wondering just what Reenie—and her aunt Edith—had gotten me into. Especially when I heard Daddy say, "You know the problem with Baptists, don't you? They don't hold 'em under the water long enough!"

If it hadn't been part of the normal rituals in a Baptist church, our baptismal experience would have qualified for a *National Geographic* special. It had all the right elements: virgins, water, ritualistic language, loud singing, and white robes.

We were dressed by the senior members of the Circle of Ruth Society, women who were old enough to have known the biblical Ruth personally. They fussed over us like mother hens, clicking their tongues and patting our cheeks saying, "Bless your hearts!" The baptismal robes were white choir robes drafted for use in the festivity and they were four sizes too big for Reenie and me, so safety pins were used to keep them from flapping around us. Nothing could be done about the length, however, so Reenie and I held the robes away from our bare feet as we made our way through the labyrinthine corridors behind the pulpit and choir loft to the main sanctuary. Our heads were covered with white bathing caps. In the black church, sanctity is important but God help the minister who messes up a good press.

The back corridors of Second Baptist were cool, quiet, and dark. They reminded me of the descriptions of the catacombs beneath Rome and held the same kind of mysterious aura. I shivered with fear and cold. Baptism was part of a tradition of symbolic rebirth, at least that's what our Sunday school teacher had told us. So why did I feel as if we were going to our execution?

"Vaughn!" Reenie's loud whisper penetrated the spooky darkness.

"What?" I nearly shouted back. My voice was shrill from fear.

"Don't forget to take a . . ."

"No talking, girls," came the stern voice of a Sister of Ruth. I felt her fingers tighten on my shoulders as she pushed me along the narrow corridor. "Quiet now."

"But I need to tell her . . ." Reenie sounded desperate. *What was wrong?*

"Did you hear what I said?" The peach-and-pecan-shaped vowels did not soften the sharpness of the voice.

"Yes, ma'am," we murmured back.

I wondered what it was that Reenie was trying to tell me. We continued down the shadowy corridor in cowed silence.

When we emerged from the bowels of the church into the light of the sanctuary, we were like bats flying into the morning. My glasses were safely tucked away in Sister Ogletree's purse. I couldn't see anything and blinked furiously to focus. Even Reenie was dazzled for a few seconds and stumbled over the trailing hem of the tentlike robe. Her tiny face was white with fear, nearly as white as the swim cap she wore. That was not helpful. If Reenie who feared nothing was scared to death, I should be petrified. I started to shake uncontrollably.

Reverend Tharp's face loomed before me. I jumped. He placed a reassuring hand on my shoulder and smiled. When my eyes focused, I noticed that he was wearing a black robe and boots.

I should have known then.

He began to speak and the organ played softly in the background. I didn't hear a word he said because my heart was pounding like the tell-tale heart and I was standing on a ledge in front of a pool of water that looked to be hundreds of feet deep. I panicked. *When did Second Baptist have a swimming pool installed?* I'd stood on this very place a million times for this Easter program or that and I'd never seen a deep pool of water here! Was he going to push me in? Drop me in? *Throw* me in?

The minister smiled down at me and patted me on the shoulder. I took a deep breath and began to relax. *What's the matter with you?* My conscience chided me. *This is Reverend Tharp, for God's sake! He's your grandfather's friend. Your dad and his son grew up together! He's not going to murder you in front of all these people! Vaughn, you're so stupid sometimes!*

Of course I was. What was I thinking? This man was scholarly, genteel, and stately. He had blessed babies and played baseball with my father at the church picnic. He and his wife often came to our house during the holidays. He wasn't a homicidal maniac. I was just being silly.

Despite the singing and the swelling chords of the pipe organ behind us, I thought I heard Reenie's voice. I turned around and saw her mouth moving and her hands waving in the air. She was trying to tell me something. But the singing and preaching and the organ blanketed her words and with the swim cap fastened tightly around my head, I couldn't hear her. She looked even more frightened, if that were possible. I tried to lip read like we did in class when we ran out of scrap paper for passing notes.

"Vaughn! Take . . . a dip . . ."

Take . . . a . . . dip?

Reverend Tharp touched me lightly on the shoulder. I looked up at him and he gestured toward the water. He took my elbow and helped me step onto the first ledge where the water wrapped itself around my ankles. He smiled benevolently at me. It was then that genteel, stately Reverend Tharp grabbed me around the shoulders, pushed me backward into the coldest water I've ever felt in my life, and tried to drown me.

I fought him off the best I could, flailing my arms and kicking just like the swim teacher taught us at the Y. But I was no match for him. He held me down for at least a half hour before releasing me and bringing me to a standing position. OK, a semistanding position. I had not taken a breath so I was spitting, gasping, and snorting in an attempt to breathe. Water poured out of my mouth and my nose, and because I was nearly blind, I stumbled and almost fell in again trying to escape from my assailant, who uttered the triumphant words of my rebirth and led me to the other side of the pool to be greeted by a Sister of Ruth and a warm towel. I felt as if I had been born again after escaping the attentions of a serial killer.

The organ music swelled around the huge sanctuary as the choirs proclaimed our rebirth in beautifully coordinated tones of alto and mezzo-soprano and majestic bass. Reenie and I sat in the chairs of honor, wrapped in towels, looking like "drowned rats" according to my sister Patty, and shivering as if we'd been refrigerated for an hour.

We didn't dare look at each other. The piety of the event dictated somber expressions and regal demeanor. But seriousness can be overdone.

I sneaked a glance at Reenie, who had chosen the same moment to sneak a glance at me. Her dark eyes danced with laughter.

"Vaughn! What I said was . . . take a *deep breath*!"

We dissolved into giggles and tears. The proud Sisters of Ruth told our parents that the Spirit had overwhelmed us. Somehow, I think my parents knew better.

Mohair sweaters and Motown, sour apple hard candy and double-Dutch ropes, kissing boys for the first time and knee socks; we were so young. We worried about what Connie Lopez would say when we wore an orange sweater instead of a yellow one and whether or not Mike so-and-so thought we were cute. We studied current events in social studies class but they were about places and times far away from the flat squares of cornfields that surrounded us and the bustle of the homey neighborhoods that protected us. In the spring of 1968, we were in our last year of junior high school, anxiously anticipating the ninth-grade spring dance and the advent of high school just over the horizon.

We lived in an oyster world, protected as much as we could be from the daily indignities of living in a society that took it for Gospel that you were stupid, dirty, immoral, and incapable, while not really believing it and surrounding itself in an oyster of fear. Our parents had created a place where we could be human and grow. We could be everything and anything great as long as we prepared ourselves.

In April, Martin Luther King, Jr., was assassinated, and Detroit, Chicago, and Los Angeles burned. In June, Robert F. Kennedy was murdered. And in August, Chicago police fired on demonstrators at the Democratic National Convention. The voices that called for another solution to the foreign war got louder and louder. And in 1968, after years of being Negro and colored, we became *black*.

EIGHT

I've got sunshine on a cloudy day . . .

"You are so boy crazy," Patty commented as I hung up the phone. She'd hovered over me as I talked, breathing down my neck with the mistaken notion that I would get off the phone sooner. Ha!

"No, I'm not." I still had my hand on the receiver. *No way am I giving up the phone.* I'd forgotten to tell Su what Linda said that Debbie said about her going with Bradley. "Anyway, it takes one to know one." Patty had a new boyfriend every other month if you believed what she said in her letters and phone calls from college.

The phone rang again. Faster than you could spit, I picked it up. "Hello?" It was Su again. Patty stalked off.

"Boy crazy," she muttered.

We'd first discovered boys in the sixth grade. By the way we'd acted, you would have thought we'd found Atlantis in the middle of the pool at the Eastside Y. It's not as if they hadn't been there all the time. But in sixth grade they began to look slightly more interesting even though they still did the most disgusting things imaginable. No bodily fluids were exchanged, this was the era of quick stolen glances only. By junior high, the boys our age were still three years behind us on the maturity scale, but they were taller and had learned to clean up nicely and behave themselves. No more farting as a quartet, smearing boogers across book bags, or scratching their butts then smelling their fingers. They probably still did those things, but they no longer made a production of them. By the time we reached high school, we thought boys were spectacular.

And there were so many to choose from. In the fall of 1968, we went from being ninth graders to high school sophomores at Southeast High. Kids from all the junior high schools on the near east side joined together to form one class, over three hundred fifty of us, nearly half of them male. It was like having Christmas every day. We couldn't have known that our friendship was about to change forever.

Reenie Keller, always pretty, always talented, and always charming became the closest thing SE High had to a femme fatale. The tiny, delicately made doll baby with curling black pigtails and the cherub's smile had become an exotic Polynesian flower with fabulous hair, bedroom eyes (I'm using this term in hindsight), and the figure of a brick house. She was a man-trap and she trapped at least one every month, sometimes two. Seniors, juniors, sophomores, and even teachers fell under her spell. Reenie had sex appeal with a capital S-E-X and used it to full advantage. She was in love with being in love and got bored easily. "Where did our love go?" was Reenie's theme song. Only, the refrain was usually sung by the abandoned boy in an Eddie Kendricks tenor rather than Irene in a Diana Ross–like mid-soprano.

There were fights. Lots of the boys who thought Reenie was the sharpest thing in a bra were going with other girls. Reenie was just so gorgeous, they couldn't help themselves. And these girls, miffed and feeling inadequate because Reenie was (a) light-skinned and (b) the sharpest thing in a bra, often raised their fists not in a Black Power salute but in a threat. How many times were we walking down the hall and Reenie got into a word fight with a gang from Champion or hijacked going home by a rejected girlfriend of one of Reenie's new admirers?

"You think you're cute 'cause you're high yalla," one of them cackled.

"Stuck up bitch," another one growled.

Reenie would beam at them and curl her fingers into a fist.

This slight would have cut deep had it been leveled at anyone else. But what these girls didn't realize was that they were dealing with "Reeniedarling," who, despite her hothouse-flower appearance, could kick your ass just as well as any boy without breaking a fingernail.

"Honey," Reenie would say in a voice dripping with it, "I don't think I'm cute 'cause I'm high yalla. I'm just . . . cute, that's all." The fist made contact with one well-aimed blow. I have to say that my classmates might have been slow in algebra II, but they were fast learners as far as Reenie was concerned. By the end of tenth grade she wasn't being sent to the principal's office anymore for fighting. Any girl who lost her boyfriend to Irene Keller just let him go.

"I don't understand it," Audrey said as we trudged to morning band and cheerleading practice. It was August of our junior year, hot as an armadillo's armpit in Arkansas, and the air was stuffy. "Of all the boys, you choose Lamar. Reenie, you know he's going with Cara Sparks!"

An indignant sniff came from behind us.

"I didn't go after him, he came after me," Reenie answered brightly. "I didn't do anything."

"You don't have to *do* anything," I grumbled, remembering how my last boyfriend drooled every time Reenie came within sniffing distance. "You just . . . are." This was jealousy talking even though Henry and I broke up for other reasons.

"Look, I told him I wouldn't talk to him unless he broke up with Cara. If he didn't want to break up with her, he wouldn't have done it!" Reenie Keller had an answer for everything.

"Yeah, right," said Su. "Ow!" She stopped to rub her ankle. "Here, take these." She handed her duffel bag to Audrey, who shook her head.

"I don't know why you're wearing those things now," she said, referring to Su's white majorette boots, the ones I coveted. "They're as stiff as plywood, they've got to be hurting your feet."

"Ouch, ouch! They are," Su whined. "But I've got to break 'em in." She grimaced.

Audrey and Reenie rolled their eyes. I was sympathetic since I'd have given both my big toes to be one of the six girls marching with a high step in front of the band in those white tasseled boots. As it was, I would march with the band in the standard issue white bucks blowing my brains out on the clarinet. I'd tried out for majorette but after knocking myself in the head with the baton and passing out from a near concussion, the selection committee wisely chose other candidates.

"They'll soften up once summer practice ends," Reenie advised. "Good grief, if you don't take 'em off, you'll have blisters."

"It's too late, I have blisters already," Su moaned, limping along, holding on to Audrey for support because she was the only one of us who was tall enough.

"Good thing Bradley's in the band," Audrey commented. " 'Cause I can't walk you home from practice, I have a hair appointment."

"Ooooo," we all howled in unison. Su batted her eyes. Reenie made dramatic kissing sounds.

Audrey's cat eyes narrowed.

"What?"

"Getting pretty for King Edwards, huh?" I mocked. "Only Audrey would get a boyfriend who's the captain of the basketball team, a straight A student, a senior for God's sake, and, adding insult to injury, the finest boy in school. Whose name, it just happens, is King! It's not fair!" I wailed.

Audrey blushed.

"He's really nice," she offered as if that would make it better.

"Oh, yeah," Reenie grumbled. "And he has the nerve to be really nice, too."

I sighed again, bouncing my clarinet case against my thigh.

"Audrey gets the best boyfriends and never leaves anyone good left over." I was still whining.

"I do not!" she exclaimed, her cheeks now the color of Red Delicious apples. "Richard Long." She threw out Richard's name just to get us off her back. He was absolutely adorable but I'd picked blades of grass that had more intelligence.

"OK, Richard Long," Reenie echoed. "Dumber than the bottom of my shoe. Really, Audrey, that's only after you've dated practically every fine senior and junior in the whole school!"

We'd stopped calling Audrey "Mary Poppins" and started referring to her as the "Barbie" doll because she dated only guys who
were practically perfect just like she was.

"I have . . . standards," she would say in her own defense.

Did she ever.

She dated only basketball players, because they were the only
boys tall enough (she was now five feet nine inches tall) and because
the football players acted like Neanderthals. She preferred boys who
were smart (poor Richard) and tended to date the ones who were either in the orchestra or the choir. Musical talent was important to
Audrey. That they had to be good-looking was a given. Whenever
Audrey and her new boyfriend, whoever he was, appeared at a
party or event, they looked like chocolate Barbie and Ken. It was
sickening.

"Only the best will do," I teased my friend. Audrey grinned and
swatted at me.

"Well, Miss Bookworm, you're the one always quoting those dead
white men. Which one of 'em said, If you expect only the best, you'll
get it?"

"Yeah, yeah," I grumbled, "that was Maugham. 'It's a funny thing
about life. If you refuse to accept anything but the best, you'll often
get it.' While I get stuck with . . . the insane and the ugly."

Giggles broke out even from Su who was still limping.

"Bobby Powell isn't insane," Su offered with a quick look at
Audrey. She could barely stop laughing long enough to get the
words out.

And he wasn't. Bobby Powell was very sane and damn near brilliant. He could play the trumpet like Dizzy Gillespie and was already taking advanced calculus. He was fluent in Spanish. But, call
me shallow, Bobby Powell was really ugly.

"Give me a break, Su," I shot back. "Bobby Powell looks as if he's
been hit by a bus, sideswiped by a semi, and run over, twice, by a
train."

My romantic record was the opposite of Reenie's and Audrey's.
Like the man magnet she was, Reenie attracted every male within a
hundred yards. Audrey attracted the boys, too, but selectively picked

only the cream of the crop. And then there was me. The sign that used to hang on my back, the one that read "Beat me up—*please!*" had been exchanged for one that read "Only the stupid or the hideous are welcome." Every moron, every nitwit, every boy who picked his nose for a hobby or neglected to wipe his mouth after gulping down a carton of milk asked me out. I'd given up on having a decent boyfriend and settled for the companionship of friends. Earl Carlisle, Tommy Metz, and other boys I'd known forever and couldn't imagine kissing without throwing up acted as my dates when I needed one. It wasn't romantic but it kept me from staying home on Saturday nights and put me on the dance floor. Someday my prince would come along. Until then I had to get that damn sign off my back.

The laughter continued down the street.

"OK, OK, there's Leroy St. John, he's not what'd you call handsome . . . but he is really nice. And he's in the Honor Society," Su suggested.

There's that phrase again "really nice" . . .

I sighed and looked at Reenie, whose eyes were filling up with tears as she doubled over in laughter.

"Well thanks a lot, Su, for recommending a boy whose face would send the sun behind a cloud," I snapped back.

"Looks aren't everything, V, you know that. Books by their covers and all that jazz," Su reminded me. As if I needed to be reminded.

"A lot you'd know about it, Susan," Audrey chimed in. "We have trials and tribulations while you're practically married. *You* have Bradley, who's cute, smart, and funny. It really is a jungle out there for the rest of us. Especially with Bobby Powell lurking in the bushes."

"You and Bradley have been together long enough to have anniversaries, for God's sake!" I commented.

Now it was Su's turn to blush. We were all jealous of Su and Bradley, even Reenie, who turned over boyfriends for blowing their noses the wrong way, and Audrey, the queen of perfection. But it was a good kind of jealousy. Su had the kind of romance that we wanted and kept looking for. She and Bradley met in fifth grade and hadn't looked at anyone else after that. By sixth grade, they were best friends, except for us. By eighth grade, they were sweethearts, and now, in our junior year of high school, they had already decided to go to the same college and get married when they graduated. It was so Cinderella perfect that it made us sigh. And since Bradley didn't have brothers who were our age, we searched for boys who measured up. Reenie never found them. Audrey stumbled across a few from time to time. And I kept kissing the ones who masqueraded as princes but turned into major toads after sixty seconds or when they got wet.

Boys weren't the only thing that consumed us. It was the beginning of the seventies. The cities had burned and were beginning to rise again. The ooh baby, baby of Motown had taken a left turn on a purple road, leaving behind the neat, safe structures of music we'd become used to. Now the Temptations sang about a "Ball of Confusion" and we exchanged "My Girl" for "Excuse Me While I Kiss the Sky." Our older brothers and cousins were returning from Indochina with "contents slightly damaged" stamped on their foreheads while our male classmates didn't worry about going. The beauty parlors and barber shops on Long Street quieted because we'd traded hot combs for afro pics, pleated skirts for dashikis.

And it wasn't just the way we looked. Our nurturing, protective community had always told us that Negroes needed education to get ahead, even girls. They preached that we could do anything, but before 1970, we'd never bothered to read between the lines.

The inequities that surrounded us had seemed far away when we were small. The boundaries of Parsons Avenue, Lockbourne, and Nelson Road kept us safe. We didn't realize that they also kept us contained. Now we didn't want walls or fences whether they were seen or unseen.

Without giving it a second thought, we dreamed dreams that pushed apart the fence posts of our former world. Audrey wanted to run a business, Su was going to be on television, Reenie would design haute couture, and I would write the great American novel. In our diaries we wrote about the pinnacles of our dreams. We saw Audrey's name on the door, Su with a microphone, Reenie in Paris with needle and thread, and my as yet untitled masterpiece at the top of the *New York Times* bestseller list. We forgot about the lives that would unfold between the lines and the sighs.

We were in the process of becoming. The city, the neighborhood, the high school, the boys, and the times were like the confluences of rivers forming a swift, strong force of nature. This was a lot more than just growing up. It didn't occur to us that the times were changing and that we were changing with them, all of us moving into place like the alignments of stars that cause wonderful and terrible things to happen. We didn't understand any of it. But we moved with the crosswinds.

> *When the moon is in the Seventh House*
> *And Jupiter aligns with Mars . . .*

We supported one another regardless of the problem, activity, or weather.

If I needed a pale blue mohair sweater to go with my plaid skirt, Reenie loaned me hers. Of course, it didn't fit well, since Reenie had boobs like Mae West and I had no boobs at all. But it was the thought that counted.

And Reenie liked the way I styled hair (not my hair, hers), so I was the official hairdresser of the Girls Most Likely, pinning, spraying, picking, and curling just like the real thing. Even Su, whose aunt Leila owned a beauty parlor, said that I was pretty good. Reenie still teases me about a French twist I did for her once.

"By the time V got through with me, my neck was twisted, too! It took one hour and a whole package of bobby pins to get my hair up in that do!" Reenie winked at me. "But I was cute."

And I could still remember the smell of Reenie's perfume on the soft fibers of mohair when I pulled the borrowed sweater over my head.

The girls provided standing ovations and calls of "Bravo!" at my piano recitals. I think Beethoven would have been fine with that even though my piano teacher wasn't amused. And Su and I were the official cheerleaders for the cheerleaders during basketball season when the majorettes hung up their tasseled boots. We drove through snowstorms and torrential rains to get to the games.

Actually, we were scouts. We took notes on the appearance, uni-

forms, and cheers of the opposing squads in case there was something
new and useful we could learn.

We watched the cheers of Buckeye Ridge with interest.

"What are they doing?" Su said, her lips not far from my ear.

I shrugged my shoulders.

The Blue Devils cheerleaders moved with jerky robotlike motions
that were very different from the sashaying, soulful dance moves that
the Purple Tigers used.

"Heck if I know. Maybe it's some kind of karate."

"Go! Go, team, go!"

The cheers of the Buckeye Blue Devils cheerleaders sounded
more like barks than words of encouragement. Not only that, but we
were really intrigued by the sharp motions they made with their arms.

"They have apoplexy," I said simply. The word just popped into
my head. It was my new favorite word of the week after reading an already forgotten early-nineteenth-century English novel. About the
only item of interest that I'd taken away from the book was a diagno-
sis made by the doctor character.

Su giggled.

"What's apoplexy?"

I started giggling, too. The cheering Blue Devils looked more
like eight girls having a collective fit than a cheerleading squad.

"It involves foaming at the mouth, high-pitched barks, and jerky
motions."

One of the blondes grinned and barked out, "Go! Blue Devils!
Go! Yeah. . . . Blue Devils!"

> *We like Southeast High, We like Southeast High!*
> *Let me tell you now!*

Audrey, Reenie, Connie, Retha, Jennifer, Linda, Karen, and Barbara
moved together smoother than the Temptations, Four Tops, Mira-
cles, and Supremes all together.

There was no comparison. They swayed from side to side,
clapped to the beat, and sang the cheer. The walls of the auditorium
vibrated with the sound.

I've never heard anything like it since.

And then, on Saturday mornings, we got up early to support Su and the debate team at home events. Su was the only debater who had her own cheerleading squad—and for these, I was the head cheerleader.

———

It was our senior year at Southeast High. And like the planets aligning themselves for a millennium of peace, it was the year Reenie, Su, Audrey, and I moved closest together. It was also the year we pulled completely apart.

Our friendship had survived rough spots and separations before, but these were only superficial distances, different homerooms, Su was a majorette, Audrey and Reenie were cheerleaders. I was in the choir, Su wasn't. Audrey traveled with the Spanish Club. The rest of us took French. And we didn't walk home together as much anymore. Our schedules and our boyfriends (yes, even I had one or two in that year) prevented it.

But some things never changed. Su and Bradley were still inseparable. Every hair in Audrey's afro was perfectly arranged. Reenie was the homecoming queen (Audrey and Su were on the court, of course), and I was still getting into trouble for using the wrong word at the wrong time.

I don't want to make it sound as if I survived the Inquisition, but the principal of Southeast was trying pretty hard to hold to the old traditions. Someone said that traditions are often used as an excuse by people who don't want to change. If that's true, the changing winds of our senior year definitely caught Mr. Marvin, the principal, in a bind. God rest his soul. He'd been turning out well-behaved, clean-cut, articulate, college-ready Negro boys and girls since 1960. With discipline, focus, and hard work, he had managed, along with some of the most dedicated teachers ever, to rebut the negative image that our school carried on its back. We were the "colored" high school. We had an antediluvian building, ten-year-old band uniforms, and a Stone Age chemistry lab. We dodged the smirks and low expectations of the rest of the city. With those odds, most administrators would have either given up or simply passed the time until retirement. But that wasn't Mr. Marvin's way. He literally took lemons and made margaritas. Many of his kids went to college. Our dropout rates were low. And our community support was high. He refused to give up on any student no matter what the problem or the personal situation.

But, Lord Almighty, I think he might have thought about giving up on the Class of 1971.

The student council threatened to sue him *and* the school board unless afros could be worn by students, including cheerleaders, majorettes, and newspaper editors (me). The dress code was challenged in 1970 after an unusually cold December forced most of us girls to trudge through snow and ice to get to school, carrying skirts or jumpers in our bags and trying to change before the homeroom bell rang. Mr. Marvin threatened to expel us, but since over half of the student body was female (not to mention sixty percent of the teachers) he lost again. Pants were written into the school dress policy. We lobbied for and got a student lounge. WXCO broadcast over the PA system at lunch with everyone's favorite DJ, Su, on the mike. And I spent the better part of the year going up and down several flights of stairs to the principal's office, usually to explain the text of the *Purple Tiger Chatter* editorial. Censorship was alive and well. What First Amendment?

It got to be such a regular occurrence that Mrs. Copley, the secretary, told me that the principal actually put my name down on his calendar at 2:00 p.m. every second Wednesday of the month. The paper's adviser, Mr. Swift, who was also the vice principal (he could have taught the CIA a few tricks) thoughtfully sent the drafts down to the office so that they could be censored, er, edited.

"Well, Miss Vaughn," Mr. Marvin would say, smiling. "What are we going to do this month?"

Intense negotiations followed with the result being that one paragraph was taken out and one sentence rewritten. Sometimes I was able to sneak some of the forbidden text back into the paper, but not usually.

It's the ides of March that Shakespeare warns against, and astrologers send out e-mail warnings now about the Mercury retrograde—stay in your house and don't make any major decisions. But in the spring of 1971, it was the usually gentle month of April that turned our lives upside down.

When you are sixteen going on seventeen or seventeen going on eighteen, the slightest misstep back can send you into the depths of despair. A grade of C on a world history quiz or uncooperative hair were enough to have me quoting Edgar Allan Poe for a week. We didn't know that the dramas, real and imagined, that touched our lives then weren't even warm-ups for what real life would hold for us. That would have been like comparing catsup to hot pepper sauce— they're both red but that's it. Our senior year in high school was mostly like that. The histrionics were wasted on situation comedies that I can't remember the plotlines of anymore.

We sailed through the first half of the year and survived home-coming, the SAT, college applications, boys, the ACT, more boys, driver's ed (Audrey and I passed, Su was too busy to take it but since Bradley chauffeured her everywhere she wanted to go, it didn't matter, and Reenie had to take it twice), the Sadie Hawkins Dance, and Mr. McClain's *Problems of Democracy* project. We were always going and coming and doing and talking on the phone. By the end of January we were talking like Reenie, running our sentences together to save time, and barely taking breaths in between. By February we were on one another's shoulders, sobbing, as we finally realized the impact of all the tests, application forms, interviews, and prom dress shopping. The epiphany was devastating. We just had not realized that we wouldn't be together as much in the years to come.

Su applied to Florida, Mt. Holyoke, the University of Michigan, and Columbia. Audrey was headed to Fisk, her mother's alma mater. Reenie was going to nursing school and, in typical Reenie style, had applied to every school that had a nursing school *and* an inviting cover photo. I was going wherever I could get a scholarship since my parents would have both Patty and me in college at the same time. The schools I'd applied to had nothing in common except my name on the application forms.

At lunch and in the stolen moments of our busy weekends, we studied the road atlas. No religious scholar ever perused sacred texts as closely as we examined the maps of the states. We plotted the shortest routes—by Greyhound since none of us had a car—between our various college choices. The possibilities were endless: two hours here, four hundred miles there, Dayton in between and on and on.

We had a discussion on this topic on a snowy afternoon in late February. There were the four of us plus Brenda Mitchell sprawled across chairs, desks, and tables in Miss Nolan's room, eighth period. She was in a meeting, leaving her empty classroom to us as squatters. We'd all cut a class or study hall to be there, senior's prerogative. Instead of debating the current affairs topic that Mr. McClain said would make us "erudite" and "well informed," we plotted out the shortest distances between Nashville and Cleveland where Reenie had just applied because she liked the ivy-covered administration building on the brochure cover.

"Reenie *darling*, I don't know how to tell you this," Audrey drawled, "but most college administration buildings are ivy-covered."

"Audrey *Jane*, this one had particular charm," Reenie drawled back, mispronouncing Audrey's middle name and mimicking the Tennessee molasses-slow speech that Audrey now used since her visit to Fisk. "Besides, the guy who led the student tour was cute."

"I thought you were going with Bobby Amos," Brenda said, flipping through a magazine that had nothing to do with college admissions or being erudite.

"That was second period," I informed her. "As of fifth period, it's Wyatt Chambers."

Reenie stuck out her tongue.

"Oh, I wasn't hip to that . . ." Brenda's voice trailed off.

"Quit it, Vaughn, you make it sound as if I change boyfriends every month," Reenie charged, frowning.

"No, every week," Su murmured, her head bowed and her eyes planted on the spring collection page of *Vogue*.

Reenie shot her a nasty look.

"It's not like I'm fast or anything," she threw out.

As the old men used to say at Second Baptist Church when the preaching got really close to the bone, "Well . . ."

"And anyway, I think I'm in love," Reenie said with a deep sigh.

Yeah, again?

"With who?"

Reenie seemed surprised by the question. She shook her head.

"It's a secret. Someone . . . new." For Reenie, every boy was some-one new and special. But not usually secret.

"You don't think she's really having . . . well, *sex*, do you?" Audrey asked a few moments after Reenie left for an appointment with the college counselor.

Su, Brenda, and I exchanged looks. We were seventeen and eigh-teen. This was the one topic that we thought about a lot, wrote about in our diaries, and persistently questioned older sisters, cousins, and younger aunts about. But we seldom talked about it with one an-other. The terminology was just too . . . well . . . *nasty.* And we never ever used the s word aloud. Until now.

And none of us knew anything about sex firsthand. At least, that's what I thought then.

"If she is, she hasn't said anything to me about it," Su answered. She sounded hurt. "But then, she just broke up with Robbie."

"No, she *just* broke up with *Bobby.* Robbie was last month."

"Right. I forgot about him," Su responded.

Brenda's lips formed a silent "Oh." We looked at one another again. The thought of Reenie having . . . well, doing it with more than one boy was too much for our brains to process. After all, we were good girls. Kissing was all right. And that fondling that we all did in cars was, well, OK. (It was really "groping" but why get picky about words?) We were still trying to understand what this sex thing was all about. It was surrounded in mist and mystery. Sort of.

I kept quiet. Like the rest of the girls, I'd had health with Mrs. Bar-nett and had the birds and bees conversation with my mother, who had blushed so deeply that it made me squirm. But I was lucky. I had an older sister to give me the real untold story. Of course, after Patty finished telling me, I preferred Mom's version with its birds, bees, and flowers.

I just stared at my sister when she finished giving me the details.

"The boy puts . . ." I couldn't get the words out. "He puts it . . . where?"

Patty's laughter filled the room. She was home from college for a rare weekend visit. She was like a stranger now, my sophisticated sister, cooler in personality and calmer than she used to be. She used words I heard only teachers use and she didn't dress like Sandra Dee anymore. Blue jeans, a flimsy floral top (and I don't think she was wearing a bra) and her hair, blue-black like Mom's, was curling around her face in a huge Angela Davis–style afro. Our parents were horrified. I was thrilled. But this sex thing . . . well, I hadn't counted on it being so, well . . . so *graphic*. After hearing Patty's explanation, I wanted the gauzy blurs and syrupy violin music back. Seeing the logistics of it in my head made me a little queasy.

"Are you . . . sure about this?" I asked.

"Vaughn, are you really this dense or are you pretending? You've seen dogs mating."

Mating. My sister the biology major.

"Yeah, well, I just thought that was . . . dogs."

"No. That's the way people do it, too. Only in different positions. I have this book called the *Kama Sutra*."

There were different . . . positions? I was still trying to get over the logistics of one thing going into another.

Patty was disgusted with my obtuse behavior.

"Look, Vaughn, if you and what's his name decide to do it, use these. At least that way you won't get pregnant."

Patty rummaged around in her knapsack and, finally, after scratching something up from the bottom, handed me two small foil-wrapped packets.

Pregnant. Yet another word I wasn't ready for—and I'm a words person. "Having a baby" I could deal with. But "pregnant"?

"What are they?" *And why do you have them?*

Patty sighed.

"Birth control, Vaughn. Rubbers. Condoms. Don't you know anything?"

Apparently not.

I was still in Never Never Land applying the laws of physics of the *Karma Sutra's* cow position to my recent backseat encounter with Davis, so I didn't hear Su's question. I was also thinking about something that Reenie had told me last week.

"Huh? What?" *Where was I?*

"Eloquent words from the poet laureate of SE High," Audrey commented sarcastically. The girls laughed.

"I *said* . . ." Su stuck her hairbrush toward my face like a microphone. Her dark eyes twinkled. "Please tell us, Miss Jones, our listeners want to know if you're having sexual intercourse with Davis." She used her radio voice, low and mellow with exaggerated rounded tones, especially on the *o*'s.

I thought back to the wrestling match with Davis Benson that took place last Saturday night in the backseat of his father's Fairlane. After what Patty'd told me, the answer was a definite "No."

"Audrey?"

Audrey shook her head.

"Mark's away at school, remember?"

Su snorted.

"Yeah, and there was Thanksgiving break and Christmas vacation and Washington's birthday . . ."

I joined in.

"I remember that he's away, but does Paul know that?" I asked. "I saw you making eyes at each other in choir. Long, sultry gazes."

Audrey blushed.

"Shut up, Vaughn."

"What about you, Su?" Audrey turned the ball around quickly.

"Yeah, you and Bradley are practically married."

Su's smile faded into a pained expression.

"Well, we have talked about it . . . but we haven't, well, done anything yet." She glanced at the open door to make sure there weren't any nosy students or teachers hanging around. She lowered her voice.

"Actually, now don't tell anyone . . ." *The kiss of death to any secret.*

"But we kinda had . . . a fight about that." Su's eyes suddenly filled up. "He wants to. I don't. At least, not yet."

"Oh, Su," we gasped. How many times had we heard this story? How many times had we lived this story?

"I-I haven't said anything to anyone." She blew her nose. "I . . . we . . . we've never argued before. It was terrible! I just felt so . . . bad. I don't know what to do!"

"You didn't break up, did you?" I asked, shocked by what Su had just said. She and Bradley had been going together since the last Ice Age. If they couldn't make it, what hope was there for the rest of us?

We looked at our friend. Su nodded wordlessly and sobbed into a fistful of pink tissues. We were just about to offer the appropriate words of condolence when the ninth-period bell rang.

"Su, I'm so sorry."

"What are you going to do?"

We murmured words of encouragement as we grabbed our books, notebooks, purses, and other stuff and dashed into the hall toward our classes. Audrey headed downstairs for her Spanish V class. I trudged through a sea of incoming students to my biology class in the lab like a salmon swimming upstream. I felt bad for Su. She was heartbroken. And then, for some reason, I remembered what it was that Reenie had told me.

It was on one of our usual ten-thirty weeknight telephone conversations, the ones that went past my ten o'clock phone curfew.

"Vaughn! Are you still on the phone?" Mother's voice penetrated the darkness of the living room where I was ensconced in the easy chair next to the bay windows.

"Noooo!" I yelled back. To this day, Mother chides me for lying to her about this.

"I have a new boyfriend." Reenie's voice was low but I could tell she was excited.

This was not real news. Reenie always had a new boyfriend.

"So what else is new, Irene?"

"No, this time, it's forever," she'd gushed. I could hear her breathing heavily into the phone. "He's perfect. Just perfect."

Well, that didn't sound like any of the boys we went to school with, so I figured she'd met up with a boy from Eastmoor or Linden.

But when I said so, Reenie just laughed.

"No. He's from good old SE High."

"Is that right?" I'd answered in true surprise. "Well, don't keep me in suspense, who is this perfect person?"

"I can't tell you" was the answer.

That's not helpful, I thought.

"Why not?"

"Because it's a secret. We're keeping it a secret. If his friends find out . . ."

"That's *his* friends," I commented, prodding her to feed me what had to be the hottest tidbit in high school history. "I'm *your* friend, you can tell me."

Laughter at the other end.

"I can't tell you, V, not yet. I can't tell anyone yet. There are some . . . well, things we have to work out. But when we do, we're getting engaged."

Now that was a scoop. I had never ever heard Irene Darling Minerva Keller talk about a commitment to a boyfriend for longer than four weeks. She had the attention span of a flea when it came to boys.

"Reenie!" I whined. "That's not fair!"

"I feel bad not telling you, V, I know you keep secrets better than anyone. But I just can't. Not right now."

By the time I got to my ninth-period class I realized what Reenie's secret was. But it wasn't our telephone conversation that gave me the clues. It was something I'd seen three weeks earlier on my way home from school. I was coming out of the girls' restroom, one last stop before trekking home from school. It was late, I'd had debate practice and, except for the team, Mrs. DeSouza, and the janitors, the school was empty.

Except for Reenie Keller and Bradley Garcia, who were standing very close to each other, talking in the recessed doorway of the chemistry lab.

NINE

Attention deficit disorder is a condition that affects (a) three-year-olds, (b) menopausal women, and (c) high school seniors. Only for the time it takes a fly to fart did I think more than twenty seconds about anything. My mind was overloaded with a million other things. Su and Bradley kissed and made up. Audrey broke up with Perfect Boyfriend number twelve and was a National Merit Scholar. Reenie went back to boyfriend-of-the-week mode, and it was late April, which meant college acceptance letters, preparing for final exams, and, most important, prom dress shopping. There were class trips to take, the senior day outing to attend, and graduation speeches to make. The class rankings had been tabulated: Audrey and Bobby Powell were neck and neck for valedictorian with Su not far behind. I was a solid fifth out of three hundred forty-two students, which wasn't shabby, and Reenie was safely in the top ten. The grades that really mattered had been turned in. The time for serious studying was over and senioritis was widespread. We did as little as possible. It was smooth sailing now; even the weather was cooperating. After a freak snowstorm in early April, the earth tilted on its axis and led us into a spring that was warm and full of sunshine. My mother's tulips came up early.

"What color tux is Tommy wearing?" Su asked as we scurried toward our third-period class.

"Watch it, twerp!" I growled at the tenth grader who'd stepped on my heel. "Black tux, white shirt, what d'ya mean what color? He'll look like a penguin just like the other boys."

Su's eyes twinkled and she grinned.

"Bradley's wearing a lilac cummerbund and bow tie to match my dress," she cooed. "Isn't that sweet?"

So sweet it makes my teeth hurt. Su and Bradley's lovey-dovey antics were giving us all gas. Lilac cummerbund? I was in a bad mood (first-day-of-my-period blues) but I tried to be nice for Su's sake.

"Sounds . . . cute. I'm still trying to put the sleeves in my dress," I said with a sigh. That was the other reason why I was cranky. I was making my prom dress. Only God knew why I'd decided to put my eighth-grade-level sewing skills to work on a Butterick pattern I'd seen in the sewing room. The problem was the advanced level of the dress I'd chosen. I had stayed up past one o'clock fiddling with the lining in the bell-shaped sleeves. So far, it was sleeves, "ten"; Vaughn, "zero."

After listening to my tale of woe, Su chided me.

"Get Reenie to help you. She's practically a tailor the way she sews. She could put those sleeves in, like that!" Su snapped her fingers.

And she was right. Reenie was making her prom dress, too, but I'll bet she was having a hell of lot less trouble than I was. And she was using a *Vogue* pattern.

"Well, I really wanted to try it on my own . . ." I murmured.

Su gave me a "get over that" look.

"Yeah? V, that's OK if you're planning on wearing that dress by Christmas. Ask Reenie to help you." We turned in to Miss Nolan's class. "Or else you'll be wearing your band uniform to the prom!"

This was the class I lived for. Every Monday and Wednesday of my senior year, I sat in rapt attention in Miss Nolan's creative writing class along with twenty other privileged individuals. The class that almost wasn't (because Mr. Marvin didn't see the point of students spending their time studying storytelling) had become the sanctuary of my spirit. We read short stories, excerpts from novels, essays, and poetry. We debated Dickinson and Faulkner and Hughes. We practiced writing about telephone poles and flowers and made characters out of people we saw downtown. We created newspaper articles, haiku, editorials, short stories, and novellas. I filled up dozens of spiral notebooks with parts and pieces of works by "December Jones" and "Veronica Highwarden," the pen names I'd chosen because my own name seemed too dull.

"Settle down, people," Miss Nolan directed in a voice that was soft, feminine, and no-nonsense all at the same time. "I have your stories. Jerome, what are you doing back there?"

The last major assignment of the year was to write a short story (no more than five pages, please) on any subject we wanted. Miss Nolan had guided us through writing on certain topics and about particular characters, helping us focus our attention on details and our imaginations on diversions and improbabilities. Now she'd sent us out with these tools to create a story that would be completely ours, from theme to format to content. I started four different stories before I decided which one to work on. I rewrote it at least ten times. I changed the names of the characters then changed them back again. I threw out pages of not-so-brilliant prose only to decide they were brilliant after all and dig them out of the trash can. Finally, I finished my story only to realize I hadn't given it a title. I'd written about a little boy, his mother, and his dog. I stayed up past midnight before I decided to call it "The Puppy." How's that for literary?

"Class, I want you to know that I was very impressed with your efforts. The pieces that you wrote showed heart, focus, imagination, and diligence. I applaud you. Good job. Now I'm returning your papers to you. I urge you to review my comments but not to be handcuffed by them. You are the authors; these are your creations. My remarks are purely supplemental."

We all sat up taller in our chairs. Miss Nolan's words made us feel respected and grown-up.

"Some of the stories are worthy of individual mention. I've decided to read the A plus stories and I urge you to listen carefully. Think about what you are hearing, the story, the theme, the personalities of the characters. Now, I'd like to start off with 'The Puppy' by Vaughn Jones."

Everyone in the class turned to look at me. I thought I'd heard her wrong. *An A plus? My story?* My ears started buzzing and my mouth dropped open. I think my heart stopped.

"V, close your mouth," Su whispered loudly.

The class was silent as Miss Nolan read. I'll admit it wasn't a bad story when I wrote it, but when she read it, I didn't recognize it. Had I really put those words together like that?

A movement caught my attention. I noticed Mr. Swift hovering near the open doorway. He was writing one of his innumerable detention tickets to some poor undeserving student. I looked away.

A few of my sentences brought murmurs and sideways glances from my classmates, but I was glad Miss Nolan hadn't edited out my words. I had put them there for a reason.

When she finished reading, the class applauded. Su winked at me. I had my mouth open again.

It was still open when I was summoned to the principal's office later that day and threatened with suspension if I didn't change one of the words in my story.

"Miss Jones." Mr. Marvin waved a sheaf of papers in the air. His face was red and his eyes were angry. I remembered the Victorian-era novel I'd just read. He looked as if he were about to have an apoplectic fit. "I've read your story. For whatever reason"—his voice took a sarcastic turn—"Miss Nolan has seen fit to give you an A plus. But this is unacceptable. Completely unacceptable. And vulgar. And you know what I'm talking about."

OK, I have to admit I didn't at first. My story was about a little boy, his mother, and his puppy. What was vulgar about that?

"Um, no, sir, I don't."

"This word, Miss Jones. This word, on . . . page two, last paragraph, second sentence."

Oh. That word.

"It's . . . it's inappropriate, completely out of line," Mr. Marvin continued. "Now, I want it changed. Immediately. Or you will be suspended from school."

Suspended? In the next to last month of my senior year? Because of one word?

In those days, I was respectful to adults, but this time I forgot the manners my parents had taught me and said, "You've got to be kidding." I couldn't help myself.

"I assure you that I am not" was the principal's reply.

I left his office in a daze, neither angry nor frightened. Just confused. And frustrated. First my prom dress, now this.

I wasn't the only one having a bad week. Reenie had been home sick for a few days. Today she'd come back to school but she looked like death warmed over. I really had intended to take Su's advice and enlist Reenie's help with my dress, but as she approached me I thought better of it. Reenie's face was a soft shade of pea green. A great color for a bridesmaid dress or elegant stationery, but a bad color for a face. I wondered if she was contagious. Audrey had been in the nurse's office last week with something and everyone seemed to be fighting off a cold or complaining about upset stomachs. The last thing I needed was the flu with my period.

"You look like the Bride of Frankenstein," I commented, trying to make her smile.

Reenie exhaled wearily.

"This is the third time today I've thrown up. Mom's picking me up, I'm going home."

"Not staying for prom committee?" I asked.

She waved and shook her head as she trudged down the hall. It was strange to see Reenie move slowly. She was usually like quicksilver, here, there, and everywhere. Today, she seemed tired, sick, and sad. Very un-Reenie-like. I hoped she would be all right.

By the next morning, my family and the school were in an uproar. My father was ready to pummel Mr. Marvin into the ground. Mother was not amused and planned to call the school that day. Miss Nolan and some of the other teachers were furious that I'd been placed in such a position. And Mr. Swift, the tattletale, strutted through the halls with a smug expression on his face.

I was nervous all morning. Every time the bells rang, I was ready to fly out of my skin. By lunch period, I was too keyed up to eat. By seventh-period choir, I had relaxed a little. So far that day, there'd been no ominous summons from the principal's office and no police to escort me from the building. And I still hadn't changed "the word." None of my teachers barred me from class for using dirty language in a short story. In fact, they seemed to be sympathetic. By eighth period, my stomach had settled down and I was back to my old self. I spent most of world history class figuring out a way to put my impending suspension in a good light. By the beginning of ninth period, I'd written a workable explanation for the colleges I'd been accepted to. This was the seventies, everything was changing, and what was a one-week school suspension compared to a sit-in at the administration building? It was just one lousy word. Besides, I rationalized, I was a writer, an artiste. Words would be my business. What good did it do to be allowed to use only the words on an approved list?

I'd just finished blocking out the last sentence of my defense in my head as I headed toward my locker. As I passed the huge open doors of the school, I could have sworn that I caught a glimpse of my mother on the last step outside walking toward the parking lot. The woman disappeared behind a hedge before I got a really good look at her. *What was Mom doing here?* I moved toward the huge open doors to call her back.

"Miss Jones."

Mr. Marvin's voice stopped me in my tracks.

"Yes, sir?" I took a deep breath and clutched my books to my chest. *Here it comes . . .*

"Would you step inside my office for a moment?"

My heart was thumping so hard in my chest that any minute I expected it to break through my skin and sprint down the hall on its own. On very wobbly legs, I walked into the principal's office.

When I came out ten minutes later, not only were my legs not wobbly but my heart had settled into a calm, steady rhythm. I was not going to be suspended. Mr. Marvin had been "persuaded" (his word), he said, that my use of the inappropriate word was part of the writer's privilege and therefore it would have been wrong of him to ask me to remove it. These were enlightened times, he said. And while he didn't approve of my language, he didn't want to seem, well, unenlightened.

I couldn't understand it. It was so out of character for Mr. Marvin even to use words like "enlightened." But you don't look a gift horse in the mouth, so they say. I got out of there as fast as I could in case he changed his mind. The principal wasn't a bad man. In fact, he was a great one, an educator who had managed a large urban high school toward a standard of excellence that was nearly unprecedented at that time. But he could be a bit reactionary. And he was definitely a man of traditions. Not that he'd ever admit it, God rest his soul.

In later years, I learned that Miss Nolan, and at least five other teachers, had argued in my defense. Not only that, several community leaders got wind of the situation and called the principal, including Mrs. O'Neal, the mother of my journalism teacher. Whatever it was, whoever it was, it worked.

But I have a theory and it involves a glimpse of a retreating woman wearing a hot pink Audrey Hepburn–style shift and dark glasses. My mother swears she did not come to the school or, at least, she doesn't remember coming to the school. A very convenient senior moment, if you ask me. My mother and Mr. Marvin grew up in the same neighborhood and went to school together. When I'd first told her of my impending suspension, she exclaimed, "Jeffy Marvin! I knew him when he was wearing short pants!"

Despite the myths and legends to the contrary, I like to think that it was my mother who kept the principal from suspending me. Never underestimate the power of the person who remembers what you were like in fourth grade and can call you "Jeffy" to your face when you're forty. To this day, Mother smiles and shrugs her shoulders. She says nothing.

I didn't get much time to gloat over my victory.

The girls and I sat under a tree in Franklin Park. It was third-period study hall. We were off school property. Senior privilege. Reenie and Su on one blanket, Audrey and I sprawled across another one, drinking Cokes and munching on potato chips. It was a storybook setting. I couldn't have written it better. But the dialogue was all wrong.

"I'm pregnant."

The words fell like a hailstorm of boulders, smashing the serenity of the moment. The honeysuckle-scented air filled our nostrils when there was a breeze. The rich, pleasant smell seemed out of place and mean-spirited, as if Mother Nature were playing a bad joke on us.

For a few moments, no one said anything. No one *could*. She hadn't said, "I think I'm having a baby." She hadn't said, "I'm doing it with so and so." She'd said, "I'm pregnant." It sounded final. It sounded lethal.

Audrey's eyes glowed with all their colors but her face was pale. She looked panic-stricken. Reenie's expression wasn't much better. Her ivory-colored skin was so white she nearly looked blue, and there were dark circles around her eyes. Su's mouth was still open but for once "the Voice" was silent. She looked away, her fingers nervously twisting the strands of her ponytail into tight coils. Her dark eyes were damp. My breath stopped. I was the words person. Was I supposed to say something? And what would I say? The syllables caught in my throat. And slivers of memories that I had stuffed into the already full pockets of my cluttered mind began to spill out.

"Are you sure?" I asked. My mouth was dry. Three one-syllable words that came out sounding fractured.

"I'm sure. I had . . . the test done."

I pressed my lips together. I kept my eyes down. I couldn't look at her. I couldn't look at the rest of them either.

"W-What are you . . . going to do?"

The question hung in the silky May air like a Chinese kite floundering in its efforts to catch the breeze and take off for the sun.

The answer was smothered with sobs.

"I-I don't know! *I don't know!*"

Again the rest of us said nothing. The sound of her crying and the trilling of a cardinal made an unlikely duet on the late spring stage.

We were all thinking the same thing: *It could've been me.* We were really naïve about the logistics of sex and completely unsophisticated when it came to birth control. But we knew all about the fate of high school girls who found themselves pregnant before graduation.

Augusta Green, junior year. She'd been going out with an older boy, now in college. Bright, funny, cute, and a genius with clay, she wanted to go to art school. Augusta almost got away with it. But a fifth month of pregnancy is a tough thing to hide when you're barely five feet tall and weigh eighty pounds after a full meal. The tent dresses that were briefly fashionable that year weren't any help at all. Augusta was found out and sent home. She finished high school at the night school across the river. Oh, and now she had an eighteen-month-old son and worked nights at White Castle. No more sculpting for a while.

It was May 15. The prom was next week, even my dress was finished. Graduation was three weeks away.

"Have . . . you told your mom?"

"No. No! She'd kill me! I haven't told anyone."

There were more sniffles, then Su spoke again.

"This will be between us, only us."

"No one needs to know . . . It's still early, right?" Audrey asked. Her face did not look as hopeful as her voice sounded.

"I'm worried," I ventured. And I was. There were so many things that could go wrong, so many snoops around. Mr. Swift came to mind.

"Vaughn, you're *always* worried," Reenie snapped at me. "It's because of those mysteries you read."

"I guess so . . ." Twenty days, a long time to keep a secret in high school. "You have a tent dress, right? I could loan you mine . . ."

"V, it won't fit! What are you thinking?"

The absurdity of my comment sank in. Of course it wouldn't fit. *What had I been thinking about?* For just a moment, the gut-wrenching crying was replaced by the relief of laughter.

The Class of 1971 chose "On the Wings of the Future" as their prom theme. The prom and my dress, the sleeves finished with Reenie's help, were a success. Commencement was held in the auditorium on June 7 and all four of us graduated as planned. The billowing black robes were hot but very concealing. Su was the valedictorian (by two points) over Audrey, who was put on punishment by her father for being second. We moved the purple tassels from left to right then threw our mortar boards in the air and rejoiced.

When I was seventeen, I didn't understand paradoxes and contradictions. My Baptist Sunday school training didn't allow for it: a thing either was or it wasn't. Only now do I understand that things can be the same only different. And that nothing is ever really black or white.

The summer of 1971 was like that. It was the same as nearly every summer we'd had in our lives. Central Ohio has lukewarm springs with lots of rain for the crops. May is warm and June is warmer. July is when the lightning bugs come out, and the August heat is strong enough for you to lean on. Add a little humidity, some mosquitoes, and a pinch of locusts near the end and you have a standard Midwestern summer. But this summer had something else, too.

Our town wasn't a river town but there was an undercurrent flowing through our July lives that left us restless and uneasy. It was like being near a river that's running high but isn't quite at flood stage. The water's still pretty, not muddy, and people still go boating, but they have to be careful. There's a strong undertow, you can't see it from the surface, but it's there. And if you're walking along the banks and lose your footing, you can be swept away in seconds.

The undertow curved its way through our downtown shopping trips, our midnight marathon telephone conversations, and what would be our last slumber party. There was a lot going on. But not much said. Until the very end.

In the middle of August, Audrey left for freshmen orientation at Fisk. After much debate and a careful review of our family finances, I was packed off to Ohio Methodist instead of Radcliffe. Su, who'd been accepted at all the schools she applied to, decided she needed to get out of the Midwest altogether. With the money she'd earned as a radio disc jockey she bought a suitcase full of shorts and short-sleeved tops and accepted a scholarship to Florida University.

And in September, Reenie and Bradley Garcia got married in Huntington, West Virginia. Their son was born in November.

Girl Most Likely

TO MARRY A PRINCE

Reenie

TEN

There are a lot of ways to describe the mess I was in. As if your senior year in high school isn't a soap opera by itself with homecoming, calculus, SATs, college application deadlines, and all the other stuff that keeps you speeding along. You live in the Land of Extreme Emotions. You're either crying your eyes out or laughing until you pee your pants, and there isn't much in the middle. But as my daddy would say, "My girl don't do anything halfway." Boy, was he right about that. I took the usual tragedies and added a doozie to the bunch: I got pregnant by my best girlfriend's boyfriend.

I look back on it now and see the train wreck a mile away, but then? Talk about clueless. Vaughn's the literary one, she knows the right words. She could tell you how I felt with gentle, thoughtful prose that would sound so nice that the situation might seem downright charming. I'll sum it up in plain English: It was awful.

Being a pregnant eighteen-year-old girl really sucks. I felt alone, sad, and so stupid. The moment I got the pregnancy test result back, I saw a gray concrete wall go up in front of my face separating me from everything I loved: my parents, friends, dreams, and a life. I went from being a carefree cheerleader to a wife and mother in six months. It wasn't even a roller-coaster ride. I felt as if I'd been dropped off a cliff into a deep, dark place with no way to get out. No elevators, ladders, or footpaths around. And no chance of being helicoptered out either. I was in an abyss.

Don't get me wrong, I adore my son. Javier is the best thing that's ever happened to me, no argument about that. Throughout all the ups and downs and just plain stupid things I've done in my life, my son has been there, supporting me, cheering me on, giving me advice.

"Whatsa matter, Mommy?" he would ask sometimes when I collapsed onto the couch and began to cry from frustration and loneliness. I think Javier has been more of a parent to me than I have been to him.

I was able to hide my "condition" under the roomy nylon graduation robe in June, but by July the game was up. Mommy came into my room one morning with the sternest look I'd seen on her face since Calvin died and said, "Reenie, who's the father?"

Not "Are you pregnant?" not "Let's go to the doctor." Just "Who's the father?" My mother knows how to get right to the bones.

Except for my cantaloupe-size belly, I felt as if I were six inches tall.

I didn't want to tell her at first. I couldn't even look at her. It was bad enough being delusional enough to think I could go on to nursing school in the fall without anyone noticing that I had a baby. But when I told her who the father was, well, Mommy looked disgusted. I felt horrible.

"Bradley Garcia? But that's . . ." Then she looked away.

But that's Su's boyfriend.

The unsaid words hung in the air like helium balloons with grotesque faces painted on them.

My mother sank onto the bed and lit a cigarette. Now I *knew* things were bad. Mommy smoked but she never lit up in my bedroom. It was off-limits for my brothers' dirty tennis shoes, food, Coca-Cola, and cigarette smoke. But not this morning.

"Have the two of you thought about what you're going to do?"

Do? I said to myself. *I have to do something?*

How stupid was I? No, not stupid. We were just so young.

"No . . . um, Bradley and I haven't really . . . talked since March."
Mommy frowned.

"He doesn't know you're pregnant?"

I shook my head. The tears kept me from speaking.

"Well, you're going to have to tell him, and soon." Mommy blew
the smoke out in a forceful *whoosh*. Her dark eyes bored into mine.
I looked away. "He needs to know so that you can make some plans."

Plans?

The making of "plans," it sounded biblical to me. Something
people did in the old days when there were covered wagons and
horses in every garage and burning bushes. Besides the sewing I did,
I wasn't a planner, never had been. Of the four of us, Audrey was the
planner. I worked best under pressure. I studied for tests the night before, wrote papers the day before. And now my mother was telling
me that I had to make "plans." Not plans to make a blouse, a life
plan. I felt as if I had swallowed nails. I put off calling Bradley for a
week, lied to Mommy and said he hadn't called me back. I thought,
maybe, I could just do this by myself. Stall for time until Bradley
went away to college, then have the baby quietly somewhere. Work,
go to school at night. Did I think about babysitters? Did I consider
the cost of diapers or a doctor if the baby got sick? Where would the
baby and I live? Had I used my pea brain to consider being an unwed
mother in 1971?

Hell, no.

It's not that girls didn't do it then, they did. But in those days, girls
who did had a lot of baggage to carry and my parents were not having that. Shotgun weddings were still real events. After a week of
putting it off, Mommy threatened to call Bradley's parents. In fact,
she'd almost finished dialing the number when I stopped her.

"Irene, call the boy and tell him that you have to see him." She
stuck the receiver in my face. *"Now."*

I could count on one hand the number of times my mother had
called me "Irene."

Poor Bradley. He couldn't imagine why I was calling him. He
was working at the zoo over the summer and taking a precollegiate

program at Fort Hayes. Both he and Su had scholarships to Indiana University and were driving out there together in the fall. Vaughn would say that my timing was "Shakespearean" tragic.

Bradley stopped by on his way to work wearing a white shirt that had his name on it. He yelled at my brothers, Ernie and JC. Said hello to my mother who did not smile or speak. Kept looking at his watch to let me know he was in a hurry. Bradley Garcia was a kid who was on his way to a wonderful life. He had no idea what was about to hit him.

"Reenie, I hope you're not going to hang me up asking me about Greg," he said impatiently. "I gotta be at work in two hours and it's a hike to Dublin." Gregory, the boy I had been seeing, and Bradley were good friends, second cousins, actually. Bradley had acted as go-between. Poor Greg. Poor Bradley.

It was midafternoon, late July, hot and humid, and I was sweating like a pig. My tip to mothers-to-be: try *not* to be pregnant in the summer. I had on a pair of shorts, the zipper open because my belly was too big, and one of my brother's C-State T-shirts. I told Bradley what I had to tell him without looking at his face. That would have been more than I could stand. I didn't want to watch his expression change as he learned that life as he knew it was ending.

I sent my mind on a trip and just let my mouth talk. I didn't listen to my own words, just followed the fat, white clouds across the sky as far as I could. The breeze was warm and gentle and carried with it the smells of summer: corn, dirt, strawberries, and manure. I thought about Indiana, flat and full of fields, and Chicago. Daddy had cousins who lived there. I got excited every time I saw the Sears Tower and the other tall buildings and the lake. I'd never been to places like Nebraska or Colorado, but I tried to imagine what they looked like. And then I sent my mind to California. I'd dreamed about moving to Los Angeles when I finished nursing school. I wondered now if I'd be a hundred years old before that would happen. I just sent my mind on a trip across the country while I told this boy that his plans for college and his childhood sweetheart were going straight down the toilet.

You have to hand it to Bradley Garcia, he's not one of those folks who studies long on a problem. He did not interrupt me. And when I was finished talking, he didn't say "How do you know it's mine?" He didn't say "Sorry, Charlie, you're on your own." He just said "OK," in a deathly quiet voice. And that was that.

We drove to West Virginia in early September and got married. Our honeymoon, the only one we would ever have, was a one night's stay in a Holiday Inn and the three-hour drive back. We moved into my bedroom. While we were gone, Mommy and Daddy moved my white French country furniture to the garage and replaced the canopy twin beds with one double bed, an oak dresser, and matching chest of drawers. Mommy cleared out my doll collection and packed up my cheerleading letters and trophies, homecoming queen crown, and Nancy Drew collection. I cried when I saw my room. I was so angry and hurt. But my parents were right. I wasn't a homecoming queen anymore. I had a husband who worked nights and went to school and a belly large enough to orbit a planet. Reenie Keller was gone forever.

If you're going to get knocked up in high school, Bradley Garcia is a damn good choice. He's the hardest-working husband I ever had. He declined the scholarship, took on two jobs, and enrolled part-time at Franklin. There wasn't anything that the baby or I needed that he did not provide. Well, except for love, but I couldn't blame Brad for that. That would have been asking for too much.

I grew to the size of Ohio Stadium. The only clothes I could wear were my brother Ernie's jeans and football jerseys. My feet swelled so much that wearing street shoes was a thing of the past. I lived in fuzzy baby blue house slippers. Not that I was going anywhere. I was so embarrassed that I didn't want to leave the house.

In early November, I went with Mommy to Town & Country to look at baby furniture. I'd been putting it off, thinking that if I just refused to buy anything baby related, maybe this whole drama would turn out to be a bad dream. But Mommy dragged me out of the house, saying we couldn't put it off anymore.

I managed to squeeze my pancake-size feet into a pair of sneakers, hid my girth under a football jersey, and pulled my hair back into a ponytail. I'd cut my near waist-length hair sophomore year, but with the pregnancy, I'd let it grow back even longer. At Mommy's request, I put on some pale lip gloss. It didn't help. I looked like a Goodyear blimp with legs. I forgot about our Girls Most Likely rule. When you take a chance and go out in public not looking your best, you are guaranteed to run into every damn person you don't want to see.

I saw one of my boyfriends from junior year; Marcia Stapleton, who hates me; the Spanish teacher; and Audrey, her mother, and her sister, Andy. Everybody stopped and spoke. Everyone was polite. We talked about the weather. We talked about Halloween pumpkins and weren't they puny this year? We talked about the winding down of the war. In fact, we talked about every damn thing except the one-thousand-pound rhino that stood among us, the one that everybody saw but refused to acknowledge. They all very pointedly did not look me in the face. I might as well have not been there. For Senora and Marcia, that was OK. But for Audrey to look past me was too much. I cried all the way home and refused to go out in public again until after Javier was born.

Bradley did what he could to be helpful, but with his schedule, he didn't have much time for me or the baby. It was probably better that way. I was the daily reminder of the scattered fragments of his dreams, the pieces now flung so far away that he would never be able to gather them up again. Mommy and Daddy tried very hard to help but there was only so much they could do. My situation embarrassed them. It embarrassed me. Even the boys, my brothers, treated me, well, differently. They made me laugh and kept me up to date with the gossip, but there was a barrier there that hadn't been around before.

And then, when the baby came, well, I just felt, and looked, like a blob. A blob sitting on a deserted island somewhere in the South Pacific. A blob with dripping, watermelon-size breasts. And no, I am not exaggerating.

Javier ate on a two-hour schedule and his little mouth was always open. I felt like a huge cow. If I wasn't feeding him, I was getting ready to feed him or had just finished feeding him. If it had been warmer, and if I hadn't been living with my parents, I would have gone around the house topless. I mean, what was the point of even putting on a bra? I was a dairy.

Eventually, we all settled into a routine and Javier grew like a dandelion. My figure began to even out and my breasts got smaller. By smaller, I mean they came down to the size of Indiana muskmelons rather than watermelons. Nearly a year went by and I barely noticed the time passing except that Javier was now old enough to climb up into my lap, unbutton my blouse, reach into my bra, and pull out my breast all by himself.

"You need to wean him," Mommy said.

"I think we should have sex again," Bradley said one night as we undressed for bed.

You must be out of your mind! I said to myself. *That's what got me into this shit in the first place!* But then I remembered that this man was my husband and that I'd had sex with him only twice in my life. Our baby was nearly ten months old and Bradley was ready. I wasn't.

But I did it anyway. After all, I was married now. If I could do it when I wasn't married, I sure as hell could do it when I was. It hurt because I wasn't aroused or prepared to enjoy myself. And when Bradley fondled my breasts as he had a millennium ago when all this mess got started, they responded like they always do when they're fondled: They gushed. So much for marital sex.

I had a handsome, hardworking husband; a beautiful, easygoing son; a car of my own; free babysitters—and I don't think I ever felt so lonely. I wanted to die. I missed being just seventeen, just eighteen, just nineteen. Mostly, I missed my friends. Su was gone forever, I'd accepted that. No way would she forgive me and I couldn't blame her. She and Bradley weren't together when he and I slept together, but I should have pushed him away. I knew it then, I know it now. If Su wasn't "doing it" with him, there sure was no reason why I should have. Audrey had pulled away too, hurt because Su was hurt, wondering what kind of person I was to do such a thing. We still spoke if she saw me out in public someplace, but our marathon midnight phone calls were a thing of the past. And so were the slumber parties where we shared gossip, Fritos, records, and magazines. I wasn't invited anymore. And my bedroom wasn't set up for that kind of entertaining.

Vaughn was in between as only Vaughn can be. I know she felt guilty, I could read it on her face whenever she came to visit. Her eyes filled with tears when I told her about seeing Audrey at the shopping center. She would start to tell me something about Su then stop and change the subject. I know she visited me out of guilt. After all, I'd told her that I was seeing Bradley, even though I didn't mention him by name. It wouldn't have been too hard to figure out. And V saw us together once, but in her usual nearsighted way, and despite her love of mystery novels, she missed the clues of what was really going on. Vaughn was never good at math, when she put two and two together she got five. But guilt can be a good thing, too. When Vaughn went away to college, she wrote me letters.

She became my window to the world even though there were days when I hated her for it. I would dread reading her scribbles from college, but then I also lived for them. She chatted on about roommates and English comp class and stuck-up professors and road trips to OU. I held Javier with one hand and V's letter about frat parties with the other. Thanks to her, I followed the lives of my friends through college and beyond. And even though I was jealous, very jealous, of their carefree, uncluttered lives, I treasured every word she wrote because it kept alive the fantasy that someday I'd be able to join them again.

ELEVEN

While I was dealing with grown-up problems like day care, paying rent (we had our own apartment now), and croup, Su, Audrey, and Vaughn coped with the ups and downs of college life. They were living my life, the one I could have had. The letters I hated the most were the ones about Su. And I read them voraciously as if I were starving to death. Out of all of us, Su seemed to be having the most fun. No filthy roommates, only one or two hangovers worth writing home about, several promising boyfriends (how could I be jealous of her over that?), and decent grades not to mention a gig as a disk jockey on the university's radio station, her dream job. Considering what she'd been through with Bradley and me, I figured she deserved some happiness. She made the Dean's list (of course) and was nominated for homecoming queen her junior year. By the time Su was a senior, she was up for a fellowship for television journalism.

Audrey's accomplishments were just as good, but it's Audrey, for God's sake. What would you expect? Vaughn, on the other hand, had a different experience. V was a words person, not a science person. She struggled through the botany and genetics courses that her liberal arts college required. About the only thing Vaughn can do with science is spell it.

It was Su I watched from a distance with an equal mixture of pride and envy. She was the girl most likely to succeed at anything she put her mind to. If only she'd been able to choose her parents.

After a few years of back and forth and "situations" with her mother, Su lived with her aunt Leila and her cousins through junior and senior high, and by the time she graduated, she considered Leila's duplex her home. But Barbara Penn wouldn't let go of her little girl that easily, not that anyone could blame her. Su didn't talk much about her mother anymore, that was understandable. But we knew what was going on because our parents talked when they didn't think we were listening.

In and out of treatment centers, drunk tanks, and the beds of men she thought she knew, Barbara Penn no longer sang or danced or discussed art with the insight of a college professor. She was either at one end of the spectrum or the other and it broke our hearts to see Su wrestling with the delight of seeing her mother after many months blended with disgust and shame because Barbara smelled as if she'd taken a bubble bath in whiskey. When she wasn't drinking, Miss Penn worked as a secretary from eight to five, wore conservative navy blue suits and polished pumps. Her dark hair was styled primly like Lady Bird Johnson's. When she was drinking, her skirts were tight, her blouses were tighter, and she didn't wear a bra underneath. Her panty hose, if she was wearing any, had runs in them and lipstick, bright and clown-red colored, was mashed across her face like a child had finger-painted it on. She'd drape herself over Su and slobber kisses on her cheeks. Su's face burned cinnamon with embarrassment. Living with an alcoholic is like living with identical twins with opposite personalities: You never know which one will show up. Unfortunately for Su, the Miss Penn who drank liked to show up the most, especially for public events and social occasions.

When our high school commencement ceremony was finished, as many of the graduates and parents as could fit gathered in the hall, on the steps, and in the courtyard of SE High taking pictures, offering gifts and congratulations. It was a happy mob of black robes, somber black suits, and Sunday best clothes. Miss Penn was the only mother who was wearing a cocktail dress, smoking a cigarette. The sharp acrid scents of Winstons and wine wrapped around the sweetness of Chanel No. 5 swirled around Barbara Penn like an invisible fog.

"Hi, baby," she cooed as she practically licked Su on the cheek.

"Ahem," Mrs. Aherns, the guidance counselor, said. "Hello, Su, Leila. Um, Barbara, there's no smoking on school property." The guidance counselor glanced from Su and Leila to Barbara, her expression friendly but her eyes wary.

Barbara Penn snorted and waved her off. She nearly lost her balance in the process. She staggered slightly on the uneven slate slabs of the courtyard. Leila grabbed her elbow. Barbara blew a loud raspberry at Mrs. Aherns.

"Well, shit, if you say so." She stamped the cigarette out with a tap of her patent leather high heel, but scuffed the back of the shoe leaving a deep ugly gash in the black shininess. Leila and Mrs. Aherns exchanged glances filled with meanings that would exceed the circulating capacity of most libraries. Su looked away.

This was the Barbara Penn Su both felt sorry for and hated. She was as skinny as a stick but her face was puffy and her eyes were bloodshot and watery. She'd applied her makeup generously with an uneven hand, trying to focus with vision made unreliable by eighty proof, so she looked more like a seductive circus clown than a woman who had once modeled for Fashion Fair. Her hair, now colored brassy auburn with dark roots, was smashed on one side as if she'd been sleeping on it and forgot to comb it out. Her sheath— shiny, tight, and low-cut—was slightly undone. When Su thought no one was looking, she quickly zipped it up.

"Barbara, let's go . . ." Su's aunt touched her sister's arm gently, but her facial features had hardened and her lips were set in an angry line. I could tell that Leila was ready to drag her sister away by her hair if she had to.

"Go? What the fuck for? My baby's graduated, I'm here to take pictures!" She staggered away. "Leelee! What you standin' there looking like you got shit for brains for? Take the goddamn pictures, will you?"

Su lowered her head; her cheeks were flaming. Leila grabbed Barbara by the upper arm, not gently this time, and tried to move her along, but it's easier to take a Brahma bull on a stroll down a garden path than to get a drunk to go anywhere. Barbara protested very loudly.

"Will you leave me alone? I'm celebratin', goddammit!"

My mother glanced over her shoulder then looked back quickly without an expression. She had positioned our family Olan Mills–style for the formal graduation photo that she wanted for her album.

"Reenie, stand closer to Ernie, that's right. JC! Stop scratching!" Mommy snapped the picture with her usual precision, which meant our heads and shoulders would be cut off but the photo would be an excellent study of waists, trouser legs, and shoes.

We tried to ignore Barbara Penn's continuing outbursts, Leila's firm coaxing, and Su's anguished pleas. All I could think of was a very different scene years before when we'd been treated to a night-club evening in Barbara's tiny apartment. We were eleven.

She'd rolled back the rug and pushed the furniture against the walls. The small kitchen table had been transformed with a red-and-white-checked tablecloth, tiny votive candles, and an ashtray filled with M&Ms. This was the VIP table, Miss Penn told us.

"Here's your cocktail, sweetie," she said, grinning as she handed me a paper cup with pink lemonade in it. A plump maraschino cherry perched on a blue skewer floated on top. "It's a Barbara Penn special!" She winked at me. I felt special and grown-up.

Drinking straws became cigarette holders like the one Audrey Hepburn used in *Breakfast at Tiffany's*. The hazy sound of Miles Davis's muted trumpet played in the background. We were elegant and sophisticated and in with the in crowd. Su beamed with pride at her sparkling mother who chatted with us as if we were twenty years old. Barbara encouraged us to think beyond the boundaries that society was squeezing us into. She listened to our girlish dreams without laughing and commented seriously on both the outlandish and the practical.

"Let me see now, who do I have here in my club?" She pulled her daughter's face toward her and planted a kiss on the tip of Su's nose. "My baby, Susan Elizabeth Penn, on the air every evening from five-thirty until six with Mr. Walter Cronkite, giving America the latest important news from the front. Well, let's hope there isn't a front by then."

She moved on to Audrey, her dark eyes shining in the flicker of the tiny candles that she'd placed in a circle in the middle of the table.

"Hmmm. I see a tall, stunning woman, dressed in Givenchy, *bien sur*! A hat, sunglasses like Mrs. Kennedy, and a Mark Cross briefcase. Yes. A briefcase." She winked at Audrey, whose dimples showed in her cheeks. "Is she a lawyer? A corporate executive? A high-society real estate broker selling mansions in L.A.?"

We giggled. Yes, we could see it, too. Audrey wanted to be elegant, rich, and successful in business. She didn't know what business. And with Audrey, it wouldn't matter. Whatever it was, she would be good at it.

"Ah, Irene, Irene. Let me see your palm." Barbara Penn was telling fortunes that evening for our amusement. She slipped on a pair of outrageous-looking rhinestone-accented glasses and pretended to study my hand with the most serious intentions. She raised her eyebrows in mock surprise. "I see . . . a rich husband; mink stole, no, *two* mink stoles, and a big house. Oh, and six children. *All* boys."

We'd laughed at this. My dream was to marry a millionaire and have six children. Six! I must have been out of my mind!

"And Vaughn, the quiet one." She looked at Vaughn's palm, put her hand on her forehead, and closed her eyes and chanted a few strange words that Su said were "Do you have any calamari?" in Italian. Then she looked at V and said, "I see a smart, funny woman who makes people smile with the words she writes and the pictures she paints."

"But will I have to wear glasses forever?" Vaughn couldn't help asking.

Very wisely, Barbara Penn replied "No."

On that evening and on many evenings like it, we fell in love with a beautiful woman dressed in black Capri pants and a sleeveless black top, who showed us how to do the bossa nova. Su's mom was a beacon whose laughter came often and generously. She never made us go to bed on time because she didn't want to interrupt her lecture on DuBois and why so much of Picasso's art looked so much like the wooden carvings that my missionary grandfather had brought back from Ghana. My mom, Ellie Taylor, Audrey's mother, and V's mother, Carol Jones, were wonderful, too, in their own ways but it was Barbara who gave us girls a sense of possibilities beyond what society expected for us in the 1960s. She told us that it was all right to dream those dreams.

But alcohol is strong, seductive, and overwhelming. Like quicksand, it sucked Barbara down into its depths and would not give her up. The rubber band–like recoveries, when Barbara sobered up, began to disappear like pandas in the wild. Very soon there were so few of them that no one could remember what Barbara was like when she wasn't drinking.

Vaughn probably shouldn't have, but she sent me some of Su's letters. They were fascinating and I loved reading them. But I was surprised that Su spoke so little about her mother. As I read further, I learned why. When Su went to college, her mother started showing up out of the blue. The front desk buzzed Su's room and announced "Susan Penn, your mother is in the lobby. Susan Penn." And Su's shoulders tightened and her stomach churned. Which mother was waiting in the lobby, "good mommy" or "bad mommy"? In time, Su began to dread seeing either one of them.

Years of experience had made Su an expert at dealing with "bad mommy." She didn't take it personally anymore. Her mother's provocative dress or filthy language no longer embarrassed her. Su had learned to block out the stares of the other students and close her ears to the insults and nonsensical comments Barbara made. I felt bad for her when I read that, many times, Su had to physically escort her blubbering mother out of the student union. She wrapped a turtle-hard shell around her feelings to protect them and often found herself looking at Barbara as if she were a stranger and not her own mother. I saw my mom in a new light. I had taken her ordinary, average Mom-like presence for granted. I didn't know how lucky I was.

"Who is that woman over there?" a student in the lobby observed. "She's smashed."

Visits from good mommy were harder to deal with because they were so tragic. It broke my heart to read about them.

"Susan Penn, please come to the lobby, you have a visitor."

The familiar signs of anxiety kicked in as quickly as the click of a light switch. Su's stomach muscles tightened and her shoulders felt as if steel bands had been riveted to them. Her throat closed and she was swallowing hard and taking gulps of air at the same time, trying not to hyperventilate. Her heartbeat increased to the point that her chest hurt. She clenched and unclenched her fists after she pushed the button on the elevator. The lobby was directly across from the elevator banks. In a few seconds, she would know which mommy had come to visit her that day.

"Hi, baby." Barbara's voice was soft and tentative. Her smile was slight and she opened her arms wide to give her daughter a hug. "Ohhhh, yes. That's my beautiful baby."

Barbara smelled like cigarettes and Jergens lotion and Chanel No. 5. Her navy blue pantsuit was neat and boring. Her hair was sprayed into control and the tarnished copper color had grown out except for the ends, which sparkled in the daylight that streamed through the floor-to-ceiling windows of the dorm lobby. Barbara wasn't wearing any makeup to speak of except for lipstick. Her fingertips with their unpolished nails fiddled with the tiny gold cross that hung on a chain around her neck.

She sighed as she sat down and her eyes swept hungrily over Su as if she hadn't seen her in months.

"You look so good, Susan, so grown-up. I can't believe how beautiful you are."

"Thanks, Mom."

Barbara reached out and touched the large, dark afro that framed Susan's face. She had finally given in and adopted an Angela Davis–styled mane.

"This is new."

"Mom . . . it's not new. I had my hair this way the last time you were here. Remember?"

Too late, Su realized that she had forgotten one of the cardinal rules of dealing with "good mommy": Never ask her if she remembers.

Barbara went pale and her eyes filled with tears.

"The last . . . time . . . When was that?" she croaked out.

Su looked away.

"A month ago, Mom."

Now it was Barbara's turn to look away, her fingers pulling on the slender gold necklace chain so hard that it might have broken. She gulped back the sobs in her throat and finally looked up at her daughter. Tears rolled down her cheeks.

"I . . . I don't remember! I don't remember being here then. I don't remember seeing your hair!"

Su sighed and reached out to pat her mother's hand. Barbara's wet eyes bored into her until she looked away again. This was the bad part about "good mommy." Good mommy wore a sad expression and her eyes were filled with pain and remorse. Not regrets that could be shrugged off and quickly forgotten but remorse that was soul deep and sharp in its bite. Barbara didn't say anything. She didn't have to. Her expression spoke for her. She looked as if her soul was haunted by cruel and persistent ghosts.

"I'm sorry," she said in a whisper, wiping the tears away with a tissue that she'd pulled from her purse. "I'm so sorry, I just don't remember. When I . . . drink, I forget things." She looked away again. "I forget life."

"I know, Mom, I know." But Su knew that her words of comfort weren't enough.

"I don't mean to hurt you, Susan. I never intended to hurt you." Barbara's eyes were filled with confusion. "I . . ." she swallowed hard. "I don't know what I'm going to do."

Su wiped her eyes with the back of her hand and looked at her mother with as much tenderness as she could bring to the surface, even though she felt as if she were talking to a concrete wall.

"Then don't drink anymore, Momma, just don't drink."

Barbara nodded quickly, turning the tissue around and around in her fingers until it began to fall apart.

"No, I won't. I won't drink."

"Please go back to AA meetings. Please? They seem to help you so much."

"Yes, yes, I'll go back," Barbara said mechanically, her dark, sad eyes staring down into her lap where her fingers lay. Their work on the tissue was finished. Now she'd begun to smooth her pants legs repeatedly. "I'll attend the meetings. Yes, that's what I'll do. Go to the meetings."

Su watched her mother talk to herself and repeat phrases over and over. She saw her hands shake uncontrollably. When they talked about normal things, day-to-day life, Su couldn't help but notice that even though Barbara laughed once in a while and actually initiated conversation on certain topics, she never lost the haunted glaze in her eyes. It was as if there were someone else living inside her mother, a monster who peered out at the world winking at her, teasing her, and reminding her that the demon still lived.

TWELVE

The Ivys stood on line for inspection and exchanged worried glances. This was an important moment in the pledging process and each girl felt a mixture of excitement and dread. The girl from Tuscaloosa took deep breaths to keep her stomach from quivering. They all wondered which Big Sister they would have to please tonight. When the hall door opened, the pledges' dread turned into terror. Audrey Taylor, the best of the best, super soror and AKA empress strode into the room and surveyed the line with the steely gaze of General Patton. Inwardly, her recruits moaned. They were in big trouble now. There would be no pleasing this Big Sister.

I got a case of the giggles when I read this section of Vaughn's letter. It was late spring; I was working part-time at Lazarus and dead on my feet most evenings. It had been a busy day and now I was pacing the floor with Javier perched on my hip. He had chicken pox and was miserable despite the baking soda baths (my mother's remedy) and Benedryl. Bradley had a class at seven-thirty so it was Mommy-on-duty. If it hadn't been for V's letter, I don't know how I would have gotten through that night.

I bounced and walked my baby and got hysterical when I read about Audrey terrorizing those poor girls and running off roommates who didn't have the surgical nurse–style cleaning skills that she did.

I can imagine how those poor Ivys felt. I've been on the receiving end of Audrey's evil eye. She's tough, skinny as a blade of grass, and hard as platinum. But she's always been tougher on herself than anyone else.

You can say what you want, there is something powerful about a girl who owns—and uses—a full set of matching luggage on every trip, short or long. Audrey was the only person I ever knew who had her 'fro washed and styled at the beauty parlor. I didn't see it but Vaughn told me that Audrey's dorm room was a replica of her bedroom at home, and just as clean. When Su and Vaughn visited Fisk for homecoming, V was jealous because Audrey's room was not only neat and showroom quality, it was also *all* hers. But, please, can you really imagine Miss Neat, Prim, and Proper sharing a bedroom with anyone?

"I've been on the waiting list for two years trying to get a single but no such luck! Zero, nothing, nada," Vaughn wrote. Until her sister Patty left home, she hadn't even had her own room at home. And now that she was away at school, Mrs. Jones had turned their bedroom into a crafts room.

Audrey dusted off Vaughn's worn-out backpack and stashed it, out of sight, on a shelf in the closet where her clothes were arranged by color.

"Just lucky, I guess," she said innocently.

Su snorted and started giggling.

"Bullshit. Don't let her fool you. Luck had nothing to do with it."

Audrey stuck her tongue out at Su.

"What you don't know is that Miss Super Neat Freak drove her last roommate crazy with all of her wiping and dusting and Windexing and her color-coordinated closet. You know that she irons T-shirts? The poor girl was so intimidated that she moved out, just down the hall. She'd rather squeeze into a room this small with two other girls than live with this insane woman. What does that tell ya?"

"Oh, shut up!" Audrey countered, grinning. "BJ and I were just . . . incompatible."

Audrey had pretended to be hurt. But later Vaughn noticed that she swept the floor and dusted her desk before they went out for the evening.

I can only imagine my mother's expression if she saw me pressing T-shirts. But Miss AKA was as flawless as an alabaster statue I saw once in a museum.

During the summers, Audrey worked two jobs so she could have all the clothes she'd need to measure up to her sorority's standards. Or at least that's what she said. By the time Audrey was a junior, her sorority sisters had to measure up to her—and the standard was high. Sometimes even Audrey had trouble reaching it. And after she perfected everything else, Audrey went to work on herself. One look in the mirror at her five-foot-ten-inch, one-hundred-twenty-five-pound body told her all she needed to know. She was too fat.

I was still in exile during this time, so I came in at the tail end of this story. Vaughn filled me in on the beginning.

It was Christmas break of her junior year. Christmas is the one holiday when practically every college student spends at least part of the time at home, or so I've been told. They met at Rubino's and ordered the usual: pepperoni with green peppers, black olives, and mushrooms; a vegetarian for Audrey; and Cokes all around. Vaughn was drinking 7-Up that year thanks to what Eddie Dunlap said about what went on at the bottling plant when he worked there the previous summer.

"I am not kidding, that's what he said," Vaughn commented after describing a specifically disgusting employee practice. Audrey made a face and stirred the straw around in her Coke. Su shook her head.

"I can see Eddie doing something like that," Su responded. "That sounds just like him. But I can't believe the company could get away with it . . . and not get caught? Someone has to have seen it happen."

"Besides Eddie, of course," Audrey commented sarcastically. She slurped down some Coke. "I wouldn't worry about it, Vaughn. The acid in Coke can take the rust off a car, I'm sure that whatever they dropped in the vat has been dissolved into nothing by now." She smiled. *We were so gullible then!*

"I'll just drink this, thanks," Vaughn said. Eddie Dunlap did have a tendency to exaggerate sometimes, but what if he was telling the truth this time? Vaughn glanced over at Audrey's drink to see if there was anything floating in it.

Audrey caught her and laughed.

"Quit it, Vaughn." She shoved the oversize glass toward her. "Here, look all you want, I'm going to the restroom."

For a few moments, it was quiet at the table. Vaughn picked the mushrooms off her pizza, sprinkled them with salt and pepper, and popped them in her mouth. Vaughn has a thing for mushrooms. Su played with her straw, looking at something going on over Vaughn's shoulder. Su isn't a daydreamer so her fixed expression caught Vaughn's attention.

"What are you looking at?" She turned around to see a table of Bexley blondes giggling and kids at a corner table blowing spitballs at one another. Besides a glimpse of Audrey's retreating form, that was it.

"Did you notice that Audrey spent the past hour pushing her salad from one side of the plate to the other? I didn't see her actually *eat* any pizza, did you?"

What does this have to do with the price of tea in China? I had wondered when I first read this. Vaughn glanced at Audrey's plate. The salad was mostly still there and the pizza looked as if it had been nibbled on by a very small animal, like a chipmunk or something. V counted one . . . two . . . three tiny bites from the crust.

"Maybe she's not feeling well. My sister's home with a cold," Vaughn had offered hopefully. "That can ruin your appetite. When you can't smell anything. I never eat much when I have a cold . . ." She wasn't sure what Su was leading up to.

"No, V, look past the nose on your face. Audrey slurped down the Coke, took one or two nibbles, if you can even call 'em that, and said she was full. Full! But look at her! She doesn't look full of anything to me. She looks like a clothes hanger with legs. A wire clothes hanger."

"But Audrey's always been skinny," Vaughn replied, hurt by Su's comment. I imagined her trying to focus her contact lens–covered eyes past the tip of her nose. Vaughn finally got rid of her glasses our senior year in high school. But contact lens technology was in its infancy then and the hard plastic lenses seemed to fit like condoms on V's corneas. (Sorry, but that's the way it seemed to me.) Her eyes were always bloodshot and she still squinted a lot.

Su shook her head.

"Not *this* skinny. Something's not right. I wonder if she's really sick . . . like with a disease or something. Shhh, here she comes."

This time, Vaughn did look past the nose on her face. V quickly realized that she'd been so glad to see Audrey and Su, happy to talk with old friends about other old friends and new friends and high school days, that she hadn't really *seen* Audrey. Su looked fine, of course, Su always looked fine. But Audrey? The description in Vaughn's letter was almost too painful to read.

Her afro, more curly than nappy, was symmetrically shaped as always. She was wearing the latest shade of lip gloss, the one I coveted but couldn't wear because it made me look like Dracula's wife, and a fabulous pair of gray bell-bottoms underneath a gauzy bell-sleeved tunic. Audrey always had on hip clothes. I'd seen the outfit at the store so I knew how expensive it was. And on Audrey, it looked as if it was still hanging on a hanger.

Her collarbones protruded and Vaughn noticed that she wasn't wearing her class ring anymore, but since her fingers looked like chicken bones, it probably wouldn't have fit. Audrey has one of the most beautifully sculptured faces you've ever seen; she looks like the bust of Nefertiti. But her cheekbones were so prominent that it made her eyes look as if they were sinking into her face. Her forehead poked out because her skin stretched like cellophane across her skull. Actually, that's kinda what she looked like: a beautiful, green-eyed skull.

Vaughn can keep secrets if you're not looking at her. Otherwise, you'll see her thoughts moving across the top of her forehead like the ticker board at the New York Stock Exchange. She is that transparent. Audrey didn't notice as she settled back into her seat. But Su caught on and gave V a kick under the table.

"Ow!"

"Oh, sorry," Su said too quickly. She narrowed her eyes to keep Vaughn from blurting out something.

Audrey looked up and smiled.

"Didn't mean to be so long. What movie are we going to see?"

It hurt them both to look at her. She really was skin and bones and not much else. Looking at Audrey made Vaughn hungry. She wanted to scarf down another piece of pizza on her behalf. Me? I think I would've just said, "Audrey Jean, what the hell is going on?"

"No hurry, it's a nine-thirty show," Vaughn said, fishing the newspaper out of her junky purse.

Su pulled off another slice of pizza and dropped it on Audrey's plate, then looked at her pointedly.

"Yeah, we've got plenty of time. Eat another slice of pizza."

Audrey looked as if she was ready to throw up right then and there, but she didn't. She just said that she wasn't really hungry, mumbled (very un-Audrey-like, Audrey never mumbles) something about eating a big lunch that day and then she drank down another glass of Coke. At the movie, they ordered the biggest tub of popcorn sold at the concession stand and soaked it with butter and salt. In the dark, Su watched Audrey carefully. Later, she told Vaughn that Audrey took one kernel of popcorn, licked off the butter and salt, and slipped it into a napkin.

By summer, the little things they'd noticed about Audrey began to add up to something strange and terrible. Audrey had a funny relationship with food: She didn't eat any. She survived on what she called the model's diet. She said she'd read about it in *Vogue*. She drank Coca-Cola and smoked Benson and Hedges. Oh, and she liked very dry martinis from which she did eat the olives. But that was the most anyone saw her actually swallow. And in such a hollow stomach, most of the time, the alcohol went straight to her head; the cigarettes began to affect her smooth speaking voice, and the Coke wound her up. She cleaned everything, she talked a transcontinental mile a minute, and she could not sit still. Riding in a car with her was like being on a carnival ride. Audrey said that she was just doing what anyone would do for self-improvement. *Self-improvement? Audrey?* What was there to improve?

But Audrey had grown up with perfection as her goal. Perfect, perfect, perfect, the Colonel had ground that into his children with a relentless millstone. Audrey's sister, Andy, told the old man to stuff it up his nose and took off for college on the other side of the world, working her way through because her father refused to help with her tuition. Her brother's response was drugs and eventual oblivion. Audrey's rebuttal to her father was typical Audrey. She would not just be perfect, she would be divine. And like Daedalus soaring giddily and too high on wax-coated wings, Audrey flew too close to the sun.

She stayed in Nashville the summer before her senior year in college. She'd gotten a summer internship at PepsiCo, the next step in her march to an M.B.A. But she came home briefly in early August and the girls made plans to get together. Well, all the girls except for me. I remember feeling antsy when I heard that they were going out. Was worried about Audrey. I wanted to know how she was doing. In March, she had been vivacious, quirkily neat, and excited about her summer appointment. She'd also been ten pounds heavier, according to Vaughn's assessment. On Audrey, ten pounds is like two for the rest of us, but it had made a difference: her complexion was glowing, her eyes bright, and her slenderness had a tautness to it that was lean but not skeletal. She'd eaten in her typical Audrey way—a little bit of this, a little bit of that—but at least she'd been eating.

Mrs. Taylor greeted Vaughn warmly when she stopped by to pick up Audrey.

"Audrey should be down in a second, she heard the doorbell," Mrs. Taylor informed her. "Where are you girls going?"

When Vaughn explained, Mrs. Taylor chuckled.

"Oh, I remember that place," she said, her eyes shining with pleasurable memories of fat, calories, and gravy. "It's a dump but the food is marvelous." In a lower voice, she added, "If you could get Audrey to eat a little something, it would be nice." The smile had been replaced by a slight frown.

Vaughn said later that all she could think about was Mr. Bones from health class. The clicking sound that the plastic bones made when they touched and the smiling skull that the teacher used to demonstrate the way the jaw and neck bones worked.

She'd watched Audrey come down the stairs with a mixture of amazement and fear.

"I've never seen a skeleton walk on its own," she told me, "much less come down a flight of stairs."

Audrey's face was so thin that her cheekbones jutted out like the ridges of slate you see in the raw, strip-mined foothills of the Appalachians. You could see the muscles of her jaw working when she spoke. I was only being slightly mean when I said that she didn't need to worry about buying necklaces anymore because her collar and breast bones were so exposed, they became accessories. Her arms looked like bones with skin painted on and even her feet had lost flesh. Her sandals barely fit.

Vaughn said that Su closed her eyes and winced when she hugged Audrey. She was afraid of hugging her too hard. Su didn't say anything, just brushed away a stray tear. "The Voice" was silent for once. Her horrified expression said enough.

They got a table at the Chartwood. My family used to eat there — it's gone now — I loved the place, especially the corn fritters. Even years later, you can feel your arteries hardening when you mention the name of that place. They settled in for a high-calorie, high-fat, high-flavor spread of country fried pork chops and gravy, mustard greens and corn bread, and, for dessert, sweet potato pie and peach cobbler that only your grandmother could make. They got caught up on with one another while dipping squares of corn bread into melted butter. They talked about classes and the law school application that Vaughn was thinking about (because she couldn't think of anything else to do when she finished college) and Su's Jewish boyfriend whose mother had said, "Oh! I'm so glad you're not *too* dark!" Su and Audrey learned that Audrey's sister was writing for a newspaper in London and was going on assignment to South Africa. The girls talked about the Supremes busting up, how bored they were with afros, and how Marcia Hampton, a Methodist minister's daughter, had joined the Black Muslims and was baking bean pies now. (I already knew about that tidbit, ha!) They traded useful information about birth control pills and near misses they'd had and giggled when Donna Cunningham came in with her four layers of makeup, blond wig, and four-inch-high platform shoes. She sashayed by, headed toward a table of men (of course), leaving the girls choking and coughing with laughter and respiratory distress due to the stench of very cheap perfume that she wore. Nothing worse than an old whore.

"Mercy!" Audrey exclaimed, fanning the overpowering scent of perfume away.

Vaughn had a hard time eating from her plate of pork chops and gravy because, sitting directly across from her, sat a girl who made the babies from Biafra look as if they'd been overfed.

"Audrey, aren't you going to eat anything?" Su asked with her mouth full of peach cobbler. Su likes to eat her dessert first.

"No, Mom made dinner and I ate before I left."

But V knew that was a lie. Mrs. Taylor's words rushed back.

"If you could get Audrey to eat a little something, it would be nice."

Audrey drank a Coke, lit a cigarette, and tapped her fingers on the table as they talked and ate. Just the thought of Miss Norma's country fried steak makes me hungry. But that evening Audrey was immune. Su gave up trying to tempt her with a bite of this or that. They watched her chain smoke and sip her drink and when the Coke ran out, she chewed on ice chips like they were pieces of steak.

"Well, well, if it ain't the girls most likely."

They turned around to see Eddie Dunlap bounding over to their table. Tall and goofy, Eddie's grin had enough wattage to light a stadium and his sense of humor (and the lies he told to support it) was endless. Everything and everyone made Eddie laugh and no party started without him. He had a story for every situation, he knew everybody and had been everywhere. Believing him was not important. Eddie told (and still tells) such good stories that it didn't matter.

"Su, you a sight for sore eyes, as always. Audrey Jean, girl you need to sop up some of that gravy with a biscuit, you look like you ain't had a decent meal in a week! V, V! My girl! I heard you and Tony B were going together. What's the deal, honey? Y'all seen Irene lately? I heard . . ."

Tony B, the bane of Vaughn's (and every SE High girl's) existence. Through three years of high school, he had attached himself to nearly every human wearing a skirt. Once he convinced himself that you were madly in love with him and ready to elope, you were in trouble. Tony was harder to get rid of than shit on a shoe. Tony thought (and still thinks) that he is the cream of the crop, the best of the best, and the knee of the bee. His positive opinion of himself did pay off in good grades, acceptance to a prestigious college, and an M.B.A. But it also contributed to his being one of the biggest assholes you'd ever hope to meet. Tony and I had had one disastrous date sophomore year. It was so bad that I almost swore off boys altogether. I didn't go that far, but from then on I did avoid Tony like he was cholera. Poor Vaughn.

"Eddie, where'd you hear that lie?"

The Kool-Aid-size grin only got wider.

"Loose lips sink ships, V, you know that. My sources are protected!"

"Tony prob'bly told him that himself," Audrey said under her breath.

Eddie plopped down on the seat next to Audrey, nearly bumping her out the window with his butt, not hard to do since she only weighed ten pounds.

"I knew the minute I saw you girls, you'd want to know what was happenin'. Where the party at?"

"Not 'where the party at,' " Su corrected Eddie. "It's where the party *be* at. Get it straight!"

It was the question that had dominated our Friday and Saturday nights in town when we were in high school. Not old enough to go to clubs, our primary source of social activity was a party, usually at someone's house, hopefully when their parents were gone or upstairs for the night. I cringe as I think about this because I have had a teenager and the last thing you want is an unauthorized and unchaperoned party at your house. But that's now. Things were different back then, and the only real vice going on was someone spiking the punch with cheap wine.

They were headed out to a birthday barbecue. Somebody's cousin's boyfriend or was it somebody's boyfriend's cousin? Vaughn's sister had a car and she was going to drop them off. Eddie, always in the know, gave them the word on two more parties that he had tracked down like a scout following the trail of a wounded animal.

"North on Cleveland, past Fifth, then turn right. It's a brick house, I think, six-something Ontario Street." Su wrote down the number. Whose house was it? It didn't matter. Parties were open affairs, the more the merrier.

"See you pretty ladies there later?"

"You can count on it!" Audrey replied, touching up her lipstick after she'd taken one last gulp of Coke.

At the barbecue, there were burned hamburgers, respectable chicken, and decent ribs along with the usual pork and beans, potato salad, and ice-cream sandwiches and watermelon for dessert. The music was loud, the backyard was small and crowded, and the jaws were flapping. The host's uncle cooked his secret recipe over a homemade grill and the air smelled wonderful. Su and Vaughn were full but hoped that Audrey would get hungry enough to nibble on a rib or two.

"Hey, hey, Vaughn."

It was Tony B. Vaughn's heart sank. Resistance was futile.

Tony was enough to ruin an appetite. He thinks his poop doesn't stink. I am here to tell you it would make your eyes water.

"What do you want, Tony?" Vaughn said shortly. There was no need to keep up the pretense of being polite with Tony. He was so self-centered and arrogant it never occurred to him that his attentions weren't wanted.

He moved in on her like a heat-seeking missile. She sidestepped him, hoping to avoid the feel of his sweaty hand on her butt. No such luck.

"You lookin' good, girl, lookin' good. Listen here . . ."

"Not listening, Tony. Will you excuse me? I've got to pick my nose."

"I was just thinkin'," Tony continued, "I read that romantic poem you wrote for the *Dispatch* contest. I know you were talking about us."

Vaughn had entered a poem in a newspaper contest and won. We were so proud of her. Our English teacher was ecstatic. Vaughn said she'd written about a love that she hoped to have *someday*. Someday did not equate to Tony B.

"Tony, listen here," she said, using his own words. "There is not now an 'us,' there has never been an 'us,' and as long as I breathe there will not *be* an 'us.' Get it?"

He laughed and wrapped his arm around her shoulders then leaned close to her ear.

"I know you want it, Vaughn, I could tell by that poem. You want me, I want you. You and me, right? Let's get away, just the two of us. I know a little motel off 161 . . ."

The same line he used on me in high school.

"Vaughn? Vaughn?"

It was Su and she looked worried.

"Audrey's sick to her stomach, says she wants to go home. Can you call Patty to come and pick us up?"

But this was 1974, the beginning of the Age of Aquarius. There may have been a lot of psychic communication but there weren't any cell phones. Vaughn called home on the outside chance that Patty had stopped there but she was out of luck. And calling Audrey's parents to come and get a drunk daughter was not the cool thing to do. None of the other kids were interested in leaving the party, which had now moved into full swing.

"In a minute."

"After they play 'Ball of Confusion'!"

Frantic, Vaughn zipped through her brain for all the telephone numbers that she knew by heart: her grandmother, aunts, Lester, a former boyfriend (she'd have to erase that one from her memory), Su, Audrey, and . . . me.

I'd just put Javier back to bed. He was teething, molars, and the pain sometimes woke him up. I'd rub bourbon on his swollen gums, let him chew on a cold washcloth for a bit, then tuck him back into bed. Bradley wasn't home.

I had just settled back on the couch with a glass of iced tea when the phone rang. In all my life, I don't think I've ever heard so much terror in a person's voice.

"Reenie! What are you doing? Do you have a car?"

I set my glass down and sat up straight.

"Vaughn? Is that you? What's the matter? What is it?"

"Do you have the car?"

"Yeah, why? V, what's going on?"

She was so scared I only got bits and pieces of sentences but I'm pretty good at stitching things together. They were at a party, Audrey was sick, they didn't have a car and needed to get her home fast. Could I come?

I scribbled a note to Brad using a purple crayon, grabbed my sleeping child, and dashed out the door. I don't think anyone has driven a 1968 Buick Skylark as fast as I did on the city streets that night. I flew up Livingston Avenue and roared into the driveway. There was loud music, laughter, the sound of meat sizzling on the grill, and car horns blaring in the distance and, bless his heart, Javier didn't move a muscle. He still sleeps like a stone. I bundled him into my arms and made my way up the crowded driveway toward the backyard to find the girls.

"Reenie! Hey, girl! How you doin'?"

"Fine, fine. Listen, have you seen Su or Vaughn?"

"Reenie! Hi! Oh, the baby is so cute."

"Yeah, um, do you know where Audrey is?"

"Reenie! Reenie, over here!"

In the flickering light of the tiki torches, I saw the trio, Su's hand waving me over, Vaughn, shorter in height, jumping and yelling to catch my attention. I ran to them as fast as I could carrying my two-ton little boy. I stopped just long enough to look Su in the eye and take a deep breath. It was the first time I'd seen her since July 1971.

"Reenie, we need to get her home. Fast." Vaughn was out of breath.

"What happened? Did she pass out? What were you guys drinking?"

I handed the baby to Vaughn and knelt down to get a closer look at Audrey. I must have gasped. When I looked up, Su was looking back at me. Her expression wasn't accusatory. It was panic-stricken.

Audrey was deathly pale, her eyelids fluttering, her lips moving but not making a sound. It takes a lot to shock me. But one look at Audrey came pretty close. I hadn't seen her in a while. She was thinner than a Pringle. She didn't look human. When I touched her child-size forearm, I felt a chill go down my spine. I've seen a few drunks in my life, mostly Bradley. I wasn't sure what this was, but I was sure it wasn't too much drinking.

My mother had been a nurse before she had my brothers and me. All our lives, she had managed our family's kazillion medical emergencies with the cool by-the-book efficiency of her training. I had seen her work so many times on one or the other of my brothers' calamities that I knew just what to do. I could mimic her step by step. I felt Audrey's forehead, damp and clammy. Her lips were dry. I checked her pulse. What pulse? Vaughn was yipping in my ear, dancing around with the baby. I couldn't concentrate.

"Hush up, V!" Su had picked up on my agitation. "She's trying to get a pulse."

Finally, I felt it: light, slow, and faint, very faint.

"Has she puked up the alcohol?"

Su's eyes were filled with tears. She shook her head.

"That's the thing. No . . . I-I don't think she's had anything to drink! Except Coke at the restaurant. I didn't even see her with a cup!"

"We gotta get her out of here."

This wasn't a case of just too much spiked punch. One of the boys had to carry Audrey to the car. She was as limp as a wet towel. She was beyond vomiting. By the time I got to Broad Street, Audrey was delirious, talking gibberish, and her eyes, deep-set and haunted-looking, held no sense of coherence at all. I grabbed for her wrist, trying to keep my eyes on the road at the same time. There was barely a pulse.

"Audrey? Audrey, can you hear me? We're takin' you home, OK? OK?"

I was at a stoplight. I glanced over my shoulder.

Audrey looked at me but did not see. It was August, eighty-plus degrees outside with high humidity, and I felt cold. Audrey's eyes looked like the ones I'd seen on stuffed animals in Orton Hall: empty, dull, and blind.

I detoured to St. Anthony's. Sometimes, clichés have to be used. I drove like a bat out of hell.

The admitting nurse took one look at Audrey and called for help.

They laid her out on a gurney and flew past us to a cubicle behind white curtains. Vaughn and I stayed close by while Su called Colonel and Mrs. Taylor, but they weren't at home. Later, we took turns using the pay phone while we waited. Javier snoozed on. It seemed as if the entire Paleozoic era went by before a nurse came to get us.

"We've gotten her stabilized and brought up her heart rate," the woman announced. "She's hooked up to an IV. We need to get some fluids into her, she's dehydrated." The nurse looked us up and down as if she was trying to make up her mind about something. Then she said, "What did you girls do this evening?"

In the interests of protecting the spiked punch at the party, I could see that both Su and Vaughn considered telling a very small lie to protect the guilty. But they only considered that for half a second. V explained the evening's activities as plainly as she could. The nurse's eyebrows rose when she mentioned going to Chartwood for dinner. But she didn't ask them what Audrey had eaten.

"Do you want me to write down what Audrey had to eat or drink?" Su offered.

"That's not necessary," the nurse replied. "From what I can tell, I would say your friend hasn't had anything to eat in at least a week. Maybe longer." Somehow, I wasn't surprised. When Su gasped, the nurse cocked her head a bit and looked at us. "Don't tell me you didn't notice that this girl is slowly starving herself to death?" When we didn't answer, the nurse's expression grew even sterner. "You've heard the term *wasting away to nothing*? Well"—she gestured toward the curtained area—"your friend is an excellent example."

It was 1974. None of us watched much TV. Su and V were college students and I just didn't have the time. But even if we had, the television movies about the tragedy or disease of the week hadn't been produced. We hadn't heard of "anorexia nervosa" or "bulimia." The term *eating disorders* wasn't in use yet. Both Su and Vaughn had done the "freshman fifteen," picking up extra weight their freshman year and holding on to it. I'd had a baby so that didn't count. It never occurred to any of us that someone would eat and then make herself throw up. Or, as in Audrey's case, not eat anything at all.

"She's in a lot of trouble," the nurse continued. "Her pulse is still very weak and if we don't get her kidneys going strong again soon . . ." The woman stopped, looked at us and sighed. "I'm going to try her parents again."

. . . *if we don't get her kidneys going strong again soon, she's going to die.*

I heard the rest of the sentence as if it had been spoken. I watched the nurse walk away; my vision was blurry and tunneled as if I were watching life unfold in a house of mirrors at the state fair. Su and I looked at each other and then at Vaughn. Su's face was ashen and her lips were white. I can only imagine how I looked. I felt as if a large straw had sucked all the life out of me, leaving me hollow and airless. Vaughn was so pale I thought she was going to faint.

Die.

The nurse's words fused my feet to the floor. I guess I'd been so busy, we'd all been so busy, living and growing and, in my case, watching someone else grow, that we had forgotten about death. It did take vacations. But it was never gone for very long. And it always seemed to find new conscripts. It just hadn't occurred to us that Audrey would ever be one of them.

She recovered. She spent a week in the hospital "regaining her strength," the Colonel told us. She returned to Fisk five pounds heavier and was the homecoming queen. When we saw her again at Christmas, we watched her eat with the scrutiny of researchers examining a specimen under a microscope. Audrey was not appreciative.

"Will you quit it? I'm eating, OK?" She would scold us and stuff a piece of meat or half a roll into her mouth, chewing in an exaggerated fashion to let us know how irritated she was with us.

"Sorry," Vaughn would mumble, averting her eyes.

"Just keeping you honest," I snapped, glaring back at Audrey. She could unnerve V with those glowing eyes, but not me.

But from that point on, we watched her when she didn't know we were watching. We always knew when she was under stress: she would smoke more, drink more, eat nothing, and her weight would plummet. And we worried. When life lightened its load, she'd eat, trash the Benson and Hedges, and guzzle Diet Pepsi instead of dry martinis and sangria. But as Su, Vaughn, and I learned, life does march on and if you're busy looking out for someone else's footsteps, you might fall into a ditch yourself.

THIRTEEN

My banishment was only partial now. Audrey would call me once in a while and started dropping by if she was home visiting her parents. Vaughn still took her job as the scribbler seriously but now her letters were more open if she was talking about Su. After the incident at the hospital, I didn't really have a conversation with Su again for years. But, in my heart, I thought the glacier was beginning to melt.

I've known Vaughn longer than the other girls. Met her in the neighborhood when we were in fourth or fifth grade, or was it at church? Anyway, I remember something about Timmy Early and . . . yeah, that's it. Timmy Early, the creep. He was a bully then, saying he would beat you up and wipe boogers on your dress, nasty stuff like that. Vaughn was skinny and small then. She wore glasses and was quiet and afraid of everything. She didn't think much of herself; sometimes I believe she still doesn't. Timmy chased her home a lot and one day I got into the middle of it. Timmy just about turned white when I threatened to have my brothers kick his ass. Whatever. It worked and Timmy didn't bother V again.

Vaughn often talks as if she's in our shadow, me, Audrey, and Su. Funny thing, she doesn't realize how bright, funny, and interesting she is. Just takes for granted her ability to put words and complicated concepts together and make them funny or poignant. She's still skinny and kind of small, but Vaughn is strong like a fishing line they use to catch marlin or swordfish. Skinny and resilient. That's Vaughn.

And don't tick her off either. Sometimes those words she uses cut like razor blades.

She wrote to me a lot about college and how different it was from high school. At SE, we were pampered and protected and told by our teachers and counselors that we could do anything. So almost fifty percent of the graduating class went to college. Out of that group came engineers, lawyers, doctors, college professors, administrators, a lieutenant governor, and a few writers, including Vaughn. Black was beautiful *and* smart and we had no reason to think otherwise. And no reason to believe other people thought differently.

At least, that's what Vaughn believed, until she got to college. She says she had the most boring college career ever, but I'll be the judge of that. I read her letters and sometimes they made me laugh so hard I cried. There were other times when they really pissed me off. Nothing that V did, just some of the crap she had to put up with.

She had a major inferiority complex over it, though. Su and Audrey had been on the homecoming courts, but V was derailed by Tri-Delts, who didn't feel she quite fit the mold, kind of a Sandra Dee versus Angela Davis thing. She also struggled through some kick-ass science courses, which left her GPA in ruins and her mind in despair. Vaughn had always been a decent student and this was a real blow to her self-esteem.

"Why the hell do they make us take these damn science courses!" she wrote. "If I was interested in science, dammit, I'd major in biology! I'm an English major! The only thing I know about science is how to spell it! And Reenie, if I hear 'Maggie Mae' or 'Been through the desert on a horse with no name' again, I will *scream*! My suitemates play them over and over and over and over . . ."

Ohio Methodist admitted more black students in the fall of 1971 than they had in the previous one hundred years of its existence. The funny part is, the affirmative action they were trying to achieve ended up being "unaffirmative reaction" according to Vaughn.

You see, none of us thought of ourselves as "deprived" or "underprivileged." My dad got a good job, and he and Mommy owned their own home as did Vaughn's and Audrey's parents. Colonel Taylor had been awarded a Bronze Star for his service in the Second World War. Su's mother studied dance in New York and her aunt owned one of the largest beauty parlors on the east side. We went to church on Sundays, knew where our grandparents came from, and spoke proper English. We thought we were normal eighteen-year-old kids. Vaughn found out that "normal," like beauty, is in the eye of the beholder.

The college forgot to mention to the incoming black students that a fair number of the faculty, administrators, and students thought they were (a) born and raised in a housing project with no running water or electricity, (b) didn't know who their fathers were, (c) graduated from substandard public schools, and (d) didn't know who their grandfathers were either. This left Vaughn and many of the other black students in a state of continual introduction. As V would say later, "When you don't fit the stereotype, you become a problem."

It got to the point that she almost decided to have note cards printed to hand out:

Hi! I'm Vaughn Jones.
My parents are married.
They live in a house (which they own) and both of them have jobs.
My parents are college graduates.
Two of my grandparents are college graduates.
I know who my father is.
I know who my grandfathers are. Actually, I know the name of my
  great-grandfathers, too.
I am literate and, yes, I speak very well.

"God, Reenie! If I had those cards in my hand, it would save me so much time! It's senior year and I'm going to throw up if I hear one more person tell me, 'You're *so* articulate!' in the patronizing, looking down your nose at me way. Give me a break."

It came to a head during midterms her senior year. One of her professors reviewed her project using third-grade-level language and a sappy tone. Vaughn was about ready to slug him right then and there when he slipped and used a reference to Mozart. Then, realizing his mistake, he backtracked and said, "I'm sorry. You probably don't know who Mozart is."

What did he say that for?

Vaughn is the most reserved of us. She's not mouthy or brash as I am. Mrs. Jones always told her girls to count to twenty if they weren't sure about saying something. V said that she was so mad that she just counted to five, said "To hell with it!" and let the man have it with both barrels.

"I'm not sure what you know about my background . . ." she began.

Dr. What's-his-name would not be diverted.

"I'll understand if you don't want to talk about it," he said. "My other students from deprived backgrounds are dealing with some heavy family concerns as well."

Lord, Lord, Lord. Heavy family concerns. I read this and started giggling right then. Just writing about it was making Vaughn angry, I could tell by her handwriting. It always looked like someone writing from a penal colony to the folks at home, but now it was like the scratches you see on the pictures of lie detector test results.

"Reenie, I thought I was going to smack him upside his fat head. I can be diplomatic about it, but sometimes you just can't be nice to people. I told that man that, and I quote, 'I not only know who Mozart was, I'm also familiar with Beethoven, Schubert, Bartók, Tchaikovsky, Rimsky-Korsakov, Haydn, Handel, Bernstein, William Grant Still, and Verdi. My father played the piano. My sisters and I took classical piano for ten years so I've heard the music since I was old enough to fart. I studied ballet, so I kinda learned about the Russian style versus the French. My mother can speak Spanish and a little Italian. My father learned Italian during the war and speaks a little Spanish. Oh, I know who my grandfather was. And I know who my seven-times great-grandfather was. He was born in 1740 on a small farm in northern Virginia and fought in the Revolutionary War."

Ain't being underprivileged wonderful?

V's letters were wordy, predictable (every other week like clock-work), and quirky. I learned a lot about northeast Ohio. I now know more about Thomas Hardy and James Baldwin than necessary. I didn't hear racy details about V's sex life or her latest boyfriend be-cause she hardly had a sex life or a boyfriend. Many of the black men on campus dated only white women and the white men on campus were as interested in the black women as they were in visiting Antarctica. So Vaughn spent a lot of time studying and reading and counting the days until graduation.

V's senior year was spent as the RA in a dorm named Austin Hall. Vaughn says that she ended up with the assignment because no one else wanted it. Built in the 1920s on the northwest side of the cam-pus near a quarry, Austin had atmosphere: turrets, a bell tower, and a parklike setting. And, according to Vaughn, it also had ghosts.

I took Javier and drove up once, just on a whim. Bradley had exams, the weather was nice, and I was bored. In Ohio, September is about as pretty as it gets. Bright blue skies, fat white-on-white clouds, and the brilliant oranges, golds, and reds of the changing leaves. The old dorm looked like a regal English manor house that you'd see in movies, with its topiaries and beds of vividly colored impatiens. We spread out a blanket, played with the baby, and talked and nibbled on potato chips and drank Cokes. Javier could run as fast and as far as he wanted. Frisbees whooshed in the air and badminton nets were set up here and there, their grids reminding me of sheet music against the clear blue skies.

But, as Vaughn would write later, in November that all changed. The Midwestern skies turned an angry, slate gray color, the clouds picked up weight, darkened, and got ugly and menacing. The trees became caricatures of themselves once they lost their leaves. Stripped of color and flesh, they loomed sinisterly over the once welcoming park. Vaughn said they now looked like a forest of Grim Reapers painted on the November sky like Chinese characters on platinum silk. By the end of that month Austin Hall resembled the backdrop of a scene from *The Fall of the House of Usher.*

On Saturday afternoons V had the place to herself because half the kids went home and the other half went to the football game.

She did a walk-through at three p.m. on weekends to make sure doors were locked, et cetera. This one Saturday V had the head cold from hell, so she was going off duty for a while to grab a nap. The other RA, a kid named Neville, was taking over. As she passed the girls restroom again, the sound of the shower got her attention. It was empty just a minute ago.

Probably Charlotte, V thought. *She's got a thing about being clean.*

But when she peeked in, the bathroom was empty. She turned off the water. Back in the hall, she heard music. She poked her head in the room expecting to say "hello" to one or the other of the first-floor residents. No one was there. V clicked off the TV set and left.

Halfway down the hall, she heard the sound of the shower again.

The usual suspects were out. Bob, on the men's side, had gone home for the weekend. The first floor was deserted.

"Neville!" she yelled through the intercom.

"I thought you were taking a nap." Neville's voice came through despite the static.

"Say, Neville? Have you been foolin' around with the shower or the TV down here?"

"Fooling around in the shower? Yeah, I've done that a few times."

"Not *in* the shower, *with* the shower. Turning it on and off. The TV, too. As a joke, maybe? If so, it ain't funny." Neville liked practical jokes.

The static and the rumble of thunder in the distance were the only answers V got for a few moments. Then Neville said, "No, Vaughn. Micro quiz, Monday. No showers or TV for me."

"You must be pretty ripe."

"You bet. Want a whiff?"

"I'd love to but I'm pulling my toenails out right now, thanks."

"Must be the ghosts." Neville's words were punctuated by more static. "Don't worry, they won't hurt you. Just tell 'em to stop, that you want to take a nap or study or something."

"I felt really stupid doing it," she wrote. "But my head felt like a pillow stuffed with wool, my eyes were drippy, and my throat hurt. I was so tired I would have climbed into a coffin to get some sleep. Well, maybe not a coffin . . ."

"I need a nap! Leave me alone!" Vaughn whined loudly, standing in the middle of the hallway. Heather in room 118 poked her head out the door, made a face, and then closed the door again.

"Please?" Vaughn figured that even ghosts could appreciate good manners.

She heard the rain clicking against the windows and the sound of water dripping in the women's shower. The TV was still off. She took her nap.

The next week, Vaughn spent time at the library in the archives. It didn't take long to dig up stories about Austin. There were lots of them. Two students who'd drowned in the quarry in the early 1920s were sometimes seen playing croquet on the grounds at dusk. A maintenance man who died in the early 1950s still checked the locks on the windows and doors. The belle of the campus whose father lost everything in the crash of 1929 had killed herself because she couldn't face the loss of status. There were other whispers that she had been pushed into the deep quarry by a jealous lover. V took the stories, myths, and urban legends, stirred them up, added extra fog and innuendo for flavoring, and wrote a short story about a haunted college dorm. But the review committee rejected it for the college literary magazine—they thought it might be "taken out of context" by the parents of prospective students. V submitted it to a magazine and it was accepted for publication. Her writing career had begun.

I was in a completely different league. While my friends bought matching bedspreads for their dorm rooms and spent hours in the stacks of the library searching for primary or secondary sources, I raised a child, worked as a secretary, and "kept house." I couldn't channel my energy into school until Bradley finished so I threw it all into decorating. Martha Stewart has nothing on me. I can take throwaways from a flea market and turn them into collectibles, pull the nondescript from the sale racks at Kmart and decorate an apartment that could be part of an *Architectural Digest* spread. (Actually, I have!) But once the apartment was finished and Javier was in pre-school, I was out of things to do. So I got another job.

I sold junior fashions on the third floor of Lazarus and set the trends myself. Since I made clothes, I knew how to put the patterns and colors together. The head buyer for the department saw the out-fits that I wore and, the next thing I knew, I was dressing the man-nequins for the floor and the display windows. I was promoted twice and the assistant store manager tried to hit on me. He told me I would run the department if I slept with him. I told him to go fuck himself. He got fired, I ended up running the department anyway.

Mostly, I was oblivious to men. There had been a ripple effect from my surprise pregnancy and shotgun wedding. The last damn thing I wanted was to get involved with another man. Anybody's man or nobody's man.

Bradley and I had a quiet marriage. We talked about Javier. We talked about the weather. I washed the dishes, he dried them. I folded towels, Bradley ironed his shirts. We had sex once a week rain or shine and when it was over, we went to sleep. Our marriage was tidy and polite. There was no love lost because there'd been no love to begin with. We were married roommates.

Now, if this sounds out of character, you're right. In the old days, I would have smelled a rat from day one. I'd had enough boyfriends to know when the thrill was gone. Not that we'd ever had one. But these days, Mrs. Irene Garcia was too busy to pay attention to the clues that were thrown into her path even though they glowed like neon: Bradley's extra evening law classes on days he didn't have class, hang-up phone calls, and lots and lots of overtime at work.

But no party lasts forever.

One OSU football Saturday, the store was dead. No one was shopping. They were either at the game or watching it at home on TV. The manager sent some of us home early. I decided to go home and relax a little bit before picking up Javier from the sitter.

It was a cool, brilliant afternoon, the leaves had already begun to turn and the sky was as blue as turquoise. For a minute, as I put the key in the lock, I thought about changing clothes, throwing on a pair of sneakers, and taking a long walk.

The drapes I had left open were closed, which was strange, and there were glasses on the counter, wet rings around their bases. The ice cubes had melted into a blob at the bottom of the glass. I had cleaned up the kitchen before I left. I opened the drapes and let some sunshine in.

Oh, well, Bradley prob'bly forgot something and stopped by to pick it up.

In the cool, quiet dusk of the living room, I pulled off my jacket and slipped out of my shoes. *But why pull the curtains . . .*

The sound was unmistakable even though I could count on one hand the number of times I'd heard it personally. The moans and groans of a woman's voice, throaty and guttural, hit my ears, the man's voice . . . I stood up straight.

"Oh, God, yes!"

I have to admit it; yes, I did stand there and listen for a while. The two times Bradley and I had had sex before we were married, one of which had resulted in Javier, were fumbling backseat affairs that were exciting if you like having a gear shift rubbing up against your butt. The sex we shared now was quick, quiet, and damp.

Not like this, I said to myself. *So this is what it's supposed to sound like* . . . I felt a pang in my heart, part anger, part jealousy, part sadness.

I opened the bedroom door in time to see the shocked face of my husband and Janice Griffin, a girl we'd grown up with. Bradley was scrambling out of bed to explain, Janice was too shocked to do anything, including cover herself up.

"Reenie, honey, Irene . . ." Bradley stammered trying to figure out what to call me. Thank goodness, he didn't say "darling."

One of my husbands (number two or number three, I've forgotten which) told me that if a man gets caught, even if he's midthrust (so to speak . . .), he should deny it. Bradley started to do just that.

I held up one finger and grinned at the fool.

"Bradley, don't even try it. Put your drawers on. And Janice, cover up your titties, honey. They look like deflated footballs."

"Reenie . . ."

I gave him a look that I hoped would stop a train. I slammed the door then leaned against it. My heart was pounding, my fists were clenched so tightly that my palms hurt, and even my toes were curling up. My thoughts were zooming around my head like cars on a racetrack. I realized then that I wasn't angry, wasn't really hurt or embarrassed either. Well, maybe a little angry. I mean, what was he doing with Janice Griffin? God, my boobs are so much prettier than hers! But I wasn't jealous.

I heard them bumping and thumping around in the bedroom as they located their clothes and dressed. I felt like a lioness about to pounce, lit a cigarette (something I rarely do), and sat in the living room, blowing out the smoke in concentric rings. I opened the blinds.

Bradley came out first, of course. He was making sure the escape route was safe for Janice. I waved him away and smiled as Janice tiptoed out, her face ashen, her eyes filled with worry.

"Reenie, I'm . . . I don't know what to say. I, uh . . ."

"Well, I know what to say," I interrupted, blowing another smoke ring out to join its friends.

Bradley decided to assert himself.

"Now, Irene, there's no need to get ugly about this . . ."

I laughed. And it wasn't a bitter, cackley sound like you might expect from a woman who's been scorned. It was a warm, delicious, belly laugh that had no anger or hostility anywhere in it. It even felt good. I could see that Bradley was confused. Or else he thought I was crazy.

"Shut up, Bradley," I said, giggling. I looked at Janice, whose knees were shaking. That was nice to see. "Jan, you forgot something, doll. You take those sheets in there with you. I sure as hell don't want 'em." I glanced at my husband. My soon-to-be-former husband.

"Take . . . the sheets?" Now Janice was confused.

"Yeah, take the sheets. You fucked on 'em, they're yours. You don't think I'm going to use them again, do you? And I'm certainly not going to wash 'em for you!"

Janice was almost indignant. She probably would have been more forceful had she been in her own apartment. But this was my place—and Bradley's. And to run into the injured wife who was now calmly smoking a cigarette and laughing, well, Janice wasn't sure what kind of evil spirit she might be dealing with, and I did have a bit of a reputation from high school.

"Irene, what am I s'posed to do with . . . the sheets?"

I smashed out my cigarette. Rhett Butler's classic line came to mind but I decided to update it.

"Janice, honey, you can stuff them up your ass for all I care. But they aren't staying in my house another minute. And when you go, take *him* with you!" I pointed toward Bradley.

"Now, Irene . . ." I just hate it when someone says "Now, Irene." Somehow folks got it into their heads that calling me by my proper name will get them somewhere.

I looked at that man as if I were going to take his head off with one bite. He and Janice left in a hurry.

⸺

"Can I say something?"

Almost a year later, I was sitting on a bench outside the Clerk of Courts office looking at my freshly stamped divorce decree. The attorneys had collected their fees (Bradley had paid both of them) and departed. The judge was on her next case. And I was still Reenie Garcia but single again.

"Sure, sit down." I scooted over to make room for my ex-husband.

Bradley's light brown eyes were soft. His expression, one that I would see on future former husbands, was contrite.

"Reenie, I feel bad about this. It didn't have to end this way. We could have . . ."

"What way, Bradley? There was no muss, no fuss. Just a quick divorce and you and Janice and me, myself, and I are on our way."

Bradley smiled wistfully. That was one of the things I always liked about Brad, that smile.

"Yeah, yeah, I know this is my fault. But Reenie, I don't love Janice."

Or Barbara or Joyce Ann or what's her name who works for IBM. In the past few months, I'd learned that Janice Griffin was one of several women Bradley had been involved with. I chuckled at the irony of it. He and Su had been like two peas in a pod. Now I had to wonder. Would Bradley have been the same way with Su? I'd now experienced enough to know that the answer was "probably." But did it matter anymore?

"I know that, Brad. But you don't love me either. Not like that, anyway. You love me as Javier's mother but that's it. We got married because we had to. Now we're divorced. Maybe . . ." I felt a lump forming in my throat as I thought about the ancient past when I was seventeen and a cheerleader and had everything wonderful ahead and hadn't known that a self-inflicted wound would derail my life. "Maybe one of us will get a chance to really love someone." I looked past him at a future that could be. "Maybe . . . both of us. What do you think?"

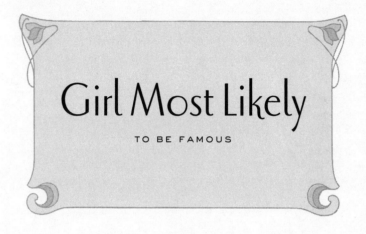

Girl Most Likely

TO BE FAMOUS

Su

I remember the day I began to confront my feelings about Reenie and Bradley. It was the day I opened the purple-and-white envelope containing the invitation to our tenth high school reunion.

I was the roving reporter at Channel 7, which meant I covered every gang fight, trailer fire, VFW musk melon eating contest, lost Chihuahua, and extreme weather situation that occurred in our tri-state area. I pulled more of the weather stories than anything else. So many of them, in fact, that it got to be an inside joke between me and the janitors at the station.

"Got us a winter storm warning, I see," Mr. Glover would comment with a chuckle and a knowing grin. "Guess they'll be sending you out there, huh?"

If there was a weather emergency, you could be sure that "the black girl" would cover it. I covered every tornado, heavy rainstorm, sleet storm, hailstorm, locust invasion, and blizzard there was. And that's just what I was doing that day in late June. The TV station van was speeding down the highway following up on a tornado sighting from the northwest edge of the county. I held on to the strap to keep from falling over as I sorted through my mail.

We'd had a spell of bad weather lately. It was good and bad at the same time. I was always on the air, reporting about downed power lines and trees crashing through roofs. On-air time was good for my career but bad for me personally. I had no social life. I took showers on the run, pulled my hair back in ponytails, and smeared on lipstick seconds before the camera lights went on. Ran home long enough to grab clean underwear.

Electric bill, Nordstrom's, junk mail, junk mail, letter from Aunt Leila, what's this? The envelope looked intriguing. I turned it over.

I didn't recognize the return address but the handwriting was familiar. It was a cross between calligraphy and Greek. Only Vaughn writes like that.

Hey, Hey, Hey! Purple Tigers, Class of 1971!
It's time for our first ever and only Tenth-year REUNION!!!

Oh, dear.

"Shit!" Bobby, the cameraman, had slowed down. The rain had started up again and this time it was streaming down the sides, front, and back of the van like someone pouring water from a huge watering can. You couldn't see anything. Bobby brought the van to a stop under an overpass. "I'll radio in, Suzanne," he said, looking over his shoulder at me. "It's going to take a while. Maybe the tornado's hit closer than we thought."

We can only hope, I said to myself. The last thing I wanted to do was stand in a cataclysmic rainstorm and tell "the viewing public" that we were having a cataclysmic rainstorm. I turned my mind back to the invitation.

I hadn't been home in a while. "Home" was a word that always had funny connotations for me. I thought about my aunt's old duplex, the room I had shared with my cousin Sharon, and the huge dining room table that we used to do our homework on. I thought about my aunt pressing my hair in her salon on Thursday nights and the stack of *Ebony* and *Jet* magazines on the coffee table in the front room. I thought about my aunt's vanity table. She owned every cosmetic Estée Lauder made. Aunt Leila was retired now, she did only a few hours a week at the salon, mostly just her closest friends and a few ladies from church. Sharon had married and moved to D.C. My other cousins had moved out years ago.

I thought of home with my mother. Her little apartment on Clifton Avenue and the copies of Picassos and Kahlos and the African carvings she had around the combination living and dining room. I thought about my mother's closet, filled to bursting with her "outfits" from her dancing days and the ornate Miriam Haskell pins she'd let me wear for dress-up play. And the way her clothes smelled, L'Interdit, Chanel No. 5, something by Balenciaga. I thought about Vaughn's house, too, five blocks away, and Reenie's mother refereeing all those rowdy boys. And Audrey and her mother's dining room that smelled like someone had lit a lemon fresh Pledge candle in it. These places were all part of the "home" I treasured in my mind and dreamed about when I needed to focus on peace and contentment.

It had been ten years since high school graduation. Ten years since Bradley told me that Reenie was pregnant and that he was going to marry her. Ten years since my heart broke, and there are still some pieces missing. But everything is different now. I'd overheard my grandmother say that time heals all wounds. I was never sure what she meant then, and I'm not sure I know now. I look at the train wreck that I thought had ruined my life in a different way now that the distance of time and place have worked their magic. But I'm still not sure how I feel about Reenie.

I looked up from the invitation to see a wall of water in front of us where the overpass stopped. Bobby was listening to the producer on the radio, then said, "OK. It's your call," and clicked off. He turned around to look at me with an apologetic expression.

"Time to rock and roll."

Have you ever broadcast from the eye of a storm? It's like being the embedded reporter on Noah's ark. Only wetter.

"Jim, you're right, it is an incredible sight, water everywhere! We're standing on I-Eighty-five and Monroe Avenue. As you can see . . ."

With a Chanel red lipsticked smile, a bright yellow rain slicker, and a massive black golf umbrella, I informed our television-viewing audience of what they already knew: It was windy and raining very hard. I gave my report on automatic pilot, trying to divert my thoughts to forget about how wet my feet were, how cold it was getting, and how much I was shivering. Thinking about Reenie was the best diversion I could have had.

Sure, I was going to the reunion. I hadn't seen Audrey in a while; Vaughn had married, had twins, and divorced; and, of course, I wanted to see the rest of the kids, even though we weren't kids anymore. I also wanted to see Reenie again. I just wasn't sure why.

I hadn't seen or talked with her since that awful summer night at the barbecue when Audrey was so sick and Vaughn called Reenie to pick us up.

When I first saw her, picking her way through the crowd, carrying that beautiful child, I nearly forgot about what had happened between us: her and Bradley, their marriage, everything. For a few seconds, I was transported back to May of our graduation year, before it all happened, when we were still best friends, before I'd been run over by that train, my emotional life completely destroyed. All I saw on that muggy night was Reenie, the same old Reenie, dark hair pulled into a ponytail, blouse, shorts, white sneakers, gold hoops in her ears. And that baby.

Once she spotted us, she rushed over and knelt next to Audrey, who'd slumped onto the grass against the fence. Vaughn was talking, I don't know what she said because my ears were buzzing and I thought I was going to pass out. I was so scared. Reenie looked up at me for a moment, her dark eyes calm but questioning, but she didn't say anything. I didn't either.

I like to think I'm capable, calm, and quick-thinking in a crisis. But that time I couldn't think at all. I felt as if I were falling to pieces.

Reenie took over. It wasn't until later that I remembered that Mrs. Keller was a nurse and that Reenie had always wanted to go to nursing school. Marriage to Bradley and a baby put that dream on hold.

She stuffed the baby into Vaughn's arms and went to work. She opened Audrey's collar and checked her breathing, touched her forehead, took her pulse. And, in the car, when Audrey began to babble incoherently, Reenie made a U-turn that James Bond would have been proud of and sped off to the hospital.

I guess we got Audrey there just in time, and after a long night, her parents and the doctor came out and told us she would be all right. Reenie drove V and me home, the baby slept on, bundled up into his little car seat. The sun was coming up, I remember that. Its rays were warm: a neon orange Popsicle-like color. None of us had slept, it was a wonder that Reenie was awake enough to drive. We were so tired we could barely mumble "good night" to one another. She dropped me off last. My aunt had left the porch light on. It looked out of place now that it was seven-thirty in the morning and daylight.

I closed the car door quietly because I didn't want to wake Javier.

Reenie and I looked at each other for a few moments without speaking. In the background, I heard birds squawking. Their cries reminded me of slumber parties that we'd had years ago at Reenie's house. The volume of our chatter would get so loud that Mr. Keller would stumble down the hall and bang on the door.

"You girls keep it down! Lord, have mercy, you sound like the blackbirds in the trees outside!"

I longed for those days.

"G'night . . . and thanks," I managed to mumble. Just before I turned away, I caught a glimpse of the baby in the back. His round face was peaceful in sleep and he had his thumb in his mouth. My heart ached to look at him. "You have a pretty baby, Reenie."

"Thanks," she murmured.

It would be six years before I'd see her again if we both went to the reunion. I came back to myself just in time to sign off.

"This is Suzanne Penn of WKBR, the voice of the tristate. Back to you, Jim."

"Suz-*anne* Penn, *the voice of the Tristate!*" Audrey mocked my sign-off in a dramatic Tallulah Bankhead drawl. "How siddity is that, I ask you?" she asked the group, blowing water at me from the tip of her straw. Audrey was pregnant and not smoking that year. "What is up with that name change, hon? Suz-anne, I mean, who do you think you are anyway?"

I gave her the finger.

"Look. 'Susan' didn't work for me, OK? There was another 'Susan' at the station and I wanted to be different."

"You're the only chocolate drop that station has on the air, cutie," Audrey commented. "It isn't likely they'd get you and Blondie mixed up. Suzzzz-anne!"

"Quit it." I swatted at her.

Vaughn lifted her chin as high as she could, also trying to imitate my on-air persona. Very badly, I might add. I don't think I'm that melodramatic.

"Thank you, Jim. As you can see by the seven-foot snowdrift I'm standing on, we're having a blizzard! I have snow up to my ass!"

Nothing had changed, thank God.

"You have some nerve, missy," I challenged Audrey. "Talkin' about folks' names. What's up with this Audrey Taylor-North stuff? How stuck-up is that?"

Vaughn giggled. Audrey stuck out her tongue.

"It's Mizzzz Audrey Taylor-North to you," Vaughn interjected. "Her subjects call her 'the Hyphenated One.' "

"Shut up!" Audrey swatted Vaughn. "I honestly planned to use my own name, you know, for business. Like *Mizzzz Jones* here, but Tommy had a conniption."

Now it was Vaughn's turn to stick out her tongue and make a face.

"Yeah, yeah, well, the hyphen makes it sound as if you can't make up your mind. Make a decision!"

What we knew but didn't say was that Vaughn's decision had been made, at least partly, because of her divorce. Her husband walked out on her when the twins were barely a month old, and life had been very hard ever since. She was determined to eliminate every trace of the jerk that she could. And that meant changing her name back to Vaughn Jones.

Audrey squirmed in the hard-backed banquet chair, trying to get comfortable. The cantaloupe-size lump around her midsection made it nearly impossible. But Audrey pregnant was almost ridiculous. She looked like Olive Oyl with a watermelon for a belly and whined all the time about all the weight she was carrying. One hundred thirty-five pounds, to be exact. Vaughn, who had gained fifty with the twins, was ready to slap her.

"Shut up, Audrey! You don't know when you have it good! Those twins ruined my navel and my boobs now hang to my waist, it's awful! They fought so much prenatal that it felt like I was having World Federation Wrestling matches in my belly!"

Audrey sighed dramatically and mourned aloud the loss of her eighteen-inch waist. Vaughn picked up the butter knife and pretended to stab her.

"Hey, hey girls!"

It was Nicey Powell, one of the other girls on the cheerleading squad. She looked the same except for the extra fifty pounds she was carrying. And she *wasn't* pregnant. We chatted awhile about old times and Darleen Howe's third divorce and how one of our teachers married one of our classmates and how we couldn't possibly do the splits anymore when Nicey blurted out, "Reenie here?"

I opened my mouth then closed it. Audrey's eyes quickly shifted to my face then to Vaughn's.

"Um, no, haven't seen her yet," Audrey said pleasantly.

"Bradley isn't here either." Nicey looked furtively around then leaned in close. "You heard that he and Irene are divorced. God, do you believe him? I mean, who knew he would turn out to be the biggest dog in the senior class!" She patted Su on the shoulder. "Girl, you were smart to dump him when you did. He was screwin' around with every girl who'd let him! Not what you would have thought, huh? Bradley always seemed so quiet, proper, you know, kind of straitlaced. A Boy Scout. You just never know . . ."

"Shut up, Nicey," I heard V say under her breath.

Not what you would have thought. I hadn't lived here in seven years. And Vaughn and Audrey were always careful about what they said, if anything, about Reenie or Bradley. So, no, I didn't know that Reenie and Bradley were divorced. No, I hadn't heard that he'd married Janice Griffin, "for a minute," as Nicey said, then was divorced again when she caught him with some *other* woman. And, of course, I almost had indigestion when Nicey rattled on about Bradley trying to hit on half the cheerleading squad and all the majorettes our senior year.

Bradley?

I'd heard rumors. I'd heard whispers. But this was the first time I'd heard the details. When Nicey finally waddled off, I turned to V and Audrey.

"Why didn't you tell me?"

Audrey's gold eyes lit up with indignation.

"What was I going to say? That your beloved Bradley, the cutest, smartest, nicest boy in school was really a two-timing—"

"Son of a bitch," V interrupted. "That's what he is. A supreme asshole and son of a bitch. You were lucky not to have married him. Reenie found him and Janice in their bed together." V giggled. "Reenie told Janice to strip the bed and take the sheets with her."

I could only imagine how hysterical it would have been to see Janice Griffin scrambling to get dressed and strip a bed before Reenie kicked her behind.

But Bradley? How could I have been so wrong about Bradley?

"But . . ." My question was hanging in the air. I glanced at Audrey, who was rubbing her swollen belly. "Nicey said . . . he hit on every one of . . ."

Audrey shook her head.

"She was exaggerating—"

"Only a little," Vaughn interrupted.

Audrey glared at her.

"What?"

"He never said anything to me, probably because he knew I would tell you," Audrey said finally. "I'd see him in once in a while with Anita or walking Karla to her car. But I didn't think anything of it. I mean, ninety-nine percent of the time he was huddled up under you."

But now I was angry. And feeling foolish. Had I really been the last to know?

"But you should have told me," I challenged them again. Audrey glared back at me. Vaughn looked away. I knew she'd felt guilty because she had actually seen Bradley and Reenie together but hadn't made the connection.

"Told you what exactly?" Audrey snapped back, beaming one of her best "Audrey" smiles at Marilyn Shore. "Hi Marilyn! How are you? *Never liked that bitch.* Really, Suzz-anne, there wasn't anything to tell. No smoking gun. We knew when you knew. And besides, whether you like it or not, Reenie got the worst of it."

No, Reenie didn't get the worst of it.

"Still . . ." I glared back at Audrey. I took a sip of the sangria because my throat was dry. Too sweet, yuck.

"Still what?" Vaughn interjected. I could tell that she was getting impatient with me and was ready to move off this subject. "Su, it's been ten years, four months, and a few days. Who cares now?"

I took another sip of wine to avoid answering her.

I don't believe in time travel, but for that moment, I felt the walls of the room close in on me as I flew back across the ten years, four months, and days to my dorm room and a weekend I would never forget. So many omens pushed into a three-day period and my life moved onto a road that it has never detoured from. Amazing.

It was my first and last blind date. And it was Dorice's fault. Dorice was my roommate, a phys ed major from Charlotte, a dynamo of a girl packaged in a petite body. She was bright, vivacious, and helplessly addicted to matchmaking. Dorice always had a boyfriend, always. And, in her view, it was practically against the Ten Commandments for any girl to attend an event without an escort. Talk about old-fashioned Southern social values.

"Honey, y'all will just love 'im! He's a doll baby!" she said in a soft North Carolina drawl. "He meets all your requirements. He's tall, y'all like tall; he's smart; he's in the honors program; and he's cute. Now what else could y'all want?"

As I glanced at the wall clock in the student union ballroom where the party was taking place, I remember thinking that verbal skills might be nice. Jimmy Lawrence was tall, smart, and cute if you liked the wire-rimmed glasses and lopsided smile type. But he walked like the Scarecrow from the Wizard of Oz and he had the social skills of a turnip. It had been at least fifteen minutes since either of us said anything. Not to mention dancing.

"No, I don't dance," Jimmy had said, looking panic-stricken when I mentioned it.

Okeydokey, I thought to myself. *Dorice, I'm putting your mattress out in the hall.*

Not that I was really looking for a boyfriend. The breakup with Bradley had been catastrophic, I'd cried for a month, was still crying all the way down I-75 when Aunt Leila drove me to school. There was a huge hole in my heart where Bradley had been. I liked boys but I didn't want a boyfriend. Jimmy and anybody else would just be something to do. But really . . .

"What courses are you taking again?" I asked him, trying to be polite and wanting to strangle Dorice at the same time.

Jimmy's eyes lit up behind his thick-lensed glasses.

"Paleogeology, advanced astronomy, physics . . ."

"Oh" was all that I could say. Talk about way over my head! I had actually taken physics in high school so I understood a little bit of what he was talking about. But it didn't take Jimmy long to get way past my second-grade level of understanding.

"Whoa. You're beyond me, now," I told him. *Just make him stop.* "I'm sure you'll be nominated for a . . . what's the name of that prize again?"

"The Brinkman Award," he told me. Then he smiled. Jimmy wasn't as cute as Dorice had marketed him to be. But he did have a nice smile. "Sorry. I bore everybody when I start talking about pale-ontology. Most of the kids aren't interested in what I'm studying. That goes both ways, really. Except for you," he added quickly. "You want to be on television someday, don't you?" He shook his head, still smiling. "I'd be afraid to stand up in front of people and . . . and talk. I'd freeze."

I laughed.

"It's nothing, really. You speak into the mike as if you're talking with a friend. That's the trick, y'know. Make the listener or viewer think you are talking only to them."

The next time I looked at the clock, I realized I had been talking for ten minutes and Jimmy had listened attentively without interruption for the entire time.

"I'm sorry. Now I'm boring *you*. I've been running on and on . . ."

"No, no, it's fine," he said, nodding. "I like to listen to you talk. You have a beautiful voice."

It was very nice of him to say that, considering what a change it was from Jurassic lizards and asteroid dust. I had a lot more to say to my dear roommate when I got hold of her by the girls' restroom.

"Dorice, you'll have to do better than Jimmy Lawrence."

"What's wrong with Jimmy Lawrence?"

"Nothing that a rudimentary knowledge of quarks, black holes, and Jupiter's moons won't fix. Dorice, he's an egghead, OK? A nerd. Not my type," I said, emphasizing the last few words.

Dorice grinned, dimples appearing in her cheeks.

"I thought I told you he was into science . . ."

"Into science! He is a science project, Dorice. No more blind dates, OK?"

I dumped Jimmy Lawrence that night and walked home with some of the kids from the college radio station.

It was hot; Florida is always hot. And the dorm wasn't air-conditioned. I woke up at three o'clock in the morning, dripping wet, to the sound of a humming fan and insects chirping in the distance. A few cars rushed by on the interstate several blocks from campus. I sat up all at once, shaking my head and gasping for air in the dark stillness. At first, I wasn't sure what had awakened me.

Then I felt them. Cramps. Awful, back-breaking cramps. Great. My period. I sighed, tumbled out of bed, and clicked on the light. My stomach was upset and I felt as if I had to use the bathroom. I rummaged around in my drawer until I found a package of pads and tampons and got myself together for the trek down the hall to the communal bath. It was when I turned around to close the door that I saw my bed.

The sheets were soaked in blood.

I did make it to the women's bathroom and managed to clean myself up, but by the time I'd finished, I was so weak that I could barely drag myself out of the stall.

"Susan? Susan?"

I recognized Dorice's voice. She'd spent that Friday night with her boyfriend at a motel at the edge of town, as usual.

"Susan! Are you all right? I saw the sheets . . ."

When she saw my face, which was probably as white as the sheets had once been, she ran for the RA. I remember hearing her footsteps sliding down the hall as a soft, warm heat oozed down my thighs and the sounds of bees filled my ears. I thought I saw stars. I saw the ceiling lights in the bathroom hanging like giant bowls upside down. And then I saw nothing at all.

"Susan? Susan?"

The voice was soft but professional. I wiggled my toes, yes, they were still there. I fumbled to touch up my hair and remembered feeling a heaviness in my belly but no cramping. Good. Maybe my period was over. But I was tired. I don't think I'd ever felt so tired. My body felt as if it had no energy at all, just lumpy and limp like a big sack of sugar I'd once carried from the store with my cousins.

"Susan, can you open your eyes?"

I did as I was told. The woman sitting by the bedside smiled at me. Her brown eyes were comforting behind tortoiseshell glasses. She wore a white coat. "Eva Bryson, M.D." was stitched in navy across one of the pockets. She took my hand in hers. Her touch was warm. I closed my eyes again; my lids didn't have the strength to stay open.

"Susan, how are you feeling? Are you comfortable?"

"Yes. I'm OK." I slowly opened my eyes again. The doctor was studying me.

"Good. I'm glad to hear it. You've had quite an evening. You aren't in any pain?"

"No."

"You've had a miscarriage but you'll be all right. Do you know how many months along you were?"

I felt the air go out of my lungs with a *whoosh*.

"W-What do you mean?" This time my eyelids did stay open.

The doctor studied me again before she spoke. I'll never forget the look she gave me. Amazement with a good dose of pity at the end.

"You . . . you do know you were pregnant? I'm thinking, maybe three, four months. When was your last period, Susan?"

Oh, God. I couldn't talk. I couldn't breathe. All I could think of was my last period, months and months ago. And I hadn't thought . . . My mind flew back again to me and Bradley, tongues and sweat and my thighs opening on their own because I was dripping for him. My arms stretched above my head and his warm breath on my neck. And a warm, deep feeling that started between my legs and moved quickly to my lips, but Bradley had kissed me instead and so my screams of pleasure became moans and then silence and then . . .

This.

"I-I didn't . . ." The words caught in my throat and scratched it as if someone had poured sand into my mouth.

The doctor smiled slightly.

"You aren't the first patient who's told me she didn't know she was pregnant. And you won't be the last one either. When was the last time you and . . ."

"Four months ago," I said. How could I have forgotten that night?

She wrote something down in her notebook then patted my hand.

"Well, Susan, you're going to be all right. I want you to stay here overnight just for observation and then you can go tomorrow. The nurse will make an appointment for you, I want to see you again in a week. And then . . ." She paused and studied me again as if there was more that she could say but wouldn't. "And then, perhaps you and I will talk about contraception?"

Tears rolled down my cheeks. I shook my head vehemently. *No, No, No. I wouldn't need any contraception. I wasn't going to do that again. Never. Ever.*

"We'll talk later," Dr. Bryson said quietly and left the room. I turned my face toward the window and cried myself to sleep.

He had told me that I needed to make a decision. We had been dating for years and he'd said that it was time to become adults about it. He had arranged for places for us to do this and flowers and cheap wine and rubbers. And several times he had stroked me and kissed me and rubbed me in places that made my lips part in gasps that never created sound. My panties got damp with his caresses but I was scared. Really scared. What if I ended up like . . . my mother? A baby and no husband?

And then we broke up. I wouldn't speak to him. He wouldn't call me. We managed to avoid each other for weeks even though we had some classes together. And then, one evening, he showed up on my aunt's porch with a dozen roses and a bracelet that he'd bought me using earnings from his weekend job.

My thighs parted for him that night and many nights afterward. We kissed until our lips were sore. My body tingled every time he touched me. My nipples stayed hard for hours after he licked them. And, sometime later, when he told me that Reenie was pregnant, I threw him out of my aunt's front room and never spoke to him again. Four months later, I miscarried.

No, Reenie hadn't gotten the worst of Bradley. She had Javier. She'd gotten the best of him. I had nothing at all.

"Su, listen, you and Reenie . . ."

My visit back in time ended abruptly.

"Shhh! Reenie just came in." Vaughn was never good at whispering.

"Is it me or does she look like a . . ."

I saw Reenie standing in the doorway. She looked like a miniseries movie queen with a little bit of trash thrown in. Later, Reenie would say that she was going through her Joan Collins stage. She'd been the good wife and mother long enough and wanted to have some fun, to make up for lost time. That night, the class of 1971 saw Irene Keller with her to-die-for figure, short skirt, four layers of makeup, and fabulous coal black hair styled in Farrah Fawcett curls. The "boys" flocked around her like bees on honey. The "girls" either spoke to one another or cut their eyes because they, unlike Reenie, hadn't been able to unload the extra twenty pounds that their pregnancies had brought.

As for me? I didn't see a femme fatale or a slut or the former homecoming queen. I saw the woman who had what I had lost. I saw Javier's mother. And it was too much.

Without saying anything, I got up, grabbed my purse, and left the room.

FIFTEEN

The girls really let me have it the next day. Audrey called me everything but a child of God, Vaughn nearly skinned me alive with her words. But I refused to tell either of them why I'd left so suddenly. It just hurt too much. They both assumed it was because of Reenie, because I hated her for taking Bradley away from me, for breaking my heart. And I did not enlighten them further.

"Well," Audrey snorted when she called me the next morning, still miffed and unable to pull any confessions out of me. "All I can say is you ruined my ten-year reunion experience." *Only Audrey would call it a reunion experience.* "I fly in to see my girls, gossip, and relax. Vaughn hires keepers for her two monsters, by the way, did you see *The Omen*? And you stay long enough to take two sips of bad sangria and walk out! You're not getting off that easy. When does your plane leave?"

She was right, of course. I'd been looking forward to the reunion, too, to see everybody, to catch up, gossip and reminisce about the baton maneuvers or Chinese splits that none of us could do anymore. As only Audrey could, she made me feel ashamed of myself.

"I'm flying out Monday morning, Oh Hyphenated One," I told her, using Vaughn's new nickname for her.

"Kiss my butt," Audrey retorted and gave me chapter and verse on where to meet her and Vaughn. "Oh, and bring an extra ten.

V's not in the money right now and since you walked out on us last night, it's your fault she has to hire another zookeeper. And remember, we want to hear all about your television career. *Every* detail."

I sighed. *Like your lives aren't more interesting? What is it about being on TV that makes people lose perspective?*

You're just a face on the screen, the voice that brings disaster and doom or tells you about a change in your trash pickup day or that the mayor is sleeping with his secretary. That's all. There was nothing about my life that was any more interesting than what was going on with Vaughn or, especially, with Audrey. The only difference is that my job involves splashing my face all over the airwaves. Other than that? My life is dull, quiet, and very uninteresting.

Not like Audrey's.

She never told us about Tommy North, of course. We found out when she sent us detailed memos about our responsibilities as brides-maids. When I say "memo," I mean *"Memo."* Audrey is nothing if not businesslike and organized. The memo set out the date, the deadlines, the dress, the cost of the dress, the shoes, the cost of the shoes, etcetera down to the name and telephone number of the hair salon for the day of the wedding.

"Memos?" I shrieked with laughter. Audrey could be so obsessive sometimes. "Audrey, this is your wedding and you're doing memos!"

"Audrey Jean? Is this a wedding or a work project?" Vaughn's voice cut through the litany of follow-up conference calls, meeting updates, and fitting schedules. "And turn off the damn speaker-phone!"

Vaughn hates speakerphones.

"Don't be an idiot! I just find it easier to manage the event as if it were a long-term project. I've got it blocked out on spreadsheets, with supporting memos and meeting updates and . . ."

Meeting updates? Audrey wasn't planning a wedding, she was or-chestrating a corporate merger.

"Audrey, since I haven't met the husband-to-be, is he as much of a corporate robot as you?"

Giggles filled the air. Audrey's giggles, now that was something new.

"No, he isn't," she said, and she sounded a little disappointed by that. "But I still love him."

And when we met him, we understood why. They say that opposites attract and I agree, but usually, they don't stay attracted for long because there isn't enough glue to keep them together amid all the differences. I wondered about this when I saw Tommy and Audrey together. Audrey had not strayed too far from type: Tommy was tall, slender, handsome, and impeccably dressed. He was a prep-school boy but his dad worked for Ford and he'd won a scholarship. Cornell and Vanderbilt followed and Tommy was now an engineer of a type that I can neither remember nor pronounce if I could! He was smart, articulate, funny, and warm. He liked classic jazz, camping, poetry, and staying home.

Physically, they were perfectly matched. They looked like a tan Ken and Barbie. But on an emotional level it was a marriage of opposites: something like pairing a brown bear with a gazelle. Their temperaments were very different and they disagreed about a lot of things, not the least of which was the wedding.

Tommy wanted a small, quiet, elegant affair with a honeymoon on Maui. Audrey wanted the wedding of the year with a send-off to New York, Paris, and London. They tossed a coin to settle the argument and Audrey won, of course. She probably supplied the coin.

In June (only the perfect wedding month would do for Audrey), Vaughn and I followed her down the aisle dressed in soft peach silk and satin gowns designed by somebody from Paris who lived in New York. We looked like apricots with legs. Audrey looked as if she'd stepped from the pages of *Bride's* magazine.

"My feet hurt, these flowers are making me sneeze, and I have to pee again," V mumbled through clenched teeth just before she stepped across the threshold of the church. "This isn't a wedding, it's an ordeal!"

Since I was struggling to keep from laughing and in a losing battle with the floral headpiece that Audrey had chosen for us to wear (it kept falling across my right eye) I was in no shape to argue. It was an ordeal.

But it was Audrey and we did it for her.

"She owes me for this," V had grumbled later at the reception.

It's so funny, that saying about the grass being greener. Audrey was an executive with a huge insurance company, her husband was an engineer, and she was now glowing with what Vaughn called—a snarl in her voice—the perfect pregnancy. She had a fabulous home, drove a Beemer that didn't look as if it ever got dirty, and had already decorated the nursery even though the baby's arrival was several months away. Audrey had baby clothes folded and tucked away in the drawers!

Vaughn had struggled through a bad marriage, pregnancy with twins that sent her to bed for three months, and, now, a teaching post with a small college where she could put her creative powers and bohemian attitudes to work. V had stories coming out of her ears about this professor or the twins or what a twit her ex-husband was. She twisted them into gothic mysteries, fantasies with alternate universes, and twisted romances in which the hero was a serial killer (her ex-husband in disguise). These were the things I wanted to hear about. Instead, all they wanted to talk about was me and my career. I guess it's the way life works. I'm on TV so that makes me more interesting than the average person. It was hard to convince them that it was just a job. And that the face you see on the evening news is really a mask.

By the time I graduated from Florida, I had hosted my own radio shows on the college station, emceed public television programs and school assemblies, and placed first in the Miss Central Florida pageant. (The swimsuit competition did me in.) I could operate behind the camera as a producer and, sometimes, as an engineer. But when I graduated, I found myself at the bottom of the food chain climbing my way up, working in the sales department of the local ABC affiliate.

I did my job, cut tapes, set up promos, coengineered the night owl news when the regulars were on vacation, and did my best to make myself indispensable, which no one ever is. I made coffee and copies, did makeup, and even drove the van for the breaking news segments. It took a while, but when one of the p.m. on-air slots opened up, I decided that my time had come.

If you are a scientist, you have a vitae; if you're a corporate slave, you have a résumé. The photographer has her portfolio, the chef has his book of recipes. In television, you need a tape.

I'd spent my first year at WKBR working in a cubbyhole in a corner of the basement. But it's who you know and how they can help you that propels my business. My work space was nearly invisible so I was hardly ever at my desk. What was remarkable was that no one seemed to miss me!

I used the ladies' room on the second floor—the one that female on-air staff used. I visited the first-floor water fountain because it was opposite the news director's office. The coffee machine in the basement made better coffee (perhaps because it was cleaned more often) but the career opportunities were a whole lot better at the coffee station just off the newsroom: the engineers, cameramen, producers, and reporters spent a lot of time congregating in the alcove. They talked trash, swapped factoids, and shared gossip. The stained gray-carpeted coffee nook was action central. That's where I had to be. Even though the thick, inky black coffee gave me heartburn.

But after six months of dodging my supervisor because I was rarely at my desk and chewing Tums to ward off the burning in my esophagus (I finally gave up and started bringing up my coffee with me from the basement), I got to know people. And they got to know me.

"Su, we're goin' to Cromwell's for some food after the six o'clock. Do you wanna come?"

"Hey, Su? Did you catch Channel Two last night? At eleven? What'd you think of the new weather guy?"

"Su, you wouldn't happen to have a can of hairspray, would you?"

"Ernie! Let me go out on a story?"

Ernie's eyebrows drew together. Ernie had amazing eyebrows. They looked like two woolly caterpillars having a torrid affair on his forehead. It was hard to look at them—you were either grossed out or trying to keep from laughing.

"Say what?"

"You heard me," I countered. "Let me go out on a story with you. Now is the perfect time."

Ernie dumped the contents of half a dozen pink packets into his coffee.

"It's Sunday morning, Penn. The dead zone. The two per week-end shootings are over, the GE strike is settled, and we've already covered the First Lady's visit to the museum dedication."

"Yeah, so? And you're loading up the van. Since using the company van for personal trips is a no-no, it's a safe bet that you're not going on vacation. What's up?"

"Shooting footage of the Walk for Peace. To go with a series that Torie's running next Friday."

"Who's going out? Jace . . . Wade? Bobbi?"

Ernie measured out a cup of nondairy creamer, dumped it into his quart-size commuter mug, and stirred. As the coffee turned to a putrid shade of grayish beige, I was reminded of the guy at the hardware store who mixed the paint I used in my bathroom.

"Nah. Just me and Jace."

Perfect, I thought. *A camera crew and a producer. All to myself. No pesky, paranoid anchors to deal with.*

"So let me tag along."

The furry mating caterpillars nestled closer together. They were starting to look obscene.

"What are you up to?"

I poured some motor oil into my brown Tasmanian Devil coffee cup (which was how I'd behave if I actually drank it!).

"I thought that I'd come along, observe, pick up a few pointers, and, maybe, do a practice tape. Just to get the feel of it."

"No, no, no!" The metal spoon scraped the sides of the stainless mug. "Ogden would have my head if I did that! You know how he is!"

I did. Our station was under new management. After three straight years of dismal ratings and running fourth in our market, the corporate office sent Ogden to shake up, clean up, and clear up WKBR. So far he'd done a decent job of keeping us in a constant state of anxiety and paranoia. Oh, yes, and he had implemented a set of stringent cost-saving measures: one pad of Post-it notes per person per month and one-ply toilet paper in the restrooms. *There's a lot that can be said about people who implement cost-saving measures using toilet paper, although none of it's good.*

"I just want to get my feet wet, Ernie," I said. "Who'll know? Jace won't care, he hates Ogden. It won't take any time—you'll already be set up. Look, I'll even buy my own tape."

"I don't think so." Ernie shook his head decisively and turned to walk away.

"I'll write my own script," I said. Actually, it was in my desk, typed and ready for just an opening like this one.

"Not this time, Su."

"You still owe me for babysitting the little Ernies."

I'd taken off the velvet gloves.

Ernie stopped abruptly then turned to look at me.

"You play dirty," he said.

One snowy February evening when Ernie and Mrs. Ernie were headed out to a party, I sat in for a sitter who'd come down with the flu. The "little Ernies," as I called them, were five and seven, looked exactly like their father, and were the best promo I could think of for mandatory sterilization. They are the kind of children for whom "time out" and counting to three mean nothing. At the end of that evening, I told Ernie that he owed me. Big time.

"Time to pay up, Ernie," I said, "a tape or your life."

Ernie grinned.

"Penn, I never knew you could be so ruthless."

———

"This is Suzanne Penn, reporting live from Waters Ford Park, downtown, on WKBR, the voice of the tristate."

I held my breath as the demo tape played.

"I can do this," I told the news director as he watched the tape.

"Yes. Yes, you can," he said, rubbing his chin with his hand.

Well, I remember thinking, *at least he didn't laugh and say "Hell no!"* His subdued reaction gave me hope.

It was 1977, the days before being a meteorologist was important, before you had four views of Doppler radar, satellite imaging, and The Weather Channel. We did weather forecasting the old-fashioned way—went to the window and stuck our heads out.

But the pause from Dan wasn't due to my lack of meteorological skills. It was because there had never been a black person on the air at the station before, at least not on a regular basis. The local Urban League director did a weekly community affairs program that the station aired at six a.m. on Saturdays (as if anyone who's up at that hour wants to hear about community affairs) and, occasionally, one of the football or basketball players would appear on the university's grid-iron or hoops sports show. Otherwise, the anchors were white, male, and forty. Dan knew I could do it. He just didn't know if the community would accept me. I guess he had a waking dream about KKK rallies outside the station or sacks of hate mail arriving daily at the receptionist's desk. And, of course, if the viewers clicked over to another station, we were sunk. A television show lives and dies by only one factor: the ratings—who is watching what and when.

These scenarios played across Dan's forehead like a silent movie.

"Look, Dan. It's the late evening weekend news. The weather's the last thing to air at eleven twenty-five p.m. Anybody who isn't at a bar or out for the evening isn't going to care. All they want to know is the temperature and whether or not it's going to rain or snow. Give me a shot at this."

There was a "Susan Dennis" on the a.m. show, a "Suzy Corelli" doing human interest stories for both noon and p.m., and me. I didn't look like either one of them, but I decided right then that "Susan Penn" wouldn't work. I would always be "the black girl who does the weather," so a name adjustment was also needed.

"And now, we'll hear from Suzanne Penn on the weather situation. Suzanne? What do you think? Will I be able to get in a round of golf before the rain rolls in tomorrow?" Eric's on-air voice was a marvel of human voice engineering. It was baritone, smooth, and his enunciation was so hard and so proper that it gave me a headache. Off-camera he was a tenor with a pronounced West Virginia twang. "Oil" sounded like "awell."

"Eric, I think you will be just fine. I am not expecting any rain or thunderstorms until well after nine o'clock. You'll make that birdie putt without any distractions on the weather front. Let's take a look at the national weather map, shall we?"

I eased the flat Ohio vowels out of my on-air voice, creating a vocal balancing act between a neutral Midwestern and the softness of a patrician Richmond, Virginia, drawl—without the drawl part!

There were a few phone calls the next morning inquiring about the previous weatherman who had departed for a station in Texas. The station manager received more mail than usual but it fell into two categories and the "that colored weather girl is all right" pile was a lot larger than the "Get that nigger off the air" stack. I stayed in front of the camera and eventually moved to reporter.

I met the girls (with the exception of Reenie) for brunch the morning after our reunion and endured no end of jokes and comments about my "intrepid girl reporter" status and, especially, my reporting in wild weather and in dangerous places.

"Are they trying to get you killed or something?" Audrey commented, scraping the butter off her French toast. She'd caught one of my broadcasts on a business trip. "Every time I talk to you, you're telling me that you were either almost struck by lightning or nearly shot in a gang fight cross fire!"

I shrugged my shoulders.

"It's just part of the job. It's no big deal, really. I want to hear about you, Tommy, and the baby."

"No, you don't, trust me," Vaughn interrupted, stabbing a sausage link with more violence than I'd ever give V credit for having. "She's seven months and the nursery is already wallpapered and furnished, she's got four cases of Pampers in the closet, ready and waiting. The baby clothes are folded and put away in the drawers! Shoot, my nursery for the twins was two large wicker baskets and a couple of banker's boxes."

Audrey does not just prepare for things. She overprepares.

Audrey's cheeks colored.

"I needed to get it ready in advance because . . . I'm going away on a couple of business trips and I didn't want to have to do all of that when I got back."

"Audrey! You shouldn't be traipsing around the country seven months pregnant! Will the airline let you fly?" I asked in amazement. I couldn't imagine even wanting to be on a business trip at that point, squeezed into one of those tiny seats. I love to travel but hate to fly.

"They wouldn't have let *me* fly," Vaughn said sarcastically. "I exceeded their weight requirements."

Audrey brushed off our concerns.

"I have a doctor's authorization. And besides, this is a very important proposal, a client I've been bringing along for months. I can't trust this project to anyone else."

Vaughn shook her head.

"Once you have the baby, your focus will be slightly altered, dear," she said knowingly. "All you think about is diapers, poop, feedings, and naps. Lots and lots of naps. Business meetings will fall by the wayside."

"Yes, I'm sure. But I'll just have to work that into my schedule," Audrey said briskly. "It's really not that hard, V, y'know? You get a planner, prioritize your tasks and fit them into a schedule, and block out a plan. Then you work the plan."

I howled. I didn't have children, but even I knew that Audrey was being just a little ambitious.

"Work the plan?"

"Listen to me, Hyphenated One," Vaughn advised sternly. "Babies make their own schedules, and I can tell you this, it won't fit into a Franklin planner!"

Audrey sipped her coffee and raised one professionally arched eyebrow.

"V, no offense, but you had two babies, not one, and your husband, well, I'll have Tommy and a nanny. It'll work out, you'll see."

Vaughn paused for a moment as if she wanted to say something, then thought better of it and drank her juice instead. I just looked at Audrey as we moved on to another topic. Sometimes Audrey's quest for perfection took her into fairy-tale land.

But this time, we were wrong. Audrey's baby was born on a Monday morning at eleven-thirty a.m. after her staff meeting and before lunch. She took a cab to the hospital directly from the office. Taylor was a beautiful seven-pound eight-ounce girl who had her father's square jaw and her mother's eyes. The following Monday, Audrey, Tommy, the baby and the nanny boarded a plane for San Francisco where Audrey gave a presentation and lecture. Right on schedule.

SIXTEEN

In the fall of 1985, I became the evening anchor at WKBR.

"This is Suzanne Penn. Have a good evening."

I had no social life. At least, no social life that belonged to me. I was the most social loner you ever met. I went everywhere: to fundraisers, openings, galas, and events. I emceed at banquets and was dunked at county fairs. I read to preschoolers at libraries and handed out (and received) community service awards. I served on this board and that board and did my duty as the "representative" for the station. I was invited to more cocktail parties, luncheons, and dinners than one calendar could hold, especially around Christmas and New Year's. I became the obligatory "holiday negro"—the person "of color" that society mavens and city fathers felt comfortable asking to their tony homes to show their friends how open-minded they were. I suppose they also felt that I could be trusted not to steal the silver.

"The Voice" of WKBR was always "on." I began to think of her as an alter ego, an entity that I pulled out of the closet and prepared every day like a clown dressing for the center ring. The routine never varied: two layers of makeup plus extra mascara; hair rolled, combed, sprayed; panty hose pulled up; suit; jewelry; nails polished; and throat cleared by snorting, sniffing, and singing "Three Blind Mice." "The Voice" had to be warmed up since it did not sound much like my own.

I didn't mind the solitude. After the noise and business of the day, with its camera cues, events, and posturing, it was nice to come home to a silent house. I didn't even have a cat's meow to break the peace. When the curtain went down, I was alone. Dating had become more of a chore than a pleasure. Many of the men who were interested in me were only interested in "Suzanne Penn, evening anchor for WKBR" not "Su Penn" from the east side of town. Aunt Leila visited from time to time and I enjoyed treating her to fancy dinners and outfits from Neiman-Marcus that she said were too fancy for her to wear. Audrey would call and we'd meet if she was in town on business. Vaughn would write; Reenie I heard about secondhand, and Bradley's name would pop up once or twice a year at first and then not at all. I'd see my mother occasionally at Aunt Leila's when I was home and it was like old times in a perverted way. Mom was either Women's Temperance sober or falling down drunk, there was never anything in between. The stunningly beautiful, sophisticated, erudite Mommy of my early childhood faded into the fog of myth like the tales of Amazons or King Arthur's knights.

When I was thirty-five years old, I met my father for the first time. Being on television is a little like winning the lottery. You find out you have relatives and friends you didn't know anything about. Of course I knew I had a father, everyone has one. But the man, who was pointed out to me when I was seven (he was standing on a street corner and I saw him out of a car window) and again when I was twelve, was never more than a blur. His name meant nothing to me since I had been given my mother's last name. He wasn't in my life since he was married and had other children, a tidbit I found out when I was a teenager and saw his oldest son at an all-city school track meet.

I'd been humiliated, came home in tears, and went to my room. I remember Mother visiting that evening (I was living with my aunt) and me not speaking to her and how hurt she was. I regret that now. Teenagers are about the only age group that can be moralistic and hedonistic all at the same time and never see the contradiction!

Aunt Leila read me the riot act after Mother left.

"Susan Elizabeth, is this the way I've raised you? To be disrespectful to your mother? Act like a spoiled brat?"

"No, ma'am," I mumbled.

My aunt's expression hardened. In her house, mumbling was not allowed.

"Girl, you'd better look sharp." Her words hit my ears like a razor strap. "Say again?"

"No, ma'am," I answered, sitting up on the bed and looking at her.

"If you want to keep those eyes, you'll stop rolling them. Now."

"Yes, ma'am."

"Now, I don't know what's the matter with you, but whatever it is, it will not manifest itself in you being a sullen, smart-mouth little brat, is that clear?"

"Yes, ma'am."

Aunt Leila studied me for a moment. I remember thinking that I would just keep my little secret to myself. I remember thinking, how could such an old woman understand anything about what I was feeling? About illicit love and teenage embarrassment and life's other trials. It's almost too ridiculous to think about now. My aunt was no more than thirty-eight years old, younger than I am now, and I think I'm still quite with it. Oh, well.

Her antennae had risen and she knew something was truly wrong with me. She abandoned her disciplinarian stance (arms folded firmly across her chest, feet planted into the doorway of my room, and the face of an army drill sergeant) and came into the room, smoothing out the chenille bedspread on my bed. She sat down next to me.

"What's wrong, Su, honey? What you got a burr up your butt about?"

I wasn't going to tell her at first, but then the feelings just filled me up and there was no place else for them to go. The tears spilled out of my eyes as I began, at first very slowly, then in a flood of words, to tell her about the track meet and the team from Westmoor and the kid who gleefully pointed out to me a boy running hurdles on another team, a boy named Albert Clay who was the oldest son of Howard Clay, the man who was my father who didn't marry my mother because he was already married. I rambled on about how embarrassed I was and how could Mommy have, well, *been with* a man who was married and had a family and what kind of woman *did that,* and Mommy was so beautiful and talented, why did she need to date a man who had a wife and how unfair it was to me and, well, what on earth was she thinking and . . .

Aunt Leila put her hand on my arm and gently squeezed it. Her touch was warm and dry. I stopped talking for a second and took the tissue that she handed me.

"Su, I wish I could explain everything to you. All of this grown-up . . . stuff that you have to figure out and carry around with you. It's so unfair. So unfair . . ." She wasn't talking to me now, even though her eyes held mine in a comforting embrace.

"It *is* unfair! People . . . talk about me . . . behind my back. They say that Mommy . . ."

When you're young, you're dead meat if "people" talk about you behind your back. Now that I'm older, in the public eye, and don't care a fart about other peoples' opinions (except during sweeps), I have an entirely different outlook!

"Susan," Leila said quietly, "this is grown-up business, your momma's business, but it's spilled all over you like Kool-Aid at a cookout. Let me . . . try to explain." My aunt's pretty face had twisted into a frown.

She was younger than Mommy by three years, and my mother—talented, brave, brilliant, and high-strung—had been the middle child, the second of the three girls but the centerpiece of the trio. Margaret, Aunt Peggy to me, Barbara, and Leila, the Penn girls, were tall, attractive, creative, and smart in school. Peggy followed Grandmother's example and became a teacher who married another teacher. She was also the handiest person I ever knew. Aunt Peggy could cook, sew, knit, crochet, paint, sculpt, and garden any expert under the table. At age sixty, she decided that golf looked interesting and took that up before she broke her hip.

Aunt Leila used her creativity to go into business for herself. Her beauty shop's waiting room was always full; no one could do hair like my aunt Leila or keep a house either. Leila Penn knew how to put things together. She did interior design before anyone knew what that was. Fresh flowers, Oriental rugs, and antique furniture were surroundings that I took for granted but Aunt Lei-lei was ahead of her time. She went to Santa Fe, fell in love with turquoise, and came back with two drawers full of Zuni and Navajo jewelry. She decided that Rembrandt and Manet were nice but there was a place for Elijah Pierce and Romare Bearden and Elizabeth Catlett. And then there was Momma, who danced and sang and read Sartre and had cocktails with James Baldwin and got pregnant without a husband.

"It wasn't all her fault, baby," Aunt Leila began. "I know what you're thinkin', it takes two to tango, and you're right. But your momma was in love. She thought Howard was in love, too." Leila's face darkened when she spoke his name. "She had no way of knowing he had knocked up some little girl from Louisville and was already engaged. She didn't find that out until she came back from New York, pregnant with you, and there he was. Married, a baby, and a wife set up over there on the Hilltop."

I probably listened to this story with my mouth open. It was fascinating, like a soap opera, only it was my mother's life. How on earth had she felt when she'd come back to find her boyfriend already married and with a baby on the way?

"Barbara Louise was devastated, just torn up," my aunt continued. "She cried for weeks, she wouldn't eat anything or talk to anyone. Mother and Dad were heartbroken and a little Victorian about it. You know, sin, shame, fallen women. But Peggy and I, well, Peggy was already married. She offered to take you, raise you as hers and no one would know any different." Leila stroked my hair and smiled. "I would have taken you myself except, well, I was only seventeen when you were born. There wasn't a lot I could do except provide moral support for Barbie."

"W-Why didn't she just give me to Aunt Peggy? Then . . . then people would, well, not talk so much. Make such a big deal about, well, you know . . ."

Leila's light brown eyes held mine for a moment.

"Your momma wouldn't hear of it. She said you were her baby, and she would take care of you." Aunt Leila paused for a moment, probably thinking about how things actually turned out. "And she did. For a while." She said these words softly. "You were always her shining little girl, her treasure. You will always be her treasure,

Susan Elizabeth, don't you forget it. She loves you more than she loves herself, even though nowadays, well, things are hard now. But don't you worry about what people say. Honey, if I had a half penny for every discouragin' word, I could retire and buy myself an Eldorado convertible! In fire engine red!"

For all my mother's problems—and they were legion—she was there. Most of the time. And when she wasn't, I knew she wanted to be. My father had spent the better part of my life pretending I didn't exist.

And since he did not come within one hundred feet of me in the years when I was growing up, he was barely a person as far as I was concerned, not even real. I had never heard his voice. He was a man in a crowd, a man waiting for a bus, a name on my birth certificate: *Howard M. Clay.*

"Suzanne?" The receptionist of the month was a twenty-year-old strawberry blonde who talked through her nose and whose voice squeaked. She sounded like a mouse with tonsil trouble. "Suzanne, there is a Reverend Ward Clay in the lobby to see you. He doesn't have an appointment."

Who? I couldn't be blamed for not recognizing his name. After all, I'd only seen it as "Howard Clay." Not "Reverend" anything or "Ward." I paused long enough for the mouse to come back on the phone.

"He says that you'll know what this is about," she squeaked.

No, I don't know what it's about and what does he want? I was between broadcasts, it was the break when I kicked off my heels, read over my scripts, and worked on any remarks or speeches that I had coming up in the next few days. Some days I lived for this three-hour block of time between broadcasts because, outside of going home, it was the only quiet time I ever got.

And now, he was here. And I would know what "this is about."

I had forgotten that he had been called to the ministry, moved here, and now headed a mega-church on the northwest side of the city.

I fumbled around for my shoes, which had somehow escaped to the far corners of the floor beneath my desk. I was more angry than nervous. It was funny, had Howard Clay shown up ten or fifteen years ago, I would have felt differently. Now I wasn't even curious.

The Reverend was thirty-five years late on this appointment.

The mouse didn't need to point him out since he was the only black man in the lobby. He was neatly dressed in a dark suit, white shirt, and burgundy tie. His salt-and-pepper hair was closely cut and he wore the same mustache that I'd seen in the one picture I had of him with my mother. He was grinning from ear to ear and held out his hand for me to shake. I did not take it.

"Reverend Clay, won't you sit over here?" I gestured toward an isolated part of the lobby where the wall of windows showcased the station's view of the lake.

The Reverend's voice was deep, his enunciation practiced, a perfect imitation of Charlton Heston in his role as Moses.

"Ho, ho, ho," he chuckled heartily. "There's no need for us to stand on ceremony, is there, Suzanne? You can call me 'Dad' if you'd like." He smiled magnanimously. I was as tall as he was. Thank God I'd inherited Barbara Penn's height. I was able to look him straight in the eye. Something told me that he didn't like that much.

And I'll tell you another thing. I would have rather choked and died right there than call him "Dad."

"What can I do for you?" I used my on-air voice, talking as if I was covering a breaking news story on the six o'clock news. "I don't have a lot of time, Reverend. If you'd called for an appointment, it might have been better. Right now, I'm preparing for a speech I'm giving this evening."

The Reverend seemed a little put off by my straightforwardness but his smile's wattage did not dim.

"Yes, well, that's just fine. In fact, that's what I wanted to talk with you about. I see you everywhere, I'm so proud of you! You're on the TV, speaking at the museum opening, and emceeing the symphony programs. I said to myself, 'Ward, your girl is God's blessing.' " He lowered his voice and took a step closer to me. I took two steps back. "You see, the Lord gave me a vision. He told me that I need to illuminate my past transgressions more, to serve my congregation in a more authentic manner." He clasped his hands together in his lap and assumed a practiced and thoughtful pious expression. The Charlton Heston Moses-on-the-mountain voice lowered to a dignified baritone whisper. "It's up to me to make myself an example, to show them what's possible."

Reenie was the one who used to say, "What shit. He makes me want to puke." Her words would have been so appropriate right now.

"You are my daughter, there's no denying that. Why, you look just like my sister, Geraldine. Just like her. So I said, I'll ask Susan if she'll speak at my anniversary service on Sunday the sixteenth. I want to show my congregation that even a child conceived in sin can rise above the dark waters and become a beacon to all!" He was beaming again; I don't know, maybe it was divine light. And maybe it was the bullshit lit up by methane. Either way, I wasn't touched in quite the way he expected.

A child conceived in sin? Rise above the dark waters? Was he kidding? I am not a violent person, but for just one second I looked around for a blunt object. What the hell was this fool talking about? I stood up.

"*Reverend* Clay, I'm afraid you have wasted your valuable time. And mine. Yes, I understand that you are my father. But I'll be thirty-six years old in March. I am amazed that it took you that long to acknowledge your past transgression, as you call it. But I'm not kidding myself. I know that the only reason you brought your pompous fat ass in here is because I'm the evening anchor on TV. If I worked the graveyard shift at Seven-Eleven, you wouldn't know my name."

The air went out of Reverend Clay's sails faster than when you pop a balloon with a pin.

"Well, I, now, girl, you need to be respectful . . ."

"In the first place, I am not a girl. In the second place, respect must be earned."

"Now, listen here . . ."

Oh, no. He was not going to pull that respect your mother and father stuff on me.

"I've an *r* word for you: responsibility. What about providing for one's family, one's daughter? And I'm not talking about money! You could have given me some of yourself! Help with homework! Attended the games where I went to school or even take me to the zoo. You could have been a father to me. I guess I just wasn't important enough then."

I had a million other examples to give this man of things that fathers do, but life is really short and, as I'd already informed the fool, I had a speech to prepare.

"I am not a child conceived in sin, rising above the dark waters to stand in front of your congregation and make apologies for where I came from and give you any credit at all for where I am now! "

The mouse, my producer, the FedEx man, and the two salesmen in the lobby had given me their undivided attention. It was as if an African elephant had charged into the atrium.

"I will not be the poster child for your salvation. You have transgressions that you want to parade in front of your flock? Be my guest. But don't count on me to be a part of the show. You're on your own."

"Now, girl . . ."

I had turned to leave but when he said "Now, girl . . ." in what he thought was a stern, fatherly tone, I whirled around and faced him again. I must have looked like a Gorgon because he stepped back.

"Reverend Clay, time has marched on. Perhaps you haven't noticed that you completely missed the days when calling me 'girl' was appropriate. I am very busy today. If you will excuse me."

"B-But I . . ."

I left the Reverend, the mouse, and the rest of them staring after me with their mouths open in a silent "O." I returned to my desk, kicked off my shoes again, and reached for the Pepsi can that I'd left on my filing cabinet. It was still cold. Good.

That evening, I attended a banquet at the university. I was the mistress of ceremonies. I smiled at whoever was talking to me and went over my notes in my head at the same time. It was a reception honoring a group of scientists who'd been honored with an international award in paleoanthropology. I was introducing the honorees, the university president, and the mayor.

"Yes, yes, that's true," I answered one of the questions that had been put to me. "I will introduce doctors Chang and Patel, I just hope I'm able to do justice to their topics. I've been practicing the pronunciation." There was insincere laughter all around and, gratefully, I grabbed a glass of water from a passing waiter.

"Suzanne! Suzanne! There's someone I'd like to introduce to you." I recognized the distinctive voice of Kiki Hughes Porter, society maven, wife of Duncan Porter, who had more money than God's mother. Kiki was the grand patron of all lost causes, fine arts, and any charitable ventures her husband told her to be the patron of. She bought her clothes in New York and Paris, got her face lifted in Cincinnati, and had homes in Palm Springs, California; Naples, Florida; and Jackson Hole, Wyoming. She was born dirt poor in a no-name town in a no-name holler in southwest West Virginia. The distinctiveness of her speaking voice was to her credit and that of her voice coach. She sounded as if she'd been born in Atlanta, reared in Charleston (South Carolina not West Virginia), and educated in the U.K. It was quite a creation. So when Kiki said "Suzanne!" it sounded more like "Suzzz-Ahhhhnnnn." Good grief.

"Suzanne, dear, I have someone here who thinks he knows you! One of our esteemed honorees, as a matter of fact." Kiki was beaming. The tall man next to her blushed slightly.

He was pecan-colored with bright, dark eyes that greeted me warmly from behind stylish wire-rimmed eyeglasses. His face was lean and clean-shaven; his dark hair, graying slightly at the temples, was cut close to his head. He was smartly dressed in a dark suit, light blue shirt, and conservative tie. He didn't look academic at all and smiled at me warmly as he took my hand in both of his. I was startled.

"This is Dr. J. Otis Lawrence, Suzanne. He says he knows you well."

"That's not what I said," the doctor piped in. His voice was smooth and cultured. Something about it made my stomach quiver. "I said that Miss Penn and I have met before." He didn't let go of my hand. I didn't want him to.

"I'm glad to meet you, Doctor," I said, trying to figure out where the hell I could have met such a delicious-looking person and not remembered. "But I'm sorry to say, I . . . don't remember . . . I meet so many people . . ." *Lame, Su, really lame. Like you're Jane Pauley or somebody.*

He laughed and started to respond but was sideswiped in the conversation by Kiki's nasal twitter. She would not be relegated to a sideline position in our conversation.

"Dahling, he said you went to school together! Now, rewind your memory tapes—"

"Mrs. Porter, it was a long time ago," the Doctor interrupted again. "And Miss Penn meets hundreds of people, so many faces." His smile was so friendly and so inviting that I was getting lost in it.

"Doctor, I told you to call me 'Kiki'!"

"I-I . . . uh . . ." I don't know what I was trying to say. *Oh, this is good. An anchorwoman who stutters. Wonderful.*

"Don't worry about it, Miss Penn . . ."

"Su," I said. *Now, that was an interesting response. I hardly ever told anyone to call me "Su."*

"Su, please don't let Mrs., er, Kiki intimidate you. We met a hundred years ago at Florida U. At a dance. I'm not surprised that you don't remember . . ."

The expression on my face told him that I did. I felt my jaw drop open and my eyes widen. *Oh, God! Jimmy Lawrence, the nerd.*

"B-But, I thought your name was . . ."

"The 'J' is for James. My family and friends call me 'Jimmy,' as you know. But professionally, because my dad is also a doctor, I go by J. Otis."

I was having a nuclear hot flash at thirty-six. Of all the people to run into, Jimmy Lawrence. The boy I had dropped like dog turd at a college party and hardly ever spoke to again. And now, here he was, an award-winning scientist, a college professor, internationally esteemed scholar, and . . . *Could the floor open up now and swallow me whole?*

"Oh, tell me *all* about it," Kiki gushed. I wanted to take her fourteen-carat headlight-size solitaire pendant and stuff it down her throat. "Were you two lovers? College sweethearts?" she asked, as if interviewing us for *Access Hollywood*.

Jimmy took it all in stride.

"You have an active imagination. I was the campus nerd. You know, like *Revenge of the Nerds*? And Su, here, was the voice of

WKFU. We were . . . acquaintances, only." His eyes met mine with a look of conspiratorial glee.

"You're being very kind," I said, feeling like an idiot. I wanted to say more, to apologize, and to grovel at his feet for being such a bitch back then. In all my life, I've tried not to be mean to people, at least not to people who don't deserve it. But Jimmy was one of the exceptions. And now that "goes around comes around" adage that my mother and aunts had drummed into me as a child was proving true.

"Dr. Lawrence? Dr. Lawrence." A student appeared at the doctor's elbow. "Would you mind taking your seat on the dais? You, too, Miss Penn. We're getting ready to start."

"Will you excuse me?" he asked politely. His smile was so welcoming that I wanted to sigh.

"Of course," I said.

Kiki gave me a broad wink of her Bambi-size eyelashes as she tucked her arm into his and escorted him to the dais.

I was miserable throughout the evening, but not for the reason you might have thought. I managed to get through the introductions of Drs. Chang and Patel without stumbling over the complicated technical names of their projects, papers, and awards. And I listened intently to the introduction of J. Otis Lawrence, Ph.D., cum laude, Florida University; summa cum laude, Columbia; Fellowship at Oxford, research studies and accolades from every corner of the wide world. When he spoke, clearly, concisely, and in plain English (for which I was grateful), he drew us all in with analogies of his very complicated subject to daily life and ordinary things and the future of our precariously balanced planet. Amazing. He was funny, he was bright, and he was profound.

And I had treated him like a used tissue in college. *Could it get any worse?* I had asked myself. Yes, it could. I was interviewing the good doctor tomorrow for the evening news. *Great.*

SEVENTEEN

"Doctor, let me start by congratulating you and your team on your award and appointment. You must be very proud."

"Thank you, Suzanne, we feel honored to have been recognized by the committee in this way."

"Now, if you don't mind, Dr. Lawrence, for the sake of our viewers, and, frankly, for my information as well, would you mind explaining geosocial anthropology?"

Thank God for cheat sheets and teleprompters! I had stayed up nearly all night practicing the pronunciation of the theory and formula that Jimmy had developed so I wouldn't sound like an idiot. As he explained his theory, its application, and related his travels, his entire face lit up. His eyes sparkled with excitement from behind his glasses. Unlike most interviews, where I stay in focus, quartering my attention between my producer's voice in my earpiece and my notes and subject, this time, I was completely taken away. Jimmy's anecdotes triggered a memory of two college freshmen sitting on the steps, chatting on a muggy fall evening in Henderson, Florida, years ago when he and I had talked briefly at the dance and he was excited about the experiments he was doing in geology class. His enthusiasm was infectious then just as it was now. He had hooked me. I began to smile, too, leaning forward to fill in with additional questions.

"Doctor, how does that relate to the global warming situation that we hear so much about?"

"I'm glad you asked that," Jimmy responded, beaming at me as if I was the most important person in the room. "Let me explain it this way . . ." I felt the breath catch in my throat and heat rise up from the soles of my shoes. As he explained the fascinating interdependence of geography, climate, and Neanderthal bones, all I could think about was how firm his shoulders might be and whether or not . . .

"Thank you, Dr. Lawrence." I turned to the camera to my right to acknowledge the red cue light that had just come on. "If you are interested in hearing more from Dr. J. Otis Lawrence, he is speaking this Saturday at noon at the Davis Auditorium. The lecture is free and open to the public. I encourage all of you to come out and hear this remarkable man. Back to you, Dean."

The cue light clicked off and I sat back in my chair. Thank God, we were taping! The studio was quiet except for laughter in the production booth and chuckles coming from Jose who came from behind the camera, his wide brown face split with a huge grin. He was fanning himself with a sheaf of papers.

"Maybe we should leave you guys alone?" he asked facetiously, taking the minimike from my hand. "There was so much heat in here, I'm surprised you didn't set off the smoke detectors!"

"You know what, Jose? You can kiss my . . ."

The producer's voice came over the intercom.

"Suzanne, why don't you guys get a room, for Christ's sake? We have summer interns in the studio! There are children around." I could hear raucous laughter in the background. I'd never live this down. *Was it that obvious?*

"Yeah, this spot airs during prime time, Suzanne, there'll be kids watching! *Passion* doesn't air until nine o'clock, remember?" More laughter at the reference to an especially cheesy and racy evening soap. I felt my cheeks burning.

"You all need to quit! Behave yourselves! We have a distinguished guest here. Nobel Prize material!" I yelled back at them, embarrassed. I fumbled with my script as I stood up. I didn't want to look at Jimmy, who was being divested of his microphone. I mean, really, I hadn't seen him in almost twenty years! And when I had known him, well, it was still too horrible to think about.

Jimmy's eyes sparkled. He touched my hand gently and leaned in close to my face. I think I would have kissed him right then and there if it hadn't been for the audience.

"It's not a bad idea, you know," he said quietly so that Jose wouldn't hear.

My breath caught in my throat when I looked up at him.

"What do you mean?"

"Getting a room," he said simply.

Oh, dear.

OK, it's not like I hadn't had sex since Bradley, I had. And it isn't as if I hadn't dated or had relationships, I had. But . . . I hadn't *loved* making love to any man since Bradley. And I surely hadn't *loved* anyone.

I was Suzanne Penn, the voice of WKBR, high profile and very high maintenance. As such, I was asked out by pillars of the community (married and unmarried), pro athletes, entertainment types, high-powered executives and lawyers, and every other man who thought I'd make the perfect accessory for his style and status but no substance lifestyle. In this business, you learn quickly that, for these men, you're on the same level as the Porsche two-seater that he has in his garage. And I didn't want that for myself. I wanted to mean more, to *be* more. And so I would date them a few times and/or sleep with them a few times, until their true stripes showed through, and then move on or retreat back to my lair. As V's daughter, Rebecca, would say, kick 'em to the curb. I'd been doing it for so long, with long stretches of celibacy in between, that it had become a pattern in my love life. And I had gotten quite comfortable with it, too.

Once you get over the initial shock of being naked with someone, the sex part comes easy. But the intimacy, the touching, the wanting to hold and be held, the talking about nothing and everything until three in the morning, well, that's the hard part. I'd sleep with a man and then want him to leave as soon as possible. *Get out of my sight, don't ask me to scramble you any eggs and no, don't call me for lunch tomorrow. I'll call you if I want you.* It was strange. What should have been a prelude always became an epilogue.

You've got to trust people and that's my problem, I don't trust. I guess I've been hurt too often by the people closest to me to do that. I loved Mommy but she could never get it together. My father isn't even on my radar screen. Bradley, well, the less said about him, the better, and yes, I know, I need to get over that. Irene, I'm getting there. The girls would always be there, but when it came to men, well . . . Somehow I guess I just didn't feel like I could be loved, and wanted to get out before someone discovered my ugly secret.

"Suzz-anne," Audrey would chide me, exaggerating my on-air name as she liked to do. "Sweetie pie, I've never seen anything like you. You're like a black widow spider. If they don't get out quick enough, you eat 'em. And I ain't talkin' about oral sex either!"

"It's not like that," I'd protest, looking away but not before catching a flashing glare from those eyes of hers.

"Oh, please. Tell your lies to someone who can't see through them. Honestly, Suzz honey, please tell me this is not about Bradley. You should have been over his sorry ass a long time ago. Life does go on, you know."

I know. No, it wasn't about Bradley. It was all of it—Mommy, Howard Clay, all of them.

But now there was Jimmy Lawrence. This was something new.

I get a little squirmy here. I am not the kind of girl who kisses and tells, not even to V, Audrey, and Reenie. Audrey calls me a prude, V says I'm Victorian. And Reenie, well, we're polar opposites. She'll tell you damn near everything (except when she was dating Brad) and I tell you as little as possible. I love men, I love sex, and, if I may say so myself, I think I'm pretty proficient at, er, the techniques you need to . . . oh, hell. What I'm trying to say is that I'm not going to give you a finger-by-finger description of what Jimmy and I did, where we did it, how it tasted, smelled, and, well, you know. Honestly, if you're reading this, then you're a grown-up and I don't have to tell you how to have sex, do I? I stand by my motto, borrowed from some nineteenth-century libertine known for her affairs and free-wheeling behavior.

"It doesn't matter what you do, just don't do it in the streets and frighten the horses."

Amen.

Jimmy and I did things that would have frightened horses, disturbed small children, and sent old ladies to the hospital with heart palpitations. We would have had middle-aged men reaching for their blue pills and college students rereading the *Kama Sutra* to find out more about the Monkey Armadillo position! And you'll just have to take my word for it.

I've never before had an affair in the town where I live. It was kind of fun. I have a spacious two-bedroom condo but I live in the 'burbs and we didn't want to drive that far, so we went to his hotel instead, making one detour to a Walgreen's that was on the way. There was no prelude, preamble, or chapter one; we left a trail of clothing from the door of the suite to the foot of the bed and beyond. I am proud to say, with a slight blush on my cheeks, that the bed was a total wreck when we finished. I was so tangled up in the sheets that I nearly broke my leg trying to get out to go to the bathroom! At two in the morning we ordered room service. At four in the morning we twisted up the sheets again and then slept until the *Today* show came on. It was wonderful.

"This little piggy went to market . . ."

"Jimmy, stop! You're tickling me!" I tried to squirm away.

"Ummmm . . . this little piggy went home. I like the hot pink nail polish."

A warm, wet feeling engulfed my middle toe as Jimmy gently took it into his mouth.

"Eek! Jimmy!"

"And this little piggy said . . ."

"If you don't stop it, I'm going public on your . . . personal habits."

Jimmy's face burst into a wide grin, the corners of his eyes crinkled. Without his Professor Owl glasses, he looked just like a ten-year-old boy. Well, almost.

"Don't tell the Nobel committee, it would ruin my reputation." He tickled my little toe. I nearly jumped out of the bed.

"So when do we get to have this little island of sex and serenity again, Su Susan Suzanne?"

I closed my eyes and snuggled down into the covers, enjoying the foot massage.

"Hmmm . . . you tell me. You're the world traveler. Oooo . . . Jimmy! Quit it." I didn't mean one word of that.

"I go to Beijing then Hong Kong at the end of next week. You, on the other hand, will anchor the evening news at six and eleven and lend your elegant presence to the Black and White Ball on the tenth, the Joiners Luncheon on the twenty-third, and the opening of the Margaret Duncan Porter gallery on . . ."

"Wait a minute, how is it that you know my entire schedule for the next month?"

He grinned.

"I have three words for you: Kiki Hughes Porter. Gave me every detail of your professional and public life . . . for the next six months."

"Oh, Lord," I moaned. Jimmy was working his way up my leg with soft kisses and tiny licks that left my skin damp and warm in the icy air-conditioned room.

"Oh, Lord, is right," he echoed. "Given the data presented, I have calculated that the soonest you and I will be on the same continent again at the same time is when Jupiter, Uranus, and Europa line up in a triangular configuration. The year 2014, July 14, at 2:03 p.m. EST to be exact."

I stroked his cheek.

"That's not good, is it?"

He shook his head.

"No. But I'm a scientist. It's my job to figure out how things work, put them together, make something happen. If I can trace the foot-steps of a man who lived thousands of years ago from a remote valley in Tanzania along the coast of the Indian Ocean into what is now Jordan, then I can figure this out, too." He gathered me into his arms and kissed my earlobe. "I've been in love with you since that night at Florida when we met. And now that I've got you"—he nuzzled the back of my neck—"I'm not letting go. How about meeting me in the Gobi Desert? In four weeks?"

I giggled. He was tickling me again in a very improbable place.

"W-Where?" I stammered. That felt so good.

"The southeast corner of the Gobi Desert. A small village, no telephones but lots of camels."

I closed my eyes and sighed again.

"Couldn't we just meet in Timbuktu in March?"

"Timbuktu, it is," he replied. "It'll be a little warm but I'll bring a fan and we won't need . . . clothes . . ."

Get over it! Shake it off, suck it up; the self-help books and the airwave head doctors have a lot of catchphrases that they use to help people. They think. But the tough love approach never worked for me, it was too blunt. You don't heal by bludgeoning. And the "time heals all wounds" thing, well, my wounds had scabbed over long ago but not healed. There was still a lot of gooey, sticky guilt-feeling-sorry-for-myself-blaming-other-people stuff beneath my polished surface.

Audrey would have said, "See? All you needed was a decent man to help you get over that Reenie-Bradley thing." But Audrey is one of those "get over it" people and you can see what it does to her.

Getting a man is not the cure-all for everything. But forgiveness is. And those of us who hold on to extra unmatched pieces of luggage filled with guilt and blame have to say it aloud in order to get well: "I forgive you. I forgive me. I'm going forward." In my case, meeting Jimmy again showed me that forgiveness is a powerful thing. I'd been carrying around all this bitterness and pain from nearly twenty years ago, twenty years! Angry and disappointed with my parents for their failures, and thinking that it was my fault at the same time. Angry at Bradley for not being the person I thought he was. Angry and hurt at Reenie, not because she was drawn in by Brad, no, I couldn't blame her for that. It wasn't her fault. No, I was mad at Reenie, jealous of Reenie because of the child she'd had and the child I'd lost and would not have again. And even though there was no amount of money that could induce me to go back to Bradley Garcia again in this life or any other, I still carried around the anger and the hurt.

And skinny, nearsighted, nerdy Jimmy Lawrence fell in love with a snotty very shortsighted girl on a sultry night in Florida, kept a stiff upper lip when she ran out on him, and still carried the torch for so many years until he won her back.

"Jimmy, every time I think about it, I'm mortified. How can you stand to be in the same room with me?" I'd asked one night in Paris as we watched the boats sashay along the Seine.

He picked up my hand and kissed it.

"It's not complicated, Su," he said simply. "Nothing like my geological formulas. I love you, that's all."

And then, of course, there was my mother.

"Susan, honey?" Aunt Leila always called me that, but the tone in her voice told me that there was something else that she wanted to talk about. "It's your mother, sweetie. She's . . ."

Mommy had been bouncing back and forth between sobriety and Scotch and sodas for so long that I was used to it. Lately, she'd been living on the quiet side, working every day as a secretary, going home at night to her little apartment and her cats. I flew home expecting to find Mommy resting comfortably at Mt. Carmel; my aunts Peggy and Leila fussing and feuding over who would do what and when and the cats in a tizzy. Instead, I found Mommy nearly comatose, my aunts inconsolable, and the cats behaving themselves in eerie silence.

"I d-don't understand," I stammered to Aunt Leila. "I thought . . . She told me there was nothing to worry about." I looked down at Mommy. It was so strange to see her with her eyes closed.

We stood in the hall. Aunt Leila dabbed her eyes with a dainty cloth handkerchief embroidered with irises.

"That's what she told everyone; me, Peggy, her boss, everybody. We just had no idea that things were as . . . serious as they are."

The hospital had cranked up the air-conditioning so I was cold. But my chest tightened and I struggled to catch my breath.

"How serious is it?"

"She's . . . The doctor says her liver's gone and her kidneys aren't far behind. Bless her heart, I think she was just holding on . . ." Aunt Leila's eyes filled with tears. "I think she was just waiting for you to get here."

I ran down the hall, pushed the button for the elevator, and nearly mowed over a little old lady who was trying to get off. I ran outside into the hot sunshine into one of the courtyards and just stood there, coughing and gasping for breath and wondering what the hell was wrong with me.

I looked up at the statue of St. Francis. It was silent. The Madonna at the end of the walkway was silent, too.

"OK, God, now's your chance. Wherever you are, you need to tell me what I'm supposed to feel here. How I'm supposed to deal with this!" I bellowed. I was so pissed off. I was distraught. I felt guilty and sick and relieved and stupid, very stupid.

My mother had been drunk for much of my life. She had arm wrestled with her demons and, most of the time, she'd lost. And I had been left alone at night, and forced to live on crackers and water and clean up my mother when she'd passed out on the bathroom floor. But the few times that Mommy won her rounds, I had shimmering memories of a beautiful, dancing princess who sang and recited poetry and decorated her apartment like a trendy nightclub just to make me smile. A woman who had told me I could fly jets, write masterpieces, and walk to the tip of Argentina if I wanted to.

I had hated her, I had loved her, I was ashamed of her and she'd made me proud. Through my tears, I saw her face in the clouds and wondered how on earth I could match these things up and make them even.

"Why didn't she tell me she was so sick?" I'd asked Aunt Peggy earlier, after I spoke with the doctor.

Peggy shook her head.

"Honey, she didn't tell anyone. And, of course, she would never have told you."

"Why not?" I asked, angry. What gave my mother the right to withhold this from me?

Peggy smiled.

"She didn't want to disrupt your life. She didn't want you worrying any more about her, running down here all the time. Susan, she was so proud of you. So proud. All the time, she'd talk about you on television and how poised and professional you were and . . ." Peggy swallowed and tried to bat away the tears that began to roll down her cheeks. "You were all she talked about. And when she talked about you, her whole face lit up."

Mommy died when I wasn't looking. I'd stood up to stretch my legs and rub a kink out of my back. I looked out the window. The parking lot was full, it was two o'clock in the afternoon. A florist's truck pulled up and the man unloaded bushels of flowers. Nurses stood in the courtyard sipping Cokes and chatting. People came in and out of the automatic doors. And, not wanting to bother me, she just slipped away.

Two days earlier, the last time she was awake, she smiled at me and patted my face. She was talking then, not much, but a little. Mostly, she listened to her sisters chitchat and fuss and she watched me with a small smile and glistening eyes.

"So pretty," she'd said, patting my face. "So smart and pretty. My baby."

I held her hand to my heart and cried for the mommy that she was and the mommy that she wanted to be. And I let it be enough.

———

It had been nearly twenty years since I'd said more than four words to Reenie. I was tired of carrying around that baggage. I had finally emptied out the suitcase that carried all the stuff I'd felt about my mother. It was now time to get the bitterness, hurt, and jealousy out, too. I needed the room for a two-week trek to Italy with Jimmy.

PURPLE TIGERS, CLASS OF 1971!
LET'S PARTY LIKE IT'S 1999!
TWENTY-YEAR CLASS REUNION
JUNE 14–15, 1991

I was supposed to meet Audrey and Vaughn at six-thirty at the bar of the Hilton where we were having our reunion but I went looking for Reenie instead. I had a few things to say to her and I didn't want an audience.

From my window, I saw Reenie's red Firebird zoom into the parking lot. Reenie was a Realtor/interior decorator/wedding planner now and her flare for the dramatic extended to every part of her life, of course. Even to her flashy car. So Reenie.

As the fates would have it, I passed Bradley and his girl du jour on the way to the parking lot.

"Susan," he said stiffly, clutching his lady friend's arm a little more tightly, as if afraid I would snatch him away and declare him mine. *In his dreams.*

"Bradley," I answered and kept walking. He looked back, I could feel the heat of his eyes on my back. I didn't look back. Life goes forward, always.

Reenie came toward me looking like a million bucks. God, I had missed her.

Still tiny, still with the to-die-for figure and still gorgeous. The shiny black mane was chin length this year and the makeup more subdued. She wore a snazzy purple silk pantsuit and heels, always heels, to give height to the five feet three and three-quarters (don't miss that extra quarter inch!) that she claimed. She was walking briskly like a businesswoman with places to go and people to see. She nearly skidded to a halt when she saw me walking toward her.

To her credit, Reenie had not sought me out during our years of estrangement. She knew better than anyone how hurt I was. Hell, if I want to be honest about it, Reenie had moved on from Bradley when she found out she was pregnant. She hadn't intended for things to turn out the way they did. But she'd been adult about it, married, and raised Javier, who I'd heard was bright, handsome, and funny like his irreverent mother. And now, here she was, looking at me as if expecting the wrath of God to fall on her straight, small, elegant shoulders and not afraid to face it.

"Oh! Hi, Su." Her eyes flickered as they met mine and then she stepped aside to let me pass.

"Reenie, can I talk with you for a second?"

Reenie was startled. Her eyes widened, then she took a deep breath as if preparing for an assault.

"OK."

"It's nice to see you."

She paused a second.

"It's . . . nice to see you, too."

We looked at each other for a few seconds and then the words spilled out.

"Reenie, look, I'm sorry. I'm really sorry. It's been almost twenty years and that's too long to be stupid about things. You got . . . caught up in a net and, well, I did, too. Bradley had us both where he wanted us only, well, only I think things may have been tougher for you than they were for me." I put the sticky Florida night out of my mind for the moment. That was a secret I had shared with only one person and he was now taking water samples on an oasis in the northwestern edge of the Sahara. "Can you forgive me? Can we . . . be friends again? I miss . . . the ways things were."

Reenie Keller is emotional, passionate, loud, and straightforward. Don't let her delicate size fool you. This gal learned to fight from her brothers, she's tough and she doesn't cry. Except for now. Her dark eyes filled with tears.

"Oh, Su, I've missed you. And I'm sorry. Sorrier than I can say, you just can't imagine . . . Bradley and I . . . Susan, I wanted to call you so many times . . . to tell you how awful I felt and how sorry . . ."

I left tear tracks on her beautiful purple silk jacket. She left mascara stains on the lapel of my Anne Klein blouse. We sniffled, giggled, sobbed, and hugged. Then, arm in arm, we walked into the ballroom of the Hilton, grinning like two fools, gossiping about how *old* some people looked (how fat some others looked), and how Bradley's new girl was wearing very tacky shoes. Vaughn and Audrey were waiting for us, Vaughn's mouth in a huge "O" and Audrey looking as if the wind would blow her away.

The four of us bunched together in a bundle of hugs, kisses, tears, and no regrets. We were twelve years old again and going to the sixth-grade dance. We were seventeen again and riding on the homecoming parade float. That was the year I loaned my pink mohair sweater to Vaughn and she spilled hot chocolate on it. It was the year we got in trouble for squeezing nine people into a 1968 Mustang. The memories were delicious. We were the girls most likely to be friends forever and ever. And it was wonderful.

Girl Most Likely

TO RUN THE WORLD

Audrey

EIGHTEEN

I saw them first, standing in the doorway. I couldn't believe my eyes. I thought I was dreaming. I hoped I wasn't. They walked in, arm in arm, floating across the ballroom floor, laughing like fools, acting as if the past twenty years hadn't happened. I was stunned, surprised, and happy all rolled up together. I couldn't wait until they got to our table. Vaughn and I had waited for Su in the bar for half an hour but she hadn't shown up. We'd wondered why. Now we knew. Reenie and Su. They'd put the "Bradley business" behind them. Finally. We could all be together again. The quartet was back in business.

Su was exquisitely dressed, as usual, in Anne Klein, I think, black, wonderful heels, and her hair was pulled back. She'd added a reddish tint that complemented her skin and she was beaming, more from the reunion with Reenie than anything else, I'd say.

Reenie, as usual, was perfect. Tiny, so tiny, I wish I could be as small as she is. She only gets better-looking, I don't know how she does it. We've accused her of being a vampire queen, bathing in the blood of virgins.

"That means y'all are safe, huh?" she quipped.

The royal purple–colored pantsuit was perfect with her black hair (I wonder if she's coloring any gray yet?) and dark eyes. Stunning. And then there's Vaughn.

What am I going to do with her? Vaughn doesn't age, she has

great skin, a decent figure (if you can find it under all the layers, folds, and pleats), and nice hair (just too much of it). I wish she'd let me do a makeover. She needs makeup, a good tailor, and a hair stylist. I could have V shaped up in a morning's work, but Su won't let me. She's told me a million times to leave Vaughn alone.

"She's an artiste, a teacher now, and artists are . . . different."

But, really! The reddish gray corkscrews, the John Lennon wire rims, the afro–Navajo–Middle Eastern wear, all of it has to go! I would love to kidnap Vaughn, take her to Saks, and tell them to do what they can. It's frightening! Su catches me studying the strange-looking suedelike sack that's hanging from a black cord around V's neck. I'm afraid to ask what's in it. The last time I asked about V's jewelry, I got a lecture on pre-Christian Celtic goddess folklore. This year, Vaughn's studying with a shaman. I'll leave that alone.

Su slowly shakes her head and narrows her eyes. "Don't even think about it," she tells me telepathically. I look away and take a sip of my drink.

We'd ordered another round of drinks, sequestered ourselves at a corner table, and hunkered down to talk. There was a class reunion going on but we just shut it out. Vaughn and I wanted to hear about the Irene and Susan reconciliation, down to the last detail, words and sighs included. *I* wanted to know about the new man in Su's life, the scientist whose team had won a Nobel Prize or some international award, whatever it was. She's not saying much about him, which means there's a lot to tell. We all wanted to hear about the book of short stories that Vaughn had finished and Reenie's son, Javier, who was in college. Plus I wanted to know if anyone noticed the incredibly tacky white shoes that Bradley's new love was wearing, the ones that made her look like Minnie Mouse. We covered all of those hot topics and then the girls focused their sights on me. I was now a vice president; Tommy and I had a new house; Taylor was playing field hockey, and Joseph was on a traveling soccer team.

But the only damned thing the girls wanted to talk about was how skinny I was.

"Audrey, when was your last meal?" Su queried.

"You aren't on that Marlboro and Coke diet again, are you?" Vaughn wrapped her fingers around my wrist. "My eight-year-old niece's wrists are thicker than these."

"Honey, I've seen Pringles with more weight on 'em than Audrey." This from Reenie, who looked me up and down like I'd stolen the silver.

"Please tell me you're not . . . sick again, Audrey, please?" V's alto voice caught. "I couldn't stand it if . . . I've never forgotten that night. You scared the shit out of me." The look in her eyes was almost, well, mournful. I'm using a "Vaughn" word.

"You scared the shit out of all of us," Reenie added.

Su nodded, smiling to keep the moment lighter than it felt. Reenie's dark eyes bored into me. But she didn't say anything else on the subject.

They didn't have to remind me. I'd scared myself shitless that night, and now, looking back, I don't know how it happened. It just sneaked up on me. How I got it into my head that being a straight A, high-achieving, hardworking girl meant that I had to starve myself to a skeleton's weight is still a mystery that years of therapy haven't sorted out. But somehow, some way, I'd decided that if the Colonel wanted perfect, he'd get perfect. It became my way of getting back at him. Never again would I give that mean bastard an opening to criticize me for anything. And that meant every aspect of my life would be strictly controlled and managed to a dust-free, sterile perfection, from my grades and the cleanliness of my dorm room to my weight. Maybe I got the idea one day when he was doing inspection in my bedroom at home and picked up a copy of *Vogue* that I'd forgotten to put away.

"Hmmmm," the Colonel murmured, flipping through the pages and stopping at a layout featuring Veruschka, the six-foot-plus, one-hundred-ten-pound model who'd dominated the fashion world back then. "Now, there's a flawless specimen. Not one blemish. Perfect symmetry."

I'd studied the photos after he left until my eyes hurt, trying to dissect the model's formula for what my father thought was perfection.

I had a long way to go. My hair wouldn't be long enough; I hated long hair and had cut mine. But the models wore hair pieces in the photo shoots so that didn't worry me. I would never be white so that was out and my height had reached its stopping point (I thought) of five feet nine inches. I was tall for a girl; I towered over Dad when I wore platform shoes. The only thing left for me to control was weight. I made the scales groan at one hundred thirty pounds, mostly legs and feet; my size nine and a half's were the bane of my existence. I looked in the mirror and decided that if Veruschka's protruding collarbones, pointy elbows, and capsule knees were what perfection was all about, I could do that.

I didn't know anything about anorexia nervosa or bulimia—those names came later. The binging/purging routine was not for me, just the thought of vomiting makes me sick! No joke. But the controlled eating? Now *there* was something I could do. At first I counted calories, but then I started counting bites. Twelve bites total. I cut up my food until all the pieces were even. I chewed slower than snails stroll. I measured the fat content in every morsel. Cigarettes and Coca-Cola, the model's diet, I don't know where I read that. But it worked. The weight dripped off. The sugar and the nicotine kept me going when hunger was gnawing at my stomach. The summer before my senior year, the summer the girls rescued me, I weighed one hundred five pounds and I'd grown almost another inch so I was nearly five foot ten. Reenie was right. A Pringle was obese compared to me. And my internal organs, deprived of the nutrients that a still-growing girl needed, said "To hell with this" and began to shut down. My kidneys were nearly gone when I was admitted to St. Anthony's.

The treatment was exhaustingly slow. It had been so long since I'd eaten a meal that was close to containing even half the daily minimum requirements that it took me an hour just to eat a bowl of cereal and drink a glass of orange juice. Eating lunch was worse and dinner was like watching grass grow. The chewing alone sent me to my room for a nap. But the weight, well, *some* weight, crept back onto my frame. By Halloween, I'd lost the cadaver-like thinness that had made Vaughn say I looked like an X-ray. But the shame of having to be hospitalized for a psychological disorder followed me around like a shadow.

"It's an eating disorder," the doctor told my parents. "But it's very treatable. We've had a lot of success with—"

"I don't believe in disorders," the Colonel had interrupted her. He didn't believe in women doctors either, but it wasn't the time to go into that. "My daughter will buckle up and get herself together. In short order." This last comment was directed at me. The Colonel had no patience or time for recuperative periods, therapy sessions, or restoration. His dictionary had been redacted to exclude those words. You "sucked it up," "got over it," and "marched forward, soldier."

The doctor ignored my father. That was new. In my memory, no one ever ignored my father.

"As I was saying, we've had a fair amount of success with counseling, individual and family. It's important to involve the family with the patient so that everyone can participate in helping her get well. Support, nurture, and encourage the patient—"

"That's nonsense," the Colonel barked. "I don't have time for it. People who need counseling"—he said the word as if he was saying "shit"—"are weak and lazy. The way to get well is to pull yourself up, face the music, and move out."

My father had forgotten that the war was over and he was no longer in the army.

"Wallace, perhaps we should hear the doctor out and—" my mother spoke. My father silenced her with a venomous glare. The doctor continued with her recommendations and my father responded to them with scorn. My mother didn't say anything else. The doctor gave me a look that said, "I feel very sorry for you."

I am a fast learner. They didn't call me "Straight-A Audrey" in seventh grade for nothing. Starving myself to heart stoppage was not productive. Bulimia was messy and getting hooked on heroin, although effective in some circles for weight control, was expensive and tended to leave you looking less than model perfect. So, going forward, I managed my perfect look with just enough food to keep me from fainting, Pepsi and black coffee to keep my heart rate up and my mind awake, and cigarettes. It's amazing, that combination of caffeine and nicotine. Works like a charm.

There's only one problem with perfection: You'll damn near kill yourself trying to achieve it. You spend so much time trying to be perfect that you don't know what it is you really wanted to do in the first place. It takes over your life. "Perfect" becomes the goal in a race where the finish line keeps moving.

Even when I left home for good and the Colonel's grip on my neck loosened, I still heard his sharp barks in my brain: "not good enough," "excellence, always excellence," "you can do better." It played over and over like a tape on a loop.

My cum laude diploma from Fisk gave me the entrée I needed. I went to grad school then entered the management training program at SKT Global, a plum position. There were twenty coveted slots that year, 1979, fifteen men, five women. We listened to a pep talk about teamwork and project dynamics. We were warned that we would become best friends and our children would grow up together as we climbed the corporate ladder into the stratosphere of the executive offices, some ten years in the future. We were praised for being high achievers who'd "demonstrated a strong work ethic and measurable leadership skills."

None of us were remotely sure what this stuff meant, business degrees notwithstanding. But we soon found out. I'd write a book about it if I had the time. History carries the keys to many situations; you just have to know where to look. The corporate world adopted the antebellum plantation paradigm. Employees are human capital just like in the old days. You can be bought, you can be sold, you can be traded. You just can't be beaten, at least not physically. There have to be some limits. And the "teamwork" mantra? It didn't take us long to learn that it was fiction. The working motto for SKT (and other corporations, I suspect) was every man, woman, and dog for themselves. Love does not make the world go round—greed and power do.

Marti King and I were two of only ten women who had anything that even closely resembled "executive" status with the company. We were never allowed to forget (in subtle, covert ways to avoid EEOC problems) that we had taken a job away from a more deserving white male and that we'd better be ten times as excellent to justify ourselves. We wore navy suits with white or light blue Oxford-style blouses and Naturalizer pumps, pearl stud earrings (or diamonds, if we felt like being flashy), and our hair was cut in chin-length bobs. Thank you, John Molloy, wherever you are. Business school, however, had not taught us anything about being a woman in the ranks of corporate America. Sleeping your way to the top? Forget about it. It's more like working in a coal mine while running a gauntlet with a bull's-eye on your back.

Fortunately, we had Farah Malone to serve as our role model. Farah was the gold standard of women executives: B.A. from Radcliff; M.B.A. from Wharton; studied at Oxford; and then took a J.D. from Harvard Law. She was an overachiever's overachiever. She was the executive vice president of administration and had an office next to the chairman's. He thought she walked on water in high heels. Farah Malone was a legend in our industry. There was no one like her and every executive woman aspired to be her. We met at a women's support luncheon sponsored by the company and held in the executive dining room on the twenty-fifth floor.

Looks can be deceiving, I thought to myself as I sipped my water, watching the Mother of all female executives as she moved toward the podium. She, too, wore the regulation navy blue skirt suit and matching pumps. She had the figure of the *Queen Mary* and moved like an ocean liner, too. Forgive me for being shallow, but I do like some style.

"She's the best," Marti whispered in my ear. "No one works harder on a project than Farah does. She's tenacious, never, ever lets go. She hardly ever goes home until seven or eight and it's done." Marti's eyes were gleaming with admiration. "She slept in her office on the weekend of the U.K. conversion. And her baby was teething then!"

If she never goes home that would explain the runs in her panty hose and the grease stains on the front of her skirt, I thought to myself. *No time to get to the cleaners. Not to mention the hair salon or the gym . . .*

Farah took the microphone, welcoming us to the company, talking about the corporate mission and our bright futures. I'm sorry, but I'm a sucker for pep talks. I was brought up by a colonel who knew how to raise troop morale, usually by fear and intimidation, but, sometimes, by recounting tales of glory and gold. At SKT, Farah used the quest for gold to motivate us to the heights of dysfunctional human achievement: gold in the form of stock options; profit-sharing incentives; performance bonuses; promotions; and six-figure base salaries. But there is something called perspective.

Farah neglected to mention what we would be giving up. Nor did she comment on how tenuous the thread of employment could be. We were more indispensable than toilet paper. All that glitters isn't gold. And even if it is, remember what happened to King Midas.

But I ignored the yellow caution lights that started blinking in my head. "Don't breathe the air, get an oxygen mask!" they said. "The air is toxic. And for God's sake, don't drink the water!"

Farah had a golden worm on the end of her fishing line—and I swallowed it hook, line, and sinker. I thrive on challenges—no one can prove to me that I'm not good enough.

I worked ten, sometimes twelve, hours a day, Monday through Friday and half a day on Saturdays. I brought a briefcase home so that I would "have something to do" on Sundays. Four years later, when I told Tommy I was pregnant, he didn't believe me at first.

"Now, when did *that* happen?" he asked, only half teasing.

Over the next few months, we talked about the nursery, the names ("Taylor" whether it was a boy or a girl), and the nanny. The three N's, Tom called them. I was determined to do a juggling act so seamless that no one would be able to tell where the lines were. Work, husband, baby, home, work, husband, baby, home. And I had it all arranged in my planner.

Vaughn thought I was nuts.

"Listen to me, Ms. Taylor-North, babies don't give a shit about planners, schedules, deadlines, or . . ." One of the twins was coloring on the coffee table. Literally. The other one spilled a cup of juice on the Operation game. The buzzer died midbuzz.

"Drop cloths." V mopped up the mess with a worn diaper.

I tried to concentrate on what she was saying but it was noisy and Vaughn's house was, well, messy. There were toy parts scattered across the floor, popcorn hulls crunched underfoot where they were embedded in the carpet, and, for some reason, I had a difficult time ignoring a mummified apple core that had made a home on top of a stack of *Ebony* magazines.

"You have to work your schedule around theirs, that's as good as it gets." She scooped up Rebecca (or was it Candace?), threw the child over her shoulder like a sack of potatoes, and started to pat her on the back.

Candace (or was it Rebecca?) screamed, "Mommy, I spilt it!" Something orange dribbled down her chin. The combination of Barney songs, the Operation buzzer, and Rebecca screeching gave me a headache. I remember thinking that my baby would never be as, well, grubby (or as noisy) as Vaughn's.

I patted my protruding stomach.

"It's all about organization, Vaughn, I keep telling you. I have it all in here." I pulled my agenda book from my shoulder bag. "Every hour accounted for: work; the nanny's schedule; the baby's schedule."

V laughed and snorted at the same time.

"*Nanny?* Well! Some of us have it good," she said in a bitter tone. "Becca! I will not tell you again!" She sprinted after the child who had taken the centerpiece apart. "I wish I had a nanny!" she called over her shoulder.

I wished I hadn't mentioned the nanny. Vaughn hardly had any help at all.

The nanny idea came from Farah Malone, who'd used nannies for her children and raved about them. My familiarity with nannies extended to Julie Andrews as Mary Poppins.

"Motherhood isn't an ordeal unless you fail to plan properly," Farah had told me over a business-mentoring lunch. She laid open her weekly agenda. It was filled with navy, black, red, and green writing. The red and green entries represented her children, who, I think, did not have names because she always referred to them as "the children" or "the girl" or "the boy." Their lives were organized, one entry per line, five words per entry.

"You strategize, plan, and arrange for your family just as you would any other long-term project, like a systems conversion, for instance. Delegate the work where appropriate. Plan meetings. Do follow-up and updates, yes, updates are important. A nanny, house-keeper, they're essential. It's very simple, really."

I decided to follow her advice. Too bad they didn't have Microsoft Project when Taylor was born or I'd have organized pregnancy and motherhood on my PDA.

Tom had his doubts. He agreed with Vaughn and thought it was just fine to "go with the flow." "Babies follow their own schedules" was his mantra. An old-fashioned babysitter would work just fine. Mrs. So-and-So Down the Street had kept his nephews and look how wonderful they'd turned out. Plus, Tommy didn't want a stranger in our house. The entire idea of household help turned him off. Tommy was the first in his family to attend college, and his mother had done housecleaning for other families. My suggestion struck a nerve.

I'd tried to persuade him. "The nanny is like part of your family. And she'll be focused only on the baby's comfort. Nothing else."

"Sounds hoity-toity to me," my husband grumbled, running his hands along the railing of the crib that I'd set up three months in advance. "But if that's what you want . . ."

Poor Tommy, he spent our entire marriage, until the very end, of course, being supportive and very agreeable.

Unlike Vaughn's husband, Noah Gold.

We weren't the fabulous four when she met him. Su was still in Florida and I was in grad school. Reenie was divorced and she and Su weren't speaking then. But somehow or other we all got to meet Noah and, despite the geographical and emotional distance between us, we all agreed on one thing: none of us liked Noah Gold.

Vaughn met him the last semester of her senior year. She fell madly, passionately, deeply, overwhelmingly, and a few other words that ended in "ly" in love with Noah. These are Vaughn's words. I don't use adverbs.

I thought they'd be a perfect match but only if she was looking for love affair material. Noah Gold is like an expensive chocolate dessert: rich and gooey with swirls of crème fraîche and a cherry on top, kiwi sauce drizzled around the plate like a Picasso sketch. Wonderful to look at, to die for to eat, but nothing you could make a meal on without getting sick.

Noah was an artsy fartsy type, like Vaughn, a sculptor/playwright/theater arts management major who looked as if he'd stepped from the pages of the *New York Times* arts section. He had long, kinky dark blond hair and blue eyes set in a deceptively rugged and handsome face. He had a wicked sense of humor and was very popular at V's school. He knew every dance, could hum the entire boxed set of *A Love Supreme*, and dressed like a beatnik from the fifties. He was too cool. I met him over a basket of nachos and bad margaritas. Su had coffee and beignets with him at the efficiency apartment that he and Vaughn shared on campus. Noah prepared the beignets. And Reenie met him when Vaughn took Javier to the zoo. Noah was dashing, funny, brilliant, a little weird, and fine to look at. We could all see what V liked about him. But . . .

"I don't know about you, but there's something not quite right about Noah." We were talking after Su's eleven p.m. broadcast. She was still using "the Voice." It takes a while for it to wear off. "He doesn't seem very genuine. There's something that's . . ."

"He's OK as a boyfriend but not anything more?" I volunteered. Noah was nice, Noah was bright, Noah was something else that I couldn't put my finger on. That was what worried me. And Vaughn had fallen hard.

"Yes, maybe that's it. I just don't have a good feeling about him. It isn't that I think he's an ax murderer or anything but . . ."

There was always that "but."

Reenie was more blunt.

"V, just sleep with the guy, OK? I mean, the sex is probably delicious, right?"

Vaughn's cheeks colored and she looked away. I giggled. If you had read some of Vaughn's as-yet-unpublished romance novels, you would think the woman didn't have a Puritan gene in her body. But you'd be dead wrong.

"I can just imagine how he uses his—"

"Thank you, Reenie!" Vaughn interrupted what might have been a suitable-for-*Penthouse*-letters comment from our own resident Dr. Ruth. "We're engaged." Vaughn flashed a sparkling diamond solitaire.

Reenie inhaled loudly. Her dark eyes flickered at me and then she started dumping cream into her coffee.

"Congratulations. That's wonderful."

Aloud, we said no more.

It was Tommy who summed it up best.

"He's a flake. Full of hot air and pontification, really good at talking about the complicated concepts in bold print. But he can't go into detail because he hasn't taken the time to read the fine print. Long on ideas, short on elbow grease."

We hoped that Tommy was wrong. Vaughn married Noah the next spring and got pregnant right away. ("Good grief, V! They have chemicals now!" This remark from Su not Reenie.) Reenie the Tactless asked V point-blank why she married him. Vaughn was angry but her answer was scary: "Because he asked me."

Oh, boy.

Things bounced along from there. The first test was one of identity as in Noah wanted Vaughn to change hers. They fought about this for weeks before the wedding, they broke up (we rejoiced), they made up (we had a sympathy daiquiri), then they compromised. Vaughn would not convert to Judaism (she's studying Buddhism now) but did agree to change her name to Vaughn Jones-Gold. Ha, ha. She also refused to raise their children as "mixed."

That was the other problem with Noah.

His mother was black and his father was Jewish. Since he wanted to embrace his heritage, a good thing, he cultivated a persona of being "mixed." The result was, however, that he was mixed up.

He spent so much time reminding people that he was only half black (which was funny because Vaughn was fairer-skinned than he was, so people just assumed she was "mixed," too) or half Jewish or half something else that he was never really a whole anything. And in the end, it was his lack of compassion, not his genetic makeup, that buried his marriage to Vaughn and decimated his relationship with his daughters.

And Tommy was right. Noah had no sense of responsibility or tenacity. Working every day, nine to five was fine for other people, for normal, run-of-the-mill Joes who weren't as brilliant as he was. Noah was an entrepreneur. My husband said Noah spoke "wish-I-was-in-business speak," which is really bullshit wearing a Burberry raincoat. And when the chips fell, and they always do, it turned out that Noah didn't want to work. Period. When the going got tough, and it did, Noah got going. Vaughn got the electric bill.

"This is too much, man," he told V soon after the twins were born. "I can't cope; it's wiping out my art! I can't deal with the noise, the smells, the time; I never have any time for myself!"

He walked out a few days later leaving Vaughn hardly enough money to buy diapers or food.

My phone rang at work.

"What are you doing?"

Reenie never bothered with introductions or pleasantries when she had something important to say.

"Nothing, really. Just putting a six-million-dollar system in and scheduling a two-day client meeting with one of our largest customers. Other than that? I'm polishing my nails, why?"

"Vaughn's in trouble."

I clicked the "save" button on the computer and sat up at attention.

"What?"

"The fool has left her. With nothing. She's home sick today. Well, the kids are sick, she's sick, and she has no money! Audrey, he walked out on her and she's barely got enough to pay the rent for the month!"

I said a prayer of thanks for Tommy then called Su and caught her minutes before the noon broadcast.

"That SOB. I can't come down but I'll send you money. Today. Damn that man."

We organized the work like a military campaign. The Colonel would have been proud. I started the household chores; Reenie and Javier fed the babies and got them settled down. It didn't take us long to get clothes started in the washer, wash up the dishes in the sink, and clean the kitchen. I tackled the floors.

"Javier! Go pat the baby on the stomach, softly now, OK? That's a good boy! No, no, the yellow baby not the green baby!" Vaughn had dressed the twins in different colors so that she could tell them apart.

While the babies napped, we made an assault on Kroger's. And in the middle of the living room, dressed in yesterday's clothes, with an expression of grief and exhaustion on her face, stood Vaughn. She was wringing her hands and pleading with us to stop. I have never seen Vaughn look like this. It broke my heart. And despite the sharpness of her words, I knew that Reenie's heart had broken, too.

"I-I can't take this," Vaughn stammered, her cheeks red, her eyes filled with tears. She was dead on her feet; she'd been up all night. And she was humiliated both by what Noah had done and by our help. "I-I can't take any of this. It's nice of you but . . ."

"Shut up, Vaughn, we're doin' it and if you try to stop us or send it back, I'll kick your tired ass, OK?" Reenie's words were abruptly said but not mean. "Javier! Check on the babies. Quietly. That's a good boy!"

"Vaughn, you're in no position to turn down anything except the covers on your bed." I hugged her. She sobbed quietly on my shoulder. Reenie wiped her own tears away and went back to chopping and dicing. "I'm going to run you some bathwater. I want you to take a bubble bath and then a nap. Is that clear, Soldier?" I handed V a tissue.

The defeated look in Vaughn's eyes almost did me in.

"Yes, ma'am."

I wondered how I would manage if Tom walked out on me and I didn't have the position that I had. Vaughn had loved Noah. Vaughn thought Noah loved her. But you never really know, do you?

Babies or no babies, I had to work. And the position at SKT was as good as anything to keep me from the door of poverty. If Tom left me, I wanted to be able to keep moving forward, maintain the four-bedroom monster house, keep the oil changes up on the BMW.

The nanny was hired, the nursery was ready, and I prepped my staff for my six-week maternity leave.

But I was sideswiped by Farah Malone, Super Woman Executive.

"Six weeks?" Jamie Drummond, my VP, exclaimed, as if this was the first time he'd heard it. "Six? Audrey!"

Oh, oh . . .

"Ah, yes, Jamie, I've had it blocked out on your secretary's calendar for months now. But it's no problem. I have all my projects in good shape, the TRA account is being covered by Arlene, and Paul has the IT situation in hand as far as Western WY is concerned. Marc Haskell . . ."

"Yes, but six weeks." Jamie sighed. In my experience, men don't usually sigh, but Jamie did. "I mean, I understand it's your first baby, but, well, you know we were counting on you to give the presentation at the users' group meeting in San Francisco."

My baby gave me a little kick and I shifted my position. Warnings from the womb. Jamie Drummond was a SVP and knew about one-tenth of one percent of what I knew but was still promoted over me to head the division. He lorded it over me every chance he got in little ways. He could never make a decision and he micromanaged every aspect of everyone's daily life in his sphere of influence. In other words, he was a big pain in the butt. The users' group meeting had been scheduled and rescheduled so many times that I'd nearly lost track of it. It was originally set for two weeks before my due date, but Jamie had now scheduled the meeting for one week after.

"Jamie." I paused for a moment to measure my words. "You and Harold Lazar will be more than covered, every wheel is in motion. The materials have been finalized. I'll . . . I'll call in from home and coordinate with the staff. It's a slam dunk." I hate sports analogies. "I assure you that you won't even notice I'm not there."

"Farah Malone had her first child on a Sunday night and came to the merger board meeting on Wednesday morning. Did you know that?" He mused aloud. *Now there's a woman . . .* he was thinking it so loudly that I heard the words. I knew where this was going.

"Yes, I've heard the story."

Hadn't every woman in the company? It had taken on mythic proportions. They talked about it around campfires. The company was involved in a hostile takeover. The board meeting was held on a Wednesday morning and Farah's first child, "the boy" as she referred to him, was born on Sunday night. Farah dropped the baby (Jamie's words, not mine) and flew to Cleveland to coach the executive team at the board meeting that Wednesday. For that Herculean feat, she won the undying admiration of every male executive in the company and the hatred of every woman. Her second child was born, conveniently, on Good Friday, which was a paid company holiday. From those days forward, every woman who found herself pregnant had to wrestle with the myth of Mega Mother, Farah Malone.

Why, when "the girl" had ear tubes put in, Farah Malone did a deposition from the hospital waiting room. When "the boy" fell off the jungle gym and got a concussion, Farah Malone dropped him at the hospital and returned to her desk that very afternoon. Any woman who had the temerity to request a six-week maternity leave was likely to find herself "reorganized" out of a job when she returned. Any man or woman who took time off to tend to a sick child (and children are always sick with something) was labeled a "slacker" who didn't have a good "work ethic."

I'd watched all this from the sidelines while sipping bottled water and wearing an oxygen mask to keep the poisonous fumes out. The caution lights kept flashing and I heard sirens in my head, too, warning me to "Beware! You are about to sell your soul for a sack of stock options!"

Marti and I were pregnant at the same time. We'd planned joint showers, we consulted on nursing schedules and cloth versus disposable diapers, and we even figured out a contingency plan for unexpected events like sickness, nanny absences, and things like that. Like the trained corporate women we were, we mapped out our prepartum and postpartum activities with the precision of aerospace engineers planning the Mars missions. The only problem was, as Vaughn had so wisely said, babies have their own schedules.

Marti's son came six weeks early and both Marti and the baby had complications, so the six-week maternity leave stretched out to ten then fourteen weeks. In the interim, one of Marti's coworkers, in the interest of libel I'll call him "the Troll," moved in on her department to "help out." By the time he finished his benevolent aid, he'd helped himself to her vice president's promotion. Marti returned

after fourteen emotionally charged weeks to find that her department had been "right-sized" and she had been "reorganized" out of
a job.

As I've said before, I'm a fast learner. You do not have to tell me
anything twice. Taylor was born without much fanfare on a Monday
afternoon. The following Friday, on two hours' sleep and still wobbly
legs (I felt as if I'd been tackled by the Cincinnati Bengals—*all* of
them) I boarded a plane to San Francisco where I would address the
meeting as planned. Tommy came along as well as the nanny carrying diapers, blankets, and the breast pump. I was promoted to vice
president two weeks later when Taylor was three weeks old.

NINETEEN

"This place has the charm of Dracula's castle," Reenie remarked, her high heels clicking on the slate floor as she took stock of my house. She scowled at me. "*Without* the warmth." She scribbled something in her Louis Vuitton notebook.

"The verdict, Reenie, if you please," I snapped, refusing to be drawn into a defense of my home. I glanced at my watch: one p.m. I had a two-thirty meeting.

Reenie's dark eyes flickered for a moment then she turned and walked into the living room. She didn't answer but I could tell from her expression and the furious way she was writing that it wasn't good.

Tommy and I had decided to have the house professionally decorated—well, I had decided to have the house professionally decorated. We'd moved from the little four-bedroom on Willow Lane to a five-bedroom, six-bath home in the new Pines Ridge subdivision on the northeast side of town. No home had less than six thousand square feet or three garages. The streets had been landscaped in an English village style with elegant Tudors and Georgians and street-lamps that simulated the early-twentieth-century gas versions. Taylor, now thirteen, had her own suite, as did Joseph, our son, now ten. I had an office; Tommy had a studio with plenty of room for his drafting tables, plans, and equipment; and our gourmet kitchen cost me nearly half a year's salary. I hardly used it, but Mimi, our house-keeper, loved it.

Reenie, however, was not impressed.

She sighed when she saw the glass-topped dining room table and the stainless-steel kitchen appliances. She shook her head but said nothing when we walked through the master bedroom suite, which I had decorated (quite nicely, I thought) in an all-white scheme with Scandinavian-influenced furniture. The master bath was a wonder of silver fixtures, white porcelain, and white towels.

The new hot designer du jour, Irene Keller Garcia Noland (left over from her last husband, from whom Reenie was now extricating herself. "Never, *ever* change your last name," she'd told us at the last reunion. "It's a pain in the ass to change back all your credit cards, your license, and you have to buy new monogrammed towels . . ."), had been hard to get, even for me. Reenie worked all the time now, with Javier nearly grown and the husband out of the picture. Her projects had been featured in the local paper and one of her penthouses (a school buddy of ours who'd made it big in Chicago) garnered a spread in *Architectural Digest.* Little Reenie Keller had arrived and now she was in my study.

"Audrey." Reenie looked around the room then fixed her gaze on me. "Don't you think you've taken this minimalist thing a little too far? It looks as if no one lives here!"

I frowned. *What is she talking about?* I scanned the room trying to understand. OK, my desktop was clean, that was good. The books were on the shelves, arranged alphabetically and by subject . . . trash can empty, good. No unanswered faxes in the tray, fine. Pens in the drawers, no paper left out . . . I was puzzled.

"What?"

Reenie sighed again.

"Audrey Jean, if this place were any more sterile, it'd be a bio-chemical lab on a secret military base." She strolled through the room gesturing wildly. "No paintings, no photos, no . . . mementos, no . . . knickknacks . . ."

"Just more to dust," I commented drily.

"No . . . nothing to indicate that anyone human lives here!"

I looked at my watch again; maybe she'd get the point.

"Irene, the reason I asked you here? Do you want to do the house or not?"

Reenie grinned at me and put her hands on her hips.

"Oh, I'll do it all right. But when I'm finished, Oh Hyphenated One, it'll look more like a home than a laboratory."

I later found out that Reenie had shared her professional opinion with Vaughn.

"I don't know what you expected," Vaughn commented. The sound of an elephant doing the electric slide came from her second floor. "Keith! What are you doing up there?" she yelled.

"Nothing" came a confident young voice. Vaughn had remarried: a warm bear of a man named Ridge Johnson, and their son, Keith, was the source of the upstairs tumbling activity. Ridge was different from Noah Gold. Thank goodness.

"Well, please stop doing nothing or I'm coming up there." Vaughn paused for a moment, her eyes rolled upward.

"Yes, Mom!"

Vaughn exhaled loudly.

"V, it was so . . . sterile," Reenie had said. "I've seen morgues with more ambience than that place. And she's had to have paid, what, half a million?"

Yes, I had.

"At least," V commented, her eyes returning to the mélange of yarn she was trying to sort. Vaughn was always taking up something, a new religion, a new hobby or language (she'd tried Mandarin, Arabic, and Sanskrit). This month's activity was knitting—if she could get the yarn untangled.

"It was so . . . empty, not personal, like a display home only more impersonal than that!"

Vaughn set the orange yarn aside.

"I don't know what you expected," she repeated matter-of-factly. "She's never there."

And I wasn't.

You worked from seven until seven and coming in at eight (for whatever reason, day care, traffic, what have you) was a no-no. Face time had been elevated to a sanctioned employee activity at SKT. It didn't matter what you were doing at seven a.m. or six forty-five p.m. as long as you were at your desk. It was the CEO's delight to walk through the floors checking to see if there were slaves in the fields, um, bodies in the cubicles and offices. As long as you were present and vertical, you were fine. Absences, for whatever reason, including severe illness or family death, were frowned upon. As SKT employees, our job was to provide value for the shareholders and uphold family traditions. Just not our own.

And so, I juggled. With Tommy's support and after-school programs, I managed fine. Taylor and Joseph were good, healthy kids. Tommy didn't believe in simply helping out with his children, he believed in being a father, so we were able to coordinate the children's activities pretty smoothly. But it's only good when life is good. And things never stay that way for long.

Staying home with a sick child was unheard of. After all, Farah Malone's kids were strong, hardy individuals who had stayed home sick by themselves since they were eight. And despite the bereavement policy, taking time off for more than a one-hour funeral was like slapping the chairman's mother.

"It doesn't take all of three days to bury her, does it?" Jamie asked when my grandmother died. *How selfish of me! What was I thinking?* At the time, I tried to make some explanation for taking time to help my family. Mom's family was close-knit and Nan's illness and death had been a devastating blow. I mumbled some excuse like comforting my grief-stricken mother and helping her with the arrangements. But I was a good corporate soldier. I took exactly thirty-six hours off for Nan's funeral activities, writing out the obituary and the order of service myself at two o'clock in the morning.

I functioned like a robot, in at six forty-five, meetings all day, lunch, if any, at my desk, and paperwork, phone calls, and e-mail until eight in the evening. I was the first at my desk in my department, the last to leave. Audrey Taylor-North was the ultimate team player: I sang off the same page until I was blue in the face. I was such a good example of corporate womanhood that Farah Malone began to look up to me.

At home, life went on, usually without me. Mimi fixed dinner; Tommy managed the household and took care of the kids. It began to fall apart when . ∴. no, it had started falling apart before this. I noticed the cracks when Joseph got the flu. It had been a nasty flu season, everyone got hit with either the respiratory version or, worse, the stomach variety. I'd been hit earlier in the season but fortunately I'd had a mild case and was sick only over a weekend. Tommy was down for four days, Taylor for three. Joseph got hit badly.

Fever, coughing, vomiting, head hurt, you name it. He was ten and scared and wanted his mommy or daddy. And that Wednesday, Tommy was in St. Louis on business and I was in board meetings. Taylor was away on a field trip. None of my usual stopgap measures were available: Mimi was on vacation, Mommy and Dad were on their yearly trek to Vegas, Reenie was in New York, and Javier, who sometimes pinch-hitted for me, had exams. All my other sitters were either tied up or sick themselves.

I did what any loving working mother would do. I left my son at home alone.

"Here, sweetie, down it goes. Good." I poured the liquid acetaminophen down his throat and handed him a glass of ice chips. Joseph had the worst of all worlds, both respiratory and stomach flu. His head hurt and his eyes had sunk into his face. He looked like a little zombie but the worst was over. He was able to drink again, hadn't thrown up in twenty-four hours, and the fever was gone. I'd lined the wastebasket with newspaper just in case and left him my beeper number.

"Mommy, can't you stay with me?"

Joseph's eyes looked like beautiful gray orbs floating in a bowl of tears, but he hadn't been crying.

"Not this time, Joseph, but I'll be home before you know it. I just have this meeting to go to. Now, go back to sleep. Here's your remote, and I've set the TV . . ."

Toy Story, Home Alone I and *II*, ha ha, a pitcher of liquids and peanut butter crackers, the only "food" Joseph felt like eating. My meeting was at two o'clock and would be over at four. As I drove back to the office, I found myself wondering what excuse I would give

Jamie for leaving if the meeting ran long. Looking back on my ratio-
nale then, I have to wonder if I'd lost my sanity. My priorities were
completely upside down. Oh, yeah, I'd been drinking the toxic water,
all right.

The meeting ended on time, I got home at five o'clock, and was
met by my husband who was so angry that his face had begun to split
open.

"You're back early. What's the matter? Is Joseph all right?" I
threw down my briefcase and started up the stairs.

"Yeah! He's all right," my husband countered. "Considering that
he was left home alone at ten years old! He's fucking fine!"

I bit my lip.

"You don't have to be vulgar . . ." I always like to use my corporate-
speak, let's keep a calm demeanor when arguing with Tommy. But it
rarely worked.

"I'll do you one better, Audrey, I'm fucking mad as hell! What
were you thinking? He's ten, for God's sake! He was sick! Couldn't
you have stayed home just for an afternoon? A few hours?"

"I had a meeting . . ." Even as I spit out the words I knew it was
the wrong thing to say.

Tommy cocked his head and looked at me as if I had an eye in
the center of my forehead.

"You had a meeting . . . a business meeting, let me guess, you had
to pull the marionette strings on that stupid bastard Drummond so
he could speak intelligently and fool them into thinking he knows
what the hell he's talking about! No, no, probably not. I know. You
had to hold his dick while he pissed so he wouldn't dribble on his
shoes! Christ, Audrey! They have conference phones!"

"Tommy! Now, look . . ."

My husband's face loomed just six inches from mine. I wasn't
afraid of any physical violence, Tommy's not like that. But I knew
that he was angry. Really angry.

"No, Audrey, *you look*. Our son was sick. I'm out of town. That
means you as his mother have to make arrangements for him. He's
too young to be home alone sick! Period! I walked in here . . ."
Tommy's eyes blazed as he glanced upstairs. He was so angry that he

just shook his head. "The boy was drenched in sweat, couldn't find your beeper number. Beeper number! For his own mother! And wanted to come downstairs to get more ice but was afraid you'd be mad at him for leaving the bed."

I had told Joseph to stay in his room no matter what. He always did what Mommy told him to do.

"Tommy, look. He was fine. The fever had broken, he wasn't throwing up anymore, Joseph has stayed home alone by himself for short periods of time! I was just a phone call away. I—"

"You're his mother, Audrey. You shouldn't have to be a phone call away. Your job when he's sick is to be with him."

"No. My job is to be at SKT Global. That is my job. You know, I'm getting sick of this shit where I have to make these sacrifices and you don't! I juggle and arrange things and . . ."

And Tommy juggled and arranged things . . .

"You do it because you won't let anyone else do it!" My husband bellowed back. "It's General Audrey's way or the highway! The perfect everything!"

"Well, somebody has to do it," I countered, wounded by the reference to my father. "I mean, if I don't do it, who will? I'm a working woman, Tommy, in case you hadn't noticed. I guess what I really need is a wife."

Tommy's jaw tightened and his eyes narrowed. For a moment neither of us spoke. Joseph's voice floated down the staircase into the front hall.

"Mom! Dad! Are you guys fighting?"

"Nooooo," Tommy and I said in unison.

"Can I have another Popsicle, please? My throat hurts" came the little voice again.

"Whatever you want, Joseph!" I said.

"Coming up in a minute, son," Tommy yelled back. Then he turned his attention to me.

"Then you and I are in the same boat." My husband's voice was scalpel sharp and Antarctic frigid. "I need a wife, too."

I never learned to prioritize my life beyond what was in my

Franklin planner. I learned how to "drill down" when it came to work, but when it came to my personal life?

What personal life?

I was the most organized mother you ever saw except that I hardly got to spend any time with my children or my husband.

I attended the mother-daughter luncheon at Taylor's school for the first time her sophomore year. Mimi or Mother or even Tommy had gone in my place before. Taylor was so proud, showing me off to her friends, introducing me to teachers whose names I'd seen only on report cards or whom I'd talked with by trading voice mail messages. I met the mothers of her friends, voices on my message service.

"Hi, Audrey? This is Meghann's mom, Jeannie Weston. We're taking the girls to . . ."

"Mrs., er. Ms. Taylor-North? This is Catie Owens, Joseph's room mother? I was wondering if . . ."

I baked the chocolate chip cookies at one o'clock in the morning after a ten-hour day at work; I dropped off whatever-it-was at six o'clock in the morning on my way to work, often handing packages to the janitor, who was the only person at the school that early. I returned the phone calls at the end of the week because they were on the fourth page of my "to do" list.

"Oh, my God! I don't believe it! Is that actually Taylor's mom? Or a stand-in?" The loud whisper was followed by a chorus of giggles. I wanted to turn around but Taylor was introducing me to her history teacher. But I can multilisten.

"No, I think that is actually the elusive Mizzzzzz Taylor-North, in the flesh!"

"Interesting. I always thought the child was being raised by her father. He's the only parent you ever see at these things."

"He and the housekeeper."

"She's never home, works sixty hours a week for Global. Those kids are raising themselves."

The words stung.

I never saw their faces. By the time I'd finished chitchatting with Mrs. What's-it and Dr. So-and-So there was a sea of faces around me, no way to pick out the bitches. But my cheeks were burning, I could feel them. I don't think Taylor heard. At least, I hope she didn't.

My kids weren't raising themselves! I was always home by eight, spent Sunday mornings with them exclusively. Saturday mornings I went to the office, but in the afternoons I went to whatever soccer, football, volleyball, or music lesson was scheduled. I remember being in a rage about what the women had said about me. What the hell were they talking about? Why, I worked until seven o'clock the day before Thanksgiving, then stayed up until three a.m. polishing the silver, cleaning the house (the housekeeper never gets everything right), and getting the food ready. Not to mention ironing the Irish linen tablecloth and napkins. Again. And everything was perfect! Just perfect.

I vented to the girls over Sunday brunch. Su was in town to check on her aunt, who was in the hospital, so we met her at a little hole-in-the-wall nearby. It was low on ambience but had great scrambled eggs, bacon, grits, and huge blueberry muffins. After we heard the latest on Aunt Leila, Vaughn and Reenie listened patiently as I expressed my frustration with the Muffy room mothers at Taylor's school. But the girls were a tough crowd.

"Audrey, I love you but . . ." Always the diplomat, Vaughn started off. "They were right."

"Audrey Jean, you're a nut case, ready for the men in white coats, dear," Reenie blurted out, popping a piece of muffin into her mouth. "What the hell is wrong with you? You work like a fiend, I mean, workaholic doesn't begin to describe your schedule. It's ridiculous!"

"It's not ridiculous," I defended myself. "All the other men . . ."

"All the other men have nonworking wives, I know," Vaughn commented with a raised eyebrow. "But you have the next best thing. You have Tommy."

I had Tommy . . . I hadn't dropped that bomb yet.

"It's important to have a strong work ethic . . ." I tried to keep myself in the boxing ring.

Su blew me a raspberry.

"Audrey, no one will accuse you of being a slacker. You practically work yourself to death. You've got more money than God's great-aunt, household help, you're a senior VP now, what the hell are you driving yourself so hard for? You could probably retire next year!"

To be perfect. To be excellent. The Colonel's voice stung my ears.

"You're ruining your health, you're no bigger than a minute . . ." Su continued.

"Half a minute," Vaughn revised the statement.

Not to be left out, Reenie quipped, "Ten seconds."

"Listen, my physical appearance . . ."

Laughter came from all directions.

Reenie rolled her eyes and poked me in the ribs. Hard.

"Audrey, I don't know if you're still starvin' yourself or pukin' for fun or what you're doing, but whatever it is, I wouldn't recommend it. If a strong breeze comes along, girl, you are gone with the wind."

"You've given up everything for that damn company, Audrey, and what have you gotten from them in return?"

This from Su, whose soft, dark brown eyes bored into me. I heard her voice more clearly, more intimately than the others. Because Su had been obsessed like me, to be the best, to prove that she was nearly perfect and without the deficiencies of her sad mother and manipulative father. She'd given up a lot, too, for her career—a husband, children. But now she had Jimmy.

"What do you mean, what am I getting? A nice salary, bonus, stock options . . . Su, not all of us can traipse around the Galapagos for three weeks," I snapped back at her. "I have a merger coming up and . . ."

"Like that shit won't be there when you get back?" Reenie jumped in again.

I had had enough.

"Listen, this is all I'm going to say about it and then we're movin' on to another subject. I work, hard. I'm ambitious, yes. But I'm trying to build a safe, comfortable life for my family. And a career for myself."

Vaughn poured cream into her coffee and began to stir it into circles. She did not look up when she spoke.

"How *are* Tommy and the kids?"

Damn her, damn her, damn her.

Tommy and I had been on and off for several years, ever since I left Joseph home alone when he was sick. Tommy never forgave me for that. He finally moved out three years ago and bought a condo nearby. To be honest, it was a relief. His absence took some of the pressure off. The kids accepted the separation with few questions and quiet faces and spent most of their after-school time with their dad. My voice mail filled up with their messages.

"Mom, it's Joseph." As if he would ever need to introduce himself to me. "We're spending the night at Dad's, OK? We're making pizza and he's gonna help me with my science project."

"It's Taylor, Maternal Unit." This from my teenage daughter. "The rug rat and I . . ."

"I'm not a rug rat!" Joseph's voice broke through the receiver.

"The big rug rat and I are staying at Dad's tonight. OK?"

It went from being "OK" to the norm instead of the exception. And I came home at eight or eight-thirty at night to an empty five-bedroom, six-bathroom, six-thousand-square-foot house. Oh, and three-car garage.

"They're fine," I said shortly. I didn't even want to look at Vaughn, whose kids adored her, whose second husband adored her, and who, somehow, managed to be a working mother and a human at the same time. I didn't want to look at Reenie either. Her decorating career had flown into the stratosphere. She'd managed to extricate husband number two—"Mr. Noland"—from her name and her life and was now dating one of her former clients. Javier was a funny, artistic young man, just like his mom.

And even Su, who'd climbed up the media corporate ladder, had a stronger family life than I did. She anchored Channel 8, at six o'clock and eleven. And when she wasn't "the voice of the midstate" she and Dr. Jimmy were exploring wild and exotic places like the Gobi Desert or the badlands of Montana.

How could I tell them that my perfect life was a perfect wreck?

"Audrey, I just wanted you to know. It's been long enough,"

Tommy began, pacing the kitchen floor as he always did when he was thinking and talking at the same time. "We've been apart for five years, nothing has changed. I think . . . Audrey, I'm going to file for a divorce. Taylor goes to college next year, Joseph can stay with me if you want. If you want to keep the house, fine, we'll work it out. But Audrey . . ." My husband's eyes and voice were filled with longing. I felt a lump forming in my throat. Tommy reached out to touch my arm. I moved out of his reach. "Audrey, it's time for me to go on with my life. I can't keep . . . waiting for you to come home from work."

"Are you seeing someone?" I blurted out. But somehow I didn't think so.

Tommy laughed.

"Yeah, Audrey, I'm seeing someone. Someone tall, exquisitely beautiful, and model thin with a haute couture wardrobe, professionally cut hair and makeup. Yeah, I'm seeing a brilliant corporate businesswoman who manages a billion-dollar product line as effortlessly as some folks ride a bike. Oh, yeah, I found a lady just like that at the C&S last Wednesday on blues night."

Despite the seriousness of the moment, I smiled. Two seconds later, my husband's arms were around my waist.

"Audrey." I could feel his warm breath in my ear. "There's no other woman. There's never been another woman. There is only you. But you don't seem to need me." He turned me around and tipped my chin up. Tommy's voice cracked with emotion. "You don't . . . seem to need any of us. We're just in your way."

"That's not true. I love you and Taylor and Joseph and . . ."

Tommy shook his head.

"We know that. But you don't need us, Audrey. You don't have time for us. Families take time, children take time. A marriage takes . . . time."

I backed away. I guess I'd been drinking the tainted water at work too long.

"Tom, you don't understand. I'm trying to build a career. I'm the only, hell, I'm the first woman SKT has ever had in this division. Ever! It's important that I do well, that I prove . . ."

Tommy listened to my litany of corporate responsibility, work ethic theories, self-sufficiency bullet points, and Republican bootstrap philosophy without interruption. Then he exhaled deeply and gave me the saddest look I've ever seen, grabbed his keys from the counter, and walked out the back door.

The divorce papers came a few weeks later.

TWENTY

Most people can't see the forest for the trees, but not me. I can see the forest. It's the trees that I missed.

It would be easy to say that I ignored my husband in favor of my job, that I shoved my children aside in order to climb the corporate ladder in high heels, and that I didn't take parenthood seriously. It isn't true that I became a glacial cyborg coordinating multibillion-dollar transactions with the bat of a mascaraed eye. These generalizations are way too complicated. The truth is that I saw myself as a "good girl." It was part of my hard drive.

Good girls dress appropriately, enunciate their words clearly, and arrive on time. They are neither too emotional nor too reserved. They always try to do their best just like the Girl Scout pledge says and, despite the fact that most of us over forty grew up without the benefit of team sports (other than cheerleading), we are team players. The commandments that the Colonel drummed into my head from the cradle played from dawn until dusk like a broken record: *Excellence, always! Don't complain, don't explain. Suck it up, soldier! When the going gets tough, the tough get going.* I took it all to heart, gathered up those mantras, my cigarettes and Coca-Cola, my six daily cups of black coffee, industrial-size bottle of Tums, and my nerves and became the perfect executive woman. The good girl extraordinaire.

I remembered too late what Vaughn said about good girls. If good guys finish last, where do good girls finish? Answer: They don't. They crash and burn.

"I'm really sorry to hear about the divorce, Audrey." Despite the intermittent static and fade-outs, I heard sadness in Su's voice. "You and Tommy seemed, well, good for each other. He's a nice guy."

"Nobody said he wasn't nice, Su," I snapped at her. "We're just better apart than we are together." I spat back the counselor's words verbatim.

"How are the kids?"

"Just fine," I remarked. It's amazing how well you can lie when you're talking long distance. Su couldn't see the grimace on my face. The kids were "fine" if you didn't count Joseph's nightmares and Taylor's anarchic behavior at school.

"The most challenging ages are three and thirteen through eighteen," Vaughn commented after listening to a tale of woe about Taylor's latest antic: a tattoo of a griffin plastered across her butt. "God, I remember when the twins were teenagers. They were horrible. I told them that one of us would survive puberty but it might not be them."

I knew I could count on V for moral support. Su had been no help at all, sending me a postcard from Tunisia that read, "Audrey Jean, don't forget, you're going to need all the things you've given up if those SOBs push you off the corporate ladder."

"The therapist says it's a natural form of rebellion in teenagers." I sighed, lighting a cigarette. "She says I should just ignore it."

Vaughn's right eyebrow went up at this comment. Then she started fanning the air dramatically. Vaughn hates cigarette smoke. She doesn't think much of therapists either. She says all their kids are more screwed up than their patients'.

"You can stick your head in the sand if you want to." Her words were dark and crisp. Her eyes probed my face in an uncharacteristically un-Vaughn-like way. "But teenagers are a lot like three-year-olds. You have to keep your hands on them at all times. Ignoring them only means that you'll have to clean up a bigger mess later on."

So much for herbal tea and sympathy. By the time I met Reenie for lunch later that week, I'd been pretty well beaten up. Reenie moved in for the kill.

"Well, Stick Woman, we've been here"—she checked her watch—"since eleven-thirty. You've told me about the merger, the Kansas City meetings, the New York meetings, the Miami meetings, the IT . . . what was it, strategic planning session? Oh, the board chair and the United Way campaign."

"Yeah, so?"

"Yeah, so, you've told me damn near everything including what time the CFO farts, but you haven't told me what I asked you." Reenie's eyebrows rose.

What had I missed? I frowned.

"I'm sorry . . . what did you ask me?"

Reenie pushed the place setting aside and folded her arms on the table.

"I asked how *you* were, Audrey. You've told me everything but that."

Oh, is that all.

"I'm fine."

Reenie laughed until tears rolled down her cheeks. I sat back in my chair and watched her in amazement. The waiter came and went, trying not to notice the woman seated opposite me who was dabbing her eyes with the white cloth napkin.

"Do you mind letting me in on the joke?" I asked.

Reenie coughed, blinked a few times, then held up one finger as she grabbed the water goblet and took a few sips. Then she dabbed at her eyes again and settled back into the chair.

" 'I'm fine,' she said," Reenie quipped, holding up her fingers as if she were Cruella de Ville smoking a cigarette. She threw her head back in an exaggerated but elegant gesture. Her black hair, now long again, spilled around her shoulders. "I'm fine, dahling." She drew out the words. "I'm a little nervous, which is why I've gulped down two cups of black coffee in the half hour I've been here, not to mention stepping out to go to the ladies' room but grabbing a quick cigarette instead in the lounge. 'I'm fine,' she says as she taps her foot under the table, fiddles with the bread basket, but doesn't eat any bread, of course. Checks her watch every five minutes. Oh, yeah, you're fine, all right, Audrey. Tommy's gone, the kids are gone, all you have is your job, your BMW, and your nerves. Although I'll wager you're just about out of nerves, too."

"Reenie, I don't need this. I came here for a pleasant afternoon lunch, not a guillotine appointment." I wiped my mouth and started packing up my tote bag. Life was too short for this stuff; besides, I had a two o'clock meeting that I needed to prepare for. "Obviously, you're in a bad mood, why don't we get together when you're . . . feeling better?"

Su would have reached out, taken my arm, and calmly told me to sit down, that she was sorry and didn't mean to be so judgmental. Vaughn would have laughed, thrown a roll at me, and told me not to be such so touchy about everything. Reenie stayed where she was, a Mona Lisa smile on her face, watching every move I made without saying a word. But the look in her black eyes was lethal. She didn't try to stop me from leaving.

"Be careful, Audrey," she called after me.

"What do you mean, be careful?" I snapped back, angry with her for ruining a lunch I'd been looking forward to and had rescheduled two meetings to attend. "What is this . . . ominous phantom that I'm supposed to be careful of?"

Reenie's eyes bored into me.

"Just be careful. You're no bigger than a twig, it'd be easy for those toads you work with to push you off that corporate ladder you're always talking about. And twigs snap pretty easily."

"Yeah, whatever, Irene."

I was angry at her, frustrated because she didn't understand my side, disappointed because I had hoped for more empathy from friends. The caution lights were flashing and I just didn't see them.

My stomach was churning from the coffee and because I hadn't eaten lunch. By the time I got back to the office, I had a headache and indigestion. Tums and Advil, now there's a tasty combination, one that I had used more than once to get through a meeting.

Sabotage, backstabbing, clandestine meetings, poison-filled rings, rumors, and hatchet jobs were tools used in the great intrigues of the past. They were effective in toppling kings, disrupting papacies, and creating political chaos. Historically, assassination, both of body and reputation, were useful tactics, too. In the twenty-first century, corporate politics have surpassed most Renaissance intrigues. And SKT Global was one corporation where it had been elevated to an art form. At certain levels in the company, it was wise to wear a bullet-proof vest and hire a food taster. The Borgias had nothing on these people.

I, of course, was the perfect target: a woman, a minority, and distracted by paying attention to doing my job. I was too busy being a good corporate citizen and team player to notice that I'd wandered into the crosshairs of an assassin's bow.

Jay Norman was the bane of my existence. He'd been with Global since Moses wore diapers and had never worked anywhere else. When I first joined the company, responding to his memo for "cost-saving efficiencies" with a list of documented improvements, he invited me to lunch. He explained, with the grin of the Cheshire cat, that "the company" didn't really want *my* ideas for improvement. (Actually, they didn't want improvement at all.) They had their own tried-and-true formulas for success and my opinion was not needed. They had done things the SKT way for over one hundred twenty-five years and the stock price was still strong. No need to make changes, even if they would make the auditors happy.

Then why send that memo? I remember thinking.

"You'll catch on," Jay told me, his face bright with the energy it took to beam that insincere smile in my direction. He patted my hand before I could move it. I felt as if I'd caught the cooties.

I caught on, all right. I learned quickly that I could trust Jay about as far as I could throw a bull elephant. His areas of responsibility didn't overlap mine but I needed his technical group to make my projects operational. Jay did everything he could to make them blow up and managed to cover his wide, pale ass with voluminous memos to his supervisor detailing the deficiencies of whatever plan, project, or time line I had in place. He skipped meetings I called but needed him for, failed to respond to requests for technical assistance with his standard answer ("The system isn't designed that way"), and just plain made my life as difficult as he could. Shooting me would have been an improvement.

Maybe we should look into . . . a new system?

"You don't understand," Jay said. "It's the way we do things here. We'll do a work-around."

Which always took twice as long and didn't work half as well.

"It's not just you," one of my colleagues assured me. "He does it to everybody."

"OK, Marc, if it's not just me and he derails everyone's passenger train, why the hell is he still here? He is the best example of adding absolutely no value that I can think of."

Marc shrugged his shoulders.

"A lot of people have asked themselves that question, including me," he said woefully. His blue eyes twinkled behind his tortoise-shell glasses. "We think he has pictures of the divisional head practicing lewd acts with a farm animal." Mark swallowed hard. "Kinda makes you feel sick, doesn't it?"

The visual on that concept was too horrible for words.

The day of the accounts conversion was pretty nearly perfect if you're talking about the weather. It was late September and the days had stretched into a comfortable pattern of warm, dry days and cool, cricket-chorus-filled nights. It was my favorite time of year. I loved the smell of the crispness in the night air. It took me back to SE High and football Friday nights and cold knees because our cheerleader skirts were short. I loved seeing the deep burgundy and sunshine gold mums in my flower bed and the brilliantly colored maples that swayed in the breeze, giving me an occasional peek at their blond and red leaves at the top. The cool night air was beginning to work its magic.

I sighed as I got into the car. I'd started it earlier to let it warm up. It was six o'clock in the morning, a Friday. I'd been working on this conversion for months, for nearly a year, and finally, today, at four-thirty p.m. Eastern Standard Time, we'd flip the switch and do the deed. The team planned a celebratory dinner at a local restaurant afterward. The day hadn't even started and I'd already decided how I wanted it to end. I would watch the numbers come across the new system, sign off on the final documents, shake hands with the auditors, and go home to take-out Thai and a bubble bath. I wanted peace and quiet. Taylor and Joseph were spending the night with Tommy.

"How's it lookin', Marc?" I asked my manager as we walked, no, marched to the conference room where the final countdown meeting was taking place. "Any changes since noon?" I'd managed this project like a military exercise. In these last few days before conversion, we had meetings every four hours to receive updates, reconnoiter where necessary, and check and double-check the details. Marc had been my lieutenant in the campaign. I even used military time — the operation was set for 1430.

He shook his head and grinned at me.

"No, ma'm," he said crisply. "All systems go. All *i*'s dotted, *t*'s crossed, the fat lady is about to sing!"

"All staff accounted for? Everyone here?" I reached for the handle of the conference room door.

Marc shrugged.

"Everyone from our end. All the usual suspects." He moved to open the door for me then paused. "Well, except for one."

"Who's that? I don't remember anyone calling in sick," I commented.

"Not on our team," Marc informed me. He stopped for a second before continuing. "Jay's AWOL. I haven't spoken with him since the ten o'clock meeting."

I sighed. Jay had some outstanding items to finagle. As usual, he'd waited until the last minute, keeping all of us on needles and pins, before rushing in and announcing that he'd fixed the problem (and with Jay, there was always a problem) and would save the day. And, as usual, Jay had gone underground and was unreachable until it would be time for his big dramatic moment.

"OK, well, as long as Indira is here, we should be fine." Indira was Jay's second in command. She was so nice that I'd often wondered how she managed to work for such a jerk.

We entered the conference room and Indira was there. I allowed myself to exhale, counted to twenty to settle the butterflies in my stomach, and looked at the clock. It was time to start the count-down.

"People! Let's settle down, everyone ready?" I looked around the table at a sea of solemn but satisfied expressions. *Good. This was going well.* "Do we have all the teams on the conference line?"

"We're here, Audrey!" came a female voice over the speaker phone. "This is Em, Paul's here . . ." There was laughter. "Um . . . Gene just slid in, literally!" More laughter. "Tony, Martine, Yolanda, and . . . Deborah and her team just sat down. All present and ac-counted for!"

"KPMG? Are you there?"

"All here, Audrey!" Michael's voice rumbled like human thunder over the conference line. I ticked off names as I reviewed the list.

Then, I took a deep breath and started in.

Fifteen minutes later, we'd checked off every item on the count-down list. Everything was "thumbs-up." The systems people were "standing by," as they say on TV, and four-thirty p.m. EST was ex-actly two hours away. I felt like Hannibal Smith on *The A-Team.* "*I just love it when a plan comes together.*"

"It looks as if we're about done here," I commented, feeling very much like the cat that had swallowed the canary. "In about two hours, we'll have our conversion." The group around me exhaled loudly and started nodding and smiling among themselves. "Mike? You can sign off now. We'll fax over the documents at five."

"Um, Audrey?" This from the speakerphone on the other confer-ence line.

"Yes, who's that?" I didn't recognize the voice.

"Oh, it's David, on Deborah's team?"

"Yes, David, is there something else?"

There was another pause, murmurs, then silence. Then David spoke again; his anxiety was so great that I could hear it in his voice even at long distance and over a conference phone line. My stomach muscles tightened.

"Yes, there is," he said slowly. "What did you decide to do about the oh-four-oh account issue? We need to know before we convert."

The 040 account issue? *What 040 account issue?* Marc and I exchanged puzzled glances with each other. The other team members frowned and began to whisper among themselves. I put the conference phone on mute.

"Have you heard anything about the oh-four-oh account?" I asked the chief accountant on our side.

Bailey shook her head.

"What do you mean? What issue?" I asked, trying to keep my voice calm. But my insides had already begun to panic. The coffee-Tums-Advil combination was churning away like lava in the cone of a volcano.

Again, silence, then David's manager, Deborah, spoke.

"Audrey, when we checked the last quarterly report, there was a discrepancy in the accrual calculation. That's, well, that would be a huge problem and we shouldn't convert the account without addressing it."

No shit. Huge problem didn't go far enough in describing the seriousness of the issue.

"Deborah, I don't mean to be inquisitive," I said, "but we've been meeting this week on a regular basis and this is the first time any of us have heard anything about a discrepancy. When, exactly, did you discover this?" I was ready to take off heads then and there. "And when were you going to tell us?" I had an edge in my voice. Marc gave me a quick sideways glance. He was probably feeling the same way. *Things had been going so well. How could this have happened?*

Around the room, we all looked at the phone with dread. We had given the last eight months of our lives, most of our waking moments, to this project, and now, two hours from blastoff, we had this. It was incredible! Unbelievable! Diabolical . . .

"Deborah? Are you still there?"

The silence seemed to last longer than the Jurassic Age. Then David spoke again.

"Audrey, we notified Jay on Wednesday morning. At the tech meeting. Jay said he would inform your team and handle the situation on your end."

Jay.

We all looked at Indira, who was already shaking her head. She held up her hands in a defensive gesture and glanced around the room.

"No, no. I know nothing about this. Nothing." She looked panic-stricken, as if afraid that we would attack her physically. Poor Indira, Jay was always putting her in this position. She was his managing supervisor and, as such, it was assumed that she was involved in his projects, prepared to provide backup or support if he wasn't around. It was a reasonable assumption. But it was wrong. Jay kept Indira in the dark just like he did everyone else.

His modus operandi was to keep all the cards close to his chest. It was a sick kind of job security ploy. Tactically, it was brilliant. If you're the only one who has the keys, then everyone has to wait until you get there to open the door. It was the simplest form of job security and it made Jay virtually untouchable. Well, that and the pictures he had of the divisional head and a goat.

"It's OK, Indira, it's OK."

David's tone was apologetic.

"I'm really sorry, Audrey," he said. "I thought . . . we thought that, well, surely that Jay had notified you and that it was being worked out on your end. I mean, if you want to go ahead with the conversion . . . we could do that . . ." Bless his heart, he had the honesty to really sound doubtful.

Marc and the rest of the team looked at me. I was so angry, upset, frustrated, and exhausted that I couldn't focus on anything.

Oh, sure. We could convert. And KPMG would try to clean out my intestines with a rototiller, the Securities and Exchange Commission would pay me a personal visit, the Justice Department would send me a battalion of regulators and a subpoena and all of this would happen after the front-page article in bold print announcing a financial irregularity at SKT Global and the subsequent firing of Audrey Taylor-North, who, in addition to being let go, was being brought up on fraud charges in federal district court.

I was imagining a worst-case scenario and had added some drama of my own but the truth wasn't so far away. I tried to take deep breaths like the ones I'd done in Lamaze class years ago when Taylor and Joseph were born. It didn't help but at least I tried. Then, I mentally cleared my brain and began to think of how I was going to get out of this mess.

One of the auditor's spoke.

"Audrey . . . obviously, this is a difficulty."

Corporate-speak.

"No shit, Sherlock," I commented. There was laughter and the tension in the room broke. My mind flew in a thousand directions. "Hammond, can we segregate that class of assets and let the others go over as planned?" This question I directed to the lawyer.

"I think you can, Audrey," he shot back. "They're already segregated by their very nature. We can let the other groups convert. And begin the work on this . . . irregularity immediately."

"Michael, your thoughts?"

I could hear the auditors caucusing in the background then Michael's voice came over.

"Yep. He's right. You can hold those. We'll talk with our tax lawyer and with the IRS to see if there'll be a penalty situation."

"Good," I said as my mind raced through a proposed scenario and timetable. If my proposal was accepted, I'd have to sell it to Jamie by condensing forty pages' worth of material into five bullet points that his six-year-old attention span could absorb.

For twenty more minutes, we walked through the legal, auditing, accounting, and logistical threads that would need to be woven together in order to remedy the situation in which we'd found ourselves. At the end of the day, and I mean at the very end, at four-fifteen Eastern Standard Time exactly, the teams decided, along with the lawyers, accountants, auditors, and operations staff, that we had a plan that could work. The main part of the conversion was cleared to go forward. We would convene again as a group on Monday to clean up the rest.

Jay never showed.

"That was a hell of thing," Marc commented as we walked to the elevator banks that would take us back to our offices. The halls were deserted, it was eight o'clock at night. The only sound besides the echo of our voices in the cavernous lobby was the hum of the floor polisher that the janitor maneuvered in perfect concentric circles. "You were amazing, Audrey, honest."

"Brownnosing is appreciated," I told him, smiling as sincerely as I could. I was so tired by that point that it hurt to keep my eyelids open. "We did what we had to do."

Marc nodded and held the elevator door back as I stepped inside.

"Yeah, but I can't stop thinking about what would have happened if David hadn't spoken up, if you'd gone ahead with the conversion as is . . ."

Which is what that bastard Jay was hoping I would do. Maybe he thought I'd try to muscle it through. Or, even worse, he probably thought I'd postpone the conversion, which would also cost the company millions. Either way, he figured my professional life was over. I'm usually way too busy to fantasize, but this time I wondered what it would be like to mow Jay down with my car and throw myself on the mercy of the courts. I could make a case that he'd sideswiped, sabotaged, and destroyed so many people in his tenure that society was better off without him.

I shrugged my shoulders and watched the little moving white light jump from twelve to fourteen to fifteen to sixteen . . .

The team went to dinner. I had a bowl of soup at my desk.

At eleven-thirty p.m., I got a call from the head systems processor.

"Audrey? It all came over without a hitch. Everyone has signed off. Congratulations."

"Thanks, Bonnie. Thanks for everything that you've done."

"No problem." Bonnie's cheerful voice belied the twelve-hour shift she'd just completed.

I drove home on automatic pilot, let myself into the dark, quiet house, and collapsed onto the bed.

At four-thirty, I woke up to the loud chirping of one bird in the maple tree just outside my bedroom window. He chirped alone for the longest time, interrupted once in a while by what sounded like an aggravated chirp from a neighboring bird that I interpreted to mean "Shut up! It's too early for that!" By five o'clock, however, he had a duet going, and by five-thirty it was a chorus. I got up, showered, and got ready for the day. I was so brain-dead that I actually pulled a gray pantsuit out of the closet before remembering that this was Saturday. And this Saturday, I was not going into the office.

I padded downstairs and went out to get the newspaper. A man across the street waved at me.

"Hi! Just moved in?" he asked. His expression was friendly.

"No. We've lived here for a couple of years now."

The man's mouth slammed shut.

"Oh. I'm sorry. I'm Jerry Solomon. I guess our schedules are in conflict. I don't remember seeing you before."

"That's OK. Nice to meet you, Jerry. I'm Audrey."

"Oh, yeah, you must be Tommy's wife. Nice to meet you. I see Tommy all the time."

As I walked back up my driveway I chuckled to myself. He saw Tommy all the time and Tommy no longer lived here! *I* lived here — or at least I kept clothes and a pillow here — and my own neighbor hadn't ever seen me before. I stopped in the middle of the driveway.

The landscaping company I called twice a year had put in my mums and cleared away the few leaves that had fallen. The merlot- and goldenrod-colored blooms glowed. The sky was bright and blue. My house was pretty. I had never really seen it. The apple tree at the side was bowed under the weight of ripening fruit. A groundhog mother and her baby stopped midbite. Perhaps they thought I'd try to wrestle the apples away from them.

"It's OK, they're all yours," I told her.

As I closed my front door, I suddenly realized that this was one of the very few times I'd ever spent any time at home. I worked like a sharecropper, from before sunup to after sundown. And when I wasn't working, I was thinking about working. Even on Saturday mornings, I was off to the office at seven o'clock sharp as if my life depended on it. I hadn't seen my patio the entire summer. I had a window seat that I'd had Reenie turn into a reading nook that I had never used, not even to read the *Wall Street Journal*. I had a pristine white-on-white kitchen that Mimi kept spotless and that I had barely burned a piece of toast in. And as I looked out of the French doors that led to the patio, I realized that, sometimes, a doe and her fawn would step out of the woods in the back to eat the leftover apples that had escaped the attention of the groundhogs. I had a fabulous life-style that I never had time to actually live.

I felt as if I'd had a near-death experience, and I had. Jay had tried to sabotage me. He had done everything he could think of to kill me off, so to speak, to discredit me, ruin my credibility, or get me fired. And the lingering account issue was the pinnacle of his intrigue. Had he succeeded, I would have wished I was dead.

But I wasn't dead. I had survived. The question was, now that I had a second chance, what was I going to do with it?

I decided to fix breakfast. I lost myself in batter, blueberries, and bacon. Thumping and the sound of a key turning in the lock informed me that the kids were home.

"Mom, are you all right?" Taylor's eyes darted across the counter and the kitchen table.

"Yes, just fine. Go get washed up, I'm putting your waffle on now. The juice is on the counter over there, pour yourself a glass. Joseph, grits or home fries, honey?"

My children looked at me as if I were the Bride of Frankenstein. I had filled the counter with their favorite dishes: grits, fried potatoes, sausage, bacon, not too crisp, waffles, and blueberry muffins for Joseph. Now I was whipping up the eggs.

Tommy bounded in the door.

"Audrey, listen, I . . ." His eyes took in the scene. "What's this?" he asked, frowning.

"Breakfast," I answered. "The coffee's over there."

Tommy and I had been married nearly twenty years, and in that time I think I'd fixed breakfast once a year, maybe twice in 1985. On Saturday mornings, Tommy would drop the kids off to an empty house and find a note on the kitchen counter instead of a bowl of grits. Not today.

"Audrey, what's going on? Are you feeling all right?"

"Hey, Mom! Blueberry muffins. Awright!" Joseph grabbed two and put them on his plate.

"Well, Maternal Unit." My daughter kissed me gently on the cheek and leaned over my shoulder as I scrambled the eggs. "You're acting a bit mental. You're not going through menopause, are you?"

I laughed so hard that I almost peed my thong.

"Probably," I told her, handing her father a mug of coffee.

"I brought in yesterday's mail," Tommy said, handing me a stack of envelopes and ads. He brought my hand to his lips when I took them from him. I had a really handsome, kind, ex-husband.

A white envelope trimmed in purple slipped out of my fingers and onto the floor. I leaned over to pick it up.

PURPLE TIGERS, CLASS OF 1971
WE NEED YOUR HELP!
REUNION PLANNING COMMITTEE
FORMING NOW!

I started laughing again.

"What is it?" Tommy asked, taking the flyer from me and reading it. "Oh, yeah, I went to mine last year, remember? Oh, no. You didn't go . . . Thirty years, we're old! Where's the time gone, Audrey?"

Where, indeed?

The kitchen was a wreck. I'd spilled pancake batter; bacon grease had splattered across the previously pristine ceramic stove top, and my very expensive custom-made granite counter was slathered in orange juice, muffin crumbs, dirty cups, bowls, and spoons. At least I'd remembered to wear an apron, the one the kids had gotten me a hundred Christmases ago. The one that I had never worn. The legend read "Warning: Under Construction." It was now grease-stained and covered with blueberry fingerprint marks.

My family gathered around the counter. Taylor set out plates, Joseph poured and spilled coffee, Tommy made noise as he fished through the silverware drawer. My designer kitchen was a clean freak's living nightmare.

I loved it.

Perfection is an admirable trait of character but it can be overdone. I might as well have been looking for the Fountain of Youth. When you chase something that isn't real, no matter what they tell you, you lose what is real in the process.

The Colonel learned a lot in the army but he didn't learn that.

Fortunately, it wasn't too late for me.

The elevator was packed Monday morning. I had to squeeze on. Don't laugh, I have picked up some weight recently. It was an unusual elevator ride for me. When I come in at six a.m., I have the elevator all to myself. But this Monday, I checked my employee manual and noted the start time of eight o'clock and decided that seven forty-five was early enough for me.

Jay scooted his beer belly out of the way to make room.

"Hmmmm," I commented. "When is it due?"

Chuckles filled the air. Jay's pudgy cheeks reddened. He pulled himself up a bit in order to suck in the gut. It didn't work. So he tried a diversionary tactic.

"I heard there was an issue on Friday."

I checked my watch. Only two hours before coffee break. Good! That meant three and three-quarters hours before lunch!

"Only that oh-four-oh account issue," I answered nonchalantly. "Nothing that we couldn't handle."

"That's pretty serious," he shot back. "You didn't move the assets over, did you?"

Some of the chatter around us diminished as the inquiring minds listened for my answer.

I shook my head and looked him straight in the eye. He looked away.

"Can't do that, but it's taken care of. A nonevent."

The doors opened at my floor. I beamed at Jay. "I'll send you a memo."

Jay looked as if a dog had just puked on his shoe. I knew he'd been expecting to find me spitting fire or sobbing into my soup. Instead, I was smiling, lighthearted, and not trying to bite his head off (so that he could send a memo to my supervisor). In other words, I had ruined his day. *Good.*

I thought about my coffee break again.

Revenge is a latte served very warm with swirls of whipped cream on top.

TWENTY-ONE

Vaughn

I smoothed the yearbook page a couple of times then patted it gently as if it were a sleeping child or favorite pet. This book was like a favorite bedtime story for me, comfortable and reassuring. The smiles of my girlfriends were beacons emanating from the page; there was warmth there, laughter and dreams, especially dreams. And our hopes then were strong enough to transcend the limitations of early seventies black-and-white photography. The emotions leapt off the page.

Well, it was just my imagination, once again. Running away with me.

The silver thread of the Temptations song floated through my head, like a whisper of a favorite fragrance catching a ride on a rare summer breeze. A million snapshots had flooded my memory ever since I opened the invitation. I could hear the sounds of Audrey and Su leading the cheerleaders: *"We love Southeast High, We love Southeast High!"* The rumble of the bass drums over the roar of the Friday-night football crowds, the hum of voices in the lunchroom, and the smell of wet clay from the art room.

Purple Tigers, It's Reunion Time!

Thirty years had passed. Were we the same or were we different? The photo gave away no clues. This one was taken in November, before Reenie cut her waist-length hair again, before the fiasco with Bradley. Her exotic smile was both young and knowing. And Reenie is still like that, hopes always for the best, but has her cellar well provisioned for the worst.

Audrey's bony knees were the only interruption between the hem of her short cheerleading skirt and the tops of her snowy white bobby socks. Her dimples were prominent in cheeks that hadn't yet been devastated by starvation diets, cigarettes, and stress. She was skinny, there was no other way to put it. And yet, in only a few years, Audrey would look at that photo and point out how pudgy she was. How could we have known?

Su maintained her Egyptian statue face with only the hint of a smile. Her chin was slightly raised, her skin taut around those amazing cheekbones. "The voice of the tristate" had already perfected the outward image of stability, focus, and calm. And yet, almost a year later, her own personal hurricane would rip off the roof of her hope chest and send her back into a world of doubt and self-consciousness. Did Su feel the winds picking up? Did she have any idea?

I studied my seventeen-year-old face and laughed aloud. I'd taken my glasses off for the picture and couldn't see, of course, so I was squinting. I think Leonard Watkins was taking the picture and had said something to me. My hair, a trial then, a trial now, was pushed away from my face with a hair band (I've since written Congress to ban their use) and my blouse, I now notice, was rumpled. But despite the nearsightedness and wild hair, I was smiling. It was the French Club picture and we were all happy to be brilliant and headed for college and the wonderful world ahead. The road was straight and clear as far as we could see. But then we were only at the beginning of it. The sharp turns ahead were obscured by fog.

If I'd known that I would have to endure near poverty, an exhausting pregnancy, a devastating marriage and divorce, and the terrible three's to get to an exhilarating teaching career, wonderful husband, dynamic kids, and publishing contract, would I have taken this road? Did I have a choice? Or would I have been afraid to take any roads at all?

I thought about Reenie's isolation when she was pregnant with Javier, Su's miscarriage, and Audrey's illness and near professional assassination. I thought about how low I was when Noah left me with only twenty-five dollars in our checking account and two babies. But this was life. And we had managed to get through the storms and remain friends, "with our sense of cool intact" as Reenie would say.

And technology, too, apparently. Our last reunion, at least among us girls, was put together with phone calls and postcards that Su sent from whatever off-the-coast-of-Jupiter venue she was visiting with Dr. Jimmy. This time, the deed was done by e-mail.

Sub: 30th SE Hi Reunion
From: Irene@IreneGarciaEnterprises.com

Hey girls, booking a suite at the Westin for us. NO HUSBANDS. The Imperial Arms?? What was Kay Mitchell thinking? Never mind, I've seen her wardrobe. Fri and Sat. Su, do you want me to pick u up from airport? Reenie

Irene Keller Garcia
Irene Garcia Enterprises
Décor with a difference

Sub: 30th Southeast High School Reunion
From: ataylornorth@TNConsultants.com

Darling, sounds wonderful! I'll be there. (And which husband were you going to bring, Irene?) Anyone heard from Su?

Sincerely,
Audrey J. Taylor-North
TN Consultants, Inc.

Sub: PLEEZ!
From: Irene@IreneGarciaEnterprises.com

Will somebody tell Stick Woman that she doesn't need to sign her e-mail messages to US with a damn "Sincerely"? As for husband, none of your business.

Sub: PLEEZ!
From: ataylornorth@TNConsulants.com

Reenie, kiss my ass!

SINCERELY,
The Hyphenated One

Sub: SE High Reunion
From: wysewoman@aol.com

You all need to quit. Suite idea sounds wonderful, I will be there. Keith's music is making me crazy, I need a break. No husbands rule fine. -0- from Su. I'm a grandmother, Becca had the baby, eight-pound boy. Be afraid. Be very afraid.

V

Sub: Reunion
From: globetrotter1953@ynet.com

Hey girls, it's me from the Galapagos. Freezing my buns off with the turtles but loving it. Will be there with bells on! I can't bring Jimmy? ☺ Reenie, pick me up. Su

Sub: Reunion
From: wysewoman@aol.com

Where the hell are the Galapagos again? Signed geography not my strong suit

Sub: Galapagos
From: ataylornorth@TNConsultants.com

They're west and slightly south of Ecuador, official name Archipelago de Colon, with 13 major islands, June best time to visit. Check out www.galapagos-islands.net

AJTN

Sub: Who gives a #$%^?
From: Irene@IreneGarciaEnterprises.com

Only Audrey Jean would look it up
Su, send flight info.
V—what's with the Wyse woman handle?

Reenie

Sub: Who gives
From: wysewoman@aol.com

I'm studying Shawnee shamanism.

V

Sub:!

From: Irene@IreneGarciaEnterprises.com

Good grief! Reenie

The afternoon of the reunion, I was a wreck. I'd had to change my blouse (marinara sauce from a meatball sandwich), ran downstairs twice before realizing that I hadn't brought along the garment bag that had my pantsuit in it, and now I couldn't find my keys. Sometimers had set in.

As I rummaged through my purse (again), walked back through the kitchen scanning the counters (again), and then looked on the bathroom sink (again), the sound of mortars exploded over my head. Keith's feet hitting the floor. I checked my watch: four-thirty.

"KEITH OLIVER JOHNSON! If you're late to that SAT class, I will geld you!"

"Yeah, yeah" came the bass voice of my infant as he bounded down the stairs. "Like you're going somewhere without your car keys?" He dangled my key chain in front of my nose.

"Give me those!" I snapped, stuffing them into my pocket. "Where'd you find them?"

Keith snickered and patted me on the head. I swatted his ham-size hand away.

"In the linen closet. You put them on top of the towels." He didn't even make a pretense of keeping a straight face. "You're gettin' senile, Ma." He patted me on the head again and jumped out of the way before I could grab him.

"I am not! And don't call me 'Ma'!"

"OK, Grandma! Ha, ha." The bass voice rumbled as he moved into the kitchen and began circling the island counter like a white shark on patrol. "Oh! Is this your pizza?"

"No, it's your dad's," I told him, checking my purse for the e-mail that Reenie had sent. *Now, where is that paper?* "If you value your life, you won't touch it."

"OK, I see some salami and cheese anyway."

I sighed. That salami and cheese was meant for lunch next week. Now that Keith had found it, I would have to buy more. Tomorrow.

"Keith, don't be late, OK?"

"OK, Ma, I won't. Getting ready right now." I heard him plop onto the kitchen chair.

Ah, there it was. Reenie's e-mail.

Westin. Suite number . . . fifth floor. And the reunion starts at six-thirty with cocktails . . .

As I maneuvered onto the outer belt, heading south toward downtown, I glanced over at the bulky package that sat on the seat next to me. Butterflies fluttered in my stomach.

The book had taken four years to write. It had taken nearly five decades to live. I inhaled deeply to calm my nerves and tried to concentrate on the road, but it was hard. I'd brought along a copy of the galleys for each of my friends. They all knew I'd been writing a book. They just didn't know what the book was about. I was secretive about my writing, paranoid, actually, telling the girls that I was superstitious and didn't want to jinx the project by talking about it. But the truth was that I was writing about them, about Su and Reenie and Audrey and me. I'd been writing about the kinds of lives we led, our good times and bad times, the drama, betrayal, and healing. I had written about our friendship. Sort of.

But I was scared. I didn't know how they would take it. Would they be angry or feel betrayed? Would they feel embarrassed about childhood antics and teenage angst, twenty-something heartbreak, forty-ish disappointments? Or would they be able to set that aside and look back with fondness as I had, shaking their heads at our naïve foolishness?

I set the cruise control and looked out into the bright, blue sky toward the city skyline. On any other day, adjectives of beauty would fill my head: brilliant, azure, compelling. Today, anxiety flushed out the pretty words and replaced them with suspicion, mistrust, secrets, betrayal. The last word had popped up a lot these past few days. Betrayal.

I could hear Audrey's clipped, sharp corporate-speak enunciation: "There's only one right answer. You cannot publish that book."

Su would nod in agreement. Reenie's eyes would darken (if that was possible) and her face would harden into a stern expression of marblelike warmth.

"What god gave you permission to write about our lives? Who do you think you are?" Her words would be said with such coldness that they would freeze into icicles.

There was no going back. The galleys were four weeks old and had already been sent out to the four corners of literary earth, magazines, newspapers, bookstores, everyone. The printing presses were turning and, to my amazement, a small book tour was being planned. *Girls Most Likely* was a kite that was ready to fly on its own. I turned in to the parking garage and took the ticket. My insides had turned to concrete. By this evening, I would either be having a wonderful time at my reunion or I would be friendless.

"Hey, hey, girl! How are you? You look wonderful!" A big kiss on the cheek from Reenie along with a sharp twinge from the pins in her soda-can size hot rollers. "Oops! Sorry 'bout that."

"Is that V? Wait a minute, I'll be right out! Puttin' my bra on now." Su's voice had the volume of Jessye Norman at the Met.

"Lord, yes, please, put that harness on!" Reenie yelled back, grabbing my garment bag before it dragged along the floor. "Seeing you topless is too much to deal with on an empty stomach!"

"Reenie, kiss my butt!"

Somewhere in the distance I heard the sound of a toilet flushing. Reenie grinned.

"Audrey."

My breath caught in my throat.

"Oh, no. She's not—"

"No, no!" Reenie interrupted me, taking my bag toward an open door leading to another bedroom. "Says some Thai food didn't exactly agree with her. She's doing great, you'll see. Better than ever now that she ran away from the corporate plantation and started her own consulting firm."

The toilet flushed again.

"Hmmm. Might need to get her some Imodium."

The suite was beautiful, lavishly decorated, had an amazing view of downtown (Who knew it could look so nice from this high up?), and had plenty of room for a slumber party. I was sharing with Reenie, Su and Audrey had the other bedroom. Nice.

Reenie hung the bag in the closet and turned to look at me. Her cheeks were flushed with excitement.

"Girl, you look great! I love your hair! And I even like that blouse! You're not doin' that . . . what was it? Ashanti-Navajo-Celtic motif?"

"And you're doing the Victoria's Secret catalog this year?" I shot back. Reenie was wearing a purple lace bra with matching tap pants and a white silk robe. Chic. I looked down at her feet, expecting to see a pair of lavender satin mules. I nearly dropped the box of books on my toe. Reenie was wearing bright yellow fuzzy Tweety Bird slippers.

"Oh, that's a nice touch," I said, moving away and putting the books on the table. She posed for me, putting first one foot out for my attention then another.

"I know, aren't they darling? Mother's Day gift from the grand-baby."

Yes, I knew we were close to fifty, but talking about grandchildren still gave me the runs. Right on cue, the toilet flushed again.

"Audrey's having a hard time, I hope she's all right."

"Veeeee!" The duet hit my ears, a pleasant combination of first alto and second soprano. Su and Audrey bounded into the room and we hugged. For a few minutes, we all tried to talk at once. Then we moved into the living room, poured ourselves something to drink, and flopped onto the couches and love seats. Except for me, the girls were in varying stages of dress. Su in sweats and a T-shirt, Reenie still in her glamorous lingerie, Audrey in an exquisite silk kimono. I noticed that Su was limping.

"What's wrong with your foot?"

Laughter and a glare from Su was part of the reply.

"Shaving my legs. I cut my toe."

"Your toe? What were you doing trying to shave your toe?"

Reenie giggled.

"You don't want to know."

Su blushed and held up her bandaged big toe.

"Tried to cut it off," she said, shaking her head.

"Need to keep razors out of her hands," Audrey commented, peering over the top of her reading glasses at Su. "She's like a three-year-old with matches."

It didn't take long for us to get caught up. E-mail had taken the place of snail mail and long distance phone calls, and over the past five years we'd been able to maintain pretty good contact, even with Su. Since her relationship with Skinny Jimmy began, she was sometimes in places that none of us could pronounce. We'd already shared the high points: Audrey had set up her own consulting firm and was back with Tommy; Reenie's interiors had won awards and she was spending a month in Italy, and I had just become a grandmother. Oh, and the book.

I nearly chickened out. The girls knew about the book but not when it was coming out or what it was about. And only Reenie had seen the box I'd brought in and, which was totally unlike her, she hadn't asked what was inside. So I started thinking that maybe, if I didn't mention the book, the girls would forget about it and I could postpone what might be a nasty situation.

I was wrong.

I felt the intensity of Audrey's Bengal tiger gaze on my cheek.

"Vaughn? What's going on with the book? It should be about ready to come out now, shouldn't it?"

"Yeah, V, tell us! What's it about anyway?" Su chimed in.

Reenie's eyebrows rose.

"Wait a minute, ladies, I think we may be in for a news flash." She climbed out of the plush cushions of the suede love seat, slipped on her Tweety Bird feet, and scampered into the bedroom before I could stop her. Actually, there was no way I was going to stop her. The cushions of the couch were so soft that I had sunk down several inches and found myself struggling to get to my feet. By the time I managed it, Reenie was back with the book.

"Eureka! Books! Hmmm. Nice title!" She held up the navy-and-white generic galley cover where the words *Girls Most Likely* were printed. It was a feeding frenzy. All I could do was sigh, sink back into the cushions, and take another sip of my drink.

"As usual, Vaughn, you were holding out on us," Su concluded, plopping back down onto the couch and flipping the pages of the book.

"She's so damn superstitious," Audrey commented. "Every time I'd ask her what the book was about, she'd chant a spell and say it was bad luck to talk about it."

I felt my cheeks flush.

"That was the year I was into Celtic wise woman lore."

Reenie rolled her eyes.

"Whatever. Let's see what we have here." She slipped on a pair of rhinestone-accented reading glasses and began to read.

Su looked up, her eyes beaming with pride.

"I like the dedication, Vaughn. That was really nice of you."

Audrey read it aloud.

"To the Purple Tigers of SE High, Class of 1971, and especially to my friends, the real girls most likely to do everything wonderful: Irene Keller Garcia, Suzanne Penn, and Audrey Taylor-North, thank you for letting me be a part of it."

Reenie's eyes shone with tears.

"OK, you got me with the sappy stuff. Now do you want to tell us what this book is really about?"

I paused before I spoke, which was probably a mistake. Three pairs of eyes turned in my direction. *OK, what are you going to do now?* So I did what I usually do when I'm nervous and put on the spot: I blundered through my sentences.

"Well. Um. OK. It's . . . well, it's about us. I mean, our friendship, it's about our friendship. And . . ." I paused to take another breath. "Ah, it's about what it was like growing up here and high school and what happened when we went away and didn't see each other and . . ."

I stopped because the expressions had changed from interest and pride to bewilderment, disbelief, and concern.

"Wait a minute." The "Voice of the tristate" is lovely to hear when you're watching the evening news. But if it's directed at you instead of at the camera, it's not nice at all. It's like having Mike Wallace on your front porch. "Hold on. This book? It's about us? *Our lives?*"

Reenie took off her glasses and sat up straight, which I wouldn't have thought possible in the lumpy cushions of the love seat.

"V, did you actually write about us? How *much* about us? Just how personal is this book?"

Audrey stood up. Her cheekbones tightened and pulled her long face into a Siamese temple cat look of warning: *Tread at your own risk.* She didn't say anything.

"No, I didn't write about us!" I protested. "I mean, I did, but I didn't. It's kind of like our story but it isn't really." *What did I just say?*

Reenie cocked her head.

"Vaughn, you're not making a damn bit of sense. Is this book about us or not?"

"It kind of is. It's about our lives and what our friendship is like but it's not. You know, it's the same . . . but different." I stopped myself before I could go on.

"Hold on." Audrey's voice cut through the tension. She was frowning as she read from a page one-third of the way through the book. A slight smile began to form on her lips. Then she looked up at me. The predatory tiger gaze was gone. "Wait a minute. This isn't . . ."

Reenie and Su had cracked open the book, too.

"No, it isn't . . ." Reenie turned a page.

"It isn't about us." Su finished the sentence.

"But the Diane character," Audrey said, her smile growing with each passing second.

Su looked up. "What page?"

"Page seventy-five," Audrey told her. "She sounds a lot like Gladys Randolph. I mean, who else could it be? Going from a size four to the size of, let me quote from the book: 'to the size of a giant ground sloth'?"

"V! You're awful!" Su started laughing.

"You've seen her!" Reenie chimed in. "She looks like a woolly mammoth! Maybe they aren't extinct after all!"

"You would think they'd have waxing salons in Milwaukee!" Audrey's comment was peppered with giggles. She looked at me and I shrugged my shoulders. I was familiar with libel laws. I wasn't about to admit one way or another that "Diane" was Gladys. No way.

"This book really isn't about us." The conclusion came from Su. She also looked up at me. "I mean, it is about us, but it isn't our stories. Not really."

I began to sing the old Carly Simon tune with a different set of lyrics.

"You're so vain. I'll bet you thought this book was about you, you're so vain!"

Su, Audrey, and Reenie chimed in.

"I'll bet you think this book is about you, don't you, don't you?"

"It's the story of four friends growing up in an average-size city in the Midwest. It's about their friendship, their lives, their community, their hopes and dreams. That's what I wanted to write about." I told them. *About our friendship and all that friendship means to people. Not about our secrets.* "Secrets are meant to be kept, not shared."

I went to the reunion with the girls most likely. We danced the electric slide, we sang to the Supremes, we talked about old times, cried over fallen classmates, and gossiped about former boyfriends and bad wardrobe choices. Everyone wanted to know about my book and when I'd be on *Oprah* and if there'd be a movie and, of course, if the book was about them. And I told them all "no." The book was not about them; I hadn't written about their lives and loves and disappointments and secrets or about my own. Because that is a book for another time.

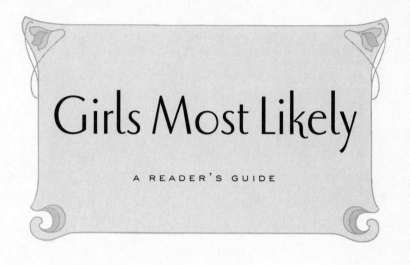

Girls Most Likely

A READER'S GUIDE

Sheila Williams

1. What kinds of things are the focus of the girls' lives growing up, and how do their interests evolve over time? Do any of your childhood interests play a role in your life today?

2. Each girl's narrative highlights something new about another girl that went unmentioned in her own chapter. What do you think the author was trying to show through this interplay of stories? Is this a realistic portrayal of a close-knit circle? How do the stories of your friends overlap in relation to your life?

3. Su's narrative is heavy with the concept of questions, secrets, and the responsibilities of truth. How does this affect her? How are secrets kept throughout the girls' lives? Who keeps them? Why? Is there ever a good reason to keep a secret?

4. When discussing their upcoming thirtieth reunion, the girls share a very telling round of e-mails. What do these e-mails reveal about their adult personalities?

5. What is it about high school that allowed the girls to express themselves so clearly? Was it who they were, or was it shaped by

the climate in which they were growing up? Is the experience of contemporary high school students similar?

6. Vaughn is "the glue" that keeps the girls together. Does she have particular character traits, strengths, and weaknesses that contribute to this function? Do you have a "Vaughn" in your group of friends?

7. Audrey is the quintessential Type A personality and an overachiever's overachiever. Why is she like this? What are the positive and negative aspects of Audrey's personality?

8. How does envy affect the girls' relationships with one another?

9. Reenie's pregnancy is a big surprise. Do you think it is the catalyst for her maturity? If not, what forces Reenie to grow up? How do think pregnancy changes a woman's way of being?

10. Some limitations were easy for the girls to get over (i.e., Vaughn not making the majorette squad). But others (i.e., Su's family problems) were not. What allows some girls to overcome disappointment better than others?

11. Reenie and Vaughn met when Reenie saved her from a bully. In what ways did the girls save one another from the "bullies" in their lives?

12. When the girls were children, what did being a woman mean? What symbolized womanhood? How were these symbols recognized, achieved, or abandoned as they became women themselves? Were they true for you as you grew up?

ABOUT THE AUTHOR

SHEILA J. WILLIAMS was born in Columbus, Ohio. She attended Ohio Wesleyan University and is a graduate of the University of Louisville in Louisville, Kentucky. Sheila and her husband live in northern Kentucky.